JESSE'S GIRL

LENNOX VALLEY CHRONICLES
BOOK 2

HANNAH BRIXTON

First edition 2024

Editor: Myranda Bolstad: https://www.mjbolstad.ca/

ISBN: 978-1-7380101-3-4 (paperback)

CONTENT WARNING

This work of fiction is intended for adults and describes mature situations that may be triggering or upsetting for certain readers.

Topics dealt with in **explicit detail** include: alcohol consumption, difficult relationships with parents, learning challenges due to dyslexia, ableist attitudes about dyslexia, sexual harassment, physical assault (a character punches someone), and explicit sexual activity (including breeding kink and a gentle hand necklace but *not* choking/breath play).

Topics dealt with in **moderate detail** include: a life-threatening medical emergency (a character's parent has a significant cardiovascular event and hospital stay/recovery), divorce, jealousy, manipulative behavior by an ex-partner, and infidelity by an ex-partner.

Topics dealt with in **minor detail** (including brief mentions and off-page events) include: poisoning, hypothermia, sexual coercion, and figurative descriptions of drowning and addiction (as well as of a gif of Artax in the Swamp of Sadness from The Neverending Story).

Note: The male main character goes on two dates with other women before he gets together with the female main character.

Please read at your own discretion.

For the snarky little bitches.

1

ADA

I squeeze the rolled-up tube of paint so hard my hands start to shake, trying to extract every last drop onto my palette. *Fuck you, Candy Apple Red.* It's an intolerably cheerful name for a color. Scowling, I chuck the spent tube into the trash can and wipe my hands on my T-shirt, blowing a wisp of turquoise hair out of my eyes. Ani DiFranco's *Untouchable Face* plays through my headphones. I'm really leaning into the *fuck you* part today. This song always makes me think of Pascal. And not fondly. He's certainly untouchable, what with being five thousand miles away and all. Not that I would touch that cheating asshole again, even if I could.

My paintbrush dipped in the last precious drops of red paint, I carefully shade around the fingertips of the figure at the center of this piece, then step back to take in my progress. It's the most haunting of the series I've been working on lately: a woman's face submerged just under the water with her hands in the foreground —the only part of her not drowning.

"Angry painting again?" Katie's voice cuts through the reverb on Ani's final guitar riffs.

I whirl around, pulling my paint-smudged headphones down to my neck. "Hey! Didn't expect to see you home."

Between Katie's twelve-hour night shifts in the Intensive Care Unit and her spending so much time with Dimitri, she's been a fairly absent best friend lately. I basically live alone in our little basement hovel—soon to be just *my* little basement hovel, unless I can find a new roommate.

"Grabbed breakfast with Dimitri after my shift." As she twists the white gold ring on her finger, the oval-cut sapphire catches in the light. She grins, her expression shining with something more than pancakes would explain.

"Okay, sparkle eyes." I lift my chin and point the paintbrush her way, drawing a small circle in the air. "The post-orgasmic glow is getting a bit blinding. You two still going at it? Novelty hasn't worn off yet?"

Katie smiles. "Engagement sex just... *hits different.*"

"Well, I'll have to take your word for it."

No way in hell I'll be finding out anytime soon.

I'm happy for her, but I'd rather get punched in the boob than get into another serious relationship. "But, I mean, it's been a week..."

"Yeah..." She glazes over, her gaze settling somewhere in the middle of the room.

I smirk. "You're having a sex flashback right now, aren't you?"

She snaps out of it, then clears her throat. "Maybe. Any luck on the roommate search?"

I sigh. "Not yet. But I'll figure it out."

Only a few boxes are left in Katie's room at this point. I can't be certain, but I figure she's been dragging her heels on moving out officially because I still haven't found anyone to rent her room. But I've known Katie since high school. She'd move in with Dimitri yesterday if she could. She practically lives at his place already, anyway.

"Where've you been?" I ask. "I mean, besides working and getting railed on the regular. Barely see you these days. I miss your ass." I take a sip of water from the glass on my nightstand. As happy as I am for Katie and Dimitri, I feel a bit like they're riding off into the sunset on a white horse while I'm left shoveling shit in the barn. But, ever since I got back from Europe, heartbroken and jaded, Katie's given me so much—support, love, a place to live... I won't ask her to put her own life on hold for me any longer.

"Just my ass, huh?" She turns and waggles her butt toward me.

I nearly spit my water back into the glass. "Shut up. But seriously," I gesture between us, "it's like I'm in a long-distance relationship again. And you know how I feel about those."

"Ada." Katie grabs me by both shoulders. "Look at me."

I meet her eyes with resigned patience.

"I might be busy as fuck with work, I might have transformed into some kind of exhausted, nocturnal she-beast, and I *might* even be slightly dick-whipped..." She trails off, glazing over again.

I tilt my head. "Uh, were you... making a point just now?"

"Right. *Fuck*, I'm tired." She sucks in a breath like a drunk trying to sober up. "My point is: I love you and I wanna see you. And... *pfft*, long distance? That's not us! You're my *bestie*. Plus, I would never cheat on you with some Spanish slut."

Fucking Pascal. The memories are still raw, even a year later.

"Right," I say. Covering the sting with dry wit, I add, "Dimitri's *Greek*."

She swats my arm.

"Hey!" I say through a surprised laugh. "I'm joking! You know I love him. And, since Pascal is to blame, let's not throw other women under the bus. Plus, we're reclaiming the term *slut*, remember?"

"*Fine*," she says, waving me off. "I'm off Friday." She points a finger at me, as if challenging me to argue. "You working? Or are you free?"

I nod. "Friday's good."

Katie's gaze lands on my easel and her face falls slightly, no doubt guessing what's fueled my salty mood yet again. She walks around me and surveys the canvas. "So? What'd they do this time? Same old bullshit?"

"Of course it's the same old bullshit," I grouse, chucking the paintbrush onto a battered tray. "Mom emailed me some shit about college applications today. And I've got dinner with them tonight. I already know they're gonna be on my ass about it. It's always like"—I affect my best impression of my nagging mother —"*when are you going to quit messing around and go to college? Or why don't you get a proper job in an office? Come work for Sitka like Marcus.*"

I frown. The last thing I want is to spend my days in a cubicle at my parents' property development firm.

"You already have a *proper job*," Katie reassures me, bumping her hip against mine. "*And* a volunteer gig on top of that. Don't let them get to you. They're just old-fashioned."

"Wanna come to dinner tonight and explain it to them? Because they're sure as shit not listening to me." I reach into my basket of paints and select pure black. It's become a real pattern recently—knowing my parents will give me shit every Sunday means I spend the entire day in a state of anticipatory dread, painting my feelings. Maybe I should have been an art therapist instead of a bartender-slash-recreation-coordinator.

Katie glances around my bedroom, studying the artwork leaning up against the walls. "I'm liking the dark and broody vibes, though. Maybe your parents are doing you a favor, y'know, fueling the whole *tortured artist* thing."

I hum a soft sound of acknowledgment. "Maybe I should lean into it—get some face tattoos, a bunch of piercings. Really *exces-*

sive eyeliner. They'd love that." I survey my cluttered room as I turn the tube of paint over in my hands, contemplating the way my emotions have flooded out of me and onto these canvases.

"Looks like you've gotten a lot done," she says, following my gaze.

"I guess." I pause, then blow out a breath. "Don't know why I bother, though. I'm barely making any sales. All I do every day is shout into the void on social media about my paintings. And my parents..." I trail off, shaking my head.

Katie's brows lift. "They've really gotten to you this time, haven't they?"

"I dunno." I toss the tube back into the basket, pulling the headphones from my neck and dropping them onto my bedside table. "Yeah, maybe."

She puts a hand on my shoulder and faces me. "Ada Russo, listen to me: you are an incredible artist, and I know you're gonna blow up one of these days. Just look at all this!" She gestures at the finished pieces around us.

I sigh, sinking heavily onto my bed. "They're never gonna see this as legit, though. They don't understand. They just keep harping on about college and comparing me to fucking Marcus. Because he's all successful and shit with his cushy office job."

That he didn't even earn. Goddamn nepo baby golden child.

My parents, both raised by Italian immigrants, have always understood success as following the classic college-to-traditional-career pipeline. A box I've never fit into. Nothing screams *traditional career* less than a tattooed artist with dyslexia and blue hair.

"Remind me again why you keep subjecting yourself to their crap?" Katie asks.

I give her a long look. "You know how my parents are. Missing Sunday dinners would be sacrilege." I pick at a bit of dried paint on my knuckle. "Plus, you've had my mom's cooking, right?"

"Yeah, but you don't need to tolerate their criticism just to get a free meal." She sits beside me and mutters, "I don't care how good your mom's lasagna is."

I throw her a sidelong glance.

"Don't stink eye me!"

"It's really fucking good lasagna." Home-cooked Italian food isn't something you turn down.

"I know." She rubs my back and tries to stifle a yawn. "But this is a *them* problem, not a *you* problem. Don't get caught up in comparing yourself to your brother."

My phone chimes in the back pocket of my jean shorts.

"What the fuck?" I mumble as I peer at the screen. "Did we summon him or something?"

> MARCUS
>
> Had to run to Seattle to pick up Jesse

Quickly, two more texts come in.

> MARCUS
>
> His mom's in the hospital
>
> Tell mom and dad I won't make dinner tonight

"Shit," I breathe, my brow knotting with concern.

"What's wrong?" Katie asks.

I turn the phone so she can read Marcus' texts.

She presses her lips together.

"You already knew," I say.

"Confidential patient information. Sorry. I couldn't."

"How bad is it?"

"Ada..." She averts her gaze and stands.

We both know she can't tell me. But she's an ICU nurse. It can't be *good.*

"Just... is it bad?" I search her face for a hint. "Blink twice for bad."

"I'm not..." she says, turning to leave.

"Katie!" I say, catching her by the arm.

"Just text Marcus and ask him like a normal person," she says, shaking me off.

Fuck. Jesse's mom was always so sweet when we were younger. *She can't be that much older than my parents, can she?* Guilt shimmers in the periphery of my mind for bitching about Mom and Dad.

"Fine." I send a quick reply to my brother then pocket my phone, chewing on my lip. "I should get ready, anyway. I'm covering part of Kyle's shift at the bar before dinner."

Katie throws me a confused look over her shoulder as I follow her into the kitchen.

"He asked me for a favor. He has a thing." *A fuck-buddy, probably.* "I could use the extra hours." Especially if I can't find someone to split the rent soon. I've known for a few weeks Katie was moving out—saw it coming a mile away, even before she gave her notice—but Dimitri proposing last week finally made it real. I admit, I've been procrastinating on the roommate search.

Katie nods, a hint of guilt flickering over her features, as she fills a glass with water. "Make sure you bleed the drunks dry for tips then?"

I flash her a playful smile. "Always do."

"Okay, I need to get the last of these boxes moved before my shift." She turns toward her room.

"I believe in you, you beautiful she-beast!" I call after her.

She spins on her heel, walking backward a few paces, and flips me off with a smirk.

I SLIP behind the bar at Carnival with two bobby pins between my lips and lift my chin at Kyle. Rising on tiptoe to catch my reflection in the mirror behind the bar shelves, I quickly pin my hair away from my face and move to the sink to wash my hands.

"Hey," I say over my shoulder, then shut off the tap and grab a towel.

"Hey, yourself." He fills a pint glass and slides it over the bar top to a woman who gives him a lingering look. "Enjoy," he purrs softly, leaning toward her. Kyle would flirt with a lamppost if it had boobs.

"Kyle," I say and, when his gaze stays trained on the woman's ass as she walks away, I snap my fingers in his peripheral vision. "Kyle!"

His eyes jump to mine.

"You wouldn't know of anyone who needs a place to live, would you?" I hate that it's come to this.

"Why?" He frowns, scrubbing at a spot on the bar top with a cloth.

"Katie's moving out."

He stops wiping down the bar. "What? Why?"

"She's moving in with Dimitri. He proposed last week." I stack a few dirty glasses in a bus bin to take to the kitchen.

He sucks his teeth. "Yeesh. Another one bites the dust."

"Hey, it's *good* news, dickhead."

He throws up his hands. "Didn't say it wasn't!"

"Just because you'd rather bone anyone who looks at you twice doesn't mean other people have to live like hedonists too," I say with a laugh.

"Ouch," he says, pretending to be wounded. "Careful. You might hurt my feelings." He pouts and dodges the towel I flick at him.

"Oh, please." I shake my head and point at him. "Don't even start."

He gives me a smirk that shows off his dimple and winks. Kyle is almost excessively handsome and, unfortunately, he knows it. I swear, half the business the bar gets on the nights he works can be attributed to how blatantly he wraps customers around his little finger. The women drool over him and the men pal around like they've known him for years. Hell, even *I* have to acknowledge he's an attractive guy. If only he never opened his mouth.

"So, come on," I press. "Anyone you know need a place?"

He thinks for a moment. "I don't think so? I'll ask my friends, though."

"Thanks." I nod with a thin smile. The idea of living with one of Kyle's friends has Plan B energy but, right now, I'll take any leads I can get.

An older man approaches the bar and orders a scotch on the rocks. I scoop ice into a highball glass. "Maybe I'll put an ad online or something," I muse.

"Uh, yeah. You could," Kyle says, closing out his sales at the till. "If you wanna end up *on the news.*"

"Shut up. I might have to." Tomorrow's July first. All the sane people must have places lined up already. "Whatever. I'll figure something out."

Kyle heads to the break room to get his things. When he comes back, he's changed from his all-black bartending getup into jeans and a T-shirt. Seconds after he settles on the barstool in front of me, a cloud of cologne wafts my way.

I scrunch my nose. *Easy, Kyle, geez.*

"So, Katie's getting married, huh?" He glances over his shoulder at the front door like he's waiting for someone. He turns back, leaning his elbows on the bar and typing something on his phone.

"Yeah."

He lifts his head. "Didn't you just go to some chick's wedding, like, a month or two ago?"

"That *chick* was my cousin." I give him a wary look. "What's your point?"

"Just seems like everyone's getting married."

"Two women I know is hardly *everyone*."

"I dunno. You're probably just getting to that age where it starts happening."

"*I'm* getting to that age? We're the same age, asshat."

"Yeah, but I'm never getting married." He leans in and gestures to his body, cocky smirk at full tilt. "Nobody's gonna tie this shit down with a ring."

"God, would anybody want to?"

"What about you?" he asks, ignoring the barb. "You don't seem like the marriage type."

"Wow," I deadpan, crossing my arms over my chest. "You know, I'm racking my brain for how that was appropriate to say to me. And I'm comin' up short, Kyle. Real short."

He holds out apologetic hands. "Ada. Dude. You know what I mean. You do your own thing. You make art, you work in a bar, you've got blue hair... You're always talking about feminism and shit. I dunno. I guess I never pictured you wanting that." He pauses. "Do you?"

I scowl. "I don't know. Maybe. No. Yes? Ugh, why are you making this about me? Can't I just be happy for Katie?"

"Are you?"

"Of course I am," I say quickly.

He seems skeptical.

"And feminism isn't about not wanting to get married. It's about equal access to—"

Kyle drops his chin to his chest and fakes a loud snore.

"Kyle!" I snap.

He lifts his head and winks.

"You're such a prick."

"You love me."

"I *barely* tolerate you," I reply as I approach my next customer.

Kyle grins and returns to his phone.

I pull a pint of beer for the man waiting at the counter while Kyle's question rolls around in my head.

Am I happy for Katie?

I try to feel it but, the truth is, there's been a weight on my chest lately. And, if I'm honest with myself, it's something more than the inconvenience of having to find a new roommate.

People all around me are doing adulthood: taking steps, getting degrees, making career moves. Even our bar manager, Ros, and her wife are expecting a baby. Katie's engagement will just give my parents yet another angle to argue I'm not measuring up —not taking those same steps. At twenty-five, I might have plenty of time to figure my shit out, but *they* don't see it that way. Hell, they were married at twenty-two and expecting Marcus a year later.

This is probably why I haven't told them about Katie and Dimitri yet, though I'll have to bite the bullet tonight if I want to stay ahead of the rumor mill in this town. But one thing's for sure: my parents will have a fucking field day when they hear the news.

2

JESSE

Marcus' double take is almost cartoonish when I finally get close enough for him to recognize me.

"Jesse? Whoa! Hey!" He falters for a beat before yanking me into a tight hug. When he pulls away, he holds me by the shoulders and leans back. "Wow. I didn't even recognize you under all that hair." He seems to shake it off. "Any update about your mom?"

"Yeah. Claire emailed. Mom made it out of surgery. She's stable for now." Not knowing how she was for the entire flight had been agonizing. When my phone finally connected to Wi-Fi as I got off the plane, the relief was so visceral I needed to sit down for a few minutes.

"Oh, thank fuck," he says, then lets go. He stares for another beat before gesturing for me to follow him toward the baggage claim.

I fall into step beside him, adjusting the strap of my carry-on. "I'll find out more when I get there, I guess."

He nods. "Still good you came."

"Yeah. Didn't know if…" I trail off, rubbing my forehead. "Didn't know which way it would go, you know?"

My older sister had raced home from Seattle as soon as she'd heard. I thought I might be hallucinating when she called me as I was standing in the Brisbane airport, preparing to board a different flight for a different trip.

Abdominal aortic aneurysm rupture.

Four words I barely understood, but the terrified way my sister spoke them was enough to send me racing to the nearest ticket counter. Mom collapsed in the grocery store, Claire had said. There'd been massive internal bleeding. A quick-thinking cashier had helped her get to the hospital in time, but they hadn't been sure if she'd make it through surgery. So I didn't know if I'd make it back in time to see her before she…

Well, thank God she didn't.

"Scary shit." Marcus shakes his head, then reaches out to squeeze my shoulder as we stop at the conveyor belt. Between the bear hug and the shoulder squeezes, this is more physical affection than I've had in months. He's always been like that, though, and comes by it honestly. The Russo family crest might as well have a hand squishing your cheeks on it.

My suitcase approaches on the belt, packed to bursting with everything I'd need for a couple months with only sporadic access to laundry facilities. For a weird, detached moment, I think about how this wasn't what I'd envisioned when packing up at the farm. I was supposed to be on vacation, fleeing the Australian winter by traveling all over Southeast Asia for the next two months. I'm still scrambling to process the sharp left turn my day—or week? *hell,* maybe my *life*—has just taken.

"Hey, thanks for coming to pick me up on short notice, man," I say, hauling my suitcase off the belt.

"Best friend duties," he says, waving a dismissive hand between us.

The truth is, he was the only person who I knew would drive an hour out of his way to collect me. The only friend here I haven't lost touch with.

"Just sorry we're not getting to hang out under better circumstances," he adds.

The automatic doors hiss as we leave Seattle-Tacoma International Airport. My bags loaded into the trunk of Marcus' car, we settle in for the drive to small-town Lennox Valley. Home, I guess, though it doesn't feel like it anymore.

"Alright, so what the hell happened to you?" Marcus stares at me from the driver's seat as he buckles his seat belt with one hand and starts the car with the other. "Like, seriously, when did you turn into blond Jesus?"

"Nice to see you, too, dipshit." Even after spending the exhausting, seventeen-hour flight in a haze of worry, I can't help but smile at how easily we fall back into this comfortable banter. I run a hand over my scraggly beard as I try to remember how long it's been since he last visited me in Oz. "I dunno, man. You work in the bush long enough, you stop giving a shit. Been a few years, huh?"

"Yeah." He blows out a breath and pulls out of the parking lot. "And, clearly, you've gone feral in the meantime." With a smirk, he adds, "Is that what Australian women are into? Long hair and a big fuck-off beard?"

"Ah, who the fuck knows," I say on a long exhale. Admittedly, it's a dodge, but I'm not ready to get into the details of my love life right now. There wasn't exactly much opportunity to date in rural Queensland.

"You sure you're cool crashing on our couch?" he asks, seeming to sense I don't want to go there. "It's a long couch, but, uh... you might be longer."

I glance down at where my knees press against the glove box and stoop forward to adjust my seat. After the nonexistent legroom on the plane, I'd barely noticed. My six-foot-three frame and uncomfortable seating are old friends. "Oh, no, man. The couch is great," I reassure him.

"You sure? Not your mom's place?"

"Don't have a key." That much is true, but I don't elaborate. I don't want to talk about how Mom practically dropped out of my life during the divorce—and how I returned the favor by leaving. We haven't exactly been close in recent years. "Besides, your place is closer to the hospital, right? Close enough to walk?"

He nods.

"Good. As long as I won't be cramping your style," I add, turning to him as he pulls out onto the highway that'll take us home. "Or Renee's. I don't even know how long I'm gonna be here. It all depends on... uh..." I trail off and look out the window, feeling the tightness in my throat return. My brow pinches together and I try not to think about it.

We both know it depends on how my mom does.

Fuck. She's only fifty-eight.

"Totally, yeah," he says, shaking his head. "Don't worry about figuring it out right this second. You can stay as long as you need. Renee doesn't mind at all; she's barely home, anyway. Real estate is wild here. She's working all the time."

"Thanks, man." I'll have to sort out the logistics later, because, right now, I feel like I could slip into a week-long coma. Preoccupied with all the *what-ifs* swirling in my head about my mom, I hadn't been able to sleep on the flight.

I pull out my phone, tapping through the process of connecting to the local network for service. When I get a signal, I send a quick text to my sister that we're en route and shut off the screen. I sigh, rubbing my eyes, then lean back against the headrest.

The scenery whips past. While the billboards have changed, the places along the side of the highway are mostly familiar, with a few new builds scattered here and there. The names and land-marks swim back into my memory so easily I almost feel like I never left. I guess the place where you grew up pulls at you like that.

Fuck, it's weird being back.

Eight years. Eight fucking years I've been hiding on the other side of the world. I press my lips together and inhale an unsteady breath through my nose, hating myself for my shit-for-brains, short-sighted cowardice. It had been easier to keep running than to think about the mess I'd left behind. I'd shut everything and everyone out—except Marcus, really. I exhale, fighting against a fresh wave of suffocating guilt.

According to a sign that sails past, Lennox Valley is another seventy-three miles away. As antsy as I am to get to the hospital, we've got time to kill.

"What's everyone up to these days?" Flopping my head in Marcus' direction, I try to stuff my internal wince about not keeping up with our friends. Not that it was easy to stay in touch with anybody—even if I'd tried—thanks to shoddy internet access in the bush. With Marcus, it was different. We'd talked on the phone here and there. It helped that our friendship has always been the kind where we could pick right up where we left off. It never felt like work.

The corner of his mouth lifts slightly. "You sure you wanna just, like, shoot the shit?"

"Yeah. *Fuck.* I obsessed about what's happening with my mom the entire flight. Need something else to think about." I bend to dig a bottle of water out of my bag.

"Okay. Well," he starts, "Kai's getting married in August. Nadine's her name. Sweet girl."

"No shit," I say, surprised. "Someone wants to marry *Kai*? Huh." I take a swig of water and cap the bottle, tucking it back in my bag.

"Yeah." He smiles. "And Adrian's in Seattle finishing his master's."

"Still political science?" I ask, squinting as I strain to remember what he was studying.

"Yeah. Wants to run for office."

"God help us," I laugh, running a hand over my face.

"I know," he says, shaking his head. "We're all fucked."

"What's Ada doing?"

"Oh, the usual. Railing against the injustices of the world. Making weird art. Getting pissed at Mom and Dad."

I blow a breath through my nose. "Sounds about right."

"She's bartending now at Carnival," he adds.

"Ada," I say, my eyes widening. "Like *Ada* Ada?"

He nods.

"Your baby sister's *bartending*?" I can't picture it.

"She's twenty-five now, man," he says with a laugh, glancing at me.

"No, she's fucking not."

"It's true." He tilts his head. "She traveled for a few years. Went all over Asia and Europe, working until she could afford her next move, y'know?"

"Right, right," I say, some vague memory forming of Marcus telling me about her travels back when he visited me.

"But she came home last year. She's been living with... you remember Katie?"

"Katie Chen?"

"Yeah."

I shrug. "Vaguely. She lived next door to Naomi."

Marcus lifts his eyebrows in silent acknowledgment of the girl who ripped my heart out.

"Fuck, man," I say, letting out a breath. "I think the last time I saw Ada, she still had braces." I run a hand through my hair, trying to imagine all this. "Twenty-five? Are you serious?" Marcus and I are twenty-seven; I know the math checks out, but *still...*

"Yeah. She's still a pain in the ass, though," he mutters, almost to himself.

I arch a brow, remembering how she could be a bit of a shit when we were teenagers. She always swore like a sailor and her tendency to run her mouth had gotten us into trouble more than once, even getting us kicked out of the local diner a few times for being too rowdy. Not that the rest of us didn't deserve it. We were always screwing around and making fun of each other—and Ada gave as good as she got. She'd called Kai *pissboy* for an entire summer after he'd accidentally spilled water on his lap.

I stare out at the blur of evergreens rushing past, trying to get my head around how long I've been gone—and everything I've missed.

Man, I really ran for the hills and never looked back.

I turn back to Marcus. "Y'know, I was supposed to spend this winter traveling." I pause, noting the sun beaming through the dusty windshield. It might be winter in Australia, but it's sure a hot-as-fuck summer here. "I was actually about to take a flight to Thailand when Claire called." The panic in my big sister's voice drifts back to me again and I clench my hands.

"No shit?"

"I'm serious. At the airport, suitcase in hand." At first, I'd been convinced I misheard her. Then my eyes had darted around the check-in line as if I'd find someone or something in the immediate vicinity to help me know what to do.

"That's freaky," Marcus says.

That's one word for it.

An invisible fist grips my stomach, wrenching it up behind my sternum. I swallow, trying to push it down.

Marcus glances my way. He must catch me frowning, because

he changes the subject. "So, uh... what were you gonna get up to in Thailand?"

"Meet up with some mates." I shrug.

"*Mates*." He snorts. "Listen to you."

"Friends, I mean. Whatever." I roll my eyes. "Anyway, I'll go once my mom's better. I just need to make sure she's okay first, help Claire with juggling her kids... But, when everything settles down, I'll fly back. I can probably still catch a bit of time in Thailand." I rub my hands over my thighs, cementing the plan in my mind, and notice one of my knees is bouncing. I consciously stop the movement.

"Hey, Jess," Marcus says, clearly picking up on my unease. "Your mom's still pretty young. She'll be okay."

My smile is tight. I nod. She'll bounce back from this. She'll be fine. She *has to be* fine.

CLAIRE TEARS up the moment she spots me in the hospital hallway and hurries over to pull me into a hug. We hold each other tight for a minute. "She's too young for this," she finally whispers into my shoulder, sniffling. "I don't know how to do this. Mom would normally be the one who—"

"I know. It's gonna be okay," I say in what I hope is a reassuring tone. She's my big sister, but she shouldn't have had to handle the weight of something like this alone.

"It better be," she says, forcing a laugh. She steps back, peering up at me. "I'm glad you're here."

"Me too." I glance at the door. "Can I see her?"

We get buzzed into the ICU and shown to Mom's room. Well, *room* might be overstating things; it's not much more than a bed partitioned off from its neighbor by a curtain the color of pale egg yolk. Machines blip and whoosh in their simple yet Herculean task of keeping the sickest people in the hospital alive.

Mom's asleep in a semi-reclined position, her jaw slack, mouth slightly open. Guilt coils around my stomach at the change in her appearance. She's pale. *Gaunt.* Like she's aged twenty years in the last eight I've been away. Her hair has grayed since I last saw her. I barely recognize the smiling, whip-smart woman who raised us. Wires and tubes protrude from the collar and sleeves of her hospital gown, attaching to machines flanking the head of her bed.

"It's okay to hold her hand, Jess. If you want to." Claire gestures, snapping me out of my state of inertia. I shuffle to Mom's side, wrapping my fingers around hers.

"Hey, Mom?" I say softly. "It's Jesse."

There's movement under her eyelids and her hand gently clenches mine. With what seems like concerted effort, she eventually opens her eyes and focuses on my face. Soft recognition blooms in her expression, and the corner of her mouth twitches with the hint of a smile.

"Jesse," she whispers, her voice rough like she's swallowed sand.

"Hey," I say again, smiling. "Heard you needed to see me."

Claire hands me a plastic cup of water, and I hold the straw to Mom's lips so she can take a sip.

She swallows, then blinks slowly and looks up at me, her eyes soft and watery. "I thought you were John Lennon."

I let out a laugh, trying to keep my voice down. "John Lennon?" I glance at Claire, who shrugs.

Mom's eyes close and she licks her lips. "John Lennon in the sky."

"What?"

"She's gonna be a bit out of it for the next day or so," a

woman's voice says from behind me. "She's still pretty sedated from surgery."

I turn, my brow furrowing. Standing at the opening between the curtains is a young Asian woman, around my age, maybe, with sleek black hair and a round face. She's familiar, but with the fatigue and stress, I can't quite place her.

She walks in, smiling at us as she works hand sanitizer between her fingers. "Hey, Jesse. It's been a while, huh?"

I check her ID badge and it clicks.

Katie?

Katie Chen is my mom's ICU nurse. *Man, I've been back five minutes and Lennox is already small towning on me pretty hard.*

"Katie," I say with a nod. "Yeah. Hi."

"How's it going, Maureen?" Katie asks at a volume probably reserved for minimally responsive patients, shifting her attention away from me. She places her hand on Mom's shoulder like they're old friends.

Mom doesn't respond, but her eyes flutter a bit at the sound of her name.

"Your mom's doing great," Katie tells us, smiling. "She's been resting like a champ, which is exactly what her body needs right now. And her vitals are getting better every hour, so that's fantastic news. She's really through the worst of it."

"Yeah?" I search Katie's face for reassurance, squeezing Mom's hand a bit tighter.

Katie nods. "Definitely. Making it through surgery after that kind of bleed is *huge*."

Mom tilts her head, opening her eyes slowly again. "You're in Australia."

I smile down at her. "Not anymore, Mom. I'm here now. Had to see what all the fuss was about firsthand."

A monitor starts to sound beside us, which Katie calmly

silences before readjusting one of the wires attached to an electrode on Mom's chest.

Mom seems to have drifted off again when I turn back to her.

"Is she…" I start, realizing I'm not sure what to ask. "How long do you think she'll be here?"

"Actually," Katie says, "she's close to moving on up in the world. Unless any complications crop up, she'll be heading to cardiology, probably tomorrow or the next day?" She looks up as a woman in a green scrub cap appears at the open curtain. "And here's your surgeon, right on cue."

After a quick review of the chart, the doctor leads me and Claire out into the hall to discuss Mom's case while she rests. The doctor explains the aneurysm was likely due to untreated high blood pressure and draws us a diagram to illustrate the placement of the artificial tubing in Mom's abdomen where her aorta ruptured.

I try to file the medical terms away to make sense of later.

"I won't mince my words," the doctor says. "Surviving this kind of rupture is rare. Only about twenty percent. She's lucky to be alive."

Over my shoulder, Mom appears to be sleeping.

Katie shuffles around her bed, writing things on her chart, adjusting the bags of fluid attached to her IV, and pressing buttons to quiet beeping alerts on nearby monitors. She gives me a reassuring smile.

"She'll have to take a few medications," the doctor continues, "but the surgery went really well and we're taking great care of her. And she's still young, which is positive."

"So what does this mean? Is she gonna be sick for the rest of her life, or disabled, or what?" Claire asks, cutting to the chase in her usual blunt manner.

The doctor smiles. "Actually, if Maureen continues to improve at this rate, she should make a full recovery."

"Oh, thank God." Claire visibly sags with relief, then checks her watch.

She must be worried about the kids.

"It won't be immediate," the doctor continues. "It'll take time. She'll need some help over the next six to eight weeks as she recovers."

Six to eight weeks. I might be sticking around longer than I thought.

We thank the doctor, who excuses herself.

A numb daze clouds my mind as I watch nurses and cleaners milling around the unit. I'd known there was a good chance I'd be stepping off that plane several hours too late to say goodbye, but it hadn't really hit me then how close we came to losing Mom. And now she's probably going to be fine? It's like several rugs have been pulled out from under me and I haven't got my footing yet.

My sister pulls me into another hug. "Mom's right, you know."

"About what?"

"You *do* look like John Lennon."

I puff out a quiet laugh.

She pats my back and arms. "But like, *buff* John Lennon."

"Minus the drugs?" I deadpan, pulling back.

"Yeah," she chuckles. "She's the one on drugs, here."

We both laugh—the kind of relieved laughter you only allow yourself once a major threat has passed.

She wipes her eyes with the heel of her hand, then checks her phone. "Listen," she starts quietly, shooting a guilty look up at me. "Now that you're here—"

I cut her off with a nod. "You go."

She exhales. "I'm so sorry. I can stay if you need me to. I'm just... I've barely eaten or slept in twenty-four hours and the kids—"

"Claire. Go home. I've got this now."

"Really? You sure?"

"Yes, I'm sure. Just text me when you get home safe. You okay to drive?" She's got an hour on the road to get back to Seattle.

"Yeah, I'll grab a coffee on the way out." She wells up again. "Thank you for coming."

"Of course." I squeeze her arm. "Now get going."

"You're a good egg." She squishes my cheeks with both hands, and I attempt a smile. "I'll be back tomorrow. I'll call you."

I wave her off.

When I pull the curtain to join Mom again, she's snoring. Not knowing what else to do, I quietly move a chair to her bedside and settle in for a long wait.

I must drift off sitting up, because a glance at the clock when I next lift my head reveals at least forty minutes have passed since I sat down. With effort, I fight off the vestiges of sleep and rub my face in an attempt to wake up. My head feels underwater.

Katie appears at the curtain and does the hand sanitizer routine, smiling softly. "Hey."

"Hey," I reply, my voice rough.

Katie's gaze lifts to the clock on the wall. "You know, she'll probably sleep through the night at this point."

"Oh, shit. I didn't even think about visiting hours. I just..."

Katie waves me off. "There aren't any visiting hours in the ICU. You can be here as much as you want to. Or need to."

"Really?"

"Yeah. Although I wouldn't recommend staying all night. You flew in from Australia?"

"Yeah. Brisbane."

"Get any sleep on the plane? It's... what, a fifteen hour flight?"

"Seventeen. And not really," I admit.

Her jaw drops. "You must be exhausted."

I hum a sound of agreement. "Yeah, I am."

"Where are you staying?"

"With Marcus. Crashing on his couch."

She nods, looking vaguely amused. "Sounds... *comfy?*"

I laugh again but try to keep it down. Stretching back in my chair, I let out a sigh. "Yeah, well. We'll see."

"It's good you won't be alone. But uh... you should go get some rest." Katie tilts her head at Mom. "Obviously, I can promise nothing, but I don't think she's going anywhere. And she needs her sleep too."

"You sure? I told Claire I'd stay..."

Katie nods. "If you leave your number at the front desk, I'll call you right away if anything changes. And they'll give you the direct line for the ICU. You can call anytime day or night to check in."

"Okay." I plant a soft kiss on Mom's forehead before leaving the ward, making sure they have my number on the way out.

Pushing into the fresh night air, I know I need to move my body. But I can't bring myself to walk over to Marcus and Renee's place—not yet. I slump down on a metal bench outside the door and drop my head into my hands. I try to fight the burning behind my eyes but, when I pull my hands away from my face, they're wet.

3

———

ADA

I let out a long sigh, holding the phone to my ear, and stare at the keys in my hand. "Sure, yeah, I can probably come in," I say to Ros.

Katie lets out a disappointed-sounding breath behind me.

I turn and mouth a silent apology, then whisper, "That okay?"

She waves me off with a nod and slumps down at the kitchen table, pulling out her earrings. She knows I need the extra shift.

"I'll need to change," I tell Ros. "But I can head over soon."

"Thanks. I owe you one, Ada." The clatter of glassware and voices in the background fills the pauses between Ros' words. "I know it's last minute, so I really appreciate it." Apparently, Kyle had gone home with a "bad headache". I'd put money on him being hungover after the Fourth of July parties last night, but I keep that to myself.

Ros lets me know it'll just be the two of us tonight, and I mentally steel myself. Friday nights are always busy.

We say our goodbyes and I hang up, cursing Ros' timing.

Katie gathers her long black hair up into a messy bun and rummages in her purse.

"Fucking timing. Sorry," I offer. "You wanna come? Hang out at the bar?"

"Nah, it's okay." She grins. "You know canceled plans are one of my love languages. I mean, don't get me wrong, I would have gone to that restaurant with you. But this"—she pulls out her Kindle, gesturing toward me with it—"is a beautiful consolation prize."

"I should go change," I mutter. "Did you wanna just hang here? Or are you gonna head to Dimitri's—or *your* place, I guess."

"Here for a bit, if that's okay. I still have my key. I'll just get it to you some other time." Apparently noticing my uncertain expression, she adds, "Honest, I could use a quiet night alone."

So much for our last official night as roommates. Katie had moved the last of her things a few days ago, but she'd been holding onto her key until we had the chance to go out and toast the end of an era. This change of plans is... anticlimactic.

"Okay. Breakfast tomorrow instead?" I ask.

"Absolutely," she says.

I nod and head to my room, trying not to frown at the now-empty bedroom beside mine. Still no bites on the ad I put online. I'm about to chuck my phone onto my dresser when a text from my brother lights it up.

MARCUS

You working tonight?

ME

Yeah just got called in, why?

MARCUS

I think Jess needs a break from the hospital stuff

I'm trying to convince him to have a little fun so we might come by

I pause before replying. It'll be cool to see Jesse again, I guess. I try to picture him but realize with surprise that I can't; he's been gone so long I'm having trouble remembering what he looks like. In my mind, there's just a blurry specter of the lanky, blond teenager who used to drive me and the guys to get fast food at 2am.

ME

Cool, see ya tonight then maybe?

Changing into my all-black work clothes, I stop at the mirror, leaning in to inspect my makeup. The inky black eyeliner I put on earlier is on point, drawn in sharp wings that make my eyes appear big and dramatic. I raise a brow. I look hot.

Throwing a light cardigan over my miniskirt and tank top, I grab my purse and phone and take the short walk to work. The summer evening is warm—it's one of those ideal temperatures that, except for a light breeze, feels like you're still indoors. I take a breath of fresh air before pushing through the staff entrance, the hum of the bar and restaurant rushing up to fill my ears.

I quickly stuff my things in the staff room and take up my post at the bar beside Ros.

"Thanks again for coming in," she says, throwing me a grateful smile as she fills a pint glass for a customer seated nearby. "You got here fast."

"Yeah, I was about to go out, so I just had to change."

"Oh, shit, sorry, Ada," she says as she wipes her hands on a towel, then smooths them over her growing belly.

"All good; it's not a huge deal," I half lie. Leaning over to another customer, I take her order and scoop ice into a highball glass. I go through the motions I've done a thousand times before, then slide the rum and coke to the woman waiting nearby.

"I actually wanted to talk to you about something," Ros says.

I finish taking the customer's payment and stab the receipt onto the metal spike next to the till. "What's up?"

"When I go on maternity leave this fall, I'm gonna need someone to take over as manager for a little while." Ros turns to the shelves behind the bar to get a new bottle of Jack Daniel's. "You interested?"

"Wow, um," I start, caught off guard. "Really?"

"Ada, you can do this job with one hand tied behind your back. I think you'd be great at it." Ros' smile is wide.

"Thanks," I say, then tell her I'll think about it. I'm equal parts flattered and reluctant, hating that my first thought is what my parents might think about a promotion.

The bar is humming for the next hour or so. Noticing a brief lull, I spot my chance to get us clean glasses from the kitchen and tell Ros I'll be right back. When I push through the swinging doors, the bright fluorescent light makes me squint. Nodding at Theo, one of the dishwashers, I grab two of the enormous plastic dish racks full of glasses and stack them before awkwardly bracing the weight against my hips. When Theo offers his help, I brush him off.

"Dude, I got it," I say with a smirk.

"Girl, you're crazy." He gives me a dubious look. "Those things are fucking heavy."

"No shit," I say, hefting the racks and ignoring how the plastic handles already dig into my fingers.

Theo shakes his head. "You really shouldn't carry two at a time, either. Ros'll rip you a new one."

"I got it. It's fine," I call back over my shoulder as I push through the swinging doors, already regretting my decision. At least this'll save me a trip later.

I retrace my winding path through the crowded restaurant, swerving around customers and servers. The glasses clink with each step I take. I scowl and puff out a breath, readjusting the racks against my hips with effort. *Theo was right. Damn him. But women can carry heavy shit. I'm doing this for feminism.*

Just as I'm passing the restrooms, the men's room door swings open and a huge body lurches out in front of me. My heavy load collides with the guy's upper thigh and he lets out a small grunt. The sudden impact drives the hard plastic back into my hip bones, the glasses rattling as I hurry to shift my grip. To my relief, I manage not to drop anything. My focus entirely on balancing the glasses, I barely get a glimpse of the guy I've just collided with, registering only a scruffy beard and long blond hair. Hobo surfer chic. Typical Lennox Valley type—even though we're miles from the coast.

"Sorry," he says in a deep voice, sounding almost amused. "I didn't—"

"Just watch where you're going!" I huff in frustration, laser-focused on the glassware that came dangerously close to shattering on the floor. My arms strain under the weight and the circulation to my fingers is getting progressively worse. I readjust my grip, pushing past him in my desperation to set down the trays. I almost lose my shit again when a loud bachelorette party swarms toward me and I barely manage to get ahead of them.

When I finally clunk the trays down on the bar's back counter, I let out a relieved breath. *Victory.* Ros is busy serving customers and doesn't notice I wrangled two racks at once. I clench and unclench my dented hands for a moment, shaking off the discomfort as the blood slowly returns to my fingers.

"Ada!" Marcus calls out, and I turn.

"Oh, hey," I say. Renee is perched on the barstool beside my brother, looking like she spent at least an hour meticulously flat-ironing her blonde hair to perfection. I scan the bar area but don't see anyone else with them. "Where's Jesse?" I frown slightly, then my brow smooths out as an amused smirk takes over my face. "What, did you do your terrible Crocodile Dundee impression and send him running back to Australia?"

"Very funny," Marcus says.

Renee ignores our sibling nonsense and turns to me. "Jesse's here; he just went to the restroom."

I glance behind me—toward the hallway where I just bumped into... I flex my fingers. *No way.*

I turn back right as a large hand claps Marcus on the back, pulling his attention. I look up.

Familiar blue eyes hold my gaze, and my jaw drops as realization rolls over me in slow motion. The shaggy beard and the long hair made him unrecognizable in the hallway a moment ago. But those eyes... Even though they're slightly older, a bit tired, with subtle lines creasing the skin at the outer edges when he smiles? Those eyes are the same. And they're smiling at me.

"Jesse?" I'm incredulous. I flip up the hinged bar top and walk right up to him. "Jesse fucking Bailey? Are you under there?" He startles as I grab him by both cheeks, pulling his face down slightly to give him a good once-over, turning his head side to side. I let go, dropping my arms, and a surprised laugh escapes my lips. "What the actual fuck."

He straightens and runs a hand over his beard, chuckling at my stunned reaction. "Hi, Ada."

Has his voice always been that deep?

"I didn't even recognize you!" I put my hands on my hips, scanning him from head to toe. I turn to Marcus, pointing a finger at Jesse. "Did you see this shit?"

"I know!" Marcus says. "Didn't register it was him at the airport until he was right in front of my face." He laughs and reaches over to tug on Jesse's beard.

"Fuck off." Jesse swats Marcus' hand away. "God, I forgot how *touchy-feely* you both are." He shakes his head, eyes finding mine again.

"Holy crap," I say, then blow out a breath, staring at him. The lanky teenager I used to know is nowhere to be found; instead, there's a broad-chested *man* standing in front of me. And he's *muscled the fuck up*. "Sorry," I say, catching myself, "I just can't get over how different you look."

"Well, shit—same to you," Jesse says, gesturing to me.

"Uh, yeah," I say again, trying to shake off my surprise. A beat passes and I swallow, then avert my gaze, suddenly self-conscious that I'm wearing a damn miniskirt. My tight black bartending outfit might be an unfortunate necessity if I want good tips from drunk assholes, but right now I feel... on display, somehow. I clear my throat and change the subject. "Hey, how's your mom? Sorry to hear what happened, by the way."

"Yeah, thanks. Uh, she's getting stronger every day. But it's slow going."

Ros calls me back to reality, nodding to a few customers waiting to be served. Returning behind the bar, I take their orders, though I'm strangely distracted by Jesse's presence nearby. I must still be in shock—processing how much he's changed in the last eight years. But, as I move around pouring drinks, I swear I can feel him watching me. I glance over and he smiles, his attention lingering on me for the briefest of moments before he turns back to listen to whatever story Renee is telling.

The crowd finally slows enough for me to offer them drinks. My brother orders a beer and Renee a glass of white wine, as always.

"What's your drink, Jesse?"

"I dunno. What's good?" he asks.

I scoff. "Seriously?"

"Yeah, seriously. Recommend something." He tilts his chin at the array of alcohol on display behind me. "Where I live, it's beer or beer. Plus, I'm too tired to decide."

I bite the inside of my cheek, thinking.

"C'mon. Surprise me," he says.

"Okay," I say, shrugging, then turn to start the drinks.

I pour Renee's wine and pull the pint for Marcus, trying to

figure out what to make for Jesse. I have no idea what he likes. Probably not the cheap shit we used to drink as teenagers. Then a thought occurs to me and a private smile tugs at the corner of my mouth. *Fuck it. Surprise it is.*

Setting out a cocktail shaker, I pour in a shot of white rum, some pineapple juice, and a shot of blue curacao. As I reach for a scoop of ice, Jesse gives me a cautious look.

"What the hell are you making me?" he asks, leaning forward on his elbows and peering into the shaker.

Beside him, Marcus huddles close to Renee, engrossed in something on her phone.

"Shut up. You said my choice, right?"

He raises a brow but says nothing.

"It's delicious. Trust me." I add the cream of coconut, then cap and shake it before pouring it over a fresh glass of ice. I flick my eyes up to Jesse, satisfied by his vaguely concerned expression when he clocks the bright blue color. Wedging a slice of pineapple over the rim of the glass, I reach for a maraschino cherry and drop it gently on top.

I'm about to hand it to Jesse when I pause.

"Wait!" I blurt out. I fish a little paper umbrella out from behind the bar and open it, adding it as a finishing touch before sliding the drink over to him.

He glances up with an uncertain smile.

"Welcome home, asshole." I smirk as I wipe my hands on a damp cloth.

He studies the drink, then raises a brow at me.

I soak in his dubious reaction, feeling more than a little pleased with myself.

He shakes his head, his smile splitting into a broad grin.

And that's when I feel it: the slight flush of heat on my collarbone. The unmistakable way my body responds under his gaze.

The warmth spreads, its treasonous tentacles crawling over my skin.

No. Nope.

I force my attention on wiping down the bar, scrambling to keep my cool. My brain races to catch up with my body, ready to give it hell for extreme insubordination.

Shut that shit down, Ada. He's Marcus' best friend.

4

JESSE

I can't believe the girly abomination of a drink Ada just slid in front of me. Her delighted smile and twinkling eyes challenge me to drink it.

"Oh, *fuck me*," I say after I swallow the first sip, screwing up my face in surprise. "That's *good*." I look to Ada but she's busy wiping down the bar, her amusement gone. I get the distinct feeling I missed something.

"Jesus Christ, Jess," Marcus says, clocking my excessively adorned drink. "Are you a 21-year-old sorority girl all of a sudden, or what?"

"Well, if this is the shit they drink, no wonder they're so bubbly," I say. "This has gotta be mostly sugar."

Ada gives a small nod of confirmation.

"It tastes like a piña colada. What's it called?" I ask her before taking another sip.

"A blue Hawaiian," Renee answers for me. "I used to drink them in college," she adds with a guilty shrug.

Marcus puts his arm around her and pulls her close, kissing her temple.

"Oh, hey," I say, lifting my chin at Ada. "I saw Katie at the hospital."

"Yeah. She mentioned. Well, sort of. She was there when I got Marcus' text about picking you up. But don't worry, she's a pro—those lips were zipped."

"Right. Doctor-patient confidentiality. Or nurse-patient confidentiality, I guess." I nod, taking another sip of my drink. "Mom's out of the ICU now, at least. They moved her to the surgical ward."

For the past few days, I've been visiting her every day during designated visiting hours—leaving me a ton of time to spin my wheels and worry. It's why I agreed to come out tonight; my life here is so nonexistent, there wasn't much else for me to do besides pester the hospital for yet another update only to be reassured she's fine. Marcus was right. I need a break.

"That's good, right?" Ada asks. "Sounds like an upgrade."

"Yeah, it's an improvement," I hedge, not really wanting to get into it here. "But we don't need to..."

"Yeah, lay off the heavy shit," Marcus interrupts, clapping me on the back. "We're out to have a good time."

Ada and I share a look. She's watching me closely, as if to see if I'm truly cool with dropping the topic.

The truth is, I'd like nothing more than to forget about all that stress... at least for tonight. I slap on a brave face.

"You still staying with Marcus?" she asks, seeming to pick up on my desire to move on.

"Yeah, on the couch."

"Still?" Ada rounds on her brother. "Marcus, what the fuck? You couldn't spring for an airbed or something?"

Marcus' eyes widen at Ada's reprimand and he shrugs, cutting a glance my way. "He says it's fine!"

"Is that how you treat your best friend? Kind of a dick move." She fills a glass with ice for another customer. "That couch is trash."

"Ada, it's all good, I swear," I say, holding up my hands with a smile.

She shifts her gaze to me briefly, then zeroes back in on her brother, giving him a dubious scowl.

Why does it bother her?

"Yeah, see? He says it's fine!" Marcus pleads in defense, gesturing at me. "Chill out, Ada. *Christ.*"

She continues, undeterred. "I mean, Mom and Dad probably have a spare mattress. You could put it on the floor for him at least."

"Ada, it's fine," I say. "Honest. I've slept on worse."

"Hey, thanks for that ringing endorsement, buddy," Marcus cuts in, chucking a light punch at my shoulder.

I throw him a quick knowing glance—I have to admit, the couch is a little uncomfortable—but don't reply. For some reason, I'm vaguely comforted that Ada came to my defense about the sleeping arrangements.

"I'd stay at my mom's, but I can walk to the hospital from Marcus and Renee's. It's just easier."

Ada studies me, though she doesn't appear convinced. "How long are you—" she starts, but Marcus doesn't notice and cuts her off.

"Look, you two wanna order food?" he asks me and Renee. We both nod.

"You'll have to go find a table," Ada says. She tilts her chin at the restaurant behind us. "No kitchen service at the bar."

Collecting our drinks, we leave Ada to the throng of waiting customers and head over to the hostess to get a table.

I turn back to raise my blue drink her way, my pinky lifted in silent thanks for the sugar rush.

She reaches up to brush a lock of equally turquoise hair away from her face and I catch her eye. Smiling, she turns back to the customer in front of her.

I watch her a moment longer, taking a few steps backward before I turn to follow Marcus and Renee. She's so... grown up. I mean, she *is* grown up now. But there's something kind of weird about seeing her again. *Good weird.*

The hostess seats us across the room, with Marcus and Renee on one side of the table and me across from them. I drape an arm over the back of the empty chair beside me.

"So, tell us more about Australia," Renee says, taking a sip of wine. Her pin-straight, bleach-blonde hair swishes over her shoulders. "Like, what kind of work were you doing on the farms?"

"Shit, pretty much everything, honestly. When I first moved there, I did this work placement program where we learned all kinds of stuff: how to ride horses, drive tractors, use chainsaws..." I trail off, searching my memory. I'd worked as much as I could then. It was the only thing that kept me from having to face the mess our family had become as my parents' bitter divorce played out. "Got a job on a cattle ranch for a couple of years after that."

Renee nods as I speak, looking almost awe-struck. There are a few small farms around Lennox Valley, but most of the population lives in the town center with no real connection to the land. I'm sure, to her, I sound like I'd been on another planet. It had felt a bit like one too. Which had been the whole point—to put some distance between me and my parents. Between me and Naomi. The Pacific Ocean had turned out to be *some distance,* alright.

"Wasn't there a fruit farm?" Marcus asks, likely remembering his visit to see me on the coast of Queensland a few years ago.

"Yup. Fruit, sugarcane, rice, corn..." I list them off, counting on my fingers. I shake my head, realizing how many odd jobs I've worked while I've been down there. I basically picked up anything I could with long hours of physical labor. The hard work wore my body and mind to the point of exhaustion, and I was grateful to not have to think. Over time, it got easier to forget what was happening back home. And then I just... stayed.

Our server appears and quickly takes our order before hurrying off into the din of the busy restaurant.

"What do you do for fun on a farm? Cow tipping?" Renee asks with a chuckle.

I give her a polite smile. "I don't think that's really a thing. More of an urban legend."

She looks sheepish.

"But uh, no, I didn't get out much. Long hours. Most of the year, at least. And we were pretty far from town. Did some dirt biking." I shrug.

"How'd you manage to date?"

I make a noncommittal sound and shake my head. I've wrangled everything from produce to horses—not a lot of dates, though.

Renee's brows shoot up as she leans in. "You mean to tell me you spent most of your twenties in the bush and barely got out? No partying or anything like that?"

"So, really, not much time *in the bush*," Marcus quips, earning an eye roll from Renee.

"I mean, when we had time off, we'd go into the city and live it up. There was this girl in Brisbane for a while. But nothing serious. I didn't really want that, anyway, after Naomi..." I glance at Marcus, who gives me a sober nod. "And my job didn't exactly give me the chance to try."

"Seems like such a *waste*." Renee pouts.

I clear my throat, suddenly aware of how much I've shared and the sad smile Renee has trained on me. "Yeah, but I love it there, honestly. It's rewarding work, actually seeing how what we do puts food on the table, y'know?" Grateful the pity has vanished from her expression, I continue. "And I've been taking on some bigger projects—some cool sustainability stuff... It's good." I smile, trying to sell it. It's not a lie, exactly.

"That's great, man," Marcus says, setting his pint on the table. "Hey, uh, and I don't wanna jinx it or anything, but maybe if... or *when* your mom's doing better," he corrects himself, "you might wanna catch up with everyone?"

I suck in a breath, considering this. *No,* I want to blurt out. *It's been too long. There's no point.* But the hopeful look on Marcus' face stops me.

"Nah," I say, trying to let him down easy. "I mean, I need to take care of my mom. I wasn't really... planning on a social visit, y'know? Plus, it's been ages. Probably have nothing in common with those guys anymore."

Because I've let those friendships wither and die. I push down a stab of regret.

He nods slowly, pressing his lips together, and says nothing. After fifteen years of friendship, he knows pushing me is a sure-fire way to get me to dig in my heels. But I can tell he's disappointed.

"Dude, I'm happy to see you; don't get me wrong," I say, trying to ease the sting. "But I wasn't exactly planning on coming back."

"Like... *at all?* Ever?" Renee asks.

"I mean, yeah? I dunno. I think so? I've got a good setup in Oz. A decent job. A place to stay." I lift my chin toward Marcus. "And you know how I wanted to steer clear of all the bullshit with my family... My life is pretty much *there* now."

"Okay," is all he says, and takes a sip of beer.

Swirling the last of my diluted blue drink in my glass, I glance over at the bar, where Ada's talking to a customer and laughing.

"You both up for another round?" I ask, draining the dregs. I try to catch our server's attention, but he's clearly slammed. I shift in my seat to stand, knowing it'll be faster if I just go to the bar myself.

"Sure," Marcus says and Renee nods. He reaches for his wallet.

"No, man," I say, waving him off. "I've got it."

Crossing the room, I can't help but watch Ada.

Nothing wrong with that. She's the bartender and I'm heading for the bar. I'm basically just watching where I'm going.

A small voice inside my head points out it's interesting that I'm feeling the need to justify looking at Ada, but I quickly stuff the thought as I close in on the bar. I'm a few feet away when she notices me.

"Hey," she says, filling a tumbler glass with soda and sliding it across the bar top to a customer. "How's that pancreas?"

Playing along, I take a seat on an empty stool in front of her. "Was that your game? Destroy my internal organs?"

"Maybe." She smirks up at me.

"Harsh," I say, recoiling. "I've only been back a few days."

She gives me a small smile, tilting her chin over to where Marcus and Renee sit with their backs to us. "Did you all want another round?"

"Yeah. Same again for those two," I say, "but let's save my pancreas this time. Maybe a gin and tonic?"

"Sure." She moves to get another wine bottle from the glass shelves behind her.

My eyes drop against my will. *Fuck, that's a short skirt.* I tear my gaze away, rubbing the back of my neck. I try to look around the room as she makes our drinks.

I can't believe this is the same girl who used to tag along with us on our idiotic, teenage escapades. Without question, she'd held her own with the group of us older guys. She could deliver some epic trash talk when she kicked our asses playing video games, which she'd done more often than I'd liked to admit. Back then, we'd all kind of thought of her as one of the guys. It had been an unspoken understanding she could never be more than that to any of us. Kai had once made a crude, sexual joke about Ada, and

Marcus had shut him down instantly. The message had been clear: don't even fucking think about it.

I turn back to Ada and catch her watching me. My lips curl in an uncertain smile. "What?"

"Nothing. Sorry for staring. Just wondering if you're cosplaying as Sasquatch, or …" she trails off with a soft laugh.

"Rough," I reply, moving back in my seat, my forearms sliding across the bar top. I smooth a hand over my beard, though I can't help but smile. Maybe that trash-talking kid is still in there. "That bad, huh?"

"*Unexpected* is more the word."

"Fair," I say, nodding as she slides me my gin and tonic. "Though I could say the same about you. Not the Sasquatch part, obviously."

She barks a laugh, wiping down the counter. "Fucking hope not."

"I was expecting that weird art kid with braces, to be honest," I say.

She glances up. "Well, the braces are long gone, but I'm still a weird art kid, don't worry."

Except you're definitely not a fucking kid anymore, I stop myself from saying.

"What kind of art?" I take a sip of my drink.

"Uh, I draw and paint. And I run these evening art classes for teens down at the community center. It's a volunteer thing. Sometimes I do other activities with them too—outings and stuff."

"Really? That's cool."

"Yeah, I really like it." She takes a sip of water from behind the bar, long seconds passing before she speaks again. "Sorry for smashing into you earlier."

"Oh, was that you?" I deadpan.

She laughs and I clear my throat. We share an awkward glance.

"This is fucked up," Ada says, scrunching up her nose with a soft laugh. "Why you're back, I mean."

"Yeah. Tell me about it." Sadness creeps into my awareness, remembering why I'm in town. I run a hand through my hair and push back from the bar, reaching for my wallet. Without looking, I gesture over my shoulder. "I should get them their drinks."

"It's on me," she says, waving me off. "Consider it a *sorry-everything's-all-fucked-up* gift."

"Thanks, Ada," I say, pocketing my wallet.

"Oh, and hey," she says. "Can I make your mom a card? Draw her something?"

"Uh, yeah. Thanks. She'd love that."

"Does she have a favorite flower or…?"

"Pink carnations."

Ada tilts her head, evidently impressed. "Wow, you didn't even hesitate. Major *good son* brownie points to you."

I laugh. "Don't give me too much credit. My sister sent me on a mission to buy her some the other day."

"Okay, well, then your brownie points are revoked."

I chuckle, and our gazes lock for a few long seconds, something I can't name glittering in those brown eyes of hers.

"It's uh… really good to see you." Not sure what else to say, I move to pick up the glasses.

"You too."

Carefully balancing our drinks, I return to the table, where our food has arrived.

Marcus relieves me of his pint glass, and I hand Renee her wine, taking a sip of my drink as I sit back down.

"You were gone a while," Marcus comments, throwing a glance over his shoulder toward his sister.

"Ada said I looked like Sasquatch. I had to defend my honor," I say, smiling before digging into my food.

"Sounds about right," Marcus says.

"Which part? Me looking like Sasquatch or Ada telling me I do?"

He shrugs. "Both."

I CAN'T SLEEP. While the jet lag has lifted, the stress about my mom has brought on its own cruel combination of exhaustion and wakefulness. Feeling guilty about going out for some frivolous social time, I called the hospital for an update when I got back from the bar. Mom's fine, everything's stable. That's good. And yet I'm still feeling so helpless.

I stare at Marcus' living room ceiling, lit by the dim orange glow of the streetlights outside. Propping one arm behind my head, I let my thoughts drift to Ada, smiling to myself as I remember her grouchy reaction to bumping into me outside the restroom. She'd barely looked up and clearly had no idea who I was—but I'd known it was her instantly. I'd been on the receiving end of that grumpy voice so often when we were younger.

Shaking off my initial surprise at our collision, I'd followed her down that hallway, hanging a few paces back. I'd watched her heft those dish racks over to the bar, the lean muscles in her arms and shoulders straining under the weight she carried. *When had she gotten that tattoo?* I'd shamelessly let myself study her as she moved in front of me, telling myself it was normal to be surprised about how she'd changed. I'd only snapped out of it when a rowdy bachelorette party lurched in front of me, cutting me off. When I'd finally made it back to the bar and Ada had recognized me, I told myself it was natural to notice that she was beautiful. Anyone could see it was true.

But now I'm struggling to stop thinking it—to stop picturing the curve of Ada's ass in that fucking miniskirt, or the way her tight tank top hugged her tits.

No fucking way did I just think the words tits *and Ada* in the same sentence.

This has to stop. *She's Marcus' little sister, for fuck's sake.* The first commandment of best friendship has got to be *Thou shalt not covet thy best friend's sibling.*

Guilt gathers heavy in my gut.

Restless and uncomfortable, I shift on the couch. It's too hot in here. I kick the blanket away from my bare feet and run a hand down my face. I can still almost feel the heat of Ada's soft hands on my skin when she'd marched over and grabbed my cheeks, inspecting me with those gorgeous wide eyes... *Shit.*

Stop. Just think about regular things. Focus on Mom. Or figuring out how to get your vacation back on track. Anything.

Not that I have much hope of getting back to my vacation; Mom's gonna need help and Claire lives an hour away in Seattle. I might be here for a while yet.

I turn onto my side and punch the pillow under my ear, trying to get comfortable as the couch springs squawk under my weight. Another smile tugs at my lips as Ada's incredulous words drift into my mind: *That couch is trash.* Catching myself once again, I clench my jaw, pushing my amusement away.

Focus on the trash couch—anything but Ada.

5

───────

ADA

Perched on a white bench outside the fitting room, I stare at the mirror across from me and scowl at the pile of men's clothing heaped on my lap. I already regret agreeing to come here.

"You almost done in there?" I call out to Jesse.

"We just got here. Hold your horses," he grouses back, mocking my impatient tone.

I roll my eyes.

This is all Renee's fault.

Apparently, Jesse had mentioned needing a few things; having packed to spend the summer traveling Southeast Asia, the wardrobe he'd brought to Lennox consisted of swim trunks, tank tops, and a collection of work-worn T-shirts and jeans. He'd felt a bit underdressed Friday night at the bar and, once it became clear he'd be sticking around to help his mom for a while, he'd figured it was time to bite the bullet and go shopping.

Renee had jumped at the chance to take him—probably eager to provide her womanly guidance to this scruffy country bumpkin. But, when she'd gotten called away to finalize a sale, she'd determined that *my* womanly guidance would suffice—although no one had been thrilled about the change of plans. I'd made sure to grumble audibly about spending my Tuesday morning doing community service.

I extract my right hand from the tangle of hangers and pull out my phone to text Katie.

ME

I'm in retail hell. Can fluorescent lighting cause brain death?? Asking for a friend.

She texts back right away.

KATIE

Medically, no. Spiritually? Sure.

I smile to myself, biting my lip as my thumb hovers over the on-screen keyboard. I know I should tell Katie about what's actually causing my brain death—this unacceptable attraction to Jesse —but I can barely admit it to myself. Before I can text back, the fitting room door clicks open. I lift my head and pocket my phone, taking a measured breath.

Ah, fuck.

"Thoughts?" Jesse asks, running a hand through his long hair as he steps toward me. He's wearing a fitted, gray T-shirt over dark jeans. He holds out his arms, turning a bit. The shirt hugs his chest muscles in a way I immediately regret noticing.

"I dunno. Turn around," I instruct.

He does a slow and patient spin as I try not to stare at his ass longer than strictly necessary. I sigh internally; he's got a great ass. I hate this.

"Well?" He looks at me, then down at the clothes, placing his hands on his hips.

"I mean, they're fine, I guess." I shrug.

"Fine, you guess? Shit, Ada, think you can manage *any* level of enthusiasm, here?"

"Sorry." I clear my throat and put on an exaggerated sing-song tone, flicking my hair. "They're fine, I guess!" I smile and bat my lashes, then let my face drop. "Enthusiastic enough for you?"

"Fuck off." He shakes his head as he turns back to the changing room, then shuts the door.

"It's a T-shirt and jeans, Jess," I call out. "That's what you usually wear, isn't it?" I feel my womanly guidance gland shriveling in real time.

"Yeah, I guess," he replies, shuffling around behind the door.

I bite hard on the inside of my cheek to distract myself from the mental image of him peeling off that shirt.

When he opens the door again, he eyes me with caution. He's got on a dark green Henley and black jeans. He looks... Damn.

Never mind how he looks, Ada.

I'm careful to project an unimpressed vibe as I inspect him. I should probably win an award for my ability to control my facial expressions. Standing, I dump the pile of clothes on the bench and walk over to him. He turns away from me to assess his reflection and I let my gaze rove over his back, definitely *not* noticing the flex of his shoulder muscles when he reaches up to adjust the tag at the back of his neck.

"Undo that top button," I say.

He laughs. "You always this bossy?"

"Hey, you wanna dress like a dork? Go right ahead."

He scoffs and undoes the button.

"Now push up your sleeves."

Studying me in the mirror, he follows my orders. His muscular forearms flicker with movement as he slips his hands into the pockets of his pants.

Lord, help me. Is it warm in here?

"Okay, it's decent," I concede, darting a glance up at his face. "Still look like Teen Wolf, though."

I'm leaning heavy on the sass pedal today.

He runs a hand over his beard, shaking his head again. "That was a cheap shot."

The corner of my mouth quirks up. *Fuck.* Why is he looking at me like that? Cheeks heating, I turn back to the bench of abandoned clothes. Then my mouth is moving before I can think better of it. "You know, I can cut your hair for you, if you want."

What the fuck, Ada? No. No touching.

I fight off a cringe and pull my features into an impassive mask before I turn around to face him again—like this is something a totally normal friend you haven't seen in eight years would offer to do.

"Wait, you cut hair?" He gives me a wary look.

"Not, like, as a job, obviously. But yeah, I cut my own and sometimes my friends'. It saves money, and I'm good at it." I shrug. "Whatever. Just saying: I could take care of that mess for you." I gesture at his blond waves.

"*That mess*? Wow. Well, excuse me for not racing to accept your generous offer." He pulls a hair tie from his wrist, placing it between his teeth as he sweeps his hair up. The hem of his shirt lifts, revealing a small glimpse of skin above his waistband—and the trail of soft hair that disappears into his pants. I avert my eyes, hoping he didn't catch me staring.

Shit. Stop ogling him. Jesse is a no-fly zone.

I finally notice his hair. "A man bun? Really?"

"What, were you hoping for a French braid?" He frowns, turning to me. "Why are you so fucking salty today?" Standing at least a head taller than me, he peers down, searching my expression. He's close enough to touch.

I shrug, backing away half a step. "Shopping's just... not my thing."

"Then why'd you agree to come with me?" he asks, clearly baffled. He moves to grab the pile of clothes from the bench, shoving them inside the fitting room. Then he turns back to me, leaning against the doorway with his arms crossed. "I could have handled this by myself."

God, what is it about that pose?

I force myself to tear my gaze away from his thick biceps.

"Oh, please. You've been in the bush for eight years. You *need* my help. You'd be hopeless without me."

A rueful smile tugs at his lips before something softens in his face, as if he's deciding not to fight this fight. "Okay," he finally says, pushing away from the doorframe and stepping toward me. "Not gonna lie. I hate this too. So let's get the fuck outta here." He tilts his head toward the exit.

"What about the rest of those clothes?"

"Fuck 'em," he says, wrinkling his nose. "I'll buy a few of these things." He motions to what he's wearing. "Good enough. Let me get changed, and we can go get lunch or something. I'm fucking starving." He pauses. "Have you eaten?"

"Uh... no," I say.

"Well, maybe if you eat something, you'll be less of a brat."

My expression flattens. "Thanks."

"Come on, Ada. My treat." He must sense my hesitation, because he adds, "For all your... *help*," doing air quotes around the last word.

"Right." I scoff. "Like I actually helped you." I've been a total boat anchor and we both know it.

"Oh, I learned a lot," he says, putting on an innocent air. "Undoing buttons? Rolling up sleeves? You gave me a real master-class in slutting it up."

I snort, unable to suppress the laugh that fights its way out. "That wasn't what I was trying to—"

"Right, right, right," he says quickly, nodding.

I narrow my eyes. "Just get dressed, dumbass."

Giving me a crooked smile, he backs into the fitting room and closes the door.

RIVERSIDE DELI IS PACKED. We order subs and wedge ourselves into the corner by the window, perching on two high stools. Loud chatter surrounds us as the patrons talk over the ambient hum of refrigerators and the clatter of dishes. For the moment, the noise drowns out my problematic thoughts about Jesse—the noise and the smell of my toasted turkey sub. Suddenly ravenous, I peel open the wrapper.

"Marcus told me about this place." He unwraps his and takes a huge bite. A sliced pickle falls out. "Oh, my God. Amazing," he mumbles around his mouthful.

I smile and take a bite of my own sandwich. It's sloppy with mayo and Italian dressing. Some splats out onto the wrapper as I hover over it. The flavors hit me, and I make a little sound of relief —almost a moan.

Jesse laughs, his voice muffled as he chews. "That good?"

"So fucking good." I hold a hand in front of my mouth, trying not to be gross about it. The top of the bun slides around precariously under my fingers and I readjust my grip, furrowing my brow as the sauce slips between my knuckles. I take another bite.

"This beats shopping," Jesse says between bites.

"Right?"

We eat without speaking for a few moments.

"So, how long do you think you'll be in town?" I ask. "Marcus mentioned another few weeks at least?"

He takes a thoughtful breath. "Yeah, that's what the doctors tell me. Trying to figure out a plan, you know?"

"And?" I lick dressing off my finger, cursing the delicious mess.

Jesse's silent for a moment. When I turn to face him, he jolts slightly, as if shaking off a momentary trance. His throat bobs as he swallows. "Uh, well, my mom's doing better all the time, which is great, but she's still going to need help once she goes home. And, at this point, I've pretty much given up on making it to Thailand."

"So... you gonna just stick around and see how it goes?" I use my pinky to coax a napkin off the counter, nudging it toward me to try to contain the chaos.

"Think I have to. Claire can't really help that much, between her job and the kids and living an hour away. Plus, her husband's out of town for work a lot. So I guess it's on me. I mean, I do have two months off work—I'm technically *available*. Just didn't think I'd be..." He trails off, looking out the window at the busy street.

"Here?"

He turns to me with a thoughtful expression. "Yeah."

"Well, Lennox Valley is certainly a far fucking cry from Bangkok." I take another bite.

"Yeah? Have you been?"

"Once," I mumble around my mouthful. "About three years ago? I traveled through Asia before I went to Europe."

"Oh, yeah. Marcus was telling me. You've really gotten around, huh?"

I arch a brow in acknowledgment as I chew. "Europe was my favorite. I spent a few months with extended family in Italy, then traveled around a bit. Went to all the art galleries I could find, worked a bunch..."

"Is that where you learned to bartend?"

"In Ireland, yeah." I nod.

"You're good at it. From what I've seen, I mean. Do you like it?"

"Parts of it. I like my other gig better."

"Right, with the teens. The, uh, weird art kid mentorship program?" His lips curve in a wry smile.

I laugh. "Yeah. Dunno if you remember, but I used to go to the teen center at West Valley when I was younger."

He frowns like he's searching his memory.

"School was always kinda hard for me," I continue, "and it gave me a place to be myself and get away from my parents." Admitting this to Jesse feels so lame. I suddenly feel like a child— Marcus' embarrassing kid sister. "It's dumb. Whatever. Forget I mentioned it."

He shakes his head and swallows. "Doesn't sound dumb. If you enjoy it, and you're helping the kids. Sounds great, actually."

I nod, and a beat of silence passes.

"Why'd you come back?" he asks. "After traveling for so long, I mean."

I swallow, not answering right away, and take a sip of my drink. I weigh how much detail to give him about what happened with Pascal. "Bad breakup. He... uh..."

"You don't have to tell me, you know," he says, his voice low enough that only I can hear him in the busy deli. And yet, there's something about the way he's looking at me that makes me want to tell him.

I grimace, brushing off his concern. "No, it's fine. I was living in Ireland. I got into this applied arts program in London and moved there for a few months. We did the long-distance thing... until I found out he fucked someone else."

Jesse nearly chokes on his sandwich. "Oh, shit!"

I use my elbow to slide him a napkin, waiting for him to regain his composure before continuing. "Yeah. It... sucked. *Really* sucked. So, anyway, when that program ended, I came back here. I'd been gone a while, and I figured it was time to stop fucking around. You know, you can only run away from home for so long..."

"Yeah," he breathes, nodding slowly.

My eyes widen when I realize what I just implied. *Shit.* "I didn't mean—"

"No, it's fine. You're... not wrong." He gives me a tight smile and we turn back to our subs, effectively dodging any in-depth discussion about why we've both felt the need to escape this place.

My sandwich is quickly losing its structural integrity. The top bun slides awkwardly off to one side, shreds of lettuce escaping and raining down from it at every opportunity. Mayo and dressing drip down my hands, over my wrists, and onto the checkered wax paper wrapper below. I give the sub a bewildered scowl. If it weren't so damn delicious, I'd give up and chuck it down—call it a day.

"You, uh... you have mayo on your face." Jesse gives me a side-long glance.

I turn to him. "Where?"

"There," he says with a smirk, pointing to one side of my mouth with a free pinky finger.

I lick around my lips, trying to clean it up without having to let go of my rapidly disintegrating sub.

"No, it's still there," he says, chuckling as I redouble my efforts. "Here," he says, setting his sandwich down and picking up a napkin.

I swallow as he turns to me. "What are you doing?" I ask, my body ringing alarm bells. I'm suddenly aware of my breathing.

"Just hold still, damnit." A slow smile plays over his lips.

"Ugh, fine," I say, realizing I need the help. "Just don't lick the napkin first like a gross grandma." I back away in a cautious pause.

His expression falls. "Do I look like a gross grandma?"

If only you did.

He leans in and gently wipes my cheek at the corner of my mouth, his gaze lifting to mine and twinkling with amusement.

My breath hitches ever so slightly in my throat as I search his eyes. I barely have time to register his wicked grin as he shoves the napkin into my face, pushing me back with it. I gasp, my entire body tensing as I try not to lose my balance and fall off the stool.

"Ugh, *asshole!*" I say, dropping my sandwich and shoving Jesse away, messy hands be damned. I sit there gaping as he laughs.

He leans in close, dropping his voice low. "That's for all your snarky bullshit back at the store." He pulls back and slowly wipes his hands on a clean napkin, smirking at me.

"You're dead to me, Bailey."

"Oh, I doubt that."

When he hands me another clean napkin, I snatch it out of his hands.

"For real, though. I'm sorry that prick cheated on you." His earnest tone takes me by surprise. "You didn't deserve it."

"Uh, yeah. Thanks." I feel like I have whiplash from the quick shift. "He *was* a prick, in hindsight."

"Sounds like a shithead, yeah." A muscle flexes in Jesse's jaw as if he's holding himself back from saying something more.

"A horny shithead," I add.

"Hey," Jesse says, looking taken aback. "Some of us are horny and *respectful.*"

I can't help but laugh. "My apologies to the *respectfully horny* men out there."

"Thank you. I'll let the other guys know at our next meeting." Jesse pops the last bite of his sub into his mouth and grins.

6

JESSE

"Don't you have something better to do than hang out with a sick old lady?" Mom asks. She takes a sip of water, then rearranges the blanket over herself on the couch. "Something with your friends?"

"Not really," I say, squeezing her knee. "I'm here to help *you* out, remember? You come first." I arrange Mom's medication bottles in a row on the coffee table next to the TV remote and her cell phone, mentally checking that she has everything she might need now that she's home. Her little ad hoc command center reminds me of staying home sick from school as a kid. She'd always set me up in a couch nest with all my toys, coloring books, snacks, and favorite movies.

"Honestly, honey, I'm fine. And if you're stuck in Lennox helping me, the least you can do is enjoy yourself in the meantime."

It's been just under two weeks since the aneurysm, and it'll be another several more until Mom's able to drive or exert herself again. I've officially abandoned all hope of making it to Bangkok.

Instead of vacationing, I'll be spending the rest of the summer playing chauffeur and errand boy whenever Mom needs me.

"Plus," she adds, "Claire's coming by tomorrow with the kids, so that'll be more than enough excitement for me."

I raise an eyebrow, unconvinced.

"I *mean* it." She gives me a serious glare. "I have nothing to do here but sleep and... probably sleep some more. And I'm cleared to shuffle to the kitchen if I want to grab something to eat." She lifts her chin at her freshly restocked fridge. "This condo is tiny. Everything's basically in arm's reach here. So you can go. I'll be *fine*."

"Yeah, but that's what you always say." I'm still nervous about leaving her alone, knowing there aren't any nurses or defibrillators just around the corner. After finally getting discharged this morning, she seems suddenly vulnerable to me. I try to let it go, remembering her doctor's reassurances before we left. She just needs to take it easy, take her meds, and keep up with her follow-up appointments. Things are looking good. With a resigned sigh, I push off the couch and head to grab my wallet and phone.

"I wish I had the space to put you up here," Mom says.

"Nah, you need your rest." It's true enough, though there's a sense of relief in shrugging off the idea of staying in such close quarters together. I'm not sure I'm ready to face everything we've been avoiding for the last eight years. "I can keep crashing with Marcus. It's fine."

As if Mom can feel the stiffness already settling in my back, she says, "Honey, twenty-seven is too old to be crashing on a friend's couch. And you're too tall for it. You need a proper bed."

Admittedly, the prospect of spending several more weeks on the *trash couch* is daunting.

My phone buzzes as I pick it up, and I unlock the screen. Distractedly, I say, "I'll figure something out, okay? Don't worry about me."

ADA

You free this afternoon?

ME

Yeah just leaving my mom's. What's up?

I lean in to kiss Mom's cheek. "Call me if you need anything, alright?" I point at her, smiling as I head to the door. "I mean it. And I'll be back tonight to check on you."

She lifts her hands in surrender, and we say our goodbyes. I let myself out and my phone buzzes again in the elevator.

ADA

Wanna come over?

My eyebrows twitch together. *She wants to just... hang out? Just us?* I hate how strong the impulse is to say yes. As I hesitate, another text comes through.

ADA

Just to like, be here? I've got people coming by to see Katie's old room.

Dropped the rent on the ad and I have three people interested all of a sudden.

Right. Ada needs a roommate. Marcus said something about Katie moving out. *Wait. Ada needs a roommate.* The thought makes me hold my breath. *No. Never gonna work. It'd be weird. Plus, I'm not here long.*

ADA

Katie was gonna come but she had to stay late at work.

It'd be cool not to be here alone with sketchy strangers. A couple of them are dudes. #notgettingmurdered

ME

> So what, you basically need someone with a pulse?

ADA

> Pulse optional, but I think a dead body might send the wrong message.

"Nice place," I say, peering around Ada's apartment. It's sparse—I assume since Katie moved out with her stuff.

"Sure," Ada says, like she doesn't believe me.

Better than the trash couch.

"So, I was thinking you could just hang out here and look..." Ada pauses, scrutinizing me. "Can you do *scary*?"

"What?" I laugh and lean back against the counter, crossing my arms. "Are you serious?"

"I told you, not getting murdered today. These are *internet* people, Jesse. God knows who the fuck is gonna walk in here." She stuffs her hands into the pockets of her jean shorts and shrugs.

"Aren't you overreacting a bit? They'll probably be normal."

She scoffs. "Men don't understand."

"What?" I frown.

"That women have to worry about getting murdered by strangers!" Her eyes are wide. "Like, *all the time!*"

I guess she's right. Lennox is a small, safe town, but not so small that everyone and their dog knows each other. And, from what I've seen, the place has grown a bit since I've been away. Maybe it's not entirely out of the question that dodgy folks could show up here.

"Okay, fine," I say, resigned. "Sorry. I won't let anyone murder you, okay? And I'll be *scary* if that's what you need."

She drops her shoulders, visibly relaxing. "Thank you."

"I doubt it'll come to that, though," I say. "When's the first person coming?"

She checks her phone. "Any minute now. Oh! We should come up with a secret signal. For if I'm feeling uncomfortable and need you to... you know... *step in*."

"A... secret signal." I smooth a hand over my beard, conjuring up visions of my little league baseball coach. "Do you mean, like, something you say, or something you do?"

"It should be something I say, right? Otherwise, you'll have to follow us around the entire time, like a weird lurker. I'll call something out."

"Okay." *Don't be a weird lurker. Got it.*

"How about: *Hey, Jess! Don't forget to wish your mom a happy birthday.*" She gives me an expectant look.

"It's not my mom's—"

"Ugh," she says, cutting me off. "It doesn't matter. It's just a line."

A knock at the door pulls her attention, and she brushes past me to answer it.

For a moment, her sweet scent surrounds me.

Jesus. No. Focus on the impromptu drama club thing, here.

"What do you want me to do?" I try to keep my voice down. "If you give me the signal?"

She turns to me, still retreating toward the door. "I don't know!" she hisses. "Pretend you're my jealous boyfriend?" Her expression is screaming *duh*, like I should know what she's thinking. As she grasps the doorknob, she adds, "Just act possessive or something!"

Instant tension knots my stomach. "Ada, I..."

Fuck. Alone in the kitchen, I run my hands down my face, bracing myself for whatever lecherous, murdering Casanova type is about to waltz in here and force me to showcase my mediocre acting skills.

How did I get wrangled into this shit so fast?

But any concern about needing to posture as Ada's scary boyfriend—whatever the hell *that* entails—evaporates the moment the guy walks in. For starters, he's not alone. An older woman accompanies him, a protective hand on his shoulder like he's a flight risk. I try to work out their dynamic. He stares at his feet a lot and at the woman—who introduces herself as his mother—the rest of the time. He barely speaks, and everything about the guy's slumped posture screams a defeated kind of insecurity.

"So, this is it, I guess," Ada says. "Did you, uh, wanna see the second room?"

They nod and follow her.

"Have you had any issues with mold?" the mother asks. "Because Alex has asthma, and these basement apartments can be quite damp."

I don't hear Ada's reply, but the glimpses of her I do catch suggest she's trying her best to be polite—and struggling.

I smile to myself and sit at the kitchen table to scroll on my phone while I wait.

Ada walks them through a perfunctory apartment tour, explaining the practicalities of Katie's old room and the common living spaces. When they finish, they return to the main entry near the kitchen.

"So, what would my Alex be needing to do in terms of chores?" the woman intones. "He's a very good boy; I raised him right, don't get me wrong!" She forces a laugh that neither Ada nor I return. "But he gets squeamish with handling yucky things like the garbage or the goop in the bottom of the sink." She makes a sour face to accentuate the point. "He has a sensitive stomach, you know."

Ada and I share a glance, then resume acting like this is a normal way for an adult man to tour a potential apartment.

"Sure," Ada says tentatively to Alex. "We'd basically clean up our own messes, I guess. We could talk about a system... if you need that."

He doesn't return her inquiring look.

"Oh, one more thing," Alex's mother ventures. "And sorry if this is a personal question, but... do you have a boyfriend?" She eyes me briefly, clearly assuming that's why I'm here.

"Uh," Ada starts, visibly fighting to keep a neutral facial expression, "sorry, why do you ask?" She throws me a quick *we-will-be-talking-about-this-later* look before returning her attention to the overbearing woman.

"Oh, it's just Alex isn't..."—she drops her voice to a stage whisper—"*sexually active* just yet."

"*Moooooom,*" Alex groans, tensing up in a full-body cringe. "Oh my God!"

"What?" his mother chirps. "I'm just saying, he's not used to being around that kind of thing. I don't want him getting upset if his roommate is... you know... *doing it.* He's *impressionable.*"

I watch a slew of reactions cross Ada's features. I'm bracing myself for what she might say in response, convinced this woman is about to get an earful.

Ada takes a slow, deep breath and holds it for a moment. "Well! It was great to meet you both," she eventually says. "I'll be in touch."

My brow creases despite the smile tugging at my lips when she extends an arm to guide them toward the front door. She reminds me of those grinning women in sparkling dresses at the Oscars whose sole job it is to usher the winner offstage after their speech.

When they're safely outside, Ada speed-walks back in, eyes bugging out.

"Holy shit," is all I say. "Did that... just happen? You were here, too, right? I'm not having some kind of fever dream?"

"Nope. That was—*unfortunately*—real life." She blows out a baffled breath.

We hold each other's gazes for a moment before we both crack up.

"Okay, so, that one's a *no*," I say through barely suppressed laughter.

"What do you mean?" Ada almost pulls off a deadpan delivery, save for a twitching muscle at the corner of her mouth. "I thought he was perfect." She can barely get the words out before losing it and has to grab my arm to steady herself.

When she catches her balance, I consciously step back, not wanting to risk her touching me again. I clear my throat, hoping she doesn't notice the shift.

"Okay," she says, looking at the ceiling and fanning at her face. Her cheeks are flushed pink from the absurd encounter. "Okay."

"When's the next one?" I ask, massaging my jaw.

She checks the time on her phone. "I think we've got another few minutes to get our shit together."

"Glass of water?" I ask.

"Yeah, thanks." She takes a steadying breath and shakes her head. "Oh, man, and I thought *my* parents were all up in my business."

"I feel bad for the guy," I say as I grab a couple glasses from the cupboard above the sink.

"Yeah," she sighs.

I fill the glasses before turning back to Ada.

She drags her hair out of her face, then reaches for the glass in my right hand.

When I hand it to her, our fingers brush, and I look away. But my traitorous eyes slide to her again, and I can't help but watch the way her throat bobs as she swallows that first sip.

"So, how's your mom doing?" she asks.

"Good!" I say, a bit surprised, albeit grateful, for the change of topic. "I was actually just getting her settled back at home when you texted."

"Oh, shit," she says. "I didn't mean to pull you away for this bullshit, I—"

"No, no, no," I interrupt. "It's fine. She told me to go. She was just gonna take a nap and didn't want me being a... *weird lurker*, was it?" I smile as I lift the glass to my lips.

"Okay," she says with a laugh, but her relief is visible.

"I'm happy to be here. Honest," I reassure her.

The knock at the front door interrupts us, and she puts her glass down to go answer it.

I let out a breath. Mentally, I jog on the spot and stretch my neck like a boxer—bracing myself to take on whoever walks in next.

"I am *so* excited to be here!" a bubbly voice croons from the front hall. The voice's owner, a blonde holding her phone out in front of her like she's filming, follows Ada into the kitchen.

Ada's eyes widen in some unspoken message to me. I can't pretend to read her mind, but *what the fucking fuck* is probably a fair guess.

"Jesse, this is... Rochelle."

I open my mouth to say hello but Rochelle is so engrossed in her phone she doesn't notice.

"I see Andre in the chat! Hiiii, Andre!" she drawls, waving at the phone screen.

She *is* filming. She's filming... *live? Jesus.*

Ada taps her on the arm and asks quietly, "Uh, do you think you could turn that off? Just while we do the walk-through?"

"Are you kidding? I'm almost at ten thousand followers!" Rochelle intones, blowing kisses at the camera. She taps the screen a few times and makes a peace sign, sticking her tongue out the side of her mouth.

What in the Miley Cyrus is going on right now?

Ada looks at me again like she's imploring me to do something. Do what? I'm frozen in place, mind reeling about this latest train wreck to enter the apartment. And I thought the last guy couldn't have been worse. I was wrong.

Who livestreams an apartment tour? I guess literally *anything* can be content these days.

"Oh, my God, this lighting is *so tragic*," Rochelle whines. "Could you get that fixed?" She gives a limp-wristed wave toward the dim yellow ceiling light.

Ada takes a beat to respond. "I don't really... uh, the landlord would usually..."

I so rarely see Ada at a loss for words. This is new—and it's both painful and hilarious.

Ada seems to catch herself mumbling and gestures with her thumb over her shoulder. "Did you want to check out the bedroom?"

When they return, Rochelle does another quick perusal of the kitchen, then pans her phone's camera around the space in a panoramic sweep.

I turn away, not wanting to be featured on anyone's social media feed. When I can assure myself I'm no longer on camera, I turn back around.

"I dunno... what do y'all think?" Rochelle taps the screen and primps in front of the camera, oozing phoniness from every pore. "Should I take it?"

Oh, fuck, this is hard to watch.

Ada and I share another uncomfortable glance.

Rochelle squints at the screen, presumably reading the live chat messages.

"Oh, wow, that's *such* a great point, Delilah96! Is there only *one* bathroom?" She directs this last part at Ada, who nods in confirmation. Rochelle pouts into the camera. "I don't think there *is* gonna be room in there for me to host my makeup tutorials. Like... not if we're *sharing*, I mean."

Ada mumbles something about the one bathroom being listed in the ad, but Rochelle, of course, remains oblivious, having returned her attention to her loyal followers.

In news that surprises no one, Rochelle decides the apartment won't work for her budding influencer career and swishes out to reign bubbly terror on other potential subletters.

After another bewildered interval where Ada and I try to process what we just experienced—applicant number three enters the apartment.

It takes only a second before I've got my guard up about the guy. He follows Ada in from the front door, staring at her ass the entire time.

Not cool, man.

When he sees me, he doesn't even have the decency to pretend he wasn't ogling her—just smirks and lifts his chin as if we share some kind of silent *bro* communication I want no part in.

Unlike the first two who came through, though, the guy has decent social skills. He isn't livestreaming or accompanied by an overprotective parent, and he isn't *overtly* a nightmare. He shakes my hand and introduces himself as Travis, sizing me up cautiously like he isn't sure of my relationship to Ada. I'm more than happy to leave him guessing.

"*Just act possessive or something.*" Ada's words from earlier have me suddenly scrambling for how to pull that off. Because this guy is the only one of the set to make me wonder if I'll need to.

As Ada shows Travis the room, I stay in the kitchen area but casually move into her line of sight so she knows I can see them both. She throws me a small smile, which Travis evidently catches, because he lowers his voice so I can't hear what he's saying. *Dick.* When he takes a half step closer to Ada, there's a perceptible shift in her body language and she crosses her arms in front of her chest. She looks fucking uncomfortable.

Say it. I send the silent plea across the apartment. *Give me the secret signal.*

I try to quash the tight feeling in my stomach, reminding myself Ada probably gets hit on all the time at the bar and must hold her own there just fine. But this is her fucking *home.* I run a hand through my hair, my stomach twisting as my imagination spins one sleazy scenario after the next about what this guy's saying.

I can't watch. I turn away—not wanting to let her down but needing to stop witnessing it all the same.

The rush of footsteps behind me has me twisting back around, right as Ada slips an arm around my waist. I try to hide my surprise at the contact as I instinctively wrap my arm around her shoulders.

"Hey, Jess?" she purrs, her voice flirtatious in a way that has me holding my breath. "I totally forgot to remind you earlier... but uh... don't forget to wish your mom a happy birthday." She nods for emphasis. "It's today, right?"

I exhale, trying to play it off as a grateful sigh. "Oh, fuck, that's right. Thanks, baby." I hug her closer, resting my chin on the top of her head. The scent of her hair floats up—coconut, with a hint of cherries—and I inhale for one greedy, mindless second where time slows. It occurs to me I could just tilt my chin down an inch, maybe two, and kiss the top of her head. *That would sell the ruse, right?* But I think about it for a beat too long and, then, like slow motion returning to normal speed, I'm wrenched back into the present. I fight to swallow the panic wrestling its way up my throat.

Travis shuffles out from the bedroom, avoiding eye contact. He looks so awkward I almost feel bad for the guy. Almost.

Dickhead.

Ada does me no favors and lays it on thick, her fingers tracing slow strokes over my waist.

A flush heats my skin where her fingers graze my T-shirt and my pants tighten. *Jesus Christ.*

"We should go get her flowers, don't you think?" She peers up at me, silently pleading for me to go along with this.

Travis clears his throat, but I can't tear my gaze from Ada's.

"Uh, yeah, baby, good idea. Let's go when this is over." I force myself to face Travis directly, my arm still slung protectively over Ada's shoulder. "This over?"

He seems to read my dead-eyed delivery as intended, because he nods and kicks into motion, pulling out his phone and gesturing to Ada with it.

"So, about the place... you'll let me know?"

Wow. The audacity of this guy.

She opens her mouth to answer but I beat her to it.

"Here's all you need to know, buddy: it's a sleazy fucking move to come into a woman's home and creep on her like she's a piece of meat." I give him a once-over. "Fix your shit. And, in the meantime, get the fuck out of here and never contact my girlfriend again."

He scoffs as he turns to go. "Fuck you, dude."

I let the comment slide, but my attention is glued to his back as he walks away.

The sound of the front door closing jolts me and Ada out of our act, and we pull apart. I pace away from her, running both hands through my hair.

"Shit. Fuck. Sorry." I'm barely able to look at her. With Travis now gone, I'm spinning out, guilt over having held my best friend's sister in my arms already causing a sinking feeling in my ribcage.

I called her baby, *for fuck's sake.* Twice. *What was I thinking?*

I rub my side, trying to quell the fizzing sensation where she touched me.

"Jesse…"

"I didn't know what to do. I shouldn't have… I took it too far. *Fuck.*"

"Jess," she tries again. "It's okay."

"It's not okay!" I throw my hands out at my sides, finally facing her.

"You're overreacting. I asked you to help me and you helped me. It was just, like, a hug or whatever. It's not like we *kissed.*"

I wince, trying to fight off the mental image of kissing her.

"What? Come on. It's fine. We're fine." She reaches out to touch my arm. "Right?"

I pull away.

"Wow," she says, misreading me. "Didn't realize I was so repulsive. Sorry."

"Fuck, no, that's not… *Shit.*" I rub my forehead. "I should just go."

"Okay," she says, crossing her arms over her chest the same way she'd done with Travis.

My heart sinks, realizing I've made her as uncomfortable as he did. I take a breath. "Hey. Sorry for freaking out. You're not…" I pause, searching for better words, but none are available. "You're not repulsive."

"Is that how you talk to all the ladies?" She arches a brow, selling the joke.

I blow a breath through my nose and shake my head. "Fuck. Come here." I open my arms and give her a pointed look when she hesitates. I know I shouldn't touch her again, but I need her to know we're cool. "Can I get a proper hug before I take off, or what?"

She smiles and steps into my embrace, wrapping her arms around my waist.

It takes everything I have to keep it brief but, when I pull away, my skin is humming again.

I'm so fucked.

"So, did I just get Punk'd?" she asks, flicking her eyes up to meet mine. "Is that still a thing?"

I laugh. "That was pretty brutal."

"*Fuck*. Pickings are *slim*."

"Guess so." For a brief second, I consider telling her I need a place to stay, but I stop myself and the moment passes by.

"You coming to dinner at my parents' tomorrow?"

"Yeah," I say. "Marcus mentioned that. It'll be good to see them again. See you there?"

"Cool." She nods. "We're good, right?"

I smile. "Yeah, Ada. We're good."

7

———

ADA

Sunday dinner is off to a great start: Mom's already made a passive-aggressive comment about my job, and Dad immediately stole Jesse for a protracted tour of the last eight years of home renos.

As usual, I'm steering the conversation toward safe territory by attending to the practical task of helping get dinner on the table. I set out a steaming dish of polenta, an enormous pot roast, and three bottles of wine. Everything smells incredible.

Mom carries a tray of fresh bread to the table, then returns to the kitchen.

"What can I help with, Maria?" Renee asks.

"Yeah, Mom, put us to work," Marcus adds. "Can we set the table or what?"

"Already done, darling." She pats him on the cheek. "No need to help. You work so hard. Go take a load off." At that, she shoos him and Renee out of the kitchen and pulls open a drawer, rummaging amongst the serving utensils.

I try not to glare openly at my brother's back as he leaves, biting my tongue before my salty ass asks why no one's ever told *me* to take a load off.

Mom pops the kitchen door open with her hip. "Frank!"

"I'm here, I'm here," Dad says with a chuckle, stopping to plant a kiss on Mom's cheek on his way into the kitchen.

Jesse squeezes past my parents, shooting me a smile as he joins the mayhem.

Mom returns to the drawer, clattering through its contents while directing some pointed muttering in Dad's direction about a missing spoon.

"Maria, I told you, I haven't seen that serving spoon in weeks!" Dad says. "Just let it go!"

"Let it go? It didn't just walk out of the house, Frank."

I roll my eyes and pull napkins from a nearby drawer.

As Jesse washes his hands at the sink beside me, he nudges my elbow. "You good?" he asks quietly, having clearly caught wind of my mood.

"Yeah, fine." I give him a thin smile as I stack napkins in a pile. I glance over my shoulder at my parents, who continue to shout over each other while hunting for the missing serving spoon. I turn back to Jesse, unable to avoid noticing how his forearms flex as he dries his hands on a tea towel. "So, did you enjoy the twenty-five cent tour of the house? How much do you know about heat-pump air conditioners now?"

"Oh..." He blows out a breath. "I mean, will it ever be enough?"

I laugh, shoving the pile of napkins into his hands. "Come on, let's go eat."

With the lot of us gathered around the table, Dad says grace—more of a tradition than a necessity in our selectively Catholic household—and we dig into the food.

"Jesse," Mom starts, scooping polenta onto her plate, "we're so glad to hear Maureen's doing better. We were shocked to hear about what happened!"

"Huge shock!" Dad adds. "Couldn't believe it when Marcus told me."

"Thanks, yeah," Jesse says. "It was unexpected, for sure. But she's recovering well."

"Marcus tells us you have some time off work?" Dad raises his gray eyebrows before taking a sip of wine. When Jesse nods, Dad swallows and gives him a thoughtful look. "So how long do you think you'll be in town?"

"The million-dollar question," Jesse says with a hint of amusement, accepting the dish Mom passes him, and explains his mom will need support during her recovery over the next several weeks.

"So, still looking like you'll be here for the whole summer?" Renee asks, eyes flitting between Jesse and Marcus before taking a bite of roast. She's got a good poker face, but she can't be happy about having such a long-term houseguest.

Jesse nods beside me. "Seems like it, yeah. But don't worry, I'm not planning on imposing on you two that whole time. I'll find a place to stay."

Renee smiles, trying but failing to hide her relief.

"You can't stay with Maureen?" Mom asks.

"I would, but there isn't really room for two there. The place she got after the divorce is a glorified shoebox. And I wanna let her rest without bumping around in her space, y'know? So I'll probably find a vacation rental or something."

"Oh, my God," Renee says, setting down her fork suddenly with a clink. She slaps Marcus gently on the shoulder. "Ada."

I look up from my food, mirroring my brother's confused expression.

"Babe, what do you mean *Ada*?" Marcus asks.

She turns to me, waving a perfectly manicured hand as if to start over. "Ada, Jesse could move in with *you*! Like, for the summer. You've been trying to find a new roommate, right?"

"Oh," I manage. That feeling returns instantly—the one where I'm hyper-aware of Jesse watching me. I risk only a sidelong glance his way.

"Uh," Marcus says, furrowing his brow, "I dunno. Would that work?" His eyes dart between us, as if trying to gauge our reaction to the idea. "I mean, I guess it would solve Ada's roommate problem. For now, anyway."

"And Jesse's problem," Renee offers, turning to him. "Not that you staying on our couch is a *problem*," she adds quickly. "It's just —Ada has an actual bedroom and all..."

"Uh, yeah, but..." Jesse trails off, shifting in his seat.

"You wouldn't have to look for a place!" Renee presses, clearly convinced, and picks up her fork. "I think it's a win-win."

I turn to Jesse. "Why didn't you say something?"

He sits back in his chair and shrugs. "Didn't want to horn in on your situation with the apartment."

I almost laugh. "Uh... you saw my roommate prospects, right?"

He smiles and tilts his head in acknowledgment.

Fuck. Could I live with Jesse? Does he want *to live with me?* I study him in profile as he takes a bite of roast, wishing I could read his thoughts.

Marcus pipes up again. "But wouldn't that..."

I pull my gaze from Jesse and face my brother.

"Wouldn't that be weird, though? You living together?" He lets out an awkward chuckle, glancing between me and Jesse.

"No," Jesse and I both say in unison—a little too quickly.

Our eyes meet. He looks like he's fighting to suppress a smile. *Shit.*

"Why would that be weird?" I ask Marcus, hoping I'm pulling off an air of disinterest.

"Well, I don't see the harm in it," Mom interjects. "You kids have been friends since high school. It might be fun! It's not like you're a *couple*."

Right. Jesus is watching.

"Yeah," I say to Marcus, pleasantly surprised to be agreeing with Mom for once. "We've known each other for, like, a thousand years."

I can't admit the truth—that it absolutely *would* be weird. Yesterday's awkward roleplay proved that. But I also can't ignore the relief I feel at the idea of not having to share my home with a stranger. This would buy me more time to find the right roommate.

"Well, I guess it makes sense," Jesse offers with a shrug. "You know, if you want a *non-murderer*." His brow ticks up.

"What's this about a murderer?" Mom asks as she tops up Dad's wine.

"Never mind, Mom," I mumble in her direction. "It was just a joke."

"We could split the rent for the rest of the summer," Jesse continues. "Probably easier to find someone for September, when the students are apartment hunting."

"I guess," I hedge.

Dad clears his throat. "Sounds like a plan, then. I think we've got a spare mattress in the attic. There should be a bed frame too. Marcus can help you bring it over to Ada's place."

"Here," Mom says, scooping another helping of roast onto each of our plates. "Eat some more."

Discussion kicks off about when Marcus can move the bed and I start to quietly spiral. Am I agreeing to this? It feels like this train has already left the station. If I say no, Marcus will ask why. And if I say yes...

I consider Jesse once more as he talks with Mom about borrowing bedding. When he reaches for a piece of bread, I study his broad chest. He looks strong—like he could pin someone up against a wall.

Fuck. Inappropriate thought. Think platonic things.

I take a breath and try again.

How would we work out the groceries? Would we share food? Would he come out of the shower shirtless and... Nope.

I tear my gaze away, dragging a hand through my hair, then reach for my wine.

"It would only be for the summer," Jesse reassures me quietly, having obviously picked up on the Ada-shaped ball of inner conflict sitting next to him.

I give him a small smile. Those damn blue eyes seem to suck up my ability to think this through.

Only for the summer. It could work. We *do* get along well. I'm overthinking things. He needs a place to live, and I need a room-mate. It's a purely practical arrangement—an elegant solution, really. Plus, he's one of my oldest friends. He's safe. Not some serial killer or human train wreck.

Probably.

"You won't leave your toenail clippings on my coffee table, or anything, right?" I ask him.

He laughs. "I promise I won't."

Is this happening? I think this is happening.

"Okay," I say, throwing up my hands and plastering on more confidence than I feel. "Why not, right? Let's live together."

A slow smile spreads over his face. I want to take it all back, because now I'm staring at his mouth and...

Stop it right now. This is exactly *why not.*

I swallow.

"Great," Marcus says, sounding cautious. "Two birds, one stone, I guess." He gives me a pointed look. "Hey, can I talk to you for a sec? In private?" Pushing up from the table, he gestures for me to follow him into the kitchen.

"Ooh, in private? Awfully formal."

"Don't be a dick."

Maybe I should get a T-shirt that says, "*When in doubt, snark it out*" because, apparently, it's my go-to fallback for any remotely uncomfortable situation. Throwing a skeptical glance around the table, I follow my brother into the kitchen, letting the door swing shut behind me.

"What's so important that we had to have a secret sibling meeting?"

"You sure you wanna do this?" He keeps his voice hushed, clearly not wanting the others to overhear us, and crosses his arms. "Have Jess move in?"

I frown. "I dunno. I guess?"

It's not like I've had much time to think about it, dumbass.

But I can sense something bothering my brother. "Why?"

He scratches his jaw. "You don't think it'll be awkward?"

"No," I lie. "Why would it be? Like Mom said, we're friends." For some reason, I'm suddenly extremely aware of my facial expression.

"Okay." He's watching me closely. Too closely.

"*Okaaay,*" I say, drawing out the word. "So, are we done here? Like, can we go finish dinner or...?"

"Just thought I was picking up on, like, a weird vibe."

I balk. "What *vibe?*"

Oh, God, he knows.

"I dunno, forget it. I'm just saying. He's my best friend. He's a good guy. And I'm not blind. Dude is ripped."

"Oh my *God,*" I say, doing everything in my power to deny Jesse's had some kind of hot Viking glow-up. But I can't let Marcus know I've noticed, so I swing my sarcastic barbs his way instead. "Does Jesse know you've been checking out his hot bod? Have you told Renee?"

"Fuck off." He shakes his head, obviously sick of my shit. "Just... don't get attached, alright?"

"What the hell!" I seethe. "What do you even mean by that? It's just fucking *Jesse.*"

He rubs his forehead. "Fine. Okay."

"Honestly, Marcus, have a little fucking faith that I can stop myself from falling on the nearest dick."

"Ugh, *gross*," he groans. "Listen, it's just that… y'know… He lives in Australia."

"Like I don't know that? Your point?"

"I mean, you and long distance… didn't go great last time."

"Holy shit. Are you serious right now?" I can't believe he's bringing Pascal into this. "Long distance wasn't even the prob—" I hold up my hands, stopping myself. "You know what? Never mind. This conversation isn't happening. You're gonna make me barf. I will barf. And I will aim for you when I do it."

"Jesus, would you chill out? I'm just trying to look out for you."

My brows shoot up. "Uh, thanks but no thanks, *bro*."

I follow the quick shift in Marcus' gaze and turn to see the kitchen door swing open.

"Sorry to interrupt!" Mom says as she hurries to the fridge. "Just need to pull the tiramisu out." It's a flimsy excuse to eavesdrop on us and we know it. "Mrs. Nicolosi dropped it off earlier as a thank you for helping with that church fundraiser last week."

"Nah, it's okay, Mom," I say quickly. "We're done talking." I head back to the dining room without letting Marcus say anything more.

Jesse lifts his head when I come in, tracking me cautiously as I stalk across the room. The thick, awkward silence only gets worse when Marcus and Mom follow me in, filing back to their seats.

"Everything okay?" Jesse asks no one in particular.

"Fine!" Mom chirps, laying the dish on the table alongside a handful of cutlery. "We've got tiramisu for dessert!"

Settling into my seat, I tune out Mom's babbling about desserts and the fundraiser, all too aware of Jesse at my side. When I turn to meet his gaze, he gives me a small smile. I bite the inside of my cheek and fix my eyes on my plate, stabbing my fork into a bit of pot roast.

"Jesse," Renee starts, casting a glance at Mom and Dad, who are momentarily distracted by shuffling some of the dinner plates to the kitchen. "I was thinking, like, if you're gonna be around for the rest of the summer? Maybe I could set you up with some of my friends?"

He looks immediately uneasy.

"Nothing serious! Just for some fun!" she adds quickly. "You said you hadn't really got out much back in Australia, right? So you should live a little while you're here! Make up for lost time?"

"I dunno," he hedges. "Is there a point, though, since I'm taking off at the end of August?"

"Uh, *yeah*. The point is to have *fun*!" Renee presses. "The dating scene is all casual these days, anyway. But the apps are a nightmare. Let me set you up instead."

He still seems unsure.

Renee goes on. "Plus, you've had such a scare with your mom; you deserve to relax. I have a couple of friends who'd be up for a casual thing. You'd *love* them—promise."

"She has a point," Marcus offers, briefly glancing my way. "It might be fun. We could even double-date."

"Who's going on a double-date?" Mom chimes in, returning to her seat.

"Uh, we were just talking about Jesse meeting some of Renee's friends," Marcus explains, notably omitting the part about it all being casual.

"Oh, that's a great idea!" Mom chirps. "And you're a catch! *Any girl* would be lucky to go on a date with you."

Jesse chuckles and looks down at his food. "Thanks, Maria."

"Mom, stop pressuring him. He can make his own deci—" I start.

"I wasn't pressuring him!" Mom counters.

"Sure, I'll do it," Jesse says beside me. I whip my head around to face him.

He shrugs as if to say *why not.*

Tearing my gaze from his, I focus on my plate once again.

"Ooh!" squeals Renee, clapping her hands together with a saccharine glee I can't share. "I'm so excited! I'll text Kristen after dinner."

"Should we serve up the tiramisu?" Dad asks, and Mom stands to pass around the dessert plates.

Murmured answers sound around the table and I stare past my glass of wine. There's too much to process from just the last ten minutes.

Did I really agree to live with Jesse? Did he just agree to go on dates with Renee's friends? Also, what the fuck is Marcus' problem? My stomach lurches again at the thought that he might be picking up on my attraction to Jesse. *Shit.*

No. This is fine. This is all fine. We'll live together— temporarily. It doesn't need to be complicated. Jesse seeing Renee's friends is also fine. He can do whatever he wants, and whoever he chooses to date—or fuck—doesn't impact me at all.

And yet, I can't help but frown at the thought.

"Ada?" Mom's voice interrupts my thoughts as she passes me a small plate. "Have you started on those applications I sent you? The deadline's long gone for this fall, but you might still be able to get in for the winter term. If you applied now—"

"No," I say, my voice louder than intended. I swallow. "Mom, I've told you, I don't want to go to college. Please drop it."

"Your mother and I are not gonna drop it, Ada," Dad says. "College isn't something you just opt out of."

"Exactly," Mom chimes in, placing a plate in front of Jesse. "Your Nonna and Nonno came to this country to give their children—and their grandchildren—a better life. An education!"

There's a burning sensation in my throat as I hold back all the incredulous words itching to be launched across the table. I've heard this a thousand times. And I've had enough. Enough of the guilt trips. The pressure.

"School isn't my thing, okay?" I grit my teeth. "It never was. That hasn't changed. The way my *brain* works hasn't changed."

Dad sighs, tossing his napkin onto the table. "Here we go again."

I'm sure Renee is used to witnessing this train wreck by now, but Jesse being here tonight is a fresh blow to the ego. When I glance his way, he looks concerned.

"It's nothing that can't be solved with a little discipline," Mom presses as she takes her seat, pulling my attention away from Jesse. "If you just—"

"Oh, if I just tried harder, right? We're back to this? Unbelievable." I shake my head, searching the ceiling for patience.

"Mom, maybe just give her a break," Marcus cuts in, sounding weary. "Do we really need to do this again?"

"She doesn't need a break!" Mom says, turning to him. "She needs to get her butt in gear!"

"You know, your grandparents sacrificed everything to give you this opportunity," Dad reminds me.

"I know, Dad!" My cheeks burn. I can't believe they're pulling this crap again. And in front of Jesse.

"So you're just going to throw that away because it's hard?" Dad asks.

"Are you kidding me? Have you listened to *anything* I've told you about this?"

"Honestly, Ada," Mom says. "Look at Marcus. He went to college and it was *fine*. And now he has a *wonderful* job at Sitka."

"Mom," Marcus groans, clearly no happier about the comparison than I am. "Not cool."

She sits back in her seat. "What? I'm just saying, Ada. The excuses have to stop."

I round on her, my anger close to boiling over. "How many times do I have to explain dyslexia is not a fucking excuse?"

Mom waves a dismissive hand my way. "Oh, everybody thinks they have *something* these days."

Dad nods. "If you'd stop being so stubborn and just consider—"

"You know," Jesse's deep voice cuts through the escalating noise, "I actually read a fascinating article on dyslexia recently. It said that dyslexic people are more likely to use the right sides of their brains—for reading and just... thinking in general."

"Isn't the right side of the brain more creative, like artistic and stuff?" Marcus asks.

"Oh, that's totally you, Ada," Renee adds. "With all your drawing and painting."

My anger wanes slightly as I realize what they've done—how elegantly they've derailed my parents' line of interrogation and shifted the subject away from college.

"I'm uh... I'm gonna go get some air." Five sets of eyes follow me as I push out of the dining room, but I can't look back.

I pace on the front porch for a few minutes, trying to calm myself down. Eventually, I settle enough to sit on the wicker bench near the living room window, hugging my knees to my chest as I stare out at the street.

The front door opens, and I smile when Jesse emerges with a small plate of tiramisu in one hand.

"Hey," I say quietly.

"Hey." There's an enviable ease in his voice.

"That for me?" I gaze longingly at his dessert as he walks over.

"Fuck no!" He pulls it away, affecting a shocked expression. "Get your own!"

I suppress a laugh and groan, peering up at him. "Don't make me go back in there."

He sighs. "Okay, fine. Shove over."

I shift sideways on the bench so he can sit beside me. The wicker crackles under his weight.

He passes me the spoon, holding the plate between us.

"Sorry you had to witness that carnage." I take a bite and pass the spoon back. It's light and creamy—one of Mrs. Nicolosi's better efforts.

"What? You eviscerating your parents with the stone-cold facts about your neurological wiring?" The corner of his mouth curls before he takes a bite of the dessert.

"Sure." I blow air through my nose, trying not to think about how he licks his lips. Or how the spoon that was just in my mouth is now in his mouth. "Thanks, by the way."

"For what?" he asks. The spoon clinks against the plate as he sets it down.

I roll my eyes. "Oh, come on. You know. For…" I pause, searching for the words. "For being my buffer."

"Buffer?" He frowns, then flicks a mosquito from my shoulder.

"With my parents." I rub my arms.

He takes another bite and nods, passing me the plate.

I scoop up another piece as I lift my gaze. "You sure about this?"

"Sharing my tiramisu with you?"

"No. *Living* with me, you ding-dong." I put the bite in my mouth.

"Ding-dong?" He raises a brow. "Wow, you must be pretty shaken up. That was weaksauce."

"Shut up." I laugh, swatting his knee. "Seriously. You wanna be roommates?"

He nods slowly, studying me. "Yeah, I think so. If you're cool with it."

For a moment, something unspoken buzzes like static in the air.

I swallow my tiramisu. "Yeah. I'm cool with it."

Jesse's lips twitch with the hint of a smile, then his expression suddenly falls. "Oh! But you should know: I don't have *any* followers." He feigns regret. "Like... not even *one*."

"Aww," I say with a pout. "No one likes your rock tumbler content?"

He shakes his head and turns away. "Nobody gets me. I cry myself to sleep every night."

"Well, you sound like you'll be an *ace* roommate," I deadpan. "I'll just get some earplugs to block out the sound of your sobbing."

"Don't forget the rock tumbler." His blue eyes slide back to meet mine.

"Right." I catch myself grinning, then bite my lip. Another long silence hangs in the air. "You really read an article on dyslexia?"

"It might have been a podcast."

I give him a look.

"Okay, it was some video clip," he admits.

"The truth comes out."

"But it was a *fascinating* video clip."

8

JESSE

"Who tied this knot, fucking Hercules?" Marcus eyes me across the roof of his car as he tries to untie the mattress.

"Hey, man, sorry," I puff up my chest. "Sometimes I just don't know my own strength."

"So those muscles aren't just for show, then? My mistake." He chuckles as the knot finally loosens and throws the rope over to me.

We disentangle the mattress and I move to lift it off the car.

"Hey, before we go in…" he says, stopping me.

"Yeah?" I ask cautiously.

"So, uh… You're gonna be living with my *sister*, right?"

"That's the plan, yeah." I step back, dropping my hands to my sides.

Where's this going?

"You sure it's gonna be okay?" He jerks his head toward the apartment's front door.

I blow out a breath. "You've picked a weird fucking time to be having second thoughts about this, man."

"Look, I don't wanna be that asshole, but... she's my *sister*, y'know?"

"And?"

"I mean, the last time you lived with a chick, you uh—"

"Wow. You're bringing up Naomi?" I fold my arms across my chest, drawing my brows together.

Shit. Is this *where his head's at?*

He shrugs. "Dude, you two were roommates, right? And you got your heart broken. I just wanna make sure—"

I cut him off. "Yeah, but I had a thing for Naomi way before we moved in together. This is *Ada* we're talking about."

"So?"

"I dunno. She was always just part of our crew of dumbasses. Basically one of the guys, right?"

The sight of her ass in that miniskirt flashes in my mind, reminding me she is anything but *one of the guys*. I stomp the image down and sell what I'm saying. "I don't think about her like that. You have nothing to worry about."

"Yeah?" He looks cautious.

I shouldn't need to put this much mental energy into appearing confident, but I have no choice. Plus, maybe if I tell myself this story enough times, it'll make it true—like some kind of keep-your-dick-in-your-pants positive affirmation.

"Dude. *Come on*," I say. Under normal circumstances, I'd be hurt he doesn't trust me, and I hate myself for knowing that, deep down, his worry isn't totally out of line. One thing's for sure: I can't fuck this up.

"Okay, okay. Sorry I mentioned it." He pauses like he's mulling something over.

I watch him closely, putting my hands on my hips. "If you've got more to say, man, just spit it out."

"I just don't want you getting hurt again. And I don't want *her* getting hurt, either. Or for anything to fuck with our friendship. Because she's family. It'd be messy."

"Marcus." I dead-eye him. "I don't know what scenario you've cooked up in your head, but let it go. Not gonna happen. Ada and I are just friends. Now, can we get this shit inside?"

He nods. "Yeah, okay. Forget I said anything."

We heft the mattress off the roof of the car and balance it between us as we walk down the stairs to Ada's basement suite.

Marcus backs through the door and I follow with my end, ducking my head to avoid hitting it on the low doorframe. "Happy new roomie day, sis!" he calls out in a cheerful tone.

When we make our way into the kitchen, Ada's doing dishes at the sink. Her turquoise hair is pulled up in a half ponytail and she's wearing a tight red tank top and snug, cut-off jean shorts.

I snap my eyes up to meet hers when she turns to look over her shoulder.

Great start, dickhead.

"Hey," is all Ada says to me, a hint of a smile touching her lips as she sets a dripping bowl on the dish rack. The shared eye contact—and the way her gaze slips from mine as she dries her hands on a tea towel—feels almost... *awkward.* Ada's usual sarcastic self is MIA, and it's a strangely uncomfortable feeling.

Marcus navigates us past Ada toward Katie's old room, glancing over each shoulder to see where he's going.

Behind me, plates clink under running water, and I try to think of something to say to smooth over whatever unease I sensed from Ada on the way in.

We deposit the mattress against the wall and return to Marcus' car to get the bed frame, each lugging one of the simple metal bed rails to my new room. I'm looking forward to a better sleep tonight, grateful to have brought my *trash couch* era to a close.

Once my bed is assembled, we head back to the kitchen where

Ada stands on tiptoe, reaching to put some dry dishes in a high cabinet.

My gaze once again falls lower than it should and… *fuck*. I guess whatever moral high ground I asserted with that prick Travis was just an act, because even *I* can't stop myself from staring at Ada's ass.

I clear my throat.

She turns as Marcus walks over to her and slings his arm over her shoulder.

"You okay?" he asks.

She gives him a tired side-eye. "Sorry. I'm in a weird mood."

After that argument with her parents last night, I think I can guess why.

"You're probably just missing Katie," Marcus says.

"I dunno. Maybe." She throws me a brief look.

"Well, let's have some beers and eat our weight in pizza," he says, squeezing her shoulder. "It'll dull the pain."

She glances my way again and I try for an encouraging smile.

"I know what you're thinking," Marcus adds, following her gaze, and tilts his chin my way. "That I've brought you just about the shittiest Katie substitute you could've hoped for."

A hint of a smirk touches Ada's lips.

"First of all, he's much, *much* hairier." He pauses, leaning toward her and dropping his voice low. "Disgusting, I know."

"I'm standing right here, man," I protest, throwing my hands out at my sides.

"Probably won't clean up after himself, either," he adds with exaggerated derision.

I roll my eyes, putting my hands on my hips. Ada's smiling, though, and I decide I'll take this one for the team.

"He'll probably leave the toilet seat up like an absolute ingrate," Marcus continues.

"Like *you* always used to, you mean?" She elbows her brother in the ribs.

He flinches, pulling his arm off her shoulder, and puts a hand to his chest like he's hurt. "Excuse me, we're insulting *Jesse*, here. Focus up."

"Oh, sorry, right," she says, returning her attention to me, a glimmer of amusement playing across her features.

I cross my arms over my chest and raise my eyebrows at her.

"He'll probably drink milk right out of the carton," Marcus says, scrunching up his nose, "and leave peanut butter blobs on the counter."

We all know I wouldn't, but I let it slide.

She grins, then jumps in. "And, when he drains the sink after doing the dishes, he won't clean out the little bits of gunk from the drain trap," she squints at me, "like an *animal*."

I shift on my feet and shake my head, trying to shrug off the way Ada calling me an *animal* made my blood rush south.

"Katie would *never* do that," Marcus says, looking me up and down. "Honestly, Jesse, *who raised you?*"

"You're one to talk, Marcus," I say. "You didn't lift a finger yesterday at your folks' place."

He scoffs through a smile.

"Your mom cooked everything," I add, "and the rest of us did all the dishes while you sat on your ass."

Marcus squints at me. "You talkin' to me?"

"Was that supposed to be De Niro, dude?"

"Shut up," he says, then nudges Ada. "Katie would never disrespect my De Niro impression like that."

She laughs. "No. Who does this guy think he *is?*"

"Okay, you two about done?" I ask, stuffing my hands in my pockets.

Ada smirks and turns to a nearby drawer, pulling out a stack of sticky notes and a marker. She scrawls something on the top note and peels it off, then walks over to me and slaps it onto the center of my chest, smoothing her hand over it to make sure it sticks.

I'm keenly aware of Marcus watching all of this.

When she pulls her hand away, I read the note upside-down.

Not Katie.

"Just so you never forget..." she says, "what a disappointment you are."

"Ooh," Marcus says from behind her, laughing into his fist. "Harsh."

I look at the ceiling. "Jesus Christ, can we go pick up the fucking pizza now, or what?"

She turns and grabs her purse, and Marcus trails her out the door.

I pause a moment, touching the note stuck to my T-shirt. I smile to myself as I remember the heat of her hand against my chest, then follow them outside.

WE COLLAPSE onto the assorted living room furniture, which consists of a few folding chairs and a small love seat, and devour the pizza. I check out the place as we eat. There's an emptiness to the apartment that's a bit grim, and I wish I had more to contribute.

"Anyone up for Mario Kart after we eat?" Marcus asks. "Ada has our old Nintendo stuff."

"Oh, fuck, yeah," I say. "I haven't kicked your ass in Mario Kart in *years*. It'll feel so good."

"Not if I kick your ass first," he replies around a bite of pizza.

Ada drops her crust onto her plate, setting it on the coffee table. "Such confidence from two dickheads who are both gonna lose," she says with her mouth full, wiping a thumb over the corner of her lips.

I smirk. Ada destroying us in Mario Kart is a fond memory.

She gets up and plods to the TV, crouching down to a low shelf and pulling out the ancient console. Marcus gets the Nintendo set up as I finish my pizza and, when the familiar plinking jingle plays, I'm hit with a flood of childhood memories. I clean my hands on a paper napkin and take the controller Marcus offers me.

"Hey, guys," Ada deadpans, taking hers from her brother, "when you lose, just make sure to wipe away your tears." She makes a pouting face at Marcus, then glances at me. "Wouldn't want your controllers to get all wet."

Marcus scoffs through a rueful smile. "We'll see who's crying in a few minutes, bitches."

"And so it begins," I say under my breath. This trash talk takes me back a decade.

The countdown chimes and we get ready to speed off the start line. When the word "*Go*" flashes on the screen, Ada curses under her breath as her character stutters, slow to take off.

"Hey, Ada, you have to press the A button to go forward," Marcus taunts from beside me on the small couch.

"Fuck off," she replies. "You gave me the one with the sticky A button."

"Only a poor craftsman blames his tools," I tease.

Out of the corner of my eye, she shakes her head. The slow start has her losing the race; she's already trailing well behind me and Marcus.

"Oh, Jesse, speaking of tools..." she says.

When she doesn't finish her sentence, I risk tearing my gaze from the screen for a moment to glance at her.

She's smiling.

I look back right as a red shell sends my cart spinning into the air. Ada's character zooms past me.

"What the fuck!" I say, stunned by her distraction tactic. "You dirty cheater."

I get going again and watch her roundly destroy her brother, hitting us both with a lightning bolt and then running him over as she speeds into first place. She cackles with delight.

"You're such a piece of shit," Marcus mutters to her.

I catch up and get in front of Marcus, but Ada's way ahead now. My only hope is a Hail Mary: a blue shell—the ones that seek out whoever's in first place. They're rare, though, and I'm not feeling good about my chances. Marcus and I circle the map trying to make headway but only manage to fuck each other up a few times each, never touching her.

"We're fucked, dude," Marcus says. We both stare in disbelief as Ada sails through the finish line.

"What's up, fuckers!" She throws her controller aside and jumps up with her arms thrust in the air. Grinning at us, she walks to the kitchen.

I rub my hands over my face. I can't believe she still won after that shitty start. "Okay, sit down," I say, squinting at her as she comes back into the living room and hands me a beer. "You got lucky."

"Think we should turn down the difficulty?" she asks, her tone blatantly condescending. "Make it easier for you little babies?"

"Eat shit," Marcus says to her, taking the beer from her hand.

The second race goes about as well as the first, except I get lucky at the last minute: the video game gods gift me with the holy grail. "Oh, it's fucking *on*," I say, rounding the final lap with my blue shell at the ready.

Ada apparently catches wind of my plan. "No, no, no, no, no!" she shouts, her words rushing out, but she's unable to stop me. She groans in frustration when she goes flying and I sail past her spinning cart, crossing the finish line just in front of her.

"Oh! *What's up!*" I gloat, throwing my arms out wide at my sides.

She shakes her head at me, looking disappointed. "Using a blue shell is such a cheap move."

"Hey, I still won fair and square," I say, holding up my hands in defense. But I'm beaming, delighted to have bested her.

"Alright, Big Lebowski," she retorts, lifting her chin at me, "calm down over there."

"Okay, now who's being cheap?" I ask.

Our eyes lock for a long moment, and I take in her broad smile. *There she is.*

I wrench my gaze away and clear my throat as I reach for my beer. "Okay, well, it's over for you nerds when we get to Rainbow Road."

Marcus groans. "Man, *fuck* Rainbow Road."

9

———

ADA

Tucked into a corner of the love seat, sketchbook in my lap and music blasting through my headphones, I'm doing my damnedest to ignore Jesse moving around the apartment in my peripheral vision. Drawing usually relaxes me, but I'm less able to unwind with him nearby.

"Hey," he says, giving me a lopsided grin as he walks into the living room.

I pull off my headphones and take a beat to absorb his appearance. His hair is combed and pulled up into that infernal man bun and he's wearing his new clothes. I'm definitely *not* noticing he looks good—like, *really* good. As he reaches for his wallet from the coffee table, the scent of him wafts my way: clean and citrusy with a hint of spice, like Earl Grey tea.

Fuck. He smells good too.

We've only been living together a few days and here I am practically salivating because he approached me. Forcing a swallow, I will myself not to show any reaction and return to drawing. "Looking slightly less like a Neanderthal than usual."

"Wow, thanks." His voice drips with sarcasm, and he shakes his head.

"What's the big occasion?" I ask, then remember it's Friday. "Ooh, is tonight the night? The big date? With what's-her-name? Renee's friend?"

He nods, tucking his phone and wallet into the pockets of his jeans. "Yeah. Kristen. Double-date with Marcus and Renee."

"Kristen," I repeat, almost to myself, nodding slowly as my gaze drops again to my sketchbook.

"What are you drawing?" Jesse asks, walking around beside me and making to peer over my shoulder.

"Nothing!" I snap my sketchbook shut.

He recoils a step at my hasty brush-off, hands out in front of him. "Whoa, top secret shit, or what?"

Embarrassed, I hug my artwork protectively to my chest, then stand and pick up my sketching pencils, zipping them into the small canvas case. "It's just..." I trail off, surprising myself at how vulnerable I feel that he almost saw my drawing.

What is wrong with me? It's not like I'm drawing anything scandalous.

"It's okay, Ada, you don't have to show me. I was just curious." His reassuring words belie his obvious confusion. He searches my face, like he's trying to figure out why I reacted so strongly to an innocent question.

Well, that makes two of us.

"It's just personal, I guess. Whatever." I shrug, flipping my hair over to one side and rolling my eyes, trying my best to act aloof.

Maybe if I make every nonchalant gesture at the same time, I'll actually feel it.

I wait for the aloof to kick in. It doesn't.

"Okay," he chuckles. "I guess... once a weird art kid, always a weird art kid, right?" He throws a light punch at my shoulder as he passes me on his way to the kitchen.

"Yeah," I reply, cringing internally.

Brilliant response.

"You working tonight?" he asks, his back to me as he stares into the fridge.

"Not tonight. But Katie's coming over for a bit to watch a movie."

"Cool," he says, turning to face me with a soda can in his hand. He holds my gaze as he shuts the fridge door behind him and pulls the tab. The *schick-hiss* sound echoes off the nearly bare walls in the otherwise silent apartment.

"So, uh... when do you think you'll be home?" I pause for a moment, then think better of the question. "I mean, if you even *come* home, right? Hot date and all." I pump my eyebrows, instantly regretting it. The thought of Jesse staying out all night with some woman he just met sits heavily in my chest.

"Uh," he says slowly, like he's thinking carefully about what I just implied. "No."

I give him a questioning look. "No?"

"That's not really my style." He shakes his head and takes a sip of his drink.

"What isn't your style?"

"Fucking on the first date, I mean."

I push down a flood of mental images suddenly fighting to the forefront of my mind—*for God's sake do* not *look at his body right now*—though I can feel my skin flushing as he watches me. Despite my burning cheeks, I relax a bit at his reassurance. "Alright. I just thought—"

"I'll be home tonight," he says, cutting me off. His expression is serious, like he's making me a promise.

"Okay," I say quietly.

He seems to give himself a mental shake and heads for the door. "Catch you if you're still up?"

KATIE and I are a bottle and a half deep in cheap rosé with the credits of *The Princess Bride* rolling in the background. She's sprawled across the love seat and I'm slumped in one of the folding chairs, balancing a mug of wine on my bare knee.

"Does it feel weird living here now?" she asks, shifting to sit up a bit, her drink held aloft as she rearranges a throw blanket over her bare legs.

"What do you mean? Like, without you?"

"I mean, yeah. I guess it's just kind of... empty." She glances around the room. "Without my stuff."

"Yeah. Jesse doesn't really have much since he's not staying." I shrug.

"Right. So, what's it like living with Jesse?"

"Yeah, what's it like living with Jesse?" His deep voice comes from behind me.

I nearly jump out of my skin and almost fall off my chair as I spin to face him, the wine in my system not helping me steady myself. "Fucking hell, Jess!" My heart thunders in my chest. Clearly, neither of us heard him come in.

Looking delighted at having snuck up on me, he smiles and tosses his keys onto the coffee table. He grabs the remote to shut off the movie.

"Hey, Katie. How's it going?" he asks, lifting his chin in her direction.

"Good," she replies, raising her mug with a slow, sleepy blink. "Hey, how's your mom doing?"

"Good, actually." Then he turns to me, crossing his arms in front of him and raising a brow. "Well? Aren't you gonna answer the question? What's it like living with me?" He nudges his foot against mine, grinning like a fool.

"Fucking charming," I say, narrowing my eyes as I pull my foot away. I turn to Katie. "Honestly, it's been torturous. He makes the whole place smell like *dude*."

"Come on, that's all you got?" Amusement plays on his lips and he stuffs his hands into his front pockets. "No Yeti jokes this time? I'm disappointed, Ada, really."

"I'm slipping," I say, holding up my mug in explanation.

Jesse cranes his neck when there's a knock at the door. "You expecting someone?"

"Yup, that's my ride," Katie says as she drags back the blanket and stands. She tries and fails to fight off a yawn as she stretches her arms over her head.

"Already?" I ask, checking the time on my phone as I peel myself out of my seat. I let Dimitri in and he follows me back into the living room.

"Hey, babe," he says, pulling Katie into a hug.

She lets out a sleepy, muffled squeak against his chest.

When he clocks Jesse's presence, he pulls his arm from around Katie to extend his hand.

Katie excuses herself to use the bathroom while Jesse and Dimitri do all the requisite dude-bro hand shaking and introductions.

There's an awkward beat of silence between the two men while I gather up the wine bottles and mugs to take them to the kitchen.

"So, Katie tells me you're just here for the summer?" Dimitri asks behind me.

"Yeah. Heading back to Australia at the end of August."

"Oh, nice. What do you do there?"

"I work on a produce farm."

"No way!" Dimitri says, perking up. "I'm a landscaper. I

should pick your brain. My boss has been looking into these small-scale urban farming setups... kind of like a starter kit for homesteading."

"Yeah? Produce only, or livestock too?"

I glance over my shoulder at Jesse, who's brightened at the topic. I smile and return my attention to my task at the sink.

"Not sure," Dimitri says. "Possibly both, depending on the property size. And what the owners are after, obviously. But he figures chicken coops wouldn't be too hard for us to put together, for a start."

I rinse out the mugs and set them beside the sink, then turn around to face what appears to be a budding bromance.

Katie emerges from the bathroom and joins me, leaning back against the counter at my side.

The guys are oblivious to us watching them and carry on, their gestures and voices becoming more animated as they talk shop. On the surface, they're the opposite of each other; Jesse's blond, broad, and beardy, whereas Dimitri's hair is short and dark, he's clean-shaven, and his wiry muscles are honed by all the outdoor physical labor.

As I rub absentmindedly at my wine-warmed cheeks, I try not to let my gaze linger on the way Jesse's Henley hugs his biceps. My teeth start to worry at my bottom lip when he pushes up his shirt sleeves and crosses his arms.

Fuck. Maybe I should slap myself.

"Ada," Katie whispers, keeping her voice low. She looks conspiratorial as she beckons me closer.

I lean in.

"Jesse got hot."

I recoil, glancing at Jesse to make sure he didn't hear her, and make a face. "Uh... how drunk *are* you?"

Be cool. Just deny it.

"Don't pretend you don't notice." She waggles her eyebrows,

giggling quietly. "And you've never been able to lie convincingly. I don't know why you bother trying that shit with me."

"Uh, I *don't* notice," I deny outright. "Besides, aren't you only supposed to have eyes for your fiancé right now?"

Katie makes a *pfft* sound. "I'm engaged, not *blind*."

"Okay, big shooter. Time to go home." Making a show of brushing off what she said, I take her by the shoulders and guide her toward the front hall—though I don't miss the knowing look she throws back at me.

As we pass through the living room, Katie reaches for Dimitri's hand and murmurs something about it being time to head out. Jesse trails us down the hall, still talking with Dimitri about soil pH.

I hug Katie and Dimitri goodbye in the doorway, and the guys shake hands again.

"Hey, it was cool chatting about this stuff," Dimitri says, tilting his chin at Jesse.

"Yeah," Jesse replies with a nod. "Great to meet you."

"Maybe I could connect you with my boss?"

"Yeah, sure," Jesse says. "Ada can text Katie my number."

"Okay," I say. "Hate to interrupt you two chatty Cathies, but it's late."

"Yeah, sorry. We should go," Dimitri says.

"Goodnight!" I call to Katie, who's already halfway up the stairs.

"Night, Ada," she says over her shoulder. "Night, Jesse!" she sings out, projecting her voice back into the apartment. She winks at me and I close the door with an eye roll.

I take a breath and turn around, slowly walking back into the kitchen. Jesse's already leaning against the counter by the sink, drinking a glass of water and looking decidedly hotter than earlier. A few pieces of hair have escaped his bun and fall forward, framing his face. Is there more stubble than before?

Damn. Maybe I'm *the drunk one.*

"So, how'd the date go?" I ask carefully. For a moment, I don't know where or how to stand. I settle on stuffing my hands into the back pockets of my jean shorts and focus on breathing like a normal human being.

"Uh," he starts, looking thoughtful. "I mean... She was nice."

"Nice?" I ask, squinting slightly. I watch him for a moment, but he doesn't elaborate. "It was shit, wasn't it?"

He lets out a long breath, dragging a hand down his face. "Oh, fuck. It was awful." He looks like he's suppressing a smile.

An involuntary laugh escapes my lips—louder than I mean for it to sound. I press a hand over my mouth, trying not to do it again, nearly snorting from the effort. "Sorry... sorry."

He tilts his head at me. "Oh, no, please, laugh it up at my expense."

"Aww, poor bunny," I say with a pout, still giggling a bit. Clocking his wounded expression, I walk toward him and add, "Hey, I'm sorry. Let me make it up to you." I touch his arm, a warm smile still on my lips.

I swear I hear him draw in a quick breath.

I drop my hand, pulling my gaze away.

Why did you touch him like that?

My eyes land on the fridge—and on a convenient cover. "Midnight ice cream? Makes everything better." I grab a tub of raspberry swirl from the freezer and fish two spoons out of the cutlery drawer before shutting it with my hip. I pry open the ice cream and hand him a spoon.

"What, we too good for bowls?" he asks as he takes one.

"Oh, yeah. Bowls are *way* beneath us," I reply with an arched brow, holding out the container to him. "Yetis first."

He studies me before taking a reluctant scoop, and I try not to stare at his lips as he puts it in his mouth.

"Mmm, okay, this was a good idea," he mumbles around the ice cream, gesturing to the container in my hands.

"Now, tell me what happened with awful Kristen." I try to suppress a smile.

"Hey, I didn't call her that," he corrects me, pointing at me with his spoon.

"Okay, yeah, yeah," I say, swirling my own spoon in his direction. "A girl can extrapolate, though."

He hesitates for a beat, like he's trying to decide what to say. "Okay, well... it wasn't *that* bad. She was just checking her phone the whole night."

"Gross," I say, around a mouthful of ice cream.

"Yeah, and when she wasn't on her phone, she and Renee were talking about real estate. But, like, *every* story was one of those you-had-to-be-there things, with inside jokes that just didn't..." He trails off. "I dunno. It doesn't matter, I guess."

I make a face. "Ew. Sounds painful."

"Exactly, right?" He shakes his head, then glances at me before digging his spoon back in. "Just not my kind of person. Whatever." He looks tired—maybe even disappointed.

The urge to comfort him rises in my throat, but I don't know how. I have to stop myself from reaching for his chest—from chucking the ice cream aside and sliding my chilled fingers over the soft, warm fabric of his shirt and feeling the breath fill his ribcage.

Stop thinking about touching him. Christ.

Taking one last bite, I push the container into his hands. "I should go to bed," I say softly, then toss my spoon into the sink before turning to leave. "Sorry your night didn't end up so great."

"Hey," he calls to me over his shoulder.

I pause and turn on my heel to face him.

We hold each other's gaze for a long moment before he

speaks. "It uh... ended up alright after all." He looks like he wants to say something more.

My heartbeat picks up, my pulse racing in my neck. There's something loaded about the way he's staring at me. Something that stirs places inside me that should be decidedly *unstirred* by Jesse Bailey.

"Anyway, thanks," is all he says, raising the ice cream container with a lazy smile.

I nod and turn back toward my room before he can see the grin spread over my face.

10

———

JESSE

The apartment's quiet when I unlock the front door, and I realize I'm both relieved and disappointed Ada's not up yet. I squeeze my eyes shut and rub my forehead.

Shit.

It's been nine days since I moved in with her and I'm fucking struggling.

I pinch the chest of my sweat-slicked T-shirt, tugging it away from my skin, and switch on the coffeemaker. Determined to settle my mind with exercise this morning, I'd found a gym several miles away and decided to run there and back. But even a long, hard workout couldn't calm the virtually permanent fizzing feeling in my stomach, and I'm just as worked up now as always.

I shouldn't be thinking about her this much. About the feeling of her arms around my waist. About how she smells like goddamn summertime. About that time I came home with a load of groceries and caught her dancing to the Beastie Boys on full blast in the kitchen. About how sneaking up on her Friday—mug of wine in her hand, tipsy smile on her lips—was the best part of my night. About how she intuitively understood why my date with Kristen had been a letdown.

Ada saw me—saw what I needed, what I wanted. And what I wanted was *her*. I *still* want her.

I open the cupboard, resolving to push Ada out of my mind yet again. As I set a mug on the counter, a sticky note on the wall catches my attention. I walk over for a closer look, then huff an amused breath at the doodle. Scrawled in red marker is a bearded guy with his hair in a bun. The cartoon me is crying, theatrical tears streaming down his face and an ominously large pair of scissors hovering over his head. Above the drawing is the word *"you"*; underneath, it says *"soon"*—underlined three times. Smiling to myself, I peel it off the wall and walk back to my room. I stick it above my bed, smoothing it flat with my hand.

An Ada Russo original.

Taking one last look at it, I shake my head and head back to the kitchen for my coffee. As I pass Ada's room, I catch a sliver of soft light peeking out from under her door and pause.

She's awake.

I imagine her on the other side, rubbing the sleep from her eyes or pulling on an oversized hoodie. I fight the urge to knock, then walk on. *Just friends,* I remind myself, returning to the kitchen. *Just roommates. Marcus' sister. Marcus' sister. Marcus' sister.*

I'm reaching for the coffeepot when her door clicks open.

"You're sweaty."

"Hey," I reply, unable to hide my wide smile when I see her standing at her bedroom door.

She's wearing cotton pajama shorts and a faded David Bowie T-shirt. I have to rip my eyes from her when I notice the hard points of her nipples through the fabric.

Jesus.

I clear my throat. "Coffee?"

"Please." She rubs her arms like she's cold and shuffles into the kitchen.

I get out another mug and pour two cups.

"Thanks." She takes one and leans against the counter, reaching out to pluck at the shoulder of my sweaty T-shirt with a grimace. "Did you go to the gym on the surface of the sun or what?"

"Pretty much."

"How long have you been up?" she asks, then takes a sip.

"Since five, I think?"

She nearly spits out her coffee, covering her mouth with the back of her hand. "Are you fucking serious?"

I smile. "That's what happens when you spend eight years getting up with the sun. That shit's in my *bones* now."

She scoffs. "You and I are *very* different people."

"Ah, I don't know about that," I say. "I have it on good authority we're both *snarky little bitches.*" I nudge her bare shin with my toe.

"Ah!" She laughs, pulling her leg away. "Get your sweaty foot off me!"

I chuckle, then sip my coffee. "So, what are you doing today? You at the bar?"

"No." She sets down her mug long enough to hop up onto the counter, letting her feet dangle in front of the lower cupboards. "Tonight I'm taking *the youths* out to terrorize the community."

"Yeah? Where?" I ask with a smirk.

"Bowling alley."

"Oh, man," I breathe. "That takes me back."

"I know, right?" She peers at me over the rim of her mug. "Gotta make sure they meet their teenage shenanigans quota."

I lift a brow. "Remember all those popcorn fights in the parking lot after they closed?"

"Vividly," she says, taking another sip of coffee, then smiles to herself. "Like that time you poured your entire bag down the back of Marcus' shirt?"

"Ha!" I bark. "Yes! Some of it got stuck in his ass crack."

"Fuck!" she exclaims with a cringe.

"He was *piiiiiissed*." I huff out a laugh. "Had to go hide behind a parked car and drop trou' just to get it all out of there."

"Fucking Marcus, always taking off his damn pants in public," she says, shaking her head and setting her coffee mug beside her.

"Yeah, well, he seems to have grown up a bit since then, thankfully."

"Yeah, we all have. *Thank God*." Her eyes slide to my sweat-soaked chest, and she quickly looks away.

"Yeah," I reply, unable to stop my gaze from wandering down to her full lips.

"Anyway, uh... you wanna come?" she asks. "Full disclosure: I can't promise any ass-crack popcorn, if you're into that kind of thing."

The corner of my mouth ticks up. "I think I'll live without experiencing that on a personal level."

"Fair enough," she says, arching a brow. "Come on. It'll be fun." She searches my expression, then her open smile falters. "Unless you're busy with your mom..."

Is she disappointed?

"Uh, no," I say. "I can come." I swig the last of my coffee and step toward her to place my mug in the sink.

She tracks my movement as I reach past her.

I lean in close, dropping my voice low. "Loser wears the popcorn."

She snorts as I walk away and, before I can turn into the bathroom to take a shower, a tea towel hits me in the back of the head.

THE BOWLING ALLEY is surprisingly busy for a Wednesday night. As we pour through the front doors, the musty scent of lane oil and shoe disinfectant mingles with the savory aroma of buttered popcorn, hitting me in a punch of nostalgia. The kids rush past me and Ada like rivers around boulders, immediately clustering around the arcade machines.

Ada searches through her backpack and pulls out a slightly crumpled piece of paper. Referring to the sheet, she murmurs to herself as she counts the kids. Then she seems to count them a second time.

"Did we lose any?" I ask, mostly joking.

She finishes counting. "No. There are thirteen kids, plus you and me... so, fifteen total. Wait—the kid in the white hat over there... that's Rolando... but does this say Rolando or Ronaldo?" She angles the list toward me. "They both signed up, but then Ronaldo couldn't come tonight."

I step closer, peering over her shoulder. "Lemme see..."

She runs a hand through her hair, sending her sweet coconut-and-cherry scent floating up to me.

I inhale, admittedly taking a little longer than necessary to check the list. "The top one is Rolando."

"Thanks. I've mixed those two up so many fucking times," she mutters under her breath, then scribbles a crooked check mark on the sheet. "I have no issue telling who's who in person, but the paperwork always trips me up." The quiet way she says the words, clearly intending them for my ears only, feels almost... intimate.

I keep my mouth shut, careful not to make a big deal about helping her out. Despite her confidence about dyslexia when she'd stood up to her parents the other day, there's vulnerability in the way she won't quite meet my eyes.

A teenage girl approaches us and we both look up.

"Do we have to wear those ugly bowling shoes?" she asks.

"Yeah, sorry, Sofia," Ada says. "I know they're kind of tragic, but it's a time-honored tradition. Plus, we'll all be equally hideous, so it levels the playing field."

"Okay." Sofia lifts her chin at me. "Is your boyfriend gonna bowl with us?"

Ada and I both physically recoil, stepping apart. "No, uh," I stammer. "I mean, yes, I'm just—" My gaze flits between Ada and Sofia.

"He's not my boyfriend," Ada corrects her, rescuing me by being able to produce a coherent sentence.

"Why not?" Sofia asks, shamelessly looking me up and down. "He's cute."

I frown and scratch the side of my neck, trying to play it cool. "We're uh... We're just friends." I hope I'm selling it.

When Ada nods her confirmation, Sofia gives me a knowing smile. "So, you single then?"

"Okay!" Ada shouts, clapping her hands together. "Come on, everyone! West Valley crew, follow me!"

Mercifully, I have time to get a handle on myself while Ada guides the kids through trading their street shoes for the ugly rentals. We take over three lanes at the far end of the alley, the rowdy teens wisely sequestered away from most other patrons.

Ada divides the group into teams of five, assigning me to a team with Sofia, Rolando, and two other girls, Dalia and Rupi. Addressing the entire group from the next lane, she projects confident authority into the murmuring group of awkward limbs, braces, and the blue glow of phone screens.

I stand off to the side, content to watch her do her thing.

"Alright, let's go over the rules, folks!"

A low groan breaks out amongst the kids.

"Thought you didn't *do* rules, Ada!" Dalia teases.

Ada gives her a skeptical frown. "That's with art. No rules with art. *Yes* rules in public places." She raises a brow. "Just bear with me. I'll make it quick, then shut up."

Dalia calls out again, "Do you mean, like, *you'll* shut up or *we* have to shut up?"

"Correct," Ada retorts with a nod, to a scattering of laughter, then smirks at Dalia.

I like how she treats the kids like equals; she doesn't talk down to them or brush them off like many adults would.

"Okay, listen up. Rule number one," she starts, holding up a finger. "Keep your ugly bowling shoes *on*, please."

Someone sucks their teeth audibly. Rolando spins his hat backward, crossing his arms over his chest.

"Rule number two," she calls out, two fingers up. "This is a family place, so mind your language around the tiny humans."

Sofia frowns. "You mean we can't swear? Like, at all?"

"Ideally," Ada confirms with a nod, then holds up a third finger. "Rule number three: you *roll* the bowling ball. You do not *throw* the bowling ball—unless you happen to have expertise in lane repair and an interest in some community service hours."

Rolando starts telling a story to the kid next to him about how his uncle does repair work at a bowling alley in Oregon.

Ada waits for them to finish with a pointed look. When they finally notice they've interrupted and stop talking, she continues. "Rule number four."

"Out of how many?" Sofia whines.

"Last one! Promise. Rule number four: keep your feet on this side of the... the red... line thing." She points toward the lane. "It probably has a name."

"The foul line," I offer quietly.

She turns to me in surprise—like she almost forgot I was here —and a slow smile spreads over her face. "The foul line," she calls out, still watching me.

I give a subtle lift of my chin toward the group of teens.

She seems to snap back into the moment and turns to them again, gesturing at me with her thumb. "You heard the man. Let's bowl."

The first frames are a chaotic mess while everyone gets into the groove, some kids learning how to bowl for the first time, others evidently learning how to take turns without arguing. Ada and I wind between the kids, offering guidance and reminders, and return to our lanes when we're up. As much as I try to stop myself, my eyes keep sliding in her direction. I catch myself staring at least once when she has a quiet, serious-looking conversation with Rolando near one of the tables behind the lanes.

It's around the fourth frame when I notice the ancient, computerized display flashing an arrow next to *"Man Bun"*. I frown, realizing Rupi and Dalia have edited the nicknames.

Rolando laughs into his fist from the bench behind the score-keeper's chair. "Alright, Man Bun!" he cheers, then cracks up again.

Rupi walks past and shoves him in the shoulder. "Did you even see *your* nickname?"

"Wait... *what?*" Rolando mumbles and peers at the screen before whirling back to Rupi. "*Ballsack?* What the f..."—his eyes jump to me as he catches himself—"what the hell?"

The girls bust up with laughter.

I'm suddenly grateful for *"Man Bun"*.

I bowl an unremarkable frame and return to the seats at the scorekeeping console. As I slide into the plastic chair, Ada flops down beside me on the other side. Her sweet scent once again drifts across the small space between our shoulders, and a magnetic hum buzzes under the sleeve of my T-shirt, enticing me to lean closer. I scratch at the skin, trying to shut it down.

I can't help but look at her. She's wearing a white tank top that makes her turquoise hair seem more vivid than usual. For the first time, I examine the tattoo covering most of her shoulder: a classic pinup girl with bright red lips and a matching bathing suit.

She turns, catching me staring. "What?"

"Nothing," I say too quickly—then clear my throat. "I was just wondering when you got that tattoo."

"Oh." Her gaze falls to her shoulder. "Few years ago."

"Any significance, or...?"

She shrugs. "I've just always liked them... pinup girls, I mean." She places her hand down next to her on the plastic seat and her pinky accidentally brushes against mine.

I pull my hand away and we share an awkward glance. "Yeah?"

"Yeah. They're classy and sexy. Powerful and still feminine." She looks away, her next words muttered, almost to herself. "Wish I could pull that off."

"I don't—" I start but stop myself the moment I realize what I'm about to say.

"You don't what?" she asks, turning to face me.

"Nothing."

"No, don't give me that *nothing* shit," she says softly, then lifts her chin at me, a slight curl to her lips. "What were you gonna say?"

"I was just gonna say..." Racking my brain, I can't think of a single convincing lie, so the truth tumbles out instead. "I don't think you have anything to worry about. You are. You're... *pulling it off.*"

Realization settles in her expression and her lips part.

I can't look away, though I'm already kicking myself. I've essentially told Marcus' little sister I think she's hot. *Great.*

She breaks eye contact and turns to the scoreboard on the screen in front of her. An arrow flashes near the name *"BigBallz"* and she glances over her shoulder.

Following her gaze, I watch a skinny kid with a buzz cut step up to bowl.

She turns back to me, her voice quiet. "I actually went as a pinup girl one Halloween a while back."

"Really?" My imagination wastes no time in serving up images of Ada wearing nothing but that skimpy red bathing suit and a sexy pout. I shift in my seat.

"Yeah. I guess I did kinda rock that costume." She nods as if revisiting some private memory.

I fucking bet she did.

"Wish I could've seen that." I immediately regret the words.

Who is the horny gremlin in charge of my mouth tonight, and why is he drunk at the wheel?

"Yeah?" Ada's voice cuts through my self-recrimination. "I mean... I probably have pictures."

"Uh, you don't need to—" I start, but she's already got her phone out.

"Hey, Man Bun! You're up," Rolando says, nudging my arm with a smirk as he heads back to his seat.

I hesitate for a second, but I'm grateful for the excuse to put some space between me and Ada. At least it'll give my horny brain gremlin time to cool off.

Despite the semi in my pants and the lingering distraction of imagining Ada done up like 1940s babe, I manage to bowl straight down the middle of the lane. Still, the ball only takes out the pins in the center, with one pin left standing on either side. The word *"split"* flashes under *"Man Bun"* on the screen above my lane. That's when a text notification chimes from my back pocket. When I catch sight of Ada putting her phone away, I get a sinking feeling I know what that text is. I don't touch my phone—don't want to seem overeager—but it's suddenly burning a hole in the back of my jeans.

Maybe if my ass catches fire, I'd have an excuse to run out of here.

Ada stands to bowl her frame in the next lane, and our eyes meet over the ball return between us. As she chooses her ball, she cuts an appraising look at my unfortunate split-frame situation and leans in slightly. "You know, you're supposed to try to knock down *all* the pins."

I huff a laugh. "Alright, Chuckles, let's see what you got." I brace my ball against my stomach and tilt my head at her lane. "Ladies first."

She scoffs and hefts a ball into her hands, and—*fuck me*—immediately rolls a strike. Victorious, she whirls around to face me. "Ooh, I *really* wish we didn't have that rule about swear words!"

"Oh, yeah? You'd use a choice few?"

"*All* the good ones." She grins, practically glittering with smug pride.

Letting out a defeated breath, I rub my forehead with the back of my hand and set up to bowl. I'll have to put some spin on the ball to have any hope in hell of a spare. I decide to aim for the pin on the left, hoping it'll shoot sideways and take its buddy out with it.

Right as I wind up, Ada says, "Oh, I texted you that picture of my costume."

Fuck.

Her words shoot through my nerve endings, tensing all the wrong muscles as I let go of the ball. It seems like a half-decent attempt at first, but I can tell I overshot it, and the ball inevitably winds up in the gutter. I straighten with a sigh and wipe my sweaty hands on my jeans.

"Thanks for that," I grumble, unable to avoid the broad, beautiful smile beaming back at me.

"Aw, don't cry, Jess. I can ask if they have one of those little ramps for you." She tilts her head toward a group of young kids several lanes away. "I think that birthday party is almost done with theirs."

Shielding one hand from view with the other, I flip her off.

"So, about that popcorn deal," she says, tilting her head at the front door. "We gonna do that in the parking lot like old times? In front of the children?"

"Oh, no," I assure her, lowering my voice. "That's just between you and me."

She flushes, a delicate pink creeping over her cheeks.

I catch myself staring again—*looks like the horny gremlin is back*—and, shaking my head, return to the benches behind the console. "Dalia, your turn," I say as I sit, then lean forward to squint at the screen. "Or should I call you... *Dalulu?*"

Dalia swats Rolando's shoulder as she heads to take her turn. "Clown."

He snickers into his fist.

My knee bounces and I chew on the inside of my cheek. Unable to wait any longer, I pull out my phone. After a quick glance over my shoulder to make sure Ada's otherwise occupied, I open the text.

Thank God I'm sitting down because my dick twitches to attention like a soldier reporting for duty. In the photo, Ada's dressed as a pinup version of Rosie the Riveter, the iconic red and white polka-dot headscarf tied above curled, dark bangs—her natural hair color. A tight-fitting denim shirt is knotted under her breasts to reveal her bare waist and unbuttoned at the top to show her cleavage. Tiny, high-waisted, button-up shorts hug her hips over fishnet stockings. And, if that wasn't enough to have me grinding my teeth, she's sporting a pair of red stiletto heels. *Fuck-me* heels. One arm is held in Rosie the Riveter's iconic bicep curl, with the other slung around Katie's shoulders. And her *smile*. Painted with bright red lipstick, it's broad, genuine, and sexy as hell.

"Whoa, dude, who's the *snack*?" Rolando's voice snaps me out of my Ada-induced vortex. I rush to shut off my phone, shoving it back in my pocket.

"You're looking at her," Ada replies from my other side, and I whip my head around, feeling the blood drain from my face.

Shit. How much did she see?

Thankfully, her gaze is fixed on Rolando, who has the decency to act embarrassed. "I think you're up next..."—she eyes the scores on the screen above our lane—"*Rizzero?*"

"*Rizzero?*" he repeats, frowning in confusion when Rupi and Dalia break into laughter nearby.

"Yeah," calls Dalia, cupping a hand to her mouth. "'Cause Roly's got *zero rizz*!" She and Rupi double over in their seats, laughing and holding onto each other for support.

Rolando scoffs and ignores the girls, turning back to me. "'Kay, hold up, though. That was *Ada*?"

"Yeah, and we don't call women *snacks*, my guy," I reply, because my hypocrisy apparently knows no bounds. "Not if you want to level up your *rizz*, anyway." I clap him on the shoulder. "Come on. You're up."

When he heads off to bowl, I immediately regret sending him away—because I'm now left alone with Ada and no buffer.

"Did the term *rizz* just come outta your face?" she asks, a smirk tugging at her lips.

"Shut up."

"So, you got my photo?" She sits beside me on the bench. It's a question, but we both know she saw me staring at it.

"Yeah," I say, trying to keep my expression impassive as I scramble for what to say. Somehow, *"that was the sexiest fucking thing I've seen in a long time"* and *"I might need a minute or several alone with that picture later"* don't make the cut. Instead of the truth this time, I aim for casual. "It was cool."

It was cool?

There's a brief, barely detectable fall in Ada's features before she quickly recovers.

Great. The horny gremlin has been replaced by an awkward penguin.

I need to put that photo the hell out of my mind. Desperate to change the subject, I clear my throat and tilt my chin in Rolando's direction. "He seems like a good kid."

She turns her head away from me slowly before her eyes finally jump to Rolando. "He is." Rolando holds two bowling balls by his crotch, posing with his tongue out while one of the other guys snaps a photo. "I swear he is." Ada shakes her head and walks over to talk to the boys—from the looks of it, giving them a reminder about appropriate behavior in public.

Damn. Even frowning, she's beautiful. I try not to stare. And I try even harder not to pull out my phone and have another look at that damn picture.

"Okay, let's get this over with," Ada sighs, turning to face me in the quiet parking lot. The last of the stragglers have been picked up and it's just us.

"Get what over with?" I ask, putting on an air of innocence.

Despite Ada distracting me in all ways possible, I managed to salvage the game and scored 114, beating her 98. I didn't waste a second gloating about it; she would've done the same.

"The popcorn?" She gestures to the paper bag in my hand. *"Loser wears the popcorn."*

"Right. Almost forgot." I'd done no such thing. I drink in her nervous smile, making a slow show of unfurling the curled top of the popcorn bag. "Well, a deal's a deal. You ready?"

"No." She braces herself, squeezing her eyes shut and scrunching her shoulders into her neck.

I chuckle as I slowly move closer, drawing it out. "Why are you so nervous? It's only *popcorn*."

"Just aim away from my ass crack, okay?" She breaks into laughter as the last words leave her mouth, cracking one eye open to peer up at me, then hastily closing it again.

"I promise *nothing*," I say, raising the bag over her head. I hold it there for a moment but, right before I dump it, I pull it back in front of me. Plucking a single kernel from the bag, I take a step back and toss it at her. It bounces off her chest and onto the asphalt.

"Wh—wha—" she sputters, staring at me. "That's *it*?"

I scoff. "Not gonna waste perfectly good popcorn on *you*." I pluck another kernel from the bag and pop it into my mouth.

"That's not how this works, Jess."

"What do you mean, *how this works*?" I ask as I chew, screwing up my face. "You say that like this is an established practice... with *rules* and shit."

"Hey," she says, putting her hands on her hips. "The deal was: you win, I suffer. So come on. Make me suffer."

I raise my eyebrows. *Putting a pin in that...*

"That came out wrong," she says quickly. "You know what I mean."

"Okay, you really want me to let you have it?" I ask, my calm drawl visibly winding her up.

"Yes!" She throws her hands out at her sides.

I'm loving this—watching her squirm as she tries to guess what I'm gonna do next. I won't lie; this power over her is intoxicating. Pondering my options, I toss a small handful of popcorn into my mouth.

"Come on, Jess, are you gonna—"

Before she can react, I toss another kernel at her chest, and, like a heat-seeking missile, it lands down her tank top, right between her breasts.

I almost choke. My coughing and spluttering laughter only intensifies when she slowly raises her head to glare at me. When I finally regain my composure, she's smiling too.

She gives me a pointed look while she reaches down her shirt and plucks out the piece of popcorn, popping it into her mouth. "Get in the damn car, Man Bun."

11

———

ADA

"You sure?" I ask, closing my sketchbook and tossing it onto the couch. "I can cut it? For real?"

Jesse smiles. His hair hangs in long ropes, wet spots darkening the shoulders of his blue T-shirt. He holds a towel in one hand and a comb in the other.

"Yeah, I gotta get you off my case about it somehow, don't I?" He works his fingers through a few tangles. "It has gotten pretty long."

"About fucking time." I push off the couch and walk to the kitchen. "You were supposed to be working *in* the bush, not *becoming* the bush." I pull a pair of scissors out of a drawer.

Jesse shakes his head and drags a chair into the center of the linoleum floor, placing it under the dim yellow light. "I feel like you were waiting to use that one."

"No way to know for sure," I deadpan. I snip the scissors in the air, then gesture to the chair. "Sit."

"Okay, smartass," he says, following orders.

I drape the towel around his neck and tuck it carefully under the collar of his T-shirt, willing myself to ignore the warmth of his skin against my fingertips.

He squints up at me as I circle around in front of him. "Is this where we make awkward small talk, or what?"

"Nah, this isn't that kind of salon." I smirk, combing out his hair.

"Okay." He blinks a few times when some wet strands fall in front of his face. "So what kind of salon is this?"

"Big talk only. In fact, you so much as mention the weather— or the local sportsball team—and I'll shave you bald."

He scoffs. "Knew I shouldn't trust you with this. We're not *one* minute in and you're already threatening me."

"Shut up. I told you: I'm good at this. And stop moving."

"Yes, ma'am." His blue eyes shine with amusement.

I walk around behind him, combing and parting his dark blond hair. "So, you gonna give me some guidance about what you want, or...?"

"Honestly, as long as you don't make me look like a dork, do whatever you want. Shorter, I guess. That's my guidance."

"Wow," I say. "First the drink and now this? Do you even *have* opinions?"

He huffs a laugh. "When it matters, yeah."

I take up the first sections, snipping carefully as his long, damp locks fall to the kitchen floor around my feet. His scalp is warm under my hands and he smells like soap. I have to remind myself not to lean down and huff the citrusy scent of his shampoo like some kind of subway pervert. I breathe quietly through my mouth instead, grateful I'm standing behind him where he can't see my face, because I'm already struggling to keep my cool. This was a bad idea. But I'm committed now.

"So, have you talked with your dad since you've been home?"

"Oof. Big talk right outta the gate." He rubs his hands over his jeans. "No. He's an asshole. Cut contact years ago."

"Okay, noted," I say. "Things must have been pretty rough after your parents split."

"Yeah. He purposely made the divorce a nightmare for Mom. Dragged it out for years."

Shit.

I frown. "Can't imagine anyone being cruel to your mom."

"I know. It was really shitty. He forced her into selling the house just to pay her legal fees."

"Really? *Jesus.* I can see why you wanted to get the hell out of here." Wet strands slide through my fingers as I take up the next section.

He makes a wry sound, somewhere between a scoff and a laugh. "That was only part of it."

"Yeah?"

He pauses, letting out a breath. "You remember Naomi, right?"

"Yeah."

"I dunno how much Marcus told you back then, but things with her got kind of ugly too."

"What happened?" I ask, too curious to keep my mouth shut. "I mean, you don't have to—"

He cuts me off. "No, it's fine. The nutshell version is: we were friends, then I thought it was growing into something more, but she was just keeping me on the hook."

"Ouch." I wince just thinking about being in that situation.

"I had a thing for her for *years*. She confused the shit out of me, though; always being so touchy-feely, blatantly flirting with me one minute then giving me the cold shoulder the next... So many mixed signals. Not knowing which version of her I was gonna get each day... I dunno. Something about that just had me wrapped around her little finger. Guess I was young and didn't know any better."

"Wow." I pause with a section of long hair pinched between

two fingers, scissors hovering. "Sounds like she was kinda manip-ulative."

He hums his agreement. "Yeah, none of it was healthy. Anyway, we ended up living together for a few months. But, when I told her how I felt, she got all weird about it and asked me to move out."

My movements slow as I take this in.

They lived together?

I comb through a tangle, frowning.

No. Different situation.

"Fuck. I'm sorry, Jess." Then, a fuzzy memory materializes in my mind. "Wait, so you never actually *dated* Naomi?"

"Nope."

"But I remember seeing you together at parties and stuff. She was always sitting on your lap and..."

"Exactly."

"Damn." I'm suddenly infused with anger at Naomi for being shitty to Jesse back then.

"It really sucked, yeah. So with that, and the shit with my parents, I decided to get the fuck outta Dodge."

"That... makes a lot of sense." I let a hand fall to his shoulder, giving it a light squeeze. When he glances back at me, I realize the touch is lingering a moment longer than necessary and pull away, changing the subject. "So, how are things with your mom? She doing okay being home?"

"Getting there. Still exhausted, and still needs my help with getting the groceries and things like that."

"So you're, like, her gofer?"

He laughs, the deep, full sound of it wrapping around me like a blanket. "Guess I am."

I smile to myself as I snip through another section and let it drop. "Is it weird being home?"

"Extremely."

I narrow my eyes. "Yeah? Why?"

"Well, this girl I know keeps harassing me about my appearance, for one."

I hum a soft laugh through my nose.

"*And*," he continues, "I've just entrusted her with scissors."

"She sounds sketchy. You sure that's a good idea?" I bite the inside of my cheek.

"Yeah. She talks a big game, but it's all an act."

I arch a brow. "An act, huh?"

"Oh, yeah. Big-time. She likes to be all snarky and smart-assy, but she's a total softie on the inside."

"And how do you know that?"

"I just know."

"What does that even mean?" I press, playfully tugging on a section of his hair. "Pretty vague."

He huffs a laugh. "Wow, okay... Well,"—he tries again—"I've known her a long time. She's fiercely loyal. Principled. Passionate."

A slight flush rises in my cheeks at the idea of Jesse describing me as *passionate*. "Why does *passionate* feel like code for *Italian*?"

"She's *very* Italian." I can hear the smile in his voice.

I push him lightly on the side of his head and he throws me an amused glance over his shoulder.

I drag the hair back over his right ear, the shorter sections falling between the comb's teeth. When he tilts his head to the side slightly, my gaze drops to his neck, and I imagine grazing my teeth over his skin there. I look away.

Stop it, Russo. Forbidden fruit.

"I dunno," he muses. "She teaches art classes for at-risk youth. That's softie territory, don't you think?"

"If you think that makes you soft, you clearly haven't spent enough time with the at-risk youth of Lennox Valley," I shoot back.

He laughs. "Well, that may be true, but I still think I'm right."

I shake my head as more long strands fall at my feet. Gently tousling the shorter hair on one side of his head, I move to his other side, picking up the comb again.

He shifts in the chair, sitting up straighter. "Speaking of your art, you ever gonna show me any of it, or what?"

"No!" I scoff. I've been keeping my bedroom door closed, effectively hiding my paintings since Jesse moved in.

"Why not?" He sounds offended. "What's the big deal?"

"I dunno. It's... It's not for everyone."

He lets out a soft grunt and pauses. "Alright, but I'm just gonna assume it's nudes, then."

"It's not nudes! Oh my God!"

"More embarrassing than nudes?" He laughs. "You're not drawing *me*, are you?"

"Shut up!" I grin behind him, heat rising to my cheeks.

We don't speak for a few minutes as I snip the last long sections away, then trim and check the evenness of the cut. I try my best to concentrate on cleaning up the shortest parts at the nape of his neck, pleading with myself to ignore the warmth of his skin, then place the scissors on the table beside us. Circling around to check the front, I lean down and run both hands up from his temples, watching the strands pass through my fingers.

Standing this close, I can't help but notice Jesse's quick, inhaled breath and the way he closes his eyes for a long moment. When he opens them again and exhales, it's almost a sigh.

The weight of his silent gaze finally gets to me.

"What?" I ask, frowning as a self-conscious flush dances across the back of my neck. That same one I felt at the bowling alley last night when I caught him staring at my tattoo, and then later at the photo I'd texted him.

"Nothing," he says, quickly looking away.

I'd felt vulnerable showing him that picture—like it fell into some gray no-man's-land between platonic and flirtatious—and I caught myself on more than one occasion hoping he liked what he saw. Then his response had been so... *deflating*.

Renewing my resolve not to think about it, I shake out the shorter hair with my fingertips, appraising my work. I pull back to take him in fully, and my stomach drops. He's even hotter with the new cut. Well, except for one thing.

"Now, what are we gonna do about this?" I ask, tugging his long beard toward me.

He sucks in a breath, the flinch almost imperceptible.

Suddenly aware of my breathing, I let go. I'd been aiming for playful teasing but clearly overshot and hit provocative flirting instead.

Keep it together.

"What, you don't like it?" His voice is thick with sarcasm. He knows damn well I don't like it; I've taken every shot imaginable at his scruffy appearance since he showed up here.

"No, it's awful." I force a casual air and scrunch my nose. "It's giving overgrown billy goat."

"Is it really that bad?" he asks with a half smile. His voice rumbles low in his throat, setting alight something inside me that I'm desperate to ignore. I dig deep for some way to shut that shit down—but the feeling doesn't go away.

Realizing cheap insults are my only remaining hope, the asshole teenager inside me pipes up. "Kinda reminds me of road-kill." I put on an air of disgust to drive the point home. "It's putting me off my dinner."

"Ouch," he says, his brow creasing as he looks away.

Regret pings like a pinball in my chest.

Too far. Shit.

I want to tell him I didn't mean it—that he's insanely sexy. But I have to stay in asshole mode. It's better this way.

"I told you. Big talk at this salon. No platitudes." Against my better judgment, I reach up again to run my hands through his hair, my fingers sliding gently in silent apology as I check my work once more. His face is so close to mine.

Shut it down, Ada. You can stop touching him now.

But my hands don't listen.

He searches my expression with a slight smirk, lingering on my lips briefly before he seems to catch himself and averts his gaze.

Abort mission.

This pull between us feels dangerous.

"Well, then," he adds in a low voice, reaching for the scissors beside us.

I freeze.

Studying me intently, he lifts his chin, leaning back slightly into my hands, and my fingers clench. He spins the scissors around and holds them out to me. "Think you can clean that up for me too?"

What's he doing? He can trim his own fucking beard.

"Um, sure," I hear myself say. Then, like I'm fucking hypnotized, I watch myself take the scissors, observing my own movements from outside my body.

His gaze on me is like a caress.

Unable to stare any longer into those blue eyes without doing something stupid, I look down. We don't speak as I snip away at his beard. My fingertips graze his face, and I feel his every breath as my hands move past his lips. When I gently grasp his jaw to guide him to turn, he yields, and when I lift his chin, he bares his neck, his Adam's apple lifting when he swallows. There's a warmth to the intimate space between our bodies. A charge in the air. I remind myself to breathe.

When I'm finished, I step back and tug the towel away from his neck, gently shaking it out over the floor before drifting to the sink in a surreal fog. I wet one end with warm water and squeeze out the excess.

Jesse is off-limits. Marcus would lose his shit—and I can't do that to my brother. Or to Jesse.

And yet, as I claw for the last threads of my rapidly unraveling common sense, my back prickles with heat. I can feel him watching me.

Walk away. Walk away right now.

I imagine the ways I could escape this. I could throw him the towel and tell him to go take another fucking shower, for example. A cold one. Or I could lie and say I'm late for work and run off...

But I don't run.

When I turn back around, my breath catches at the sight of him. He sits patiently in the middle of the kitchen, eyes trained on me with an expression that's both intense and unreadable.

Aaaaaand he's fucking gorgeous.

Shit.

What have I done? I should have left him in his scruffy billy goat state, roadkill beard be damned. Because now? Now he's like a disheveled Hemsworth brother and...

No. Not today, Satan.

Not ever.

I wipe my hands on the dry end of the towel and swallow. Then, my body betraying me once again, I find myself in front of him, the yellow glow of the overhead light casting shadows over him as I roughly brush the towel over his trimmed beard. A little too roughly, maybe.

"Easy, now." Jesse chuckles softly, blinking up at me. "No need to be so aggressive about it."

"Then hold still, jackass." I lean in, bracing a hand on the back of his neck to steady him. I shift my stance around his long legs, painfully aware that I'm basically straddling his lap.

He watches my every move, and I catch the flex of his hand as his gaze licks up my body.

I smooth the wet corner of the towel down one cheek and over the square line of his jaw. His lips pull open slightly as I work my way around his mouth.

His mouth. Fuck. I can't look at his mouth.

His pupils are blown wide and locked on me. My cheeks burn with heat.

"Almost done," I say quietly. Then, going against every rational thought screaming in my brain, I lean in even closer and drag the damp towel behind his ears, then across the back of his neck. Jesse's mouth is inches from my collarbone, his warm breath fanning over my skin. The sensation makes me close my eyes for a moment as I claw for self-control. I'm attuned to every movement—both his and my own—and his clean, citrusy scent fills my senses, making me wonder what he would taste like.

Pull away. Now.

But I don't. I can't.

His magnetic pull buzzes so loud in my ears, I half expect my hair to stand on end as every cell of my body orients in his direction. He turns his head away for a moment, the corded muscles of his neck flexing. When he looks back up at me, time seems to slow, and something in him snaps.

He grasps my hips and, with a jerk, tugs me down onto his lap. My shocked gasp slices through the quiet and the towel slips over his shoulder, fluttering to the floor. I'm straddling him, our lips inches apart and our breaths mingling. Tense at first, my stunned posture slowly melts against the warmth of his broad chest. When his hands slide around my waist, I can't help but rock my hips forward, leaning closer.

"Ada..." he whispers, his nose grazing mine. Hearing him say my name like that—so close, so intimate, so reverent—sucks the air from my lungs. He grips the back of my tank top, twisting the fabric as if he's fighting—and losing—some internal battle to stop himself from taking this further. And, when he breaks, hauling me in and slamming my core against his unmistakable hardness, I don't even resist.

My fingers fall from his still-damp hair as my gaze jumps between his eyes and his mouth, each movement asking every question our lips can't utter.

What is this? What's happening? Do you feel this too?

My body aches for more and my mind, addled by the damp heat gathering between my legs, has lost control. Without even meaning to, I arch my back, pushing my breasts into his chest. The places he's touching me blaze with heat and I drift closer still, my lips seeking his, needing to be tethered in the storm rushing around us.

Fuck, yes.

Wait. No. Fuck, no!

I push off the chair, tearing myself from his body. Scrambling to stand, I back away a few steps.

"Jesse..." I say his name on a hard exhale. "We..." I don't know what to say. I cross my arms tightly over my chest, not trusting myself. "We can't."

"Sorry. I just..." He scrubs both hands down his face. "Sorry, yeah, you're right. Fuck." Shaking his head, he frowns at the floor and stands.

"I should..." I trail off, throwing a fleeting look at my bedroom door, and back up a few more paces. My cheeks burn with a mixture of shame and arousal, and I do everything in my power to avoid those fucking blue eyes. I catch his fingers clenching, and the fire inside me blazes again at the memory of his hands on my hips, my waist, the curve of my lower back. Glancing again toward my room, I gesture behind me. "I was gonna go work on my..." I need to get away from here—from *him*.

We don't speak for a moment, the awkward, charged silence

hanging like molten lead in the air. When I brave a look at Jesse, there's a hard set to his jaw and his expression is a swirling mixture of desire and regret. He's angry at himself, I'm guessing. But there's also something more, like he can't decide whether to punch a hole in the wall or pin me up against it.

"Yeah, okay," he finally says. "Um, I'll... I'll clean this up." He gestures at the mess on the floor, then rubs the back of his neck.

"Okay, yeah," I say. I hurry to my room without turning back, quickly shutting the door behind me. My eyes close.

Oh, fuck.

12

JESSE

Renee's friend, Maya, meets me outside the restaurant and we do the awkward first date dance, introducing ourselves and making small talk. I stay mostly quiet while Maya gushes about how nice Renee is for having set us up.

When Renee texted me last night about another date with one of her friends, I accepted right away, using a few more exclamation points than necessary to convey my enthusiasm. Because *fuck*. I need to meet someone else. I need a damn distraction. It also wouldn't hurt to show Marcus I've got my eyes on someone other than his sister, in case he still feels uneasy about our living arrangement. After almost kissing Ada yesterday, my paranoia that he'll notice the way I look at her has only worsened.

I should never have let my control slip like that. I shouldn't have even asked her to cut my hair in the first place. But having her so close—surrounded by her sweet scent, feeling her hands on me—was intoxicating. I couldn't help myself. And, if I'm honest, I tried to drag it out as long as I could, desperate to keep her with me. Then my fucking dick started calling the shots. Thank God she stopped us before it went too far; *I* couldn't have pulled away at that point.

I need to get my shit together.

A pang of regret threatens as I pull open the door to Carnival; it might be a shitty move to bring a date here while Ada's on-shift, but I need to show her I'm committed to nothing further happening between us. If we're just friends, we need to act like it. Because that's all we can ever be. And bringing a date to a place where my friend bartends isn't out of line. At least, that's what I keep telling myself. I just need to push through this awkwardness and behave like a normal person around her. And, in the meantime, maybe I'll convince myself I can continue living with Ada without another serious lapse in judgment.

Maya walks ahead of me, wearing a yellow summer dress and a flowy cardigan. I won't deny she's an attractive woman—her auburn hair bounces around her shoulders and she shoots me a contagious smile. I can't help but smile back, though an unsettled feeling prickles at the back of my neck. The moment we pause in the entryway, waiting to be seated, what I've been trying to avoid becomes impossible to ignore. My eyes drift against my will to the bar.

Seeing Ada brings it all back. The way she touched me, the way she leaned in close, the way her gaze lingered on my lips... I *know* I wasn't imagining it. She felt something too—wanted that kiss just as bad as I did. The feeling of her body against mine plays through my memory on a torturous loop. For the thousandth time today, I try and fail to shake it the fuck off.

Ada doesn't spot me right away. The bar is busy and she's got a line of customers. Her coworker, a tall, good-looking guy with dark hair, pulls a pint of beer from the tap, obviously laying it on thick for the group of young women he's serving.

When she finally sees me, I have the impulse to look away but can't quite make myself pretend I wasn't watching her. I raise my hand, giving her a covert wave. At that moment, Maya leans over and lets me know our table is ready.

A flicker of realization passes over Ada's face before I can turn away to follow the hostess to our table.

Oh, God. Why did I decide to come here?

The look she just gave me felt like a punch in the gut.

Maya chooses her seat first, leaving me with the one facing the bar. *Great.* Now I'll need to crank my willpower into high gear all night to avoid staring at Ada over Maya's shoulder. I briefly consider asking Maya to switch seats, but I can't think of a reason that doesn't sound absurd.

Just muscle through. Focus on getting to know Maya.

I try my best, but I'd be lying if I said the turquoise hair bobbing in my peripheral vision wasn't constantly on my radar.

Maya and I go through the motions. Without going into detail, I explain how my mom's medical crisis brought me home for the summer. Maya listens with empathy, telling me about when her aunt had a stroke. Or was it her mom's cousin?

Shit. I'm not being a great listener tonight.

My eyes briefly dart to Ada, then back to Maya. I smile to cover up how awkward this feels, kicking myself for thinking that bringing a date here would help me put some distance between me and Ada.

Why *did I think being in the same room would achieve that, exactly?*

Maya props her fist under her chin and leans with her elbows on the table. "Anyway, enough medical stuff. It's kind of a bummer."

"Yeah, I guess." I nod, changing the subject. "So, you're in real estate with Renee?"

"Yeah, but at a different firm. We used to work in the same office, though. And I still see her for, like, wine nights and stuff."

I'm trying so hard to appear interested. *What am I doing with my face?*

"Cool," I say. A decidedly uncool response.

When we open our menus, I risk a look at the bar again, knowing it's the wrong move but unable to resist Ada's pull. The lines have died down, and the guy working with Ada is chatting to her, laughing with that sleazy smile of his again. His pose is relaxed and his attention is glued to her as he wipes down the bar. She tucks her hair behind her ear and my brow furrows.

Is she flirting with him?

I catch myself. It doesn't matter—she could be fucking the guy for all I know. The thought immediately lands like lead on my chest.

"Oh, my gosh." Maya's voice pulls me back to the table. "Everything sounds *so* good. What are you thinking of ordering?"

"Uh," I say, my smile awkward. "Not sure yet." I've barely registered what's on the menu in front of me and, when I try to focus, the words seem to swim together. My immediate and visceral dislike of Ada's coworker is uncomfortable proof I'm jealous—and the knowledge I have no right to be weighs me down. I study him and that cocky grin again. He looks so... punchable.

Let it go. It's none of your business.

Unable to concentrate, when the server comes to take our order, I order exactly what I had that first night I came here. I figure it was fine and, this way, I don't have to explain why I can't think straight enough to make an actual decision.

I coast through the meal on a steady stream of automatic small talk, something I've honed over the years working so many farm gigs with all kinds of people. But I still can't help my split focus. I'm barely connecting with what Maya's saying, and I feel like shit about it, even though it's clear we don't have much in common.

As we finish eating, Maya excuses herself to go to the restroom. I'm reminded about the first night I saw Ada here, when she crashed into me with those dish trays. Thinking back, it's clear my attraction to her was virtually instantaneous.

Doesn't matter. You can't have her, I remind myself for the umpteenth time. I sip my ice water and will the cold sensation to settle my racing thoughts.

Alone for the time being, I risk a glance at the bar and catch Ada watching me warily. I raise my chin and give her an apologetic shrug.

With a blank expression, she turns back to the customer she's serving.

I deserved that.

Things have been awkward at home since my haircut, and this stunt of mine clearly hasn't helped.

Maya reappears in front of me, interrupting my thoughts, and gathers up her cardigan and purse.

"Hey, you ready to head out?" I ask, rushing to stand.

"Yeah," she says, giving me a resigned look. "Listen, this was nice. But I can tell you're in your head about something. So I should..." she trails off, motioning toward the door. "I should get going."

"Really?" I sputter, blindsided by her sudden decision to leave —although I can't blame her. "You sure?"

She nods.

"Okay," I say. "Hey, I'm sorry for being..." Now I'm the one trailing off, not sure how to apologize. "It was great to meet you," I finally say.

She readjusts her purse, then reaches to open it.

I put out my hand. "Oh, no. I got it. Please."

"It's really okay..." she says.

"No. It's the least I can do." I'm scrambling like I've committed some horrific offense.

Fuck, have I? How obviously was I staring at Ada? Will Maya tell Renee?

"Okay. Thanks." With a quick goodbye, Maya heads out of the restaurant, leaving me to my stunned silence.

Slumping down in my chair, I rub a hand down my face in disbelief, wondering how badly I've fucked up by letting this date be such an epic flop. I drink the rest of my water and sit back in my seat, frowning as I replay the events of the evening in my mind. I try to gauge whether Maya attributed my distraction to something general, or whether she picked up on the turquoise-haired reason behind it.

I pay the bill and decide that, if I'm hellbent on acting like we're just friends, I should at least speak to Ada. Try to smooth things over. That's what a friend would do. I take a breath to compose myself and approach the bar.

"Hey," is my brilliant opener.

"Another hot date?" Ada lifts her chin toward our now-empty table.

"Uh, yeah. Another friend of Renee's. Maya."

She nods, her expression neutral. "She was pretty. Where'd she go?"

"Had to head out," I say vaguely, grateful she doesn't press me for details.

"Excuse me, darlin'," Ada's coworker croons as he slides in close, reaching in front of her to get a slice of lime. When he slings an arm over her shoulder, I stiffen, my eyes shifting between her and that punchable face.

She can flirt with whoever she wants, remember?

He gives me a shit-eating grin and squeezes her shoulder before finally pulling his slimy arm away. Wedging the lime onto the rim of the finished drink, he slides it to the customer beside me.

I try to shelve my jealousy, desperate not to feel this way, and remind myself—yet again—that I have no right to.

"Kyle, this is Jesse. My brother's *best friend*," Ada explains, holding my gaze as she emphasizes the last part in a way that stokes the guilt in my gut.

Recognition lights up his features and he extends his hand. "The dude you're living with! Hey, man, nice to meet you," he says with that charming, sleazebag smile.

I'd be an asshole to refuse his handshake. Reluctantly, I shake it, giving him a curt nod. I don't trust this guy.

No one speaks for a long moment.

When Kyle finally fucks off to serve another customer, I breathe a small sigh of relief.

"You gonna hang out here and have a drink?" Ada asks warily. It doesn't sound like an invitation.

"Nah," I say. "I'm gonna head home." I shouldn't hang around her, however much I may want to. And I sure as hell don't want to subject myself to watching Kyle flirt with her any more than I already have.

She nods. "Okay. See ya later, if you're still up."

I force a smile and turn to leave, silently resolving *not* to be up when Ada gets home tonight.

13

ADA

I'm fine. It's fine. Jesse bringing his date into my workplace last night was perfectly fine. We're just friends. Friends do that kind of thing. It's fine. Really. Super fine with me.

As I pace in my room, these thoughts play on repeat in my brain until I'm almost convinced. It *needs* to be true. It doesn't matter that we almost kissed; that was a huge mistake.

But the memory haunts me: Jesse's breath against my lips... The way he'd whispered my name... His hands gripping my lower back, pulling me close...

Forget it. It can never happen again, anyway.

Sure, I may have spent the duration of Jesse's date with Maya vaguely fantasizing about *accidentally* spilling a drink on her... but I shook it off. I let it go. It doesn't matter, anyway, because Jesse's clearly not seeing her again. I'm not sure what happened, but he didn't seem happy after she left and he hurried home soon after. He wasn't up when I got in after my shift, and I was actually relieved. The last thing I needed was more time alone with him. The less temptation, the better—because I can't stop replaying that almost-kiss in my mind. I need to cool off about it.

When I finally confessed everything to Katie yesterday, she was so invested in our little domestic drama I could practically hear the popcorn popping in the background. I'd share in her amusement if this didn't feel so... torturous.

I realize I've been hiding in my room a lot the last couple of days—ever since I cut Jesse's hair, really—and it's getting a bit ridiculous. This is *my* apartment and I shouldn't have to live like a recluse. We're *friends*. I can face him. I take a deep breath, psyching myself up to act like my usual aloof self, determined to make it clear I don't want him.

Plastering on an expression I hope communicates how little I give a shit, I open my bedroom door.

Jesse's stooped over, reaching into the fridge. He straightens when he sees me, pulling out a carton of milk.

"Hey," I say casually, walking straight into the kitchen. Straight toward him. I have one of those intrusive thoughts, like when you're up on the twelfth floor of a high-rise and think *I could jump off this balcony*. But, instead of imagining plunging to my death, I'm picturing waltzing into his arms and crashing my mouth into his—finishing what we started. Like with the twelfth floor, though, I know I won't jump.

"Hey," he replies after a long moment.

I open the cupboard next to him, hating that I'm hyper-aware of exactly how close he is, and busy myself preparing my bowl of cereal. Refusing to let on that he affects me, I force myself not to back away, and swipe the carton from his hand. I only risk looking at him long enough to catch the slight tick of his jaw—and the uneasy way he watches me move around him. When I've poured the milk, I shove it back toward him with a dry smile.

He narrows his eyes and takes it. "Thanks?"

I grab a spoon and tuck into the couch with my breakfast, pulling my sketchbook and pencil into my lap. I try to focus on drawing while I eat, but none of the ideas I had for this sketch are coming back to me. Sensing Jesse's gaze on my skin, I lift my head.

"What?" My tone is almost bitchy.

"Nothing," he says.

I take a bite of my cereal, returning my attention to my sketchbook. But I can feel him watching me again and I can't help but glance up once more, careful to appear uninterested.

He quickly looks away and places the milk carton on the counter, rubbing his forehead.

I set my bowl down on the coffee table and sigh, suddenly impatient. "Okay, are we seriously gonna keep awkwardly dancing around this? Pretending like nothing happened the other day?"

He frowns. "Uh, I mean... I don't see a point in talking about it."

"Well, you're staring an awful lot for a guy with nothing to say."

"I'm not staring!" he says, sounding annoyed.

I give him a long look.

"It was obviously a stupid mistake," he finally says. "End of story. Let's just forget it ever happened."

I almost laugh. *Fuck,* I *wish* I could. Wish I could forget how it felt to know the only thing between me and Jesse's hard cock was a few layers of fabric.

"Okay, listen," he starts, walking toward me. He slumps into one of the shitty folding chairs across from the couch, avoiding my eyes. "All I wanted to say is I'm sorry. I should never have... done that."

"It's fine," I lie. "It didn't mean anything, anyway." I flick my hair to one side and pick up my pencil again, turning to an in-progress sketch that won't require much brainpower. I will myself to sink into my art. To let it wash over me and carry this tension away with it.

It isn't working.

In my peripheral vision, Jesse runs both hands down his face, leaning his elbows on his knees. "Right. I mean, obviously."

"And *obviously*," I echo, lifting my gaze with forced confidence, the lie already stinging the back of my throat, "I don't think of you that way."

Lean into it. Sell it.

Something wavers in his expression, but he quickly reins it in, regarding me coolly. "Same."

"So, this is a *just friends* kind of deal." Maybe if I say it enough, it'll come true.

"Absolutely."

"Right."

Don't look away.

I do my best blank and bored face, hoping it'll hide the way my heart is racing.

He studies me, our eyes locked in some kind of sexually charged Mexican standoff.

"And nothing can ever..." he adds, trailing off as he gestures between us.

"No!" I force a dark laugh. "Never."

"Because Marcus was always clear about that—since we were kids."

"Ew, don't even tell me what he said." I wave a dismissive hand, picking up my bowl and then frowning at it before setting it back down. I've suddenly lost my appetite, and the roiling sensation in my gut is threatening to bring the few bites I've eaten back up.

He rubs the back of his neck. "And Ada... y'know, beyond the whole Marcus thing... Your friendship is really important to me."

I let out a scoff and put on a mocking tone. "*My friendship is really important to you?*" I give him a blank stare. "Gross, Jess. Put it in a fucking Hallmark card."

"Okay," he says, "so much for trying to be real with you." He stands and lets out a long breath. Walking past me, he pauses and leans down close. "But you don't need to be shitty about it." He smiles as he gently shoves the side of my head, then freezes when his gaze lands on the open sketchbook on my lap.

I wince.

"Holy shit, Ada," he says. "You drew that?"

I squint up at him. "No, a magical fucking forest nymph drew it."

He gives me a look.

"Yes, of course I did."

"It's..." he trails off. "It's *really* fucking good."

"Sure," I say sarcastically. "Whatever. It's not finished."

"No, I'm serious," he says. "I had no idea you could draw like this."

I roll my eyes.

"Don't do that," he says.

"Do what?"

"Act like it's no big deal. Be all *whatever* about it." He rolls his eyes, imitating me.

"It's just a hobby." I don't know why I'm downplaying this, but Jesse seeing this side of me has my guard up. Lately, my art has felt so... *personal.* Emotional. Raw.

"Looks like more than that to me." He raises his brows and inspects the drawing once more.

"What are you saying?"

"I dunno... Have you ever thought about being an artist? Like, for work?"

I bark a laugh. "In *this* economy?"

"*Ada.*"

I let out a breath and try again. "I mean, sure, I've thought about it. But the pay is shit. Hence the bartending."

"What about art school? You could apply. They'd *have* to take you."

"So? Art school isn't gonna pay the bills, dude."

"Okay, but *dude*, it could be a path to—"

I cut him off. "You're basing this off *one drawing*, Jess. Come on." I wish he'd just drop it. School isn't my thing.

"Well, let me see the rest, then." He makes a tentative reach for my sketchbook.

"No!" I recoil a bit, snapping it shut and hugging it against my chest.

"Ada, you're being ridiculous. Just humor me." His outstretched arm doesn't waver.

I am being ridiculous.

"Ugh, fine. But not these. They're too... unfinished." Tightening my grip on my sketchbook, I head toward my room. Jesse follows, my anxiety spiking as I reach my door with him at my heels. I spin to face him, my hand on the doorknob behind me. "Just... they might not be your thing, okay?"

"C'mon, just show me, Ada."

I shake my head and turn the knob, then switch on the light as I step inside.

No turning back now.

As he takes in what's on my easel, his jaw drops. "Fucking hell," he says, zeroing in on the painting—this one an aerial view of a woman lying on her back with disembodied arms clawing at her. He takes slow steps into the middle of my room, turning to take in the pieces skirting each wall, some stacked two or three deep. He crouches down to inspect the painting of the drowning woman I finished a few weeks ago.

"Ada... *this* is what you've been painting? These are... *fucking incredible.*"

"Thank you," I say, my voice cautious. I might as well be naked, standing here with Jesse drinking in my artwork.

He stands, taking a step toward me. "Some of these must have taken you, what, weeks?"

"I dunno. Yeah, I guess." I toss my sketchbook onto my dresser and rub my arms. "I know they're kinda weird and moody..."

"That's"—he pauses, shaking his head—"not what I was gonna say. But I mean, c'mon, Ada. You've obviously got real talent—or skill, or... both, I guess. You really should apply to art school."

I let out a dry laugh. "My parents would never let me hear the end of it if I went to fucking *art school.*"

"What? Why?"

"Because it's not *college.* They have this thing about college. Wanting me to get a *proper education* and a *proper career.*" I make a face. "They're already pissed I spent so much time traveling and haven't even applied yet. Besides, they don't take art seriously. They think I'm wasting my time—that it's all just doodles."

"Dude." His gaze levels with mine. "These are *not* just doodles."

"I know. But they don't listen to me."

"It's your life, Ada. Not theirs."

"I know! Just drop it, okay?"

"Okay," he says tentatively, then seems to change his mind. "Actually, no, fuck that. Go to art school. Prove them wrong." He crosses his arms over his broad chest. "Seriously. At least think about it."

What's his game here?

It's great he wants to support me, but formal education isn't what I want, not even if it *is* an art program. And the last thing I need is more pressure to apply to school. When the uncomfortable silence drags on for longer than I can bear, I let out a sigh. "Okay, show's over now, right? You can go."

He reluctantly lets me shoo him out but, as I move to close the door, he braces against it, stopping me with his lopsided smile as much as his forearm. "Just say you'll think about applying, ya stubborn bonehead."

Fuck, I can't think straight when he looks at me like that.

"Ugh, fine," I say and shut the door in his face.

"ADA, this is fucking *Zen as shit*," Rolando says, blue paint swirling and tinting the water as he dips his paintbrush in the glass.

Watercolor isn't usually my thing, but I know enough to guide the kids through a basic lesson. And they're into it.

"Mine's more shit than Zen, though," Sofia grumbles.

Okay, *mostly* into it.

Maybe it's being away from all the tension between me and Jesse, or maybe it's the Mozart concerto playing over the multi-purpose room's speakers, but I'm feeling the Zen vibes too.

Sofia sighs, sounding frustrated. "The colors are so washed out."

I walk over and peer at her painting. "I think you have a bit too much water on your paper. See how it's pooling in the corners of the tape? Here,"—I step to the sink and rip off a sheet of paper towel for her—"use this to blot some of it off. And make sure your brush isn't too wet before you do the next part."

Rolando pauses, paintbrush in the air. "Who's that guy? Y'know, the one with the afro who did all those paintings on TV? The *happy little trees* guy?"

"Bob Ross?" Dalia offers.

"Yeah, yeah, Bob Ross!" Roly wipes his brush on a paper towel and sets it down before pushing up from the table. "I'm gonna drop some Bob Ross trees on this shit when it's dry." He reaches across to the nearby counter for the hair dryer, careful not to disconnect the extension cord when he pulls it over. When he turns it on, an uproar of protest comes from Dalia and Sofia on either side of him.

Well, it's a bit less Zen *now.*

"Roly, watch it!" Sofia shouts over the noise, using her forearm as a shield. "You're fucking up my painting!"

I circle around and reach over to switch the hair dryer's setting. "Keep it on low, okay?"

He nods, aiming it carefully, then shoots an annoyed glare at Dalia.

After a couple of minutes, he switches it off, and I can hear the soft sound of classical music once again.

"Where's Man Bun tonight?" Rupi asks.

"What do you mean?" I frown, pretending Jesse isn't constantly on my mind. "I dunno."

"Aren't you two, like..." Dalia starts to ask, letting the implication hang.

"Uh, no, we're just roommates. *Friends.*" Heat creeps up my cheeks.

Well, that's fucking embarrassing.

I busy myself with washing out some brushes at the sink, trying once again to put Jesse out of my mind.

Murmurs ripple around the table behind me, and I turn to find the group of them staring. I shift my eyes between the half dozen kids who showed up for the watercolor lesson tonight. "What?"

"Y'all still pretending to be just friends?" Sofia asks.

I shake my head. "Let's just focus on our paintings, okay?"

"Alright," she relents. "But I saw how he looked at you."

"Yeah," Rupi says with a nod. "He likes you."

"Totally," Dalia agrees. "At bowling? He was into you *for sure.*"

"Okay, fools," I say, holding up a hand. "Enough about Jesse. I mean it." I glance at the clock. Forty-seven minutes until I can go home. Forty-seven minutes until I'll have to face him again. Forty-seven minutes until I'll have to act like everything is normal.

I give my head a shake. I need to follow my own damn advice.
Enough. About. Jesse.

14

———————

JESSE

Things with Ada have fallen into a more comfortable rhythm since our conversation about keeping things in friendship territory a few days ago. Trying that old *fake it 'til you make it* advice on for size, I throw myself into acting like a friend around her. When we see each other at home now, things feel less... charged.

Marcus and I visit Carnival for drinks a couple nights in a row, and we chat with Ada at the bar, joking around like we always have. She's in her element: dealing with all kinds of customers, slinging drinks with practiced efficiency, and managing the occasional drunk without missing a beat. Her usual sarcastic comments tell me she's feeling a bit more back to normal in my presence, too, and I'm starting to think we might be able to move on.

Ada's working the closing shift tonight, so I'm home alone, warm and exhausted from a day in the sun. I spent most of the day with my mom. Mentally stir-crazy but still physically exhausted, she'd begged me to take her out for a change of scenery. I drove her to the riverside where we set up a lazy picnic lunch, reminiscing about when Claire and I were kids. I hadn't seen Mom laugh like that in a long time. It's been a month since she got sick, and longer since I'd seen her happy. The relief I felt, realizing she looked like herself again, was huge.

Sticky with sunscreen, I decide to shower and head to bed, then read for a while before shutting off the light. My bones are tired but, inexplicably, my mind isn't ready for sleep—and my thoughts keep drifting to Ada's empty room. It feels strange she's working so late and isn't here. I don't know why it's bothering me; it's not like she hasn't worked late before.

What am I, some anxious mother hen? Get over it.

Insomnia isn't something I normally experience, but my sleep rhythm has been a bit fucked ever since I flew home and dealt with that initial stress and jet lag. At this point, lying awake at night has plagued me enough times that I know not to fight it. With a resigned sigh, I pull on my jeans and a clean T-shirt and head out for a walk, hoping the night air and exercise will do the trick.

I find myself passing by Carnival without even realizing that's where I was headed all along. Ada's back is to the window as she arranges liquor bottles on a shelf, and it looks pretty dead—she's only got one customer sitting at the bar. I check my phone; there's about ten minutes until closing. My hand pauses briefly on the door handle before I tell myself it's fine and go in.

"Jesse," she says, clearly surprised to see me strolling toward her. "Thought you'd be in bed by now."

"Yeah, same. Couldn't sleep, though, so I went for a walk."

She nods. "I'm almost ready to head home, if you wanna hang out until then."

"Sure." I sink onto one of the empty barstools, and Ada turns to finish restocking the containers of straws and drink umbrellas behind the bar.

The guy seated at the end of the bar tilts a bit, clearly sauced. He takes another sip of his beer.

Ada tucks a few juice bottles into a nearby fridge and wipes her hands on her skirt before tapping something onto the touch screen.

When my eyes land back on the guy, my jaw clenches. He's staring at her breasts and he's not even attempting to hide it.

I inhale a breath, straightening.

She prints his final bill and slides it in front of him, so engrossed in her closing duties that she hasn't noticed him leering at her.

"Thanks, gorgeous," he drawls in a messy slur, his eyelids at half-mast. He nearly falls off the stool trying to dig out his wallet, but rights himself at the last moment.

She ignores him and turns to me.

I jerk my head discreetly in the drunk guy's direction. "Everything okay?" I mouth silently.

She nods, darting a wary glance at him. She leans toward me and turns away so he won't hear her.

"He must've been drinking before he came in," she whispers, "'cause I sure as hell didn't overserve him… but he's not looking too good."

"Hey," the guy calls out suddenly, and we both turn. "I actually want one more."

"Nah, dude, you've had enough," she says with ease, wiping down the bar. "We're closing, anyway. Time to head home."

"Ah, fuck," the guy says, throwing an arm out at his side and leaning heavily on the other. "Come on, I'm fine."

"Nope, sorry. Gotta cut you off." I can tell she isn't sorry, but she definitely deserves some points for trying to be professional.

"You don't have to be mean about it," he drawls, taking another sip of his dwindling beer. He squints at Ada, leaning toward her with a slimy smile. "You're too pretty to be a little bitch."

"Hey," she says, loudly, and his drooping eyes widen a bit at her change in tone. "You don't talk to me like that."

I've seen enough of Ada at work to know she isn't afraid of these assholes. But I can't help noticing how my heart rate kicks up a notch.

The guy laughs, the sound ugly and disdainful, and holds her gaze as he dumps the dregs of his beer onto the bar, clearly knowing she'll have to clean it up.

Such a dick move.

The fucking nerve of this guy. I look away for a moment, my lips tight as I suppress the urge to tell him where he can shove that pint glass.

Ada crosses her arms and regards him coolly—not taking the bait. She's fucking good at this. I hate that she has to be.

"Time to go. You're done," is all she says, lifting her chin at the door.

"Okay, but I wanna watch you lick that up first," he sneers as he leans toward her. "I bet you're good with your tongue."

I stand, moving toward him. "Hey. You heard her. Time to head the fuck home."

The guy turns, taking a moment to focus on me. "Or what? Mind your own fucking business, asshole."

"Can't do that."

"Why not? Hoping she'll suck *your* cock instead? 'Cause I got first dibs."

My fist connects with his face before I even realize what I've done. He crumples to the floor on his back, groaning.

"Jesus!" Ada's voice enters my awareness and she shouts across the bar for some guy named Theo. "Jesse, what the fuck?"

My hand throbs from the impact and I shake it out. Clenching and unclenching my fingers, I reassure myself nothing's broken. I got lucky.

A big guy dressed in a white kitchen uniform appears beside me, seeming to quickly assess the situation. My ears buzz from the adrenaline but I'm vaguely aware of Ada explaining what just went down. He moves around me and picks the guy up off the floor, propping him up.

"I should fucking sue your ass," the asshole slurs through an obvious fog of boozed-up confusion and pain.

A look passes between Ada and Theo, and she shakes her head.

"Too bad no one saw what happened," Theo says. "As far as I'm concerned, you fell and hit your face on the barstool. So clumsy." Grasping handfuls of the guy's shirt, Theo muscles him toward the front door.

"Holy shit," Ada says as she watches the dirtbag get dragged outside. "That was fucked up."

"Yeah," is all I can think to say.

Her attention snaps to me. "What the hell was that?"

I open my mouth to answer but find I don't know what to say. I rub my hand, which is starting to swell a bit.

"Are you..." She looks down. "*Shit.* Is your hand okay?"

"Yeah, it'll be fine," I say, glancing at the door. Ada turns to follow my gaze, and we watch Theo exchange a few stern words with the guy as he dumps him outside. A string of muffled expletives cuts to silence as the door swings shut and Theo tromps back into the restaurant.

"You good?" he asks Ada. When she nods, he heads back to the kitchen.

The drunk tool outside staggers a few steps down the road and I sigh with relief that he's actually leaving. I turn back to Ada.

"I'd uh... grab you some ice, but I just drained the tray."

"It's fine," I say quickly. "Wanna head home? Like, can you

leave yet?" I want to get her somewhere safe in case the sleazebag comes back.

"Yeah, just..." she trails off, taking stock of what's left to do around the bar area. "Gimme five minutes to cash out." She turns, almost flustered, then goes through the motions on the touch screen.

As she finishes up the last of her tasks, I grab the bar cloth with my good hand and wipe up the dumped beer. She gives me a grateful look as I pass her the cloth to rinse out, but I catch her hands shaking slightly when she takes it from me.

Our walk home is quiet. It's clear neither of us knows what to say about what just happened.

"Hey, I'm sorry you had to deal with that asshole," I offer, glancing at Ada sidelong.

"Yeah. Thanks." She hugs her chest, rubbing her upper arms.

I bend my right wrist experimentally, testing out where and how much my hand aches in various positions.

"I'm sorry you had to deal with him too," she says, sounding bewildered—and still slightly stunned. "And I'm sorry you had to hear him say that shit."

"Fucking asshole." I shake my head. "You gonna be okay?"

"*Me?* You're the one with the fucked-up hand."

"I mean, it's only *moderately* fucked up," I say with a smirk.

She presses her full lips together and looks away. I think I catch an eye roll as her hands slide over her arms again.

"Cold?"

"It's fine. We're almost home."

Inside the apartment, we kick off our shoes and Ada hangs her purse over the back of a chair. "I guess I should thank you," she says, then drops her gaze to her hands, "for, you know, defending my honor or whatever." Her voice has a teasing tone but still seems guarded.

"I shouldn't have overreacted. I mean, the guy was a dick, but... that's your workplace."

"Yeah, that part... wasn't great." Her brows draw together, like there's more she can't bring herself to admit. The vulnerability on her face is so out of character that I have to do something.

"Hey, come here," I say, pulling her into my arms before I can think better of it. She slips hers around my waist and I close my eyes, unable to stop myself from inhaling her sweet scent. I rest my chin on her head. "What he said was *not* okay. And you did great handling it. I just..." I trail off and let out a breath, not knowing how to tell her what I felt in that moment—not wanting to think too hard about why his words hit a nerve. "I couldn't let him talk about you like that."

"I have to say, it *was* kinda satisfying to watch." Her words come out muffled against my T-shirt, her warm breath heating my chest through the fabric. With a smile in her voice, she adds, "He went down like a bag of rocks."

"It's what he deserved."

I realize she's playing idly with the fabric of my shirt, my attention suddenly attuned to the gentle graze of her fingers against my back. I force myself to pull away and clear my throat.

"I don't know why I'm upset about it," she says, stepping back and wiping away a few tears. "Sorry."

"No. You have every right to be. He was fucking awful."

"Yeah, but I usually handle that shit myself just fine," she says with a frown.

"Does that kind of thing happen a lot?" I push down the anger that threatens to rise up. I've seen her deal with a few drunks, but I hate the idea of her getting spoken to that way on a regular basis.

She shrugs. "I mean, not always that bad. But yeah, kind of. It's part of the job, unfortunately. You make good money with tips and all, but... that's the downside."

"Shit, Ada." I say, rubbing my forehead. "I'm sorry."

Her eyes flick my way and she nods.

"I could have killed that guy," I say quietly, almost to myself.

"Yeah, so where did that protective shit come from?"

I drop my gaze, keenly aware of how it must have looked—how it had felt. I don't know how to explain.

"Like, dude, I'm not exactly a damsel in distress."

I laugh wryly at the truth of that statement. "Believe me, *dude,* I know. But you're Marcus' sister. He would have done the same thing. So, I feel like I should look out for you. Plus, you're..." I trail off, biting my lip to stop myself from talking.

"I'm what?"

"You're... *you.*"

She smiles cautiously at me. "What's that supposed to mean?"

That's what I've been trying to figure out.

"Uh... You're my friend too?"

"Okay," she says, our gazes lingering a moment too long. She seems to snap out of it and glances toward the kitchen. "Sit down. I'll get you some ice."

Ada cracks the ice cube tray over a tea towel, then fills a small plastic bag with ice. She wraps it in the cloth, then pulls a chair over to sit across from me—close enough that our knees brush.

"Let me see," she says, reaching for my swollen hand. A bluish-purple bruise is already forming around my knuckles. She runs her fingers gently along my heated skin, her expression tinged with concern. "You sure it's not broken?"

"I don't think so. Everything still moves okay," I say, opening and closing my fingers with a wince. "Just sore."

She gingerly presses the bundle of ice to my knuckles, holding my palm in her other hand. Her skin is soft and warm, and for a moment, there's that magnetic pull between us that I've been working so hard to resist.

"Thanks," I say, taking the ice pack from her and shifting back in my chair. "I got this." I tip my head at her bedroom door. "You should go to bed."

"Yeah," she says. "Probably should."

She gets up and heads to the bathroom, patting my shoulder on the way by. "Night, Jess."

"Night." Realizing I need sleep, too, I let out a long breath and stand, then plod to my own room. I'm more wired than I was before, so I switch on the lamp, deciding to read a bit more. My right hand throbs as I peel off my clothes, but I climb into bed with the ice pack and awkwardly arrange my book on my lap.

I'm not expecting the knock on my door ten minutes later.

"Come in," I call out, putting my book face-down on the bed beside me. I'm only in my underwear—but the blankets are up, so... *I guess this is fine?*

Ada slowly opens the door and stands in the doorway. She's changed out of her tight black work clothes and scrubbed off her makeup. She's pulling at the hem of her oversized *Ramones* T-shirt, which hangs down over a pair of green pajama shorts.

She looks perfect.

I smile. "Hey."

"Can I—?" She asks only half the question, gesturing to the bed. The set of her shoulders and the way she tucks her hair behind her ear is almost... sheepish.

Swallowing, I nod and sit up a bit. I'm not sure she should be here—not even sure what I'm agreeing to. But I don't want her to go.

She sits on the edge of my bed and stares at the floor.

What's she doing here?

I sit up fully and lean forward, hooking my arms over my knees, careful to keep myself covered by the blanket. When I catch my gaze sliding up her bare thigh to the hem of her shorts, I tear my eyes away.

I wait for her to speak, but she stays quiet.

"What's up?" I finally ask.

"I was just wondering," she starts, "how your mom's been doing lately."

What?

I straighten, frowning. "Better."

"Good." She picks at a piece of lint on my blanket. "Is she glad you're home?"

"Uh, *yeah*... Is this really what you wanted to talk to me about at two in the morning? My mom?"

"Humor me." She looks at me blankly, but I can sense she's hiding something.

Is she nervous?

"Okay. Yeah, she's happy I'm home," I say slowly. "Why?"

"I dunno, I guess I was just thinking..." She drags her hair back with one hand, flipping it over to one side, and pulls one knee up to hug it against her chest. "Like, maybe you'd be reconnecting a bit?" She shakes her head. "Forget it. I'm not making sense. It's late." She pushes up to leave and heads for the door.

"Ada," I say, half smiling in confusion.

"Ugh, never mind," she says without turning back. "I'm probably delirious or some shit from witnessing your *heroic act*. Goodnight!"

"Ada! Come on, stop," I call out.

She's halfway out the door when she pauses and peers at me around the doorframe, looking wary.

I make a face that says I'm not letting her off the hook.

"Okay." She's clearly uncomfortable with whatever she wants to say. "It's just... been *nice* having you home again." She grimaces at her words.

The corner of my mouth tugs up. "Uh, yeah, it's been nice *being* home again." I wait for her to say more. This is rare; Ada almost never lets down her guard. Her sarcastic defenses are virtually permanent fixtures of her personality and, without them, I don't really know how to interact with her.

Isn't this what I wanted the other day, though? For her to be real with me?

She crosses her arms over her chest and studies the floor, but still doesn't respond.

"You getting all soft on me?" I ask, leaning forward. I can't help but tease her to break the tension. "Is this *you* having a Hallmark moment?"

She scoffs. "Just shut up and forget I said anything."

And she's back. Crisis averted.

A slow grin spreads over my face. "Get some sleep, butthead."

"You too, asshole." She returns my smile despite herself and bites her lip. "Night." She leaves the room, closing my door before I can respond.

I readjust the ice pack on my hand and furrow my brow, the smile fading from my lips as I think about what Ada said. If I reconnect with my mom, then what? I shake my head, my eyes landing on the door she just closed.

Is she saying she'd like it if I moved back home?

I lay back on the pillow and stare at the ceiling. My insomnia just got a power-up.

15

JESSE

This emergency trip home was never supposed to be a trial for a permanent move. I was just here to take care of my mom. Once her medical crisis was over, kicking around with my old friends was just a convenient bonus. But ever since Ada put the thought into my head a few days ago, I'm looking at my surroundings differently. I find myself wanting to see the leaves change this fall. To know what Ada ends up doing with her art. To see her doing what she loves. To be in her corner if her parents keep giving her shit.

Standing on the bank, I shield my eyes and cast my gaze across Black Bear River. I run a hand through my hair and chew the inside of my cheek, staring at—but not really seeing—the water.

Could I really move back home? What would I do here?

Talking about homesteading with Dimitri had piqued my interest. Could that be something?

Marcus is stooped over beside me, inflating his stand-up paddleboard with a pump. After parking his car downriver, we'd hiked with our gear upstream.

I check the time on my phone. "Kai said he was coming, right?"

"Yeah, I'm sure he's on his way," Marcus says. "He's always late."

"Still?"

Marcus shrugs.

"Okay," I say, crossing my arms over my chest.

"Too bad Renee had to work," he adds. "Means you can use her board, though. Silver lining?"

"Yeah." I look at the time again, then pocket my phone and puff out a breath.

"What's with you, Jess? You seem pretty stressed about the time for a guy who's basically on vacation," Marcus notes, raising a brow.

"I'm not," I say, frowning. "I don't know why I keep checking."

The truth is, I'm all in my head about what the hell I'm doing with my life. Although it hadn't even occurred to me before Ada said something, it suddenly feels urgent to figure out. What's really in Australia for me, anyway? Transient farm work doesn't make for a very compelling answer. I only moved there to run away from my family. Am I just going to stay there and avoid them forever?

As much as I want to shoot the shit with Kai and Marcus, these swirling thoughts have me too agitated to shelve it all right now. The prospect of sluggishly paddling the sleepy river feels almost painful in light of my feverish need to figure out where I belong on this fucking planet.

What's tying me to Australia? And what's drawing me home to Lennox Valley?

The memory of holding Ada in my arms swims into focus, and I hate that I even entertain the thought of her being a factor in this decision. If I move home, it should be for my own reasons. I have no claim on her and definitely shouldn't make a major move like this to be closer to her. All that would do is continue this torture, knowing it can never happen. I examine the fading bruise on my right hand.

What the fuck is wrong with me? Why can't I shake this feeling off?

Kai's Jeep convertible finally pulls into the gravel parking area abutting the river's edge. Deeply tanned and wearing dark sunglasses, he looks like some kind of surfer—or like he belongs in a beer commercial, slinging drinks poolside. When he pulls his sunglasses up to rest on his head, there's a distinct tan line along each of his temples.

"Hey, Bailey! Long time no see!" he says, reaching out for a move I can only describe as the triple whammy of male greetings —equal parts handshake, hug, and pat on the back—that has me bracing for him to call me *bro* any second.

"Kai, shit, yeah, good to see you," I say, rubbing my forehead.

He throws a look at Marcus. "You didn't tell me Jesse got ripped, dude." Kai turns back to me, shaking his head, and folds his arms over his chest.

"You should have seen him when he first showed up here," Marcus puffs, pausing with the pump handle pulled up. "What'd Ada call you? Bigfoot or some shit?"

Kai darts his dark eyes between us in obvious confusion.

"Sasquatch. Yeti. Take your pick." I gesture awkwardly to my face. "I had longer hair... big beard. Got it cut last week."

That fucking haircut... She's not even here and I can't get her out of my head.

Surprise pulls at Kai's dark features. "Well, shit."

"Hey, congrats on getting engaged," I offer, grateful to have thought of something to change the subject.

"Oh, yeah, thanks!"

"When's the wedding again? Marcus told me but I—"

"August 24th."

"Right! Pretty soon!" I say.

"Yeah, I know. How long are you in town, man?"

I frown, thinking about leaving Lennox. I have to admit, my urgency to get back to Oz isn't what it once was—though I try not to think about why. "Uh, end of August? Haven't booked my flight back yet."

Kai snaps his fingers, pointing at me. "Dude, if you're still here, you should come!"

"Oh, you don't have to—" I start to protest.

"The fuck I don't!" He screws up his features. "C'mon. It'll be great. Like old times. Ada'll be there. And Adrian's coming in from Seattle. We even invited Marcus and Ada's folks."

I cast a glance over to Marcus, who's still furiously working the pump.

"If you're still in town, you have to come." Kai holds his hands out wide at his sides. "Gonna be a killer party... and you could meet Nadine..." He waggles his eyebrows.

"Uh, sure!" I plaster on a brave face. "If I'm around, yeah. Thanks, Kai."

"Would you need a plus one?"

"Uh, no, I—"

"Kai, get your damn board out of the car so we can get a move on," Marcus interjects. "I'm sweating like a motherfucker over here." He plugs the valve on his inflated board and wipes his forehead with the back of his hand. "You two *social butterflies* can hash out the details on the water."

THE WATER LEVEL is low and calm at this part of the river, the glacier-fed chill from upstream warmed to a more comfortable temperature under our paddleboards. Marcus rides just ahead of me, and Kai paddles to my right. The sun is blazing as we drift along with the sleepy current and, even with sunglasses on, I squint at the river's sparkling surface. The odd group of teenagers bobs along past us in inner tubes, and a gaggle of drunk college students hollers enthusiastic nonsense our way as they slip past on a large floating platform with built-in beer coolers.

Floating down Black Bear River is a summertime tradition in Lennox. I smile to myself, thinking of all the summers I've spent here. I can't count the number of times we bailed off our inner tubes into this water, pulling ourselves back up, sunscreened limbs slipping and squeaking against the scalding black rubber. A sense of place—of *home*—tugs at me as I cast a look at the rolling mountains rising above the opposite bank.

A sudden desire to get back to the apartment hits me in the gut. I want to see Ada before she leaves for work.

Shit. How much longer will we be out on the water?

I clench my jaw, shifting my feet with a wobble. Renee's nearly a foot shorter than me, and her board is sized for her much smaller frame. Water laps up over my feet as I tilt a second time before finally finding my balance.

"Easy, Jess," Kai cautions beside me.

"I'm fine," I say, getting back into the groove and squeezing the handle of my paddle. Determined to keep my shit together, I put some force into paddling ahead to catch up with Marcus.

Kai follows suit, the three of us riding side by side.

"Hey, man," Marcus says, glancing my way. "Renee told me things didn't go so great with Maya on your date."

Fuck.

"Nah," I say casually and clear my throat. "Didn't hit it off."

"Who's Maya?" Kai pipes up.

"Renee's friend," Marcus explains. "She set them up."

I squint over at the mountains, not wanting to invite any more inquiry into my love life.

Marcus continues. "Maya's pretty hot, Jess..."

"Never said she wasn't," I shoot back.

"Thought you wanted to have a bit of fun this summer."

"I mean... Sure. Look, it just didn't work out, okay?"

"Maya told Renee you seemed distracted during dinner..." He lets the statement hang like an unanswered question.

My lips form a thin line as I brace for what might come next.

When I don't take the bait, Marcus presses on. "You got something on your mind, man?"

Your sister.

I shrug, grasping for a plausible story. "Uh, well... I've been talking more with my mom. I guess that's kinda been on my mind."

"Seriously? You were having dinner with a beautiful woman and spent the whole time thinking about your *mom*?" Marcus laughs and shakes his head. "Jesus, that's grim."

I roll my eyes. "Fuck off. It's not like that. You know what I mean."

"I'm just saying—"

"Just drop it, Marcus. I'm trying to figure some shit out."

"Alright." He cuts me a dubious glance.

"Man, I do *not* miss the dating life," Kai chimes in, rescuing me.

"I bet not," I say, grateful he's steering us away from the topic of my failed date.

"Nadine is amazing." Kai lifts his paddle, switching sides. "We still go out, don't get me wrong, but it's *so* much easier. No more fucking mind games, worrying about who's texting first and all that shit."

"I'm happy for you, man," I say with a genuine smile. "It sounds... pretty awesome."

"Yeah. My favorite thing now is just cuddling up with her, a glass of wine, and a movie, then going to bed early."

"Wow." I raise my eyebrows and shake my head, cutting my

paddle through the shimmering water. "Are we that old now? How long have I been away?"

Kai audibly sighs. "I dunno, man, but it's comfy as fuck."

I can't help but picture what it would feel like to have Ada curled up on the couch beside me, her warm cheek on my chest. That feeling of wanting to get home swells into an urgency I can't ignore. I forge ahead, but find myself scanning the riverbank for any sign of Marcus' car. I feel like an impatient kid on a road trip. *Are we there yet?*

It's mid-afternoon by the time Marcus drops me back at the apartment.

"Hey," I call out as I come in the door, kicking off my sandals and dropping my keys next to them.

Why does my stomach feel like it's in my throat?

"Hey! How was the river?" Ada calls back.

A glow of yellow light spills into the hall from the open bathroom door where she's getting ready for work.

I walk to the kitchen and fill a glass with water at the faucet.

"Good. *Hot*," I shout over my shoulder.

"Hot temperature? Or like,"—Ada comes out of the bathroom as I turn, tugging down the hem of her tight black tank top—"lots of sexual tension?" She starts to laugh but, when she looks up at me, her smile falters.

For a moment, I just stare.

Fuck, she's gorgeous.

Her full lips are painted bright red, and I can't tear my gaze from her mouth. I fight the urge to tell her coming home was the best part of my day. And that I want to mess up those perfect red lips.

Speaking of sexual tension...

Finally catching myself, I clear my throat.

"What?" she asks, smoky eyes widening. "Bad joke?"

"No, uh... Hot *temperature*." I look at my feet.

Nice move, jackass.

"It's been roasting lately," she says. She walks past me to go to the fridge, poking my shoulder as she passes. "You're already more tanned than this morning."

As she breezes past, I inhale her delicious summer scent. She's leaving for work soon, and I realize I don't want her to go. I turn to face her, the bad idea bubbling up to the surface and coming out of my mouth before I can think better of it. "What time do you get a break tonight?"

She seems surprised at the question. "Uh, around seven, I think. Why?"

"Wanna grab dinner?"

She gives me a quizzical smile, tilting her head. "I usually eat at the restaurant..."

"I know," I say quickly. "But there's this food truck down the street from Carnival. Thought it might be good. We could walk over."

"Uh, why the sudden interest in street food?" She pins me with a skeptical squint. "You starting a cringey food blog or something?"

"No." I chuckle and shake my head. "But there's something I wanted to talk to you about."

Her brows lift. "Ominous shit, Jess."

"Ada, fuck. I don't need a kidney, if that's what you mean. I just wanna talk to you."

Those bright red lips twist as she considers me. "Okay. Yeah... sure, I guess."

"Yeah?" A relieved warmth spreads across my chest, knowing I'll get to see her again in a few hours, and I can't help but smile.

"I mean, why not? I'm sick of the same old shit at Carnival, anyway." She rolls her eyes dramatically, almost as if to make the point that her reasoning has to do with food—and nothing else.

"Well, then let's hope it's slightly better than the food you're sick of?" I give her my best casual smirk, then take a sip of my water.

Would've been smooth if you hadn't gulped so loud.

She laughs. "Yeah, that's the bar we need to clear."

"Okay." I run a hand over my beard. "Fingers crossed."

She shifts to lean back against the kitchen counter, studying me like she's trying to figure me out.

That makes two of us.

"Alright," she says slowly, "it's a da—" she cuts herself off, shifting on her feet. "It's a plan." She shoots me a tight smile, then pushes off the counter toward the front door.

I try not to stare at her incredible ass as she walks past me to get her things.

She pauses in the entryway and turns back to me, slinging her purse over her shoulder. "See you tonight, I guess?"

Does she look hopeful?

"Be there at seven."

She nods. "Okay."

I let out a long exhale when the door closes behind her and drag a hand down my face.

It's not a date. Just two friends grabbing dinner.

So why can't I stop smiling?

16

ADA

Well, I didn't have "*Jesse fucking with my head*" on my bingo card for tonight's shift, but here we are. I keep replaying his words from earlier and can't decide what to make of him asking to meet up for dinner.

I also can't stop checking the clock on the wall above the bar. Or eyeing the front doors as the time ticks closer to seven.

Fucking Jesse Bailey.

I have no idea what he wants to talk to me about. All I know is, whatever friendship-zone groove we'd found ourselves in, everything shifted the night he punched that drunk asshole. I can't stop thinking about the way he held me—the weight of his chin resting on my head and his deep voice rumbling against my cheek as I rested it on his chest. *Fuck.* As hugs go, it may have been the best one I've ever had. I fidget with the bar cloth, remembering what I said to him that night. I should never have gone into his room and *definitely* shouldn't have blathered about his relationship with his mom.

What was I thinking? Maybe the sight of his shirtless chest melted my brain... Or I was just strung out on adrenaline after watching him deck that lecherous shithead. I don't normally get off on the knight-in-shining-armor thing but, I have to admit, it was a pretty badass punch. And it left me feeling things I'm not proud of. Cared for. Protected. I look up at the ceiling, blowing out a breath.

Ugh, I'm the worst feminist.

I scrunch my nose, remembering his earnest face last week when he told me I should apply for art school.

Why has he got to be so goddamn supportive?

I'm wiping down the bar when Jesse opens the front door and our eyes immediately meet. He looks sexy as fuck in a plain white T-shirt and well-worn jeans. Warmth coils low in my stomach, and I tear my gaze away before I start biting my lip and fluttering my fucking eyelashes. I quickly wring out the cloth and nudge Ros. Taking my dinner break suddenly feels urgent.

Dashing to the staff room to grab my purse, I give myself a quick pep talk.

Get it together. It's just fucking Jesse.

I stop at the mirror to fix a few errant strands of hair, catching myself taking longer than I should.

Ugh!

I give my arms a shake and try for bland apathy.

Perfect. Just... hold that pose.

Strolling out past the bar, I make a beeline for the front doors, heart hammering in my chest. It's only when I'm midway through breezing past Jesse that I realize I've overshot apathy and landed on rude indifference.

Shit. Too much.

"Ada?" He jogs after me. "Wait up! What the hell?"

"Come on. I'm hungry. Let's go." I throw the lie over my shoulder, hoping the excuse explains my aloofness.

He catches up to me right as I push out the door and onto the sidewalk. He grabs my arm, stopping me in my tracks, and I spin back to face him.

Fuck.

He's so close I can smell his soap. He must have just showered.

Double fuck; now I'm picturing him naked. And wet. And soapy...

I take a step back, pulling my arm away.

"You gonna tell me why you're acting like a spooked horse?" He frowns and stuffs his hands into the front pockets of his jeans.

"I'm not spooked," I say. I glance through the restaurant window, feeling like everyone must be watching us, then turn back to Jesse. "I told you, I'm hungry. Let's just go." I stalk down the sidewalk, out of sight of my coworkers.

Why am I acting like this? This isn't endearingly snarky and aloof; this is straight up drama queen behavior.

"Ada." Jesse jogs to catch up again and plants himself in front of me, stopping me in my tracks. The confused pinch in his brow suddenly smooths out. "*Wait.* Did something happen again? At work? Did someone—"

"No!"

He exhales with obvious relief.

I let out a sigh, pinching the bridge of my nose, and try to find the words. "I'm just..."

His expression is open—waiting.

"Why are you doing this?" I finally ask.

"Doing what?"

"First you're putting shit into my head about getting into art school, then you're punching some drunk guy for me, and now you're inviting me to dinner?"

He scoffs, giving me a crooked smile. "It's a food truck, Ada. And you're in the middle of a shift. We can't grab burgers?"

"But you're being all... *nice* to me." Really, how dare he be a total smoke show *and* kind at the same time? A girl's only got so much willpower.

He barks a laugh. "God, *sorry*! What do you want me to do?"

"I don't know!" I sputter. "Go back to teasing me and shoving napkins in my face!"

"You want me to shove a napkin in your face? What, you didn't get enough the first time?" He laughs again. "What the fuck are you talking about? I'm just being your friend, here."

"Jesse." I give him a look. *Don't make me say it.*

"Ada," he says, copying me mockingly. He knows.

I let out an exasperated breath. We can't talk about this. *This* is *not* friendship territory. "Never mind. What did you want to talk about, anyway?"

"Is that what's gotten you all worked up? I already told you, I don't need to harvest your organs." His teasing tone punches a tiny hole in the wall I've thrown up between us and some of the tension leaves my shoulders.

A smirk tugs at my lips despite my irritation. "Okay, then, what is it? It's been bugging me."

"Clearly," he says, crossing his arms over his broad chest.

"Fuck off. Spit it out."

What is wrong with me?

I'm not usually the anxious type. At least I wasn't until Jesse showed up.

He casts a glance down the street toward the food truck. "Listen, I'll explain. But do you think you can manage to walk *and* talk? Because I *am* actually hungry, here."

"Fine."

With the sun warming our backs, Jesse falls into step beside me and I turn to study him. His messy blond hair is lit up in a golden glow and his beard, trimmed to a short stubble on the rise of his cheek, glints in the early evening light. I look away, biting my lip until it hurts.

Damn him for being so gorgeous. So confusingly gorgeous.

"So," he starts, "the other night when you came into my room…"

I try to suppress my wince. "Yeah?"

"You asked about my mom, right?"

Worry prickles at the base of my neck. "Is everything okay?"

"Oh, yeah." He shakes his head, waving off my concern. "She doesn't need your organs either."

"Okay, good." I give him a wary smile, but the joke manages to lift another layer of tension away. "I was planning on selling them online, anyway."

His deep laugh lights me up and I can't stop the grin that takes over my face. I've always prided myself on my quick wit but, I realize now, it's different with Jesse. It matters more if *he* laughs at my jokes.

Shit. That's a bad sign.

I know I've been fighting my attraction, but I can't deny there's something more drawing me to Jesse. Probably just our friendship blurring everything. I try to put the thought out of my mind, because I neither want a relationship nor is there any possibility of one with him.

"Anyway, I guess you got me thinking about things." He runs a hand through his hair, mussing it up. I have the sudden urge to drag my fingers through it too. Maybe scratch my fingernails lightly on his scalp as I angle his head, showing him exactly where I want his mouth and—

A shiver ripples over my skin.

Holy shit.

I'm riding a rollercoaster here, swinging wildly from hoping he likes me to hoping he rails me—neither of which can or should happen. One thing's clear, though: I'm hard up for this man.

"Things?" A soft breeze blows my hair forward and I tuck it behind my ear.

We fall into line behind about a dozen people in a queue that snakes along the sidewalk in front of the food truck.

Jesse hesitates—probably wondering why I've gone from cold bitch to blushing bright pink in a matter of minutes.

"Well?" I ask, wide-eyed, and plaster on a mask of impatience to hide my scandalous thoughts. "Do you always reveal information this slowly? Fucking out with it!"

He blows out a breath. "Okay, look. I've been thinking about what it might be like if I moved back here... back *home.*"

What?

A flood of mixed emotions hits me all at once. My heart lifts for a brief second before a vise-like squeeze takes hold. Getting to have Jesse around indefinitely would be incredible. But more importantly, *torturous.* It would mean having to fight off this... whatever I feel for him... long term. I don't think I have that in me. No. He can't move back here.

I realize he's staring at me, waiting for a reaction, and I frown. "What about your job?"

"Well, yeah, there's that. But maybe I could talk more with Dimitri about that thing his boss is—"

"No, Jess," I interrupt, desperate to discourage this idea. "You can't just quit your job."

This has to be temporary. I was *counting* on it being temporary. I need to stamp an expiration date on this.

He pulls his head back. "You don't think I should?"

"No!" I say too quickly, grasping for a way to stave off the hurt quickly blooming on his face. "I mean... I just..."

"Wow. Okay. I have to say, that's not how I thought you'd react. I thought—" His lips form a thin line and he shakes his head.

I fold my arms over my chest. "How am I *supposed* to react?"

"I dunno." He throws his arms out at his sides. "Happy I might stick around?"

Of course I want you around, you asshole. That's the problem.

When I don't respond, he raises his eyebrows. "Wow, you're really in a rush to get rid of me, huh?"

"I didn't say tha—"

"It's fine! I get it. You probably wanna find a permanent roommate, anyway." He looks away. "Maybe *Influencer Barbie* is still available."

I can't help but smile at that, but something behind his sarcastic tone tells me he's trying not to let what I said get to him.

"Or maybe you can find a friendly hoarder," he muses. "Or someone who's, like, really into pickling things. Or crypto." He stuffs his hands in his pockets, studying the food truck. "So, yeah, don't let me stop you from living your best life."

I flinch at his inadvertent echo of Pascal's cruel words: "*Go on, Ada. Keep living your best life... Fuck off to London or Paris or whatever to do your drawings, but I have needs too. Did you think I'd wait around for months? For you?*"

The blood in my veins ices over as Jesse moves to close the gap in the line ahead of us. When I can force my feet to move, I shuffle forward to join him, finally finding my voice. "I'm not in a rush to kick you out, okay? That's not what I'm saying."

"So, what *are* you saying?"

I swallow. I can't tell him the truth: that I can't stop thinking about putting my mouth on his mouth. That he needs to move out of my apartment before I do something stupid.

"I dunno. I just think it's crazy to walk away from a steady job like that." The words feel weak on my tongue. "You've been there for eight years. And you love the work you're doing." I don't want him to give up something he loves just because I put some silly idea in his head. "You have a life there, right?"

"And there's nothing for me here?"

"Well, *is there?*" The unspoken question lodges in my throat: *Am I part of it?*

The answer, of course, is no. I can't be. Even if Marcus wasn't an issue, I'm not the kind of girl you move across the world for.

"I dunno, Ada." He steps closer and a muscle in his jaw ticks. "You tell me."

"What's that supposed to mean?" My voice is small and quiet. "Why are you putting this on me?"

Does he want me to tell him to stay? What would that accomplish?

He exhales a quick breath. The food truck line moves up again and we drift a few steps forward to close the gap. He runs a hand over his beard and fixes his gaze somewhere down the road.

I watch him in profile, wishing I could read his mind—wishing we could say what we're both trying not to. "It's your life, Jess. I can't tell you what to do."

"You're right," he says quietly. "That wasn't fair. I'm sorry."

"We both know you can't base this on what I think." My next words strip me bare—the closest I've come to saying it out loud. "Or what I *want.*"

It doesn't matter that I want him. It's just attraction. Nothing more. It can't be more.

He turns back to me, giving me a long look, but doesn't ask what I want. I can see in his eyes he already knows.

"I wanna fuck Jesse." I shut my locker in the staff room and slump down on a nearby chair.

"Holy crap, she finally admits it." Katie's voice is rough on the other end of the line, like I just woke her up. I probably did.

"I wanna fuck Jesse," I say again. Admitting it out loud feels good. And terrifying.

Katie's laugh is equal parts delighted and rueful. "Took you long enough. I'm totally not doing my *I told you so* dance right now."

"Gloss over that part, please!" I say, my tone agitated.

Fuck, I want him so bad, it's making me angry.

"So, you going to?" Katie asks.

"No!" I blurt. "I can't!" I pick at the chipped paint on the edge of the staff room chair. "Can I?"

"Okay, back up a step. Where's this coming from? Last I heard, you were dead set that nothing would happen between you two."

I fill her in on our food truck dinner: burgers with a side of angst.

"I'm totally, completely, and utterly fucked," I say. *And frustratingly, not in the literal sense.*

"Get a grip," Katie says with a laugh. "Nothing even happened. You just talked. It's not like you ended up in his lap—this time."

"Yeah, but what do I do?" I press, clenching my free hand into a fist. "I have to live with him for another month!"

Her long exhale whooshes a cloud of white noise through the phone. "Well, what do you *want* to do? I mean, Marcus *would* be pissed—that's a given. But, like, do you think you could keep it on the down-low? If something *did* happen? Just... not tell him?"

"I doubt Jesse's willing to go there. He's barely able to *admit* anything about this in plain English."

"But he wants to, right?"

"Maybe? I think he just... wants to do the right thing. Be honorable or respectful or whatever. And I get it. I get it. I don't want to hurt Marcus, either. But like—"

"But you still want him to rail you into next week?"

My stomach hollows and my shoulders sag at the thought. "So much," I say. "Fuck. More like next *month*."

Katie's cackle on the other end of the line lifts me up a bit, and I smile.

I don't know how I'm going to function being around Jesse at home, with my mind spinning wild with sexy scenarios anytime he's near me. I don't trust myself with him anymore. It's like I'm standing on a precipice built of rapidly crumbling willpower, about to do or say something profoundly inappropriate any minute.

Hell, I've probably already crossed that line.

"Well, I think you could pull it off," she muses. "I mean, you have an apartment together with fully functioning locks. Pretty solid, privacy-wise."

"Right?" I have to admit that had crossed my mind.

"Maybe Jesse just needs a little... convincing."

"I dunno." I chew the inside of my cheek.

"And he's leaving at the end of August, so... there's an end date."

"Right." He absolutely cannot stay here longer, looking at me with those hungry blue eyes and melting my brain into wanting to take stupid risks. Because the sight of him makes me want to throw caution, along with my panties, to the wind.

"It wouldn't go on forever," Katie continues. "Unless you want more than just sex. But I know how you feel about long distance."

"Yeah, fuck that. No. Never again." I pause, once again shoving aside the inkling that what I feel for Jesse is something more than physical. "Besides, I don't want a relationship at all," I say, fighting the way the words feel clumsy coming out of my mouth. "I'm just... *horny.*"

I'm in a fucking state, alright. This morning, as I came out of the shower, my gaze had snagged on Jesse's deodorant, sitting on the bathroom counter beside my makeup bag. Glancing over my shoulder to ensure the door was locked, I'd slowly picked it up and popped the lid, inhaling its citrusy, spicy scent like an addict taking a hit. *God damn, he smells so good.* When I caught myself, I quickly capped it and put it back on the counter, backing away a step. Apparently, my desperation has reached a fever pitch— because there I was, locked in our bathroom on a Saturday morning, turned on by huffing Jesse's man-smell off something that literally goes in his armpits.

I need to get a grip.

"Well, then," Katie says, "I think you could have a bit of fun and just... be careful not to get caught. Marcus never has to know."

"Why am I simultaneously relieved and horrified that you're encouraging this?"

She laughs. "Because you're a decent person. And it's risky. But it could also be *amazing*. I dunno. Maybe that's shitty of me to say. Am I being a terrible human? Telling you to go fuck your brother's best friend?"

"No, you're perfect. Never change." I let out a breath. "And I think you're right—about it being amazing. This energy when we're together is... wild," I add, remembering that tension between us in line for the food truck.

Kyle pops his head into the break room, pointing at his watch.

Shit, I'm late.

I jump up, stuffing my purse back into my locker.

Message ostensibly delivered, Kyle disappears around the corner.

"Katie, I gotta get back to work. Talk later?"

"I'm off this weekend. Can we get some *us* time in?"

"Yes! I'll text you. Thanks, Dollface. Love you."

"Anytime. Love you too. Now, go get some. And take notes because you know I'm gonna want details."

I smile and hang up, then hightail it back to the bar and apologize to Kyle for losing track of time.

"Something up?" he asks with a cocked eyebrow.

Only my sexual frustration.

"No," I lie. "Why?"

"You're all... *flushed* or whatever."

"I'm fine," I dodge, grabbing the bar towel from him, and try to force myself to focus on work.

He gives me a look, then turns to serve a customer without saying anything more.

17

JESSE

"What do you mean, you can't come?" Ada stands at the kitchen counter with her back to me, holding the phone to her ear.

I look up from my book as she listens to the voice on the other end of the line. We haven't talked about our ill-advised food truck dinner the other night, apparently having fallen into an unspoken agreement to forget it ever happened.

"But I've already made a whole pitcher of margaritas."

Reminding myself not to stare at her ass for probably the thousandth time, I force my eyes to the counter beside her, where an empty bottle of tequila sits uncapped near the sink.

"No, it's fine," she sighs. "I'll just put it in the fridge or whatever." She pauses again. "Yeah, okay. Have fun. What? Oh my God, shut up. I'm not... No. Bye!" She rushes to hang up, sounding flustered, and drops her phone onto the counter beside her, cursing under her breath.

"You good?" I ask.

"No." I can hear the scowl in her voice.

"No Katie tonight, huh?"

Ada turns to face me, bracing her hands on the counter behind her.

I remind myself to keep my gaze level with hers and try to ignore the way her tits push out.

"Some surprise engagement party her parents are throwing her and Dimitri." Catching my confused expression, she adds, "It's just family."

I flip my book face down on the table, then stand. Hoping to cheer her up, I puff up my chest and arch an eyebrow, putting on a comically deep voice as I stroll to the kitchen. "Well, it seems like you've got yourself a tequila problem, little lady."

"Fuck off." I can tell she's trying not to smile.

Worth it.

I drop the voice, chuckling as I run a hand through my hair. "Seriously. I can help you with that. Gimme a cup."

"Yeah?" She shoots me a dubious smirk as she passes me the glass, then gives the pitcher a gentle swirl. "Fuck, I made a lot."

"Seems so." I put my hand to my chest. "But I will fall on that sword."

"So valiant," she deadpans, filling my glass.

"Hey, wanna go sit in the backyard with these? Mr. Wozniak's out of town—said we could use it this week."

Filling her own glass, she darts a cautious look my way. "Oh, *yeah.*"

"Think I saw a couple crappy lawn chairs back there."

She hesitates.

I can't say I blame her. We both came far too close to saying things we shouldn't have the other night. When I realize I'm not only alone with Ada, but about to split a bucket of booze with her, I add, "I'll text Marcus to come join us."

"Sure." It's barely there, but something like disappointment crosses her features.

I pull out my phone and fire off the text.

Out back, we dust the spiderwebs and dead leaves off a couple creaking lawn chairs with rusty frames, carefully testing they won't buckle under our weight. Reassured, and with drinks in hand, we slouch into the woven plastic seats, settling into a comfortable silence. The heat of the day has faded and a sliver of sunset cuts through the trees.

"This reminds me of that summer we all stayed up at Adrian's stepdad's cabin," Ada says softly. "We'd sit in the backyard every night, just like this."

"Right." I give her a sidelong glance. "Was that the trip with the watermelon fight?"

She turns. "Oh my *God*! I forgot about that! With the kitchen knives?"

I laugh. "Yeah."

"What did we call it? The game?"

"Uh, I think it was *Defend Yourself*?"

"Ha!" she barks. "Defend Yourself. Fuck, we were stupid."

"Whose idea was it to throw chunks of watermelon and try to slice them mid-air?" I ask.

"Don't remember." She shakes her head, her grin slowly fading to a soft smile as she lifts her glass to her lips. "Yours, probably."

"*What*?" I almost laugh. "I was never the instigator."

She points at me. "That's bullshit, because you instigated the shit with the fireworks on that same trip."

"Did not!"

"You *absolutely* did. You and Kai went down to meet some shady guy who sold them to you."

"*Oh, yeah,*" I whisper slowly. "I'm seventy-five percent sure that guy wasn't a serial killer."

She laughs. "He was dodgy as fuck. I was just glad you came back alive."

"Just me? Or me *and* Kai?"

"You, mainly," she admits. "Fucking Kai."

We share a look, fighting off a laugh. Kai was a special brand of idiotic back then.

"Damn, those were fun times," I say, then take a sip of my drink.

"Yeah," she almost sighs. "Between the knives and the fireworks, it's amazing we still have ten fingers apiece."

I blow out a laughing breath, then hold my drink out to her. "To surviving being idiots?"

Her gaze meets mine as we clink glasses, her smile seeming to sit deeper in my chest than usual. "To surviving being idiots."

I take another sip, then sit back in my chair, trying to shake it off.

"I was thinking about what you said the other night," Ada says, snapping me back to attention, "at dinner."

Shit.

My brows draw together.

I guess we are *talking about this.*

"Which part?"

"About moving back."

"Yeah?" I peer up at the overgrown trees in the backyard and swallow another sip of my drink, letting the cold trickle past the knot rapidly forming in my throat. A drop of hope creeps in, that Ada might tell me she's changed her mind—that I should move home.

"I think you *should* stay in Australia."

I inhale, fighting off the sting of her words once more, and scrutinize the dead grass at my feet. "You already told me that."

"I know, and it's not because I don't want you around." She throws me a quick glance. "I just think things here are... I dunno. Too complicated for you." Ada slouches down further and crosses her legs, resting her glass on the chair's weathered armrest.

I nod. "Too complicated?"

"Yeah, like, you've been away all this time. Found your groove down there. Kinda lost touch with people here..."

Ouch.

She's not wrong.

"You've got friends there, right?"

"Yeah."

"I mean, think about it this way: you get to breeze into town for the summer—y'know, get a sick tan, drink, party—and fuck-ing... fly away at the end." She makes a little airplane gesture with her free hand, slipping her eyes to mine as if to gauge my reaction.

I rub the back of my neck. "Uh, yeah, I guess so."

"Plus, you have such an amazing job there that you *love*. And I bet that farm needs you back. Didn't you tell Marcus you're working on some really important stuff?"

I tilt my head but don't correct her, knowing I'd oversold it when I first showed up. I keep thinking about options for work here in Lennox. Dimitri finally texted me earlier today with a question from his boss about wood chip composting. It got me kind of excited about the possibilities of working here on sustain-ability stuff.

"And anyway, the admin stuff alone would be a nightmare, I'm sure." She seems like she's trying to convince herself more than me. "Yeah, you should definitely go back."

I frown, contemplating her words.

When I don't respond, she continues. "You don't really need to face reality, right? You could just... live in the moment while you're here. Have fun and not worry about it."

"Fuck reality? Just opt out?" My smile is cautious.

"Yeah, fuck reality!" She laughs, then takes a sip of her drink, turning back toward the sunset. Then, more quietly, she says, "Wish I could do that."

I run a hand over my jaw. "So, you're saying I should just do whatever I feel like while I'm here? Fuck the consequences?" Something's prickling at the very edge of my awareness.

She shrugs. "Yeah, basically."

"That's kind of irresponsible, isn't it?"

"Depends on what you wanna do."

I swallow. The words she's *not* saying are speaking volumes.

"And if you get caught," she adds quietly.

Oh, Jesus. Am I hallucinating?

I glance down at my drink.

How strong did she make these margaritas?

I look long and hard at her.

She uncrosses her legs and sits up, turning to face me, and leans closer. Her voice comes out slightly breathy. "I mean, you've got real life waiting for you when you get back there. You'll have to haul yourself up at the ass-crack of dawn for work every day, right? So while you're here, you can just..." She trails off, as if searching for the right word, and raises her glass halfway to her lips. "Play?" She holds my gaze as she takes a sip of her drink.

My blood heats under my skin. "So, you're saying *this*"—I gesture between us—"isn't real life?"

"I dunno. I'm probably drunk already." She laughs, examining the drink in her hand. "What do I know?"

No way she's drunk already. The excuse is pitiful and we both know it.

Shifting in my seat toward her, I sit up and brace my forearms on my knees, leaning forward with both hands wrapped around my glass.

She lifts her eyes to meet mine, her lips slightly parted.

Fuck, she shouldn't be looking at me like that.

"Is that what you want?" I ask softly. "To escape real life for a while?"

A muscle moves in her throat as she swallows, her bare, lightly freckled shoulder ticking up in a half shrug. "I mean, it's got a certain appeal."

"Just act on impulse, do what feels good? Just... *play*, like you said?"

She tucks her hair behind her ear. "Yeah, exactly."

I look down at my hands. "I did actually have something I wanted to do while I was here."

We're sitting so close together, I only have to extend a finger to touch her knee. I let go of the glass with one hand, grazing her sun-kissed skin with the back of my knuckles.

This is crossing a line.

She doesn't stop me—or speak. Suddenly silent, she seems to be holding her breath.

My heart races. Unable to maintain eye contact, I drop my gaze to her legs.

"Like, *really* wanna do." I pause, tracing the raised edge of a small scar. I exhale hard, searching her beautiful face for any hint of hesitation, but find none.

She licks her lips and my cock twitches.

"Something I can't stop thinking about."

"Yeah?" she whispers.

I drag my knuckles to the inside of her knee, unable to stop.

"Yeah," I nod. "But I've been holding off. Too many consequences, y'know?"

Sliding my hand to the swell of her calf, I squeeze my fingers into her soft skin.

Her eyes flutter shut.

"You back here?" Marcus calls out from the gate around the corner.

I quickly pull my hand back to my glass as Ada pivots away from me in her seat.

I clear my throat, turning away from her. "Yeah, man, over

here!" I run a hand down my face and command my body to change gears in a hurry.

What the fuck am I doing?

When Marcus appears around the corner, Ada sets her glass on the ground and launches from her chair. She jogs over to her brother, wrapping her arms around him.

"Whoa! Hey! Who are you and what have you done with my sister?" He chuckles, throwing me a confused look over her shoulder.

"What? I'm just happy you're here. Shut up," she says, stepping back and flipping her hair away from her face.

"Ada, I can count on one hand the number of times you've willingly hugged me. What's up?" He glances at me like I can explain her unusual greeting.

I give him a tight smile and shrug.

"I'm probably drunk, I dunno," she explains with a laugh that comes out a bit too loud.

Easy, Ada, I plead with her silently.

She seems to realize she's being weird, because she quickly busies herself searching for another lawn chair. Finding one behind the shed, she dusts it off and presents it to Marcus with a flourish. I stay in my seat, needing another moment to cool my jets, and send a fervent plea to my dick to settle the fuck down.

"Jesus Christ," Marcus says, his expression skeptical. "Am I gonna need a tetanus shot before sitting on that thing?"

Ada's laugh is higher pitched than usual, but she reins it in. "I'll go get you a margarita," she says to Marcus, then turns to head down the basement stairs.

"No, I got it," I say, finally trusting myself to stand. "You sling drinks at work all the time. My turn."

I squeeze her shoulder as I walk past, instantly regretting the touch and how my hand lingers a fraction longer than necessary.

What the hell is happening?

It's nearly two in the morning and I cannot, for the life of me, get comfortable. Shifting in my bed for the thousandth time, I'm tormented by my failure to keep myself in check around Ada. If anything, my attraction to her has only grown since living here—a fact I'm sure anyone with two brain cells could've seen coming. My own brain cells, however, seem to be missing in action. I'm struggling, replaying our conversation in the backyard earlier tonight on an agonizing loop.

Marcus nearly caught me touching his sister. Sure, it was only her leg—but it was clear where we were headed.

I can't stop thinking about Ada's encouragement to cut loose and fuck the consequences... And the look on her face. She knew exactly what she was saying. In that moment—with my fingers on her warm skin, my cock getting harder by the second—I'd forgotten all about having invited Marcus over.

I roll onto my side and stuff the pillow under my head—a bit aggressively—hoping sleep will give me some relief.

Come on, willpower. Do your thing.

Then an unmistakable sound has my eyes flying open.

Oh, Jesus.

Realization dawns on me fast and hot as all my blood rushes to my dick.

Another soft sound of pleasure comes from the next room and I'm rock-hard in an instant. I hold my breath, my heart kicking in my chest. My attention is laser-focused on that sound, waiting for more—and I'm soon rewarded with another moan. My hand is on my cock without a second thought. *Bad idea*, I think as I stroke myself, my eyes rolling back in my head at the relief of finally giving in. *Fucking hot, fucking bad idea.*

Pumping myself faster now, I know deep in my bones this is wrong. The shame coils around my ribcage but I can't stop.

Shit.

I should not be jerking off to my best friend's sister touching herself in the next room. She must think I'm asleep. Or not realize how thin the walls are. Or...

Does she know I can hear? *Want* me to hear?

Fuck. I should stop.

But the idea that Ada might be doing this on purpose—doing this for *me*—only has me stroking faster.

Oh, God. Can't stop.

I clench my jaw, painfully aware that making any noise would give me away.

Another blissful, whimpering sound from Ada's lips has me nearly on the edge of orgasm. I imagine busting through that wall, leaving behind a Jesse-shaped hole like some kind of modern-day Kool-Aid man with a boner. Because *fuck*, I'd give anything to be with her. To see her touch herself with my own eyes. To finish this together.

It's taking all my willpower not to leap out of this bed and do exactly that. The only thing holding me back is knowing Marcus would never forgive me. Or her. *Fuck*, this is exactly what he tried to warn me about.

Okay, well, not *exactly* this.

I slow my pace as I strain to listen for more. She seems to have gone quiet, and I can't help but think maybe I was hallucinating. But then Ada's muffled gasps reach my ears and I can't stop. Pumping myself again as she moans, I go over the cliff, sensation lighting me up from head to toe. I can barely contain my own hiss of pleasure as cum spurts hot and long over my bare stomach, hitting as high up as my chest.

Shit. Fuck. No. Yes.

I breathe hard while I wait for my vision to clear. One hand still on my cock, I drag the other one down my face in shame.

What the fuck have I done?

I know I've crossed a line—a strange, private line in my mind—and a sinking realization descends over me: living with Ada just got a hell of a lot more difficult.

How am I going to face her after this? After what I've heard? After what I've done?

MY HEART IS in my throat when I come out of my bedroom the next morning and see Ada. When she looks up from her phone, I swallow. "Hi."

"Hey." She's a dozen feet away, but I can feel the air between our bodies buzzing, charged with the shared knowledge of what almost happened.

I have to mentally shove away a flashback of what *did* happen—later, in our beds.

God, those moans...

"Can we talk for a sec?" I ask.

"Uh, sure." She glances at the door like she's considering running.

I walk closer, not convinced I'm capable of having any kind of rational conversation right now. But I have to try.

"Last night was..." I stuff my hands in my front pockets, stuffing down the impulse to touch her along with them. Not sure how to put it into words, I try again. "Marcus almost saw us."

"Yeah, I know."

"That can't happen again." I shake my head, hesitating before I say any more. "It was a mistake. I'm sorry. I should have never laid a finger on you."

She scoffs. "Just blame the margaritas or whatever."

"Ada. Cut it out. We both know it wasn't the fucking margaritas. But it *was* stupid. We can't—"

Something seems to snap in her. "Yeah, yeah, I know, *we can't, we can't, we can't.*"

I flinch at her pissy tone.

She pushes her hands into her hair, then drops them to her sides, turning for the front door. "I need to get out of here."

"Ada, come on... Talk to me."

She stops in her tracks and whirls around to face me. "I don't want to fucking *talk*, Jesse! That's the problem. We've talked ourselves in circles and gotten fucking *nowhere!* And *talking...*" She takes a long breath, letting it out through a pained smile. "Talking is *not* what's on my mind when I think about you."

Her admission has my heartbeat thundering in my ears.

"Ada..." I trail off.

What's there to say? We can't act on this.

We hold eye contact for another moment before she wrenches her gaze from mine. Quickly shoving on her shoes and snatching up her purse, she pushes out the front door.

18

———

JESSE

My knee bounces as I sit on the couch, waiting for Ada to get home from work. Her words from this morning have been running laps in my head all day.

"Talking is not *what's on my mind when I think about you."*

I need to nip this in the bud.

I'm on my feet the moment I hear her keys in the door. Ada gives me a wary look as she kicks off her shoes.

"Hey, listen," I start. "Sorry about earlier. I didn't mean to fuck with your head or hurt your feelings."

She drops her keys into her purse and tosses the bag next to her shoes in the entryway. "It's fine. Don't worry about it."

"I'm just trying to do the right thing, here. You know, with Marcus last night... We hadn't even—"

"Yeah, I know. Just drop it. Whatever." She moves to push past me, heading to the kitchen.

I step out of her way, careful not to touch her. I should be glad she wants to drop it. But I turn to follow her, unable to stop myself. "You're doing that thing again."

She fills a glass of water at the sink, her back to me. "What thing?"

"That thing where you just brush shit off like it doesn't matter. It's bullshit."

She straightens, then slowly puts her glass down on the counter before turning around and crossing her arms over her chest. "What exactly am I brushing off?"

I raise my eyebrows in answer, gesturing generically between us.

"No, Jess." She unfolds her arms as she steps toward me. "Say the quiet part out loud for once. You're the one who wanted to talk, so fucking *talk*."

"You know I can't do that," I say in a low voice. Admitting what's happening out loud feels wrong. My heart hammers in my chest as she fixes her unyielding gaze on me.

Fuck. I wasn't prepared for those eyes.

Her voice is quiet when she takes another step toward me and speaks, the words articulated slowly and clearly, like she's shoving them inside my ribcage, one by one. "He's not here. It's just *me*."

The silence thickens around us, and the look she's giving me eats away at my better judgment. The words rise from my stomach, wrapping around my throat. I clench my jaw, hesitating another few seconds before something in my chest uncorks. "Fuck. Fine, you want the truth?"

"Please!" she exclaims.

"The truth is, last week in my room, you got into my fucking head," I say, stabbing a finger against my temple. "About this place. About moving back. I was never planning to stay for longer than the summer. But now, all of a sudden, I'm imagining these scenarios where I quit my job in Oz and find some way to stick around here, because..."

The admission sticks in my throat. I can't take the words back once I say them.

"Because what?" She throws her hands out at her sides.

Jesus. She's really gonna force it out of me.

"Because of *you*, Ada."

She sucks in a breath.

For a moment, we just stare at each other. The sinking pull in my gut reminds me that, even if I were to uproot my life, there is *no* scenario where moving back here works out for me. For *us*. I press my lips together, shaking my head. "Because I can't stop thinking about last night, okay? About what would've happened if Marcus hadn't shown up. If I'd never texted him."

"That's why you need to go back, Jess," she says quietly. "I told you, this is too complicated."

The elephant in the room is starting to take shape.

"Complicated. Yeah." My brows knit together. I can't admit to her the idea of leaving is getting harder to swallow every day. I run both hands down my face.

"So, what are we supposed to do?" She looks bewildered.

"*We* aren't gonna do anything. Because this—whatever *this* is —stops here. Now. Before we fuck this all up. We have to be just friends, Ada. Nothing more."

"Just friends?" She almost laughs, but there's no joy in her eyes. "Yeah?"

"Yes!"

She tilts her head as she steps closer. "You need to sit down for a while after Marcus texts you a photo of *his* Halloween costume?"

"Ada…" Heat rushes up my neck.

She drifts toward me another step, frustration simmering in every line of her body. "You joke around with Kai about how he's something you wanna *do* while you're here?"

I squeeze my eyes shut. "Jesus Christ. This is exactly what I'm talking about. I should never have—"

"'Cause I can text him right now." She gestures with her thumb over her shoulder, presumably toward her phone. "Ask him to send you a dick pic. See if that gets you going."

I ball my hands into fists. "Will you stop?"

She doesn't let up. "Or was that just about *me?*"

"Ada." My voice comes out louder this time. I grit my teeth and pace a few steps away from her, feeling like crawling out of my skin.

"*Just friends,* my ass," she presses. "You want me. You're just too scared to do anything about it."

"Ada!" I shout, spinning to face her—finally losing my cool.

She startles, but her expression still burns with intensity.

"Oh, fuck it," I mutter as I cross the short distance separating us, caging her against the wall between my arms.

"Jesse," she whispers, wide eyes searching mine.

"Just shut up and listen."

She nods tightly. The rise and fall of her chest is rapid, and the space between our bodies is filled with a vital, humming pull that claws me closer.

"Yes, I fucking want you. So no, we are *not* just friends. I dunno about you, but I don't feel like *this* about my friends," I say, my gaze dropping to her mouth. "Like I'm a goddamn addict being denied my fix. Like if I have to spend another second without having you, I'll lose my fucking mind."

Her shoulders sag.

"And I'm doing *everything* in my power not to fall off that fucking wagon, Ada. Not to haul you against me and breathe you in deep. Just to get one hit." I lick my lips, suddenly unsure I can get through what I have to say without breaking. "'Cause I know, if I did that, I'd never be able to stop."

God damnit, why does she have to smell so good?

Her sweet lips part in protest. "But Jess, I—"

I cut her off with a warning look. "Touching you, being with you... would be a very, *very* bad decision." My shoulders tense as I fight to keep my hands planted on the wall. "I can't knowingly blow things up with my best friend."

"But what if—" Her voice wavers.

Oh, fuck.

"Don't," I cut her off again, my voice almost a growl. "Don't you *dare* tempt me."

She exhales, her brows knitting together.

Unable to help myself, I lean closer—and the dam breaks. "Because my dick aches just looking at you. Just being this close to you right now is killing me. And all I do, all night long, is imagine what it would feel like to fuck you."

The words knock the wind from her.

"To taste you. To make you moan... make you come." My eyes travel along the curve of her neck and I mutter a curse. I want to trace the path with my tongue and hear her breath catch. Feel her turn to liquid in my arms.

She peers up at me again, her lower lip quivering.

I want to bite it. I grit my teeth together.

"Why are you telling me this?" She searches my face. "If you won't even *consider* touching me... Why?"

"That's the problem, though," I say, my smile rueful. "I've considered it too fucking much. I can't stop *considering* touching you, Ada. You asked for the truth. *Pushed me* for the fucking truth. You wanted me to say the quiet part out loud? This is it. Cards on the table. Happy now?"

She blinks and drops her gaze.

"And," I continue, and her eyes snap back up, "I fucking *had to.*" My fingers tense, almost clawing the paint off the wall with the effort of keeping them there. "Because, if I didn't say something... I knew in my bones I'd snap. That my hands would end up doing the talking. And that I'd do something we'd both regret."

"*Fuck,*" she whispers.

"Yes, *that*," I say in a low voice, staring at her mouth.

Those lush lips twist in a smirk, but it quickly fades when she registers the intensity on my face.

I've never been more serious. It's taking everything in me not to crush my body against hers right now—not to tear off her clothes and taste every inch of her. Bury myself in her.

"I'm at my breaking point with you, Ada," I continue. "I'm done pretending there's nothing going on here. Done dancing around this. So you can be pissed at me. Fuck, blame me. Think of me as an asshole if it makes you feel better. But you have to understand: no matter how much we might want it... This. Can't. Happen."

Summoning all my remaining self-control, I push away from the wall with a groan and walk to my room. Unable to chance looking back at her, I shut the door—hard—and sag against it.

19

———

ADA

My heart thunders in my chest as I watch Jesse walk to his room and the vacuum left by his absence sucks up my ability to breathe. His last words ring in my ears: *"This. Can't. Happen."*

The fuck it can't.

He may be hellbent on going down in history as some kind of virtuous sex martyr, but I'm sure as fuck not.

For a split second, I think I might book it to my bedroom—*certainly the wiser fucking choice*—but I'm knocking on his door before my body and wisdom can get on the same page. I need him like I need oxygen and I'll take what I can get, bad idea or not.

When he opens the door, his hungry gaze pins me to the spot.

"You shouldn't be here," he says in a rough voice. "I said—"

"I know what you said." My eyes lock on his mouth.

And, in that moment, his resolve wavers.

He doesn't touch me or speak—just takes a slow step backward, the unspoken understanding crackling in the air around us.

I step inside and shut the door. The light from the lamp

behind him casts him in silhouette—a black hole I have no hope of resisting. I step toward him, placing my hand on his chest.

"Ada..." His heart is already racing beneath my palm. "This is a *bad idea.*"

"Yeah." I step closer. "I know." I curl my fingers, fisting his T-shirt, and pull him into me as I lift my face to his. "But now it's your turn to shut up and listen."

The light trace of his fingers as they slip up my arms has my knees threatening to buckle.

"Jesse..." I say his name like I'm exhausted. And I am—exhausted from waiting for this. From wanting him and fighting it. From trying to ignore every accidental touch. From every time we look at each other and the eye contact aches to break—or to hold. "I don't want you imagining it anymore. I want the real thing."

He drops his head, grazing his forehead against mine.

"Fuck me," I say.

A rush of air leaves his lungs. "Holy shit."

"Fuck me," I whisper again, brushing my cheek against his. His beard prickles against my skin. "Fuck me and it doesn't leave this apartment. We don't tell anyone. We're just... scratching an itch, okay?" I swallow, knowing it's half a lie; this runs deeper than either of us can admit. But Jesse needs to know this is temporary. The muscles in my core pulse at the realization that I've laid it out—laid *myself* out for him to take. *Cards on the table,* he'd said. I'm telling him exactly what I want. Well, mostly.

This is *what I want,* I tell myself. *Just a physical thing. This is the part I'm good at.*

"We're two consenting adults and it's just sex," I say. "Understand?"

Something shifts in him as he lifts his hands to cradle my face. His expression darkens, his pupils blown by desire and the dim light. He takes a long breath before he nods.

"Good," I say.

"It's about to be," he rasps, and his mouth meets mine hard.

My whimper of relief is only silenced by the hot crush of his lips. As our tongues tangle, I claw at his back and hips, desperate and needy. Finally touching him like this—like I've wanted to for *weeks*—is lighting me up in ways that threaten to undo me altogether, my every nerve ending firing at once. I want to consume him. Be consumed *by* him.

Fuck, forbidden fruit tastes so good.

"Oh, *God*, Ada," he groans, the words muffled against my lips, my cheek, my neck, my lips again. "I've wanted you so bad. So *fucking bad.*"

"I know," I say through a pained smile. "Me too."

I slide my hands under the back of his shirt, raking my fingernails over his skin, and delight in the growl that escapes his throat.

He sinks into the kiss, his tongue sweeping and twisting against mine. He grips my jaw, tugging it down so I can take more of him.

Oh, fuck, yes.

I'm sinking, drowning in the weight of this. Of him. The crushing heat of muscle and skin and need. Fire licks up my spine, meeting Jesse's fingertips at the nape of my neck.

"Ada… let me see you." He nips my lower lip as he lifts the hem of my sweatshirt. His fingers on my bare waist draw a pulsing heat to my core. He yanks my sweatshirt over my head, his chest heaving. When he unhooks my bra and lets it drop to the floor, desire flares in his eyes. "Jesus," he says as he palms both my breasts, his thumbs working my nipples into tight peaks. "You're gorgeous."

As he claims my mouth once more, all I can think about is how badly I've wanted this. How ready I am. How he's wearing too many clothes.

I tear at his shirt, desperate to feel his skin against mine. "Take this off," I bite out.

"Bossy," he says with a lazy grin before reaching up to the back of his neck and hauling his T-shirt over his head. His glorious chest now bare, he pushes against me again, letting out a harsh exhale. The heat of his skin against my breasts makes me ache to feel all of him.

"Jesse," I manage to say, then flick my tongue against his. "I want you inside me."

His inhale is sharp as his hips press forward, the steel heat of his cock grinding into my stomach. "Fuck. Are you sure?" He trails kisses along my neck, then pulls back to meet my gaze with heavy-lidded eyes.

I nod rapidly. "I'm sure."

"You better be." He dips his head to my neck again, scraping his teeth against my hammering pulse, while his fingers gently pinch and roll over my taut nipples. "'Cause *fuck*... I want to. *So fucking much.* Can't stop thinking about this."

"Mm-hmm," I hum, tracing the waistband of his jeans with my fingertips.

He shivers as he reaches a hand to cup my face, looking almost tortured, and brushes his thumb over my cheek. "Ada. This is a line we can't uncross."

"Cross it."

That last gasp of restraint evaporates when I drag my hand up between us, rubbing it against his rock-hard erection, and he moans.

He *moans.*

I could get off from that sound alone. My teeth skim over my lower lip.

Oh, God, if he doesn't fuck me now, I'm going to lose my shit.

With a rough, insistent kiss, he grips my ass and hauls me

against his body. His fingers slide under the hem of my jean shorts, lifting the lace edge of my panties.

I flex my hips back into his touch as if I might, just by angle alone, get his fingers to slip inside me and give me what I want.

"Say it again," he says as his fingertips graze the edge of my pussy. "Tell me again to fuck you, Ada. So I know I'm not dreaming."

Dear God.

"Fuck me," I breathe, raking my hands down his sculpted chest. I arch a brow as my fingers trail lower, over his carved stomach, coming to rest on the waistband of his jeans. His cock strains hot and hard against the fabric. I hold his gaze as I yank open the top button. "Fuck," I say as it pops, then jerk his zipper down, "me."

He growls his approval and, when I dip my hand beneath his waistband, wrapping my fingers around his thick shaft, he hisses with pleasure.

"Oh, Jesus Christ," I whisper. "I'm gonna be feeling this tomorrow, aren't I?"

His throaty laugh quickly turns into a ragged exhale at the first stroke of my hand. He runs a thumb over my bottom lip, his eyes molten. "We can go nice and slow… if that's what you need… if that's what you want. I can fuck you gently."

My lips curl up at the corner. "*Fuck Her Gently*… Isn't that a Tenacious D song?"

He's unable to suppress the smile. "Shut up, Ada."

"You want me to shut up?" I tease. "Make me." A grin spreads over my face and he pulls me into another burning kiss. My teasing tone evaporates in an instant, replaced by a feral need thrumming inside my core.

His hips twitch forward as I pump my fist, relishing the steel-smooth heat of him in my hand. He trails hot kisses over my lips, my cheek, my jawline, my collarbone—his breath shuddering with soft moans as I stroke him. "God, you're killing me," he rumbles. "And I haven't even been inside you yet."

I shiver when he slides his tongue over the ridge of my ear.

"Tell me you have a condom," he rasps against my neck.

My stomach drops, my hand pausing mid-stroke.

"Fuck," I say. "No." I whimper in frustration, letting my forehead drop onto his muscled shoulder. *This can't be happening.*

His hands tangle in my hair and he gently lifts my face, his blue eyes meeting mine in the dim light.

"Hey. I've been tested," he says. "All clear. So if you…"

"Same. And I get the shot," I say in a rush of relief.

"Oh, thank fuck," he says on an exhale.

I tighten my grip and push down again. Jesse's responding groan resonates somewhere deep inside me, somewhere low and sweet and warm, like my body can hear his call and wants more.

His lips crash against mine again and he hums his pleasure into my mouth.

God, I love the sounds he makes. I could get addicted *to the sounds he makes.*

When we break the kiss, his expression is darker than before. "Get your ass on the bed."

"Now who's the bossy one?" I tease, then reluctantly let go. I've barely taken two steps away from him when he stops me.

"Wait." He grabs my arm, tucking his body in close behind mine, strong arms wrapping around my waist.

I gasp, arching my back when he roughly grasps my breasts, pinching my nipples. The heat of his chest is like fire against my back as he squeezes me closer, his erection pressing against my ass.

Sliding his hands lower, he nips and licks the back of my neck, melting my senses while he quickly unfastens my jean shorts, shoving them down over my hips—along with my panties.

"The bed…" I step out of my shorts and kick them aside.

He grunts softly in response, skimming his teeth over my shoulder. Kneading the flesh of my ass, he says, "So, this is what you've been hiding under that fucking miniskirt."

"Uh-huh," I say, then sharply inhale as he slips his hand between my thighs from behind and drags a finger through my slick center.

He groans, his voice rumbling against my neck. "Oh, my God. So fucking wet. Are you always soaked like this?"

I whimper when he pushes his finger inside me, then swallow hard. "For you," I admit, "always."

His low sound of approval makes my core clench. He pumps his finger gently. Too gently.

"Remind me… Why aren't you fucking me yet?" I push my hips back, squirming for more.

"So greedy," he says, his smile audible. He slides his finger out with a warning grumble and gently slaps my pussy.

"Fuck!" My voice is tight—needy and impatient.

He leans in close, his breath fanning over my skin as he noses my neck. "Oh, you liked that?"

I exhale something between a laugh and a moan. "Such an asshole, making me wait."

He pushes two fingers inside me and starts pumping, slow and steady, and I widen my stance, desperate for more.

"That's it," he says. "Open up for me." With his free hand, he grips my hip, steadying me. "I want you ready."

Oh, Jesus Christ. I'm ready right now. I was ready when I knocked on your goddamn door.

I eye the bed. While it's only a few steps away, we can't seem to make it there.

I cry out softly as he adds another finger—filling me tightly, stretching me.

Fuck, that feels so good.

When I clench around him, he huffs a satisfied noise against my neck. "Yes, Ada."

I squirm, pressing down against his hand. "Please..."

"Mmm, you want more?"

"Yes, God, I need you." I make a desperate, mewling sound as his fingers speed up. "Need you inside me."

He pulls away, quickly shedding the rest of his clothes.

I turn to face him, taking in his gorgeous body as he stands naked in front of me.

He's incredible.

I step closer and reach for him, needing *all* of him.

He catches my hands and levels me with a dark glare. "Uh-uh. Bed. Now."

Letting out a small huff of frustration, I back up until my calves bump the bed frame.

He follows slowly. He takes his cock in his hand, working lazy strokes and watching me with ravenous eyes as I lower down onto the mattress. "Look at you."

"What?" I ask, blinking back at him.

"I've been imagining this for weeks," he says quietly as he climbs over me, dipping down to kiss my collarbone. "Imagining *you*... naked... dripping wet... letting me fuck you." He gently bites my shoulder, humming with pleasure, then drags his tongue up the center of my throat.

"Yeah?" I manage, baring my neck to him in a silent plea for more. "And how does imaginary Ada compare to the real thing?"

"Doesn't hold a fucking candle," he says, smiling as he nudges my legs open with his knee, then sucks and bites gently at my neck. He takes my mouth in a drugging kiss as he lowers his hips, resting the head of his dick against my slick entrance. He pulls back, gazing down at me as he rubs the tip against my pussy, coating it in my wetness.

I drag my hands down his chest, drinking in his incredible

body once more. I smirk up at him. "Manual labor has been good to you, *Farm Boy*."

He shakes his head, amusement dancing in his eyes. "Was that a... *Princess Bride* reference?" With a scoff, he adds, "Your dirty talk needs some work."

I open my mouth to argue, but he pushes the tip of his cock inside me, making my breath catch. When he stops, I try to squirm closer. "What do you want me to say then?"

He pushes in just a little more and lets out a low, "*Fuuuuuck.*" He's almost trembling as he withdraws again, like he's fighting to draw this out. "I want you to ask nicely."

I groan in frustration, feeling like I'm going to scream. Wicked amusement spreads over his face as he pushes the tip in and out, the too-shallow movement driving me insane.

"I want you begging for it. Begging for me to fill you."

"Please, Jesse." I'm ready to give him anything he asks for. I grab at his hips with clumsy hands. "I need more. Please... just *fuck me.*"

Apparently satisfied, he leans down close, his lips at my ear. "As you wish."

I'm about to give him shit, but my voice is momentarily fucked out of me. I arch up off the bed with a gasp, digging my fingernails into his back as he thrusts again, deeper this time.

"Oh, shit," I say. "Again. Hard."

He obliges and I moan, reaching over my head to press a hand against the wall. I brace myself so I can meet him, the angle filling me so completely that I almost shake with relief.

"Oh my God." His hips buck again. "You like it hard, don't you?"

As if the answer isn't screaming from every cell in my body.

"Yes," I whine, pushing against the wall, shifting down onto him. "More. Please."

He speeds up, pounding into me over and over again, seating

himself inside me fully now. Then, as if trying not to get carried away, he slows. He fists a hand in my hair and tugs my head to one side, his teeth scraping my neck. "Ada," he mumbles against my skin, fucking me in a slow and steady rhythm, "I wanna watch you come." He turns my face back to his, claiming my mouth in a fierce, hungry kiss, and his hips kick forward again—hard—just once, like he can't help himself.

I arch up. "Yes," is all I can say.

He withdraws slowly, stopping short of pulling all the way out.

"Show me what you like. How you touch yourself," he says, then leans down close to whisper into my ear. "Like when you're alone in your room and think I can't hear you." He thrusts in again.

My eyes fly open and my jaw drops.

No way.

At my stunned reaction, he gives me a devilish grin. "Did you think I was asleep?"

Heat flushes my cheeks. "It was so late."

"What were you thinking about?" he asks, dipping down to nip at my earlobe as he grinds inside me. He licks and sucks my neck, making my pussy pulse. "What kind of dirty things were going through your head while you touched yourself?"

Holy fuck.

When I don't answer, he draws back and slams into me again. My body arches up from the bed, and I let out a cry from some-where deep in my throat.

"Because all *I* could think about was *you...*"—*thrust*—"on the other side of that wall..."—*thrust*—"touching this tight..."—*thrust* —"little..."—*thrust*—"pussy." *Thrust.*

Oh my God.

He leans down to kiss my neck, whispering his next words

against the shell of my ear. "I nearly blacked out, I came so fucking hard when I heard you moan."

Air rushes from my lungs.

Oh, fuck... That might be the hottest thing I've ever heard.

He looks down at me, a lazy smirk tugging at the corner of his mouth. Rubbing his thumb against my clit, he watches my reaction, speeding up when my breath starts to skitter. "Were you thinking about *me*?"

My cheeks are on fire now. I bite my lip and nod.

"Good answer." He fills me again and again and I whimper, nearly losing it right then and there. "Show me, Ada."

I reach a shaking hand down, trailing my fingers through the slick, warm wetness where our bodies meet. As I rub it in circles over my swollen clit, my eyes roll.

He pumps inside me in a steady rhythm, clearly pacing himself—holding back to stay in control.

My fingers slip in tight circles over my clit, coaxing my pleasure until it's building to a peak, gathering as the sensations of his incredible cock and my fast fingers swim together. I hold onto the back of his neck with my free hand and yank him down, plunging my tongue into his mouth, sweeping and sliding it over his until there is nothing in the world except this moment—this all-consuming sensation of Jesse fucking me, kissing me, driving me toward oblivion. I clench around him, my fingernails biting into his skin. When I start to gasp, he responds with a throaty groan; I'm close and we both know it.

"That's it, Ada." He's almost whimpering with each bucking movement of his hips. "You feel so fucking good."

"When I come," I whisper, "don't hold back, okay?"

"Oh, fuck, okay." He can barely get the words out.

My gasps turn scattered and strained against his cheek, and I hold my breath as I start to go over the edge, clinging to his neck.

"Yes," he grits out, speeding up. "C'mon."

And then I'm undone. My release explodes across my senses, the muscles of my core clenching and pulsing around him. "Oh, fuck!" I bite out between the waves thundering through me. Lights spark behind the dark of my eyelids, the sound in my head is a deafening rush, and pulses of tingling sensation ripple outward from my center to lick the tips of my fingers and toes.

Jesse doesn't stop. His chest heaves as he fucks me relentlessly, turning me to liquid—boneless and floating.

"Come inside me," I beg him, still riding out my pulsing orgasm. "Fill me. Make a mess of me. Please." I reach my free hand around to his ass, digging my nails into his skin.

More. Oh, God, yes.

I meet him with every thrust, clenching around him, crying out with pleasure.

Losing his grip on control, he unleashes a whole new level of depth and speed. He lets out a loud groan as he comes, slamming and shuddering into me with everything he has left.

He collapses down over me, our chests pressed together and heaving, slick with sweat.

We stay like that for a while—I don't know how long. Grinning and blissed out, I softly trace my fingers over his shoulders. I feel cosmic. Sparkly. Overheated and raw... And yet, somehow, under the heavy press of his weight, I also feel calmer than I have in a long time.

"Holy shit," he rumbles against my cheek when he can speak again, then reaches up to rub a hand over his damp face. His gaze is clouded—like he's looking through me.

With those familiar blue eyes suddenly far away, I can't read him, and concern threatens at the edge of my mind. Reality is quickly solidifying; we just crossed one hell of a line and there's no going back. Suddenly self-conscious, I grasp for my sarcastic shields—spitballing biting comments I could use to push him away.

Quick, insult him before he can reject you.

"Regretting this already?" I let out a wry laugh to cover up my vulnerability.

He's still inside me, for fuck's sake.

He seems to focus on me again, and he smiles as he shakes his head. "Regret fucking you? God, no." He dips down to kiss me, his lips soft and warm in the calm that's descended over us. "Listen to me. You're perfect. That was perfect. Unbelievable. I'd do it again in a heartbeat." He kisses me again, tender and slow, and it's like a balm smoothing over the jagged edges of my uncertainty. "I *will* do it again, if you'll let me."

I exhale and nod, careful not to show the depth of my relief.

"My only regret," he says, nosing my cheek, "is that now, every time I so much as look at you, I'm gonna be remembering what it felt like to be inside you. And *that*"—he sucks in a breath as he pulls out—"is going to be an enormous fucking problem." He rolls onto his back, sighing softly, then turns to me. "What about you? Regretting it?"

"Never," I say quickly. "Bullying you into fucking me? Best decision I've ever made."

He chuckles. "I have to say, the peer pressure on your end was... impressive."

I give him a playful smirk. "But you wanted it so bad."

"Can't argue there." He raises a curious brow. "Remind me: what was the airtight argument you made that finally got me to cave?"

I pretend to think for a moment. "*Fuck me?*"

"Right." He laughs. "Shockingly effective."

20

JESSE

Ada's fingers trail a lazy path over my chest and stomach. I can't think of any feeling better than holding her like this, with her naked and nestled under my outstretched arm.

Except maybe what we just did.

"Weeks, huh?" she asks.

"What?" I may have caught my breath, but my mind is another story.

"You'd been imagining this for weeks?" Ada turns to me with obvious amusement.

"Ever since you tried to take me out with those dish trays." I brush a few strands of turquoise hair from her forehead.

She pushes up onto an elbow, lips parted in surprise. "Shut up. You mean that first night?"

"Pretty much." I give her a guilty smile.

"Jesus, your cock's quick to attention," she teases, slipping her hand back down my stomach.

I grab her wrist and shake my head as I shift to face her. "You're gonna have to give me more than five minutes."

She rolls her eyes with a smirk. "Ugh. Men."

I lean in to kiss her and palm her breast, squeezing it softly. "I knew I shouldn't think about you like that," I say, my thumb circling her nipple as it hardens under my touch, "but I couldn't stop." I slide an arm over her waist, tugging her in close, and murmur into her hair, "You've been making me crazy ever since."

"I hate to say it, but... same."

My jaw drops.

No fucking way.

"Even with your homeless Viking vibe," she says with a chuckle, "you were hot."

Gobsmacked, I pull back and search her face. "You're fucking with me. You gave me *so* much shit for looking like that!"

"Well, I couldn't fucking *tell you*, could I?" She shoves my chest. "Like, oh, hey, Jesse, I'm into that *Castaway* thing you've got going. Wanna fuck? Wilson can watch." She flutters her lashes. "Had to throw you off the scent."

I laugh, softly tracing my fingers up and down her spine, and shake my head in disbelief. "Wow. You keeping a list of insults to work through, or what?"

"I'm not revealing anything."

"Says the naked woman in my bed."

She smiles softly, grazing her fingers over my shoulder. "Jess?"

"Yeah?"

She presses a kiss to my chest, then rests her chin there, peering up at me. "Why didn't we see this?"

"See what?" I ask.

"Back in high school. Why didn't we ever... hook up?"

"I dunno," I say with a frown.

Probably because I was following Naomi around, begging for scraps.

"Did you ever think about it? Back then?" She gives me a skeptical look.

"No," I say, then immediately come clean. "Well, once."

She perks up, amusement tugging at the corner of her lips. "Once? When?"

I take a slow breath. "You remember that winter we got a massive dump of snow and went sledding at Cherry Park?"

"Oh, God. Yes." She props herself up, resting her chin on her hand. "When I ended up in the duck pond? I still have nightmares."

Ada's crazy carpet had veered badly off-course, cutting a diagonal path down the slick snow. She'd hit a rock and flown ass over teakettle into the filthy, freezing water.

I'd never run so fast in my life.

"When I pulled you out, your teeth were chattering so hard you couldn't even call Marcus an asshole. But you fucking *tried.*"

She laughs. "He deserved it. Still salty he almost assassinated me."

Though his aim hadn't been intentional, his spinning push was what started it all.

The guys had laughed about it for weeks. The phrase "*to infinity and the pond!*" even made it into the yearbook that year.

Ada's brow furrows. "Wait, so, are you saying it was somehow appealing that I was frozen and covered in bog water and duck shit?"

"Uh, no," I say with a smile. "It wasn't then. Shockingly, duck shit doesn't do it for me."

"So when was it?"

"I took you to my house, remember? So you could shower and, y'know, *not die* of hypothermia?" It had been the closest place she could warm up. "I had to lend you some sweats 'cause your clothes were soaking wet and reeked of pond scum."

I'd run a load of laundry for her, feeling weirdly nervous about the idea of her naked in my bathroom.

"Did you? I barely remember that."

I nod. "Anyway, when you came out of the bathroom wearing my clothes, I had this moment where I... Ah, fuck, I dunno. I thought you were cute."

"Cute?"

"Hot. Whatever. I was seventeen and a girl was wearing my clothes. It was a very confusing time." I laugh and squeeze her arm.

It had seemed almost intimate—like something a girlfriend would do.

I kiss Ada's cheek and smile again at the memory.

"You never told me that." Her voice is soft.

"Never told *anyone* that." I pause, tracing my fingers down her arm. "I knew there was no way. You were going out with that dude from across town—"

"Levi?"

"Yeah, and I was distracted by Naomi. I pretty much just stuffed it and moved on. Plus, Marcus would've shit a brick, so..."

Worry plays on her features at the mention of her brother. "Right."

I roll onto my back and run a hand down my face.

She tucks herself tighter under my arm and we lay there for a minute, my thumb brushing up and down her side, her fingers slipping from my chest to my stomach.

Unable to quash the guilt already brewing, I break the silence. "We can't... I mean, should we tell him? We shouldn't, right?"

"Fuck, no, we shouldn't tell him!" she blurts out, twisting to face me. "I don't want my brother, of all people, picturing us boning. Gross!"

"Boning, huh?" I shake my head. "Classy."

She makes a *tsk* sound. "You know what I mean."

"Okay. You're probably right." I nod. "I guess it would only make things weird."

"Well, I don't know about you, but I'm not in the habit of

telling my sibling who I'm casually fucking, anyway. It's none of his business. It's not like you and I are... we're not in a *relationship*."

Her words land heavily on my chest.

Interesting.

A relationship isn't an option, here, I remind myself. Not that I even want one.

"Right," I make myself say, nodding again.

"Plus, he warned me not to get involved with you. Can't give him the satisfaction of being right. You know how smug he can be."

"Wait, he warned you about me?"

She shrugs. "Not in those words, but yeah. Before you moved in. He was worried about me getting into another long-distance thing—you know what?" She cuts herself off. "It really doesn't matter. He was outta line."

I frown to myself. "You know, he actually talked to me about *you* too."

"What the fuck?"

"Yeah, I guess he thought it could end up like Naomi all over again. And he didn't want things to get weird for him, which... y'know... fair."

Ada's eyebrows lift. "Marcus is a fucking busybody."

"Hey," I say, my tone a soft warning. "Watch what you say about my best friend."

She scoffs.

"I'm sure he was just trying to look out for us. Both of us."

"Well, he doesn't need to worry. You're leaving at the end of the summer, anyway. It's not like we're a couple about to parade around in front of him holding hands or some shit."

She's right. Of course she's right.

"Totally," I say. I give my head a shake, trying to push away the guilt—or any more thoughts of Marcus, for that matter. He's the last person I want to be thinking about when his sister is naked in my bed. Whatever happens in the coming weeks, I want to enjoy this moment. I brush my thumb over Ada's cheek.

She seems thoughtful and slightly worried, like, despite her confident bluster, the same guilty thoughts are floating through her mind.

I try to keep things light. "Well, I guess we're gonna have to keep this buttoned up real tight." I trail my hand down her stomach and slip my fingers between her legs. "Tighter than..."

She grabs my wrist, eyes flying wide as she rounds on me. "Don't you dare make a joke about my vagina, Jesse Bailey!"

"Oh, come on, it's a *really* good one." I'm trying—and failing—to keep a straight face, lips quivering as a grin takes over.

She squints. "My vagina or the joke?"

"What joke?" I nearly snort-laugh.

"Asshole!" Ada shoves me in the shoulder.

"Sorry, couldn't help myself. C'mere." I gently grab her jaw and pull her to me for a kiss. She resists only briefly, her indignation melting as she leans closer.

"Okay, so, we just... don't tell him. I mean," she rakes her fingers through her hair and looks away, as if she's making a point of playing it cool, "it's just sex, right?"

I pause a moment, my playful expression faltering.

Of course it's only sex. It can't be more.

"Yeah. Just sex."

Is that really all this is? My attraction to Ada is undeniable—Jesus, *especially* after what we just did. But physical is all we can be. The complication of our shared reality rises to the surface again, reminding me there's no future between us, and I shove it down. I can't think about that shit right now.

"So, we can just..." she slides a hand over my chest, shrugging, "fuck in private and act normal the rest of the time."

"Mmm," I hum. "Well, you can bet your ass I'm gonna wanna

do *this* again," I add, drinking in her naked body. I grin and pull her tight against me, then kiss her.

"Yes, please." She chuckles against my lips.

Suddenly restless, I roll out of bed and reach for the towel hanging on my closet door. I throw it over my shoulder and clear my throat. "Think I'm gonna go take a shower."

Ada pushes up on both elbows. "Is that your half-assed way of saying you want company?"

I smile, drinking in her gorgeous curves. I rub the back of my neck as I meet her gaze, salacious thoughts running through my mind. "I dunno. Shower stall's pretty small. We'd probably have to get *really close* in there."

She puts on a dramatic pout and stands, walking over to me. Splaying her fingers over my chest, she slowly slides both hands up around my neck. "Mmm, I think we'll make it fit."

The feeling of her soft tits against my chest has my dick nudging into her stomach, ready for round two. Humming a low, almost involuntary sound, I slip my hands around her hips and slap her ass. When delight dances in her eyes, I let out a low, satisfied growl and pull her to the bathroom.

21

ADA

Jesse's reading on the couch, one arm slung behind his head in the kind of pose that makes it look like there's an expiration date on the T-shirt he's wearing.

I bite the inside of my cheek as I pad over to him, drawn in by the need to touch him. Coming up behind him, I run my fingers over the soft skin on the inside of his upper arm and press a kiss to the top of his head. "Whatcha reading?"

"Hey," he replies. Without losing his place, he turns the paperback to show me the cover.

It doesn't tell me much other than the title—*Paper Shadows*—but the vibe is dark and moody.

"Borrowed it from Marcus," he says. "Started reading it at their place when I couldn't sleep. Trash couch, right?" He glances up at me with a smirk, then back down at the book. "It's good. Kind of intense and suspenseful."

I come around the couch and he shifts so I can sit beside him. Dropping an arm around me, he explains the main character is a detective, Max, who's haunted by the unsolved murder of his former partner.

"So, there's this case where someone's leaving cryptic messages at crime scenes and he's working with this journalist, Liza, to figure it out."

"That does sound good."

"You wanna read it? You can have it when I'm done."

"Nah. I'm not a big reader," I say, scrunching my nose. Reading has always been so effortful; I tend to conserve that energy for something really worth it. "I'd probably like the movie, though."

Jesse scoffs. "But the movies are never as good as the books. They never do the story justice."

I shake my head. "Such a snob."

"I'm not a snob! It's just not the same." He quirks an eyebrow. "Look, what if I read it *to* you?"

"Like a bedtime story?" I give him a blank stare.

"*No*, like an *audiobook*."

"Are you gonna start at the beginning? Or just—"

"Just the bit I'm reading now. Like a teaser. You got the gist, right?"

"Yeah, I think so."

An almost boyish delight flashes in his eyes. "Okay, buckle up."

"Hold on a sec," I say. I jump up to get my sketchbook and pencils and settle onto the floor to draw. At Jesse's curious expression, I explain, "It helps me concentrate if I have something to do with my hands."

"Why are you sitting so far away?"

I throw him a knowing glance. "That's *also* to help me concentrate."

He chuckles, sitting forward with his elbows on his knees, and the ropey muscles of his forearms shift as he adjusts his grip on the book.

Damn. The floor was the right choice.

As he reads, I doodle without thinking too much, sketching out the rough outline of a buttercup. I've been on a flower kick since making that card for Jesse's mom weeks ago, and I guess those *Princess Bride* jokes have wormed themselves into my brain.

Jesse's deep voice is soothing, and the story quickly draws me in. At some point, I drift back to the couch, settling my head on his thigh and propping my sketchbook on my raised knees.

He plays absently with my hair as he continues to read.

"Max flipped the light switch. Nothing. The power to the building had been cut.

'I think he's gone,' Liza whispered. Then, when Max's hand found hers in the darkness, she gasped. 'What are you doing?'"

The rhythmic touch of Jesse's fingers lulls me into a sleepy trance. I set down my sketchbook and close my eyes. His hand shifts, brushing soft strokes over my neck with his thumb.

"Adrenaline still coursing through his veins from the chase, Max didn't think twice. He pulled her against—" He stops. "Wait a sec..."

I open my eyes and sit up, twisting around to face him. "What? Why'd you stop?"

He quickly scans the open pages and a flush spreads over his neck. He glances at me, then turns back to the book.

I laugh. "Jesse!"

He clears his throat. "I just... I didn't realize it was *that* kind of book."

"What kind of book?" I ask with a smirk. I know exactly what kind of book. I fake an affected gasp. "Are you... embarrassed? Honestly, after everything we did last night? Everything you said to me?"

"No!" he insists.

"But you're blushing."

His face falls. "I'm *not* blushing."

"Then keep reading," I challenge.

He gives me a glare, then clears his throat again before continuing.

"He pulled her against his chest, running his hands over the silky fabric of her dress. The dip of her waist fit his hands like her body was made for him."

As he reads, a soft, almost sheepish smile tugs at the corner of his mouth.

"Their kiss was rough. Messy. All-consuming in a way Max hadn't felt for years.

'Well, in that case...' Liza teased. Sliding her fingers over his tie, she guided him in front of the leather sofa and shoved him down. As she prowled over him to straddle his lap, her dress rode up, her pale thighs glowing softly in the moonlight."

I bite my lip and, setting my sketchbook and pencils on the coffee table, swing one leg over Jesse's lap so I'm straddling him.

He lowers the book and makes a low, humming sound. "Whatcha doing?"

"Shh," I whisper, leaning in close. "Keep reading."

He slips his free hand up under the back of my tank top and traces my spine with his fingertips, his gaze falling between my legs. "But this is very... distracting."

"I know you can do it," I purr.

He grunts and drags his attention back to the book, holding it out to one side.

"Liza traced his collarbone through his shirt, her soft lips on his neck sending all his blood rushing south."

Jesse's attention wanders to me again as I trail fingers over the ridge of his collarbone and feather soft kisses on his neck.

"You're making it *very* challenging to keep reading, Ada," he says, then moans softly when I take his earlobe between my teeth.

"Mmm," I hum against his cheek, "but I wanna know what happens between Max and Liza. Don't stop."

Jesse grabs my jaw with a warning growl. "Then behave."

"I promise nothing," I whisper, my hands skimming down his chest.

"Such a brat." He adjusts himself in his pants and continues.

"Max knew he could never have her, not really, but he didn't care. He'd take what he could get. His lips collided with hers in a searing kiss."

I kiss Jesse hard, then pause to let him continue.

"Liza tugged at his belt, the clink of the buckle and their panting breaths the only sounds breaking the silence."

I start to unbutton his jeans.

"Ada... *fuck,*" he mumbles. "I can't keep reading if you—"

"Keep going," I whisper as I trail kisses over his cheek and nip at his earlobe.

He exhales. *"When she freed him from his pants, his throbbing manhood—"*

I snort against his neck and pull back. "Sorry," I say, holding a fist to my mouth, "his throbbing *what now?"*

Jesse inspects the book cover again and shakes his head. "Fuck. Is this what Marcus likes to read about? Some dude's *throbbing manhood?"*

"I don't even wanna know. Read more, though," I say with a suppressed laugh. I gesture for him to continue. "Maybe it'll redeem itself."

He lets out a long sigh, then wrenches his eyes back to the page.

"When she freed him from his pants, his... I'm gonna say dick... sprang free, eager for her touch. Max groaned when Liza wrapped her fist around his length and..."

I pull down the waistband of his underwear and wrap my fingers around Jesse's stiff shaft.

"Fuck, Ada..."

I rub the head of his cock, watching the furrow in his brow deepen with concentration. With obvious effort, he keeps reading.

"... and he ss-sslid both hands up her so-ooft thighs,"—he's losing this battle now—*"lifting her dress hi-higher."*

Grumbling a warning, he slides his free hand up my leg, his thumb dipping into a tear near the pocket of my jean shorts.

It almost tickles and my breath skitters.

Okay. Two can play this game.

Impressively, he continues reading as I slowly stroke him.

*"Fi-iinding the triangle of lace between them, he-eee yanked it to the side and slipped his fingers through her ss-slick—*Oh, fuck, I can't do this anymore," he says, tossing the book onto the couch and crashing his mouth into mine.

His hands plunge into my hair, angling my head as his tongue searches my mouth, licking and tasting me like he's been starving.

"But what happens with his *throbbing manhood?*" I tease, my voice muffled against his lips.

"*Shut up, Ada,*" he bites out, reaching between my legs and under the inseam of my shorts. His fingers tease my clit through my soaked panties.

I moan, softly at first, then louder when he draws the fabric aside to slip a fingertip against my bare center. A pulse of heat washes over me, and when I tighten my grip, he growls into my mouth.

God. Fucking. Damn. Those sounds he makes...

He drags a finger through my wetness and circles it over my clit, increasing the pressure until my thighs are twitching. Through my tank top and bra, his lips and teeth tease the tight peaks of my nipples through the fabric. He slides his finger inside me, pulsing and pushing as I rock my hips.

The bunched fabric of my panties and jean shorts rub against my clit and I hold onto the back of his neck with one hand, pumping his cock faster with the other as I drift toward the edges of my sanity.

"Ada, fuck..." he whispers between my breasts. "Slow down or

I'm gonna come." Gently, he guides my hand away, placing it on the back of the couch. He pauses, looking like he's trying to collect himself.

"You okay?" I ask.

"Barely," he says, smiling. "But let me take care of you first. Because after I make you come..."—he claims my lips in a searing kiss—"I wanna fuck this pretty mouth."

I almost jolt when he pushes another finger inside me, curling and pumping them with aching perfection. "Holy shit," I say, my voice tight, forehead pressed into his. "Right there. Harder."

"Yes, ma'am," he purrs against my cheek, increasing the pressure.

When he yanks down my tank top and bra with his free hand and sucks on my nipple, it's more than I can bear. My entire body tenses and I dig my nails into his shoulders, feeling like I'm holding on for dear life as the tension builds. My climax slams into me like a freight train as Jesse's fingers speed up, drawing it out and carrying me through the rolling waves of blissful release.

My head is on his shoulder when it finally slows and he chuckles into my hair.

"God, I love the way you feel coming on my hand," he whispers.

"Well," I say, "can't say an audiobook has ever done *that* for me."

The rumble of his laughter wraps around me like a familiar embrace—soothing and close and... *safe.*

I sigh, sated and sleepy, and sit up as he slips his fingers out, then watch with rekindled fire burning inside me as he licks them clean with a low hum of pleasure.

If I thought I was momentarily satisfied after that orgasm, I was wrong; I already feel like I could eat him alive. Climbing off his lap, I move to kneel at his feet.

"Wait," he says as he lifts my chin with a finger. "Go put on that red lipstick you have."

"What?" I smile in confusion. "Really? You want me to—"

"Yeah, I want you to." He leans forward, drawing me into a rough kiss. His voice is low, almost a growl when our lips part. "I want that color ringed around the base of my cock when we're done."

Jesus Christ.

It's a wonder I can stumble to the bathroom to do it.

When I return to the living room and kneel between his legs, Jesse lifts his hips enough for me to tug his jeans out of the way. Gently, almost reverently, he gathers my hair away from my face. "God, you're gorgeous."

When I try to move, his fingers tense.

"Mmm, not yet," he says, his voice thick as he shifts his grip on my hair so he's holding it in one hand.

"But I want it." A twitch of confusion touches my brow.

"I know," he whispers.

"Please," I breathe, hating how needy I sound. I twine my fingers around his dick and pump in a slow rhythm, smiling when he makes a ragged, desperate sound.

With his free hand, he grips my chin between his thumb and forefinger. "Stick out your tongue."

"What?" I ask, confused by the wave of heat that ignites between my legs.

"Stick out your tongue," he repeats. "Show me how much you want it."

I swallow.

"And if you're good... I'll give you what you want."

Oh, God.

Giving into whatever hot magic this is, I open my mouth, obedient in a way I refuse to think too deeply about. And, when he murmurs his approval and spits into his hand, fisting his rock-hard cock just out of reach, I let out a soft whimper. My desperation to taste him is almost embarrassing, and the slick, wet sound of him touching himself only intensifies my desire. I squeeze my thighs together, chasing relief, and gently brush my fingertips over his balls. I know he can see me squirming for it, and the look on his face tells me he's holding me off just to wind me up tighter.

Well, it's fucking working.

Lowering me slowly, he slides the tip over my tongue, the movement torturously controlled. He groans as he pushes between my lips. "Oh, fuck, Ada."

Greedy and desperate, I suck his thick shaft and moan when the salty taste of him hits my tongue. Where my lips end, I follow with my fist, squeezing and twisting with each stroke. I hold his gaze as I shift my position and run the flat of my tongue up his length, sucking and flicking it against the tip.

"Jesus, Ada, your mouth... *fuck*... it's perfect." He grips my hair with both hands again and guides me up and down, gently fucking my face. "That feels so fucking good. Just like that."

I can only whimper my response.

He pushes in farther, filling my throat until tears threaten at the corners of my eyes. "Shit. That okay?" he asks, backing off slightly.

I manage a small nod and continue, my cheeks hollowing.

"Fuuuuck, Ada... I love watching you like this... taking me so fucking deep." Then, he pulls me off him. "C'mere." Cupping my jaw, he curls forward and kisses my swollen lips, lightly at first, then growing wilder, twisting his tongue against mine. The feeling of his soft mouth after the firm press of his cock is delicious, and a fresh ache hums in my core.

I smile when he presses his forehead against mine. "Why'd you stop me? I wasn't done," I tease gently to cover up my confusion, softly stroking him again.

He breathes a quiet laugh. "I just... needed to kiss you."

"Yeah?" I arch a brow, wiping the smudge of red from his lips.

"Yeah," he whispers, then swallows. "And I need to know... When I come..."—he pauses, grunting softly when I tighten my grip—"where do you want it?"

I exhale hard.

"Do you want it..."—he pauses as he traces a finger between my breasts—"here?" Slowly, he slides his finger lower, moving it down my stomach. "Here?" Reaching between my legs, he presses against my clit through my shorts. "Here? Or maybe..."—he pauses, reaching back up to push two fingers between my lips—"here?"

I suck them with a needy moan.

"Oh, my fucking God, Ada," he almost groans. "You gonna let me come in your mouth?"

I nod quickly when he slips his fingers out. "Yes. Fuck. *Please.*"

The moment he leans back, I dive down again, unable to get enough.

"Holy fuck..." he whispers when I drag my nails lightly over his balls, and his fingers tangle into my hair once again. When his control wavers and he pulls me down hard, I almost choke.

"God, look what you're letting me do to you," he says. "Such a good girl."

His words cut through the addled haze and my cheeks flush with indignation. I snap my gaze up, self-consciousness prickling across my chest, but I can't help but notice a traitorous pulsing between my legs.

Oh, fuck. Why did I like it when he said that?

Jesse seems to notice, because his hands cradle my face. "Did you like that?"

I pull back slightly, not sure how to respond.

"When I was filling your throat with my cock and called you a good girl for taking it?"

I moan around him, my vision blurring.

Oh, God. What in the actual fucking fuckery is happening to me right now?

"Hey. Eyes on me."

I peer up at him again.

"Did it make you wet, Ada?"

Hating myself, I nod.

"Good." His serious expression softens. "Because I love watching you like this: my cock between your gorgeous red lips, knowing your greedy little cunt is soaking those panties."

With a muffled whine, I take him deeper again.

"That's my good fucking girl," he rumbles.

His words urge me on and my strokes become frenzied—tighter, faster. I'm not sure how much more I can take. Tears stream down my burning cheeks, and I have to fight to relax my throat.

His thighs tense under me and he holds his breath, but I don't stop—I speed up, licking and sucking him with a maddening hunger that feels dangerous. Untethered.

Jesse's groan is everything as his release explodes. I swallow it all down, pumping more shallowly as he slows and starts to twitch. When he pulls me up, he wipes the tears from my cheeks and the smeared lipstick from around my mouth.

I climb into his lap once again, burying my head in his neck.

"Jesus, that was..." He chuckles as his arms circle my waist. "You okay?" he asks, holding me as our breathing slowly returns to normal.

"Yeah," I whisper, kissing his neck.

"Fuck, that was amazing." He smooths the hair back from my forehead. "You're amazing."

"Mmm." I practically purr as I nuzzle against his hand. "I love when you do that."

"You'll have to specify which of my many moves you're referring to," he teases.

I grin against his neck and bite it gently. "I meant brushing my hair ba—you know what? Never mind," I say, then snuggle closer, reasonably sure I could fall asleep right here.

"You like when I play with your hair?"

"Play with it, pull it. All the things. Just pet me and I'm happy." I kiss his neck again.

"Okay, noted," he says with an audible smile as he rubs my back. "So, about that *throbbing manhood* thing..."

I sit back. "Jesse, so help me God, I just spent that whole time trying to fight my gag reflex..."

22

JESSE

I think Marcus might actually piss himself laughing. Apparently, the book was Renee's. He hadn't read it and, like me, had no idea it got... *explicit*. Now he's doubled over on the shoreline of Black Bear River, wheezing and barely able to look at me.

"You're really enjoying this, aren't you?" I fold my arms over my chest and shake my head. Facing Marcus for the first time since Ada and I slept together has turned out to be less fraught than I'd anticipated, but it worries me how easily I'm lying to my best friend.

"Oh, shit," he says, wiping tears from his cheeks. "No wonder Renee was jumping my bones so much while she was reading that one." His eyes slip back to mine and another fit of laughter threatens.

"Just thought you were secretly into that kind of thing," I say, smacking him upside the head on my way to help unpack his car.

"What's the author's name?" he calls after me and I flip him off over my shoulder. "Aw, c'mon! Renee's birthday is coming up! Is it a series, or what?"

I meet Renee at the car and help her unload a cooler of beer and sodas for our afternoon at the river.

"I heard my name," she says as she pulls a few bags of snacks from the back seat. "What were you guys talking about?"

Marcus appears at my side, all too happy to fill her in. "Jess was just telling me about the book he's been reading." He slings an arm over her shoulder and turns his shit-eating grin on me.

Renee's interest clearly piqued, she asks, "Oh, yeah? What book?"

"Let's not set this dumbass off again." I lift my chin at Marcus.

Despite my suggestion to drop it, he fills Renee in.

"Oh, *yeah*, wow!" Renee says. "*Paper Shadows*? That one gets *spicy* in the middle!"

"Yeah, well, I... I didn't realize that when I started reading it." I heft the cooler with a grunt, bracing the weight on my hips, and turn back to the floating dock. I try not to think about what went down after that book got *spicy*.

"You need some help, man?" Marcus calls after me, probably still snickering at my expense.

"I got it." The cooler is fucking heavy but I power through, not wanting to give him the satisfaction. Slowly, I make my way back to where he's set up a few camping chairs and towels.

Marcus and Renee follow, bringing the food and picnic blankets.

Eager to change the topic, I grab a beer from the cooler and pull the tab, taking a sip for courage. I swallow, then ask in the most casual tone I can manage, "When's Ada coming?" I busy myself with shifting one of the chairs toward me and take a seat, keeping my eyes fixed on the mountains across the river to avoid seeming too interested in the answer.

"She said she had plans with Katie and could meet us here after. Like around one thirty," Marcus says. "What, she didn't tell you this morning?"

"Nah, we were, uh,"—I pause and clear my throat, trying not to hate myself as the memories of our morning together flash into my mind—"talking about other stuff. Forgot to ask."

We were talking, alright.

I press my lips together, remembering how Ada had begged me to fuck her hard. How she'd moaned my name when I'd pushed inside her. How I'd had to cover her mouth when she came so Mr. Wozniak wouldn't hear her screaming. How we'd lain in bed afterward and how easy it had felt—how it always feels—to be with her like that.

Guilt coils around my abdomen like a boa constrictor and the heat of the mid-August sun suddenly feels oppressive. I imagine Marcus staring directly into my brain, reading my thoughts and finding out the truth. I try to shove away the paranoia eating at me.

I'm the world's worst best friend. Thanks for the beer; I'm fucking your sister.

"I'm gonna go in." Too antsy to stay put any longer, I stand, then slide my beer into the chair's cup holder. A swim will help me clear my head. This dock is upstream from where we went paddleboarding, and the water's much deeper—and colder—here. I peel off my shirt.

"Jesus. Renee, avert your eyes," Marcus jokes.

"Very funny," I throw over my shoulder before taking a running leap off the dock. Cold hits me like a wall of ice and, when I come up for air, I shout, "Fuck!"

Well, that was a fitting punishment for my genitals.

I tread water and will myself to adjust.

"Did you forget this river is glacier fed?" Marcus asks, settling into one of the camping chairs and cracking open a beer of his own.

"Not exactly," I reply. Clearly, remembering the cold and experiencing it are two very different beasts. "It's just been a while."

Renee peers over the edge of the dock at me. "I don't think I'm going in. I like the heat, anyway. I'll just stay here and paint my nails." She wiggles the fingers of one hand and holds up a little glass bottle of pale pink polish in the other.

"Aw, come on," I say, still treading water and trying my best to stop my teeth from chattering. "You're missing out. It's in-in-invigorating."

I last another minute before I climb back up the ladder, shivering as rivulets of water snake down my chilled skin. I grab my towel and press it into my face, inhaling its clean scent. I'm still toweling my hair when Ada's car pulls up beside her brother's, and I pause. Quickly catching myself, I look away, focusing on maintaining a seriously neutral facial expression. No one has ever been as focused on drying off as I am right now.

I tug my shirt back on and take another sip of beer before slumping into my chair in my still-wet trunks, suddenly finding every piece of lint or stray thread on my clothes very interesting.

"Hey, sis," Marcus calls out to her. "You got the sandwiches?"

"Yeah, but hold onto your impatient ass for a sec," she grumbles. "Lemme put my stuff down."

I risk glancing her way as she slings her purse and beach bag down—and I have to catch my jaw before it hits the dock.

She's wearing a bikini top and the shortest pair of cut-off jean shorts I've ever seen. Two triangles of skin-tight fabric hug her full breasts, and her ass cheeks peek out from her shorts when she turns. A hint of a smile shines in her eyes when she catches me staring.

This woman is trying to kill me. Dead man gawking.

"Aw, fuck, yes!" Marcus exclaims. "You went to the deli?" He peers into the plastic bag Ada set down, clearly oblivious to my reaction to his sister's outfit. "I'm starving."

So am I, all of a sudden.

"Hey, Jess." Her voice is soft when she says my name.

She was moaning it this morning.

Nope. Not the time or the place.

"Hey," I reply with a cautious smile, still struggling to play it cool. I tear my gaze away from her, rubbing my forehead with my fingers. I've seen this woman naked several times now, but this is the first time I haven't been able to touch her when so much of her body has been on display. If I were rating this feeling on Yelp, it would get one star: *do not recommend.*

"Your bikini top is cute!" Renee says to Ada.

"Thanks. It's hot as balls today," she replies with a sigh, sitting down next to Renee on the dock.

I'm busy praying Ada makes no further mention of *balls* when Marcus hands me a sub, and I'm eternally grateful to have something to distract me from ogling his sister. The paper wrapper bears the Riverside Deli logo, and I'm instantly hungrier than a moment ago—this time for actual food. I unwrap it and look up.

She remembered?

"Is this the same one I got last time?" I ask her, careful to keep my focus north of her neck. "After we went shopping?"

"Yeah," she says. "Why, did you want something different?" She holds up the sub Marcus has just handed to her. "'Cause we can trade if you—"

She cuts herself off as I let out a groan of anticipation before taking a massive bite. I might have a small foodgasm as I chew.

Fuck, this sandwich.

She snorts. "Jeez, buy it a drink first."

I chuckle around the bite in my mouth and lift my chin at her with a knowing smile. "Thanks."

"Glad you like it," she says with a small laugh, then watches me for a moment. "But like, seriously, do you two need privacy?"

I flip her off.

She grins and turns to talk to Renee.

I'm almost dozing off in my chair when voices drift to me from down the riverbank, and I crack an eye open. Ada and Renee are walking toward us, each carrying a bag of cotton candy. Ada's laughing at something Renee's just said, and I furrow my brow, letting out a breath—she's almost painfully beautiful. I rub at a dull ache in my chest. While her usual sarcastic snark is as familiar to me as the back of my own hand, those moments she drops the bullshit are precious glimmers of the real Ada.

Catching myself staring, I'm grateful my sunglasses are the mirrored kind. I cut a glance at Marcus to make sure he hasn't noticed me watching his sister, but he looks like he might be asleep. I nudge his foot with the toe of my sandal, and he stirs, lifting his head.

"The girls are back," I tell him.

Stepping onto the dock, Ada throws me the bag.

"Where the hell did you get cotton candy?" I ask, snagging it from midair.

"There was a truck set up down there. A few of them, actually. Cotton candy, mini doughnuts, and popcorn."

"There was this children's festival thing going on," Renee adds. "Down the river a bit."

"I don't think I've had cotton candy since I *was* a kid," I say.

"Well, save me some. I'm going in the water." Standing directly in front of me, Ada peels off her jean shorts, revealing her tiny bikini bottoms.

I can't tear my gaze away.

The hint of amusement on her face tells me she knows exactly what she's doing.

Mirrored sunglasses or not, I quickly realize the situation in my shorts is going to give me away any second, so I force myself to look anywhere else. I shift in my seat, the twist tie on the bag of cotton candy suddenly needing my undivided attention. But even that doesn't last and my eyes drift once more to Ada.

She glances at her brother, her expression turning serious before she turns and pads to the edge of the dock and dives into the water in a graceful arc. She surfaces a moment later, gasping.

"Cold as balls, right?" I smile, pinching off a piece of cotton candy.

Now I'm talking about balls? What's wrong with me?

I stuff blue fluff into my mouth to stop myself from saying anything further.

Apparently having had enough of the water's cold shock, Ada climbs up the ladder, cursing and shivering.

Oh, Christ.

Each step up reveals more of her body, and I go still, the sugar crystals melting in place on my tongue. Her nipples have pebbled into hard peaks and a tiny river of water traces a path over her collarbone before it slips down between her breasts.

As she steps past me to grab her towel, my dick nudges against my swim trunks and I swallow. I try to look away but can't stop my eyes from bouncing right back again. She's fucking shimmering, the sun glittering like diamonds off every droplet of water clinging to her skin.

I imagine warming those nipples by sucking them into my mouth, or running my tongue over the goosebumps pricking her skin.

Patting herself dry, she walks over to me and holds out her hand.

It takes me a beat to realize she's asking for the cotton candy.

"C'mon, fork it over."

Wordlessly, I hold out the bag. She pinches off a piece and

pops it onto her tongue before sucking the melted crystals off her fingers.

And now I'm rock-hard in my swim shorts. *Great.*

"I'm gonna go back in for another round in a minute. Wanna come?"

Desperately.

"Nah, I'm good." I force a casual tone and sit forward, propping my arms on my knees. Now's not exactly a good time to stand. I run a hand down my beard and stare out over the water, trying to control my thoughts.

"Suit yourself." Ada turns in front of me, giving me a view of her ass through her soaked bikini bottoms. "Renee?"

"Nope, I'm not a masochist," Renee intones, digging a magazine out of her bag. "Y'all are crazy."

"Marcus?"

He shakes his head. "Maybe later. I'm too comfy."

Ada drops her towel, heading to the edge of the dock. As she walks away, my gaze drags along behind her, locked on her incredible ass. When she jumps back in, the sound of the splash jolts me back to reality.

Jesus.

I think I might implode if I have to wait much longer to be alone with her.

"I think we did okay," I say, staring at the slope of Ada's neck, wishing I could bite it.

She fishes her keys out at our front door and glances at me over her shoulder. "Yeah, I don't think they... noticed anything."

I hum softly in agreement. "Tell you what I fucking noticed, though," I say, stepping a little closer and dropping my voice low.

"I noticed how badly I wanna fuck you the minute we get inside this door."

Keeping my hands to myself for the drive home had been nearly impossible, and I'd found myself impatiently cursing every red light. It's all I can do now not to grab her ass out here in the open.

"Oh?" She laughs, twisting the key in the lock.

"So, what'd Katie say when you told her?"

Her hand pauses on the door handle and she turns around to face me, one brow raised. "What makes you think I told her?"

With a knowing look, I reach past her to pull the keys out. We both know the best friend code overrides any promise to keep this between us.

Well, except in my case.

She hesitates only a moment longer before coming clean. "Okay, well, let's just say I don't think I've heard a cackle quite that loud before. She was practically feral for the details."

I laugh through a cringe. "You shared details?"

"Oh, yeah." She gives me a sober nod.

I shake my head. "Remind me to avoid eye contact with Katie for the foreseeable future, then."

"Don't worry, I painted a *very* favorable picture of the uh..."— she slides her gaze down my body—"details."

There's a muffled clink of keys as I clench my hands into fists at my sides.

Oh, God, please just open the door.

"Oh, and Jess?" She tilts her head.

"Mmm?" My impatience is getting the better of me and my heart is already racing as I think about all the things I'm going to do to her.

"Before we go in..." She trails off, her voice flirtatious.

She's got my fucking attention. "What?"

"When I changed out of my bathing suit earlier," she breathes, stepping closer. "I *might* have forgotten to put my panties back on."

An involuntary groan escapes my throat. I lean down close, my voice low. "Open the door."

A slow smile spreads across her face before she replaces it with an innocent pout. "So impatient."

"Door. *Now.*"

23

———

ADA

We're barely through the front door when Jesse pins me against the wall, my keys crashing to the floor at our feet. Shoving the door shut with one hand and tangling the other in my hair, he kisses me with the urgency of someone whose self-control has been pushed to its limits, leaving me breathless.

Peeling us away from the wall, I pull us in a clattering stumble through the entryway and Jesse presses his fingers against my clit through my jean shorts.

"God damnit, Ada, I can feel how wet you are."

My knees feel weak; I'm impatient with hunger for this. For *him*. He smells like sunscreen, dust, and sweat, and I'm pretty sure I could get high on the scent of him alone.

"I've been thinking about this all fucking day," I say, nipping at his lower lip. "Don't pretend you haven't been half-hard too."

"Who says it was *half?*" He smirks, then rips my tank top over my head in one swift motion. "That bikini almost did me in."

"Yeah?" I reach behind me, unhooking my bra as he yanks the straps down my arms.

"Why do you think I had to keep my ass parked in that chair instead of swimming with you? Because my dick could have used that fucking ice bath." He tugs my bra free and lets it drop, diving for my mouth once more. His palms cover my aching, tight nipples and he hums with pleasure.

I blindly walk backward toward the kitchen as we stumble along, frantic hands tugging impatiently at each other's clothing. Clumsily pulling his shirt up, I drag my fingertips over his tight stomach muscles, letting out a soft moan. The sound turns to one of surprise when I trip over some shoes I'd left strewn on the floor.

"Watch where you're going," he deadpans as he catches me, my hands bracing against his strong forearms. When I find my balance, he peels his shirt off the rest of the way and pushes me into the kitchen, following so closely our knees knock together. "God, forgetful *and* clumsy."

"Fuck off, Farm Boy," I tease against his smiling lips before gripping his ass in both hands and hauling him into me. His erection against my stomach radiates delicious heat, and I kiss him hard.

When the backs of my thighs bump into the edge of the kitchen table, I stumble once more. I wrap my arms around Jesse's sun-warmed neck, holding on for balance.

His hands work fast, tugging open the fly of my shorts and roughly shoving them down my thighs. He lets loose a throaty, appreciative groan, evidently pleased with my lack of panties. Plunging his tongue into my mouth in a rough kiss, he cups the back of my neck, my head lolling back as my body goes liquid in his arms.

I arch into him, giving myself over, relinquishing control. After hours of not being able to touch each other, the heady feeling of his hands on my skin leaves me practically panting with desire.

Before I can catch my breath, he spins me around and pushes me down, my forearms hitting the table as he tugs my hips back against him. I'm barely aware of him shoving his own shorts out of the way before his warm, hot length is against my ass, sliding down to nudge against my slick opening.

Holy shit.

My hips lift seemingly of their own volition, my almost reflexive response eager and ready to take him. Having him inside me suddenly feels so urgent. But he barely moves.

"Jesse, fuck me now or I'm gonna scream."

"Mmm, tell you what," he rumbles low behind me, pausing to cover the tip of his cock in my wetness, "how 'bout we do both?" He pushes inside me.

I let out a soft sound of pleasure. "Fuck, Jesse!"

"'Cause I've been thinking about your tight little cunt clenching around my dick all... fucking... day." He slides in deeper with each word, burying himself to the hilt.

A cry of relief escapes my lips.

"Fuck, Ada, yes," he rasps.

"Jesse... I need you."

One hand braced on my hip, he reaches the other around in front of me, grasping my breast as his hips buck forward. He lets out a low moan of satisfaction as he buries himself inside me again. "You've got me, Buttercup."

The nickname takes a moment to register but, slowly, confusion cuts through the haze of wet, hot need. "What... what did you just call me?" I sputter.

I swear I hear a low chuckle from behind me, and he pinches my nipple, tugging it lightly. He drives in again, filling me, stretching me, and I can't help but cry out.

Did he just reference The Princess Bride *while fucking me? Again?*

"What, you mean *Buttercup*?" His hips jerk forward again.

I groan, pushing my hips back, utterly unable to maintain my indignation.

A low rumble comes from Jesse's throat. "You called me *Farm Boy*. It's only fair."

"Jesus…" I breathe, managing a rueful shake of my head before sagging into my elbows, overcome by the sensation of him slamming inside me.

"Figured I can't call you *Princess*,"—he thrusts again—"or you'd fucking deck me."

I can practically hear the stupid grin on his face.

"Decking you," I say, grinding into him, "is not off the table." My eyes roll. Sure, it might mostly be from the pounding of his cock, but it's got to be at least ten percent snark, because I'm determined to brush off that cheesy fucking nickname and, more importantly, the way it felt to hear Jesse say the words just before it: "*You've got me.*"

Why did that feel so… good?

"Ada," he bites out, "hold onto the table."

I reach shaking hands across the wooden surface and curl my fingers around the far edge, my blurred gaze landing on the empty chair where Jesse eats his breakfast.

Welp. I'm never gonna be able to eat here again without getting turned on.

"Good girl." The table shifts beneath us with each thrust of his hips. "Fuck, Ada. How do you fit me so perfectly?"

He pushes his fingers into the hair at my nape and grips tight, tilting my head back as he leans down. The planes of his chest mold against the curve of my back, his lips beside my ear.

"You're so fucking sexy like this," he whispers against my cheek before nipping at my earlobe.

I smile as warmth courses through my body.

Releasing my hair, Jesse straightens, fucking me faster. His huge hands knead the flesh of my hips and ass, bracing me in place as he hits the spot inside me that makes me hold my breath.

Oh, fuck. My orgasm is already building and... I squeeze tight, chasing it.

"Mmm," he hums. "I can feel your pussy clenching. You gonna come all over this cock for me?"

Am I? Like this?

"Yes." I barely get the word out as the sensation narrows, building to a peak, urged by Jesse's relentless, slamming cock and the primal sounds coming from his chest. A shimmering, electric aura gathers inside me, pulling ragged gasps into my lungs.

"That's my girl. Just let go."

"I'm gonna..." I trail off, words no longer available. My fingers in a death grip, my elbows dig into the table as my entire body clenches and I flex my hips to meet him.

"Yes, Ada. That's it." He speeds up, unleashing himself. "That's... fucking... it." He bites out the words between his pounding strokes. "C'mon. Give it to me."

I cry out as a flood of euphoria explodes from my core and spreads outward, enveloping my entire body. The tension melts from my muscles and I go almost limp, drowning in the rolling waves of delicious release.

"Fuuuuck!" Jesse's grip tenses on my hips, his groan guttural as he comes hard. His powerful thrusts dig my hip bones into the table's edge but, in this moment, the pleasure is so intense that I couldn't care less about the bite of pain.

When he finally slows, he bends to kiss my back. "Mmm, you're incredible," he murmurs softly between my shoulder blades, his warm lips grazing my damp skin.

"Oh my God," I say, pushing up from the table on limp arms.

He straightens, withdrawing from inside me with a soft grunt.

"I never..." I start, but trail off, apparently unable to formulate coherent speech. I shake my head and stand carefully on liquid legs, pulsing sensation still screaming from between my thighs. In a daze, I turn around. "I've never..."

He pulls up his shorts, smiling as he tucks his still-hard cock behind the waistband.

"C'mere," he says, reaching a hand to my face. With his other hand, he brushes the sweaty hair away from my forehead before drawing me into a deep, slow kiss. He hums a satisfied sound against my lips.

I slide my hands over his muscular ass and squeeze, sending silent thanks to his glutes for their valiant service.

When we break the kiss, I exhale, slipping my hands between us. He presses his forehead against mine, the rise and fall of his chest slowing under my palms. We're sticky with sunscreen, sweat, and sex. It's dirty—and perfect.

"I've never... come like that before," I manage to whisper.

"What, from being fucked?" He tucks my hair behind my ear, the gesture so gentle I feel like purring.

I swallow, letting my gaze slip away from his. "I usually... um..."

Ugh, why am I self-conscious? He's literally just *been inside me.*

He reaches down and, as he drags a finger gently across my sensitive clit, his voice rumbles low beside my ear. "You usually need *that?*"

"Yeah." I inhale sharply, gripping his forearm as he wipes up the cum slipping down my inner thigh and rubs it into my clit, then pushes it back inside me.

"That goes back where it belongs," he rasps.

My jaw drops.

Good fucking Lord. I could go again. *Right now.*

He kisses my cheek, then pulls back with a small smile.

I look down at the floor, pleasure still thrumming through my core.

"Hey," he says as he lifts my face, his expression serious. "Chin up, Buttercup." He barely gets the words out before a grin takes over.

I swat his hand away and jab a finger into his chest. "That nickname is *not* happening. You're *not* calling me that."

He shrugs, still beaming down at me. "We'll see."

"Jesse!" *The nerve of this man.*

He snorts out a suppressed laugh, then shakes his head. "Oh, come on, it's too perfect."

I glare at him.

"Plus, it pisses you off so beautifully." He squints. "Honestly, that pinched nose and angry little pout,"—he pulls my lower lip down with his thumb—"just makes me want to fuck that look right off your face." He leans in close, trying to kiss me.

I shove his chest. "Shut the fuck up and get in the shower." I try to scowl but amusement creeps over my features.

Damn it.

"There you go being bossy again," he says with a cocky smirk, then turns to walk to the bathroom. He pauses, reaching a hand back for me. "C'mon. Let me clean up that mess I made."

"Wow, I guess chivalry isn't dead," I deadpan.

When I don't move to follow him, he sighs and walks back to me. Before I can react, he picks me up and tosses me over his shoulder.

"Jesse, what the fuck!" I shout, pushing against him. "I can *walk.*"

His grip tightens on my legs and he slaps my bare ass cheek, a low grunt escaping his throat. "Can you? Still? Well, then, I haven't done my job properly *at all.*" He walks us into the bathroom and sets me down beside the shower. "Let's see if we can rectify that," he adds with a half smile, then reaches in to turn on the water.

"I still haven't ruled it out, you know," I say dryly, trying to fight the arousal already building inside me at the promise of another mind-blowing orgasm.

"Ruled what out?" He tilts his head in confusion before stepping out of his shorts.

I can't help but rake my gaze down his naked body. With effort, I lift my eyes again, staring him down as I step into the shower. "Decking you."

WITH WET HAIR AND WARM, flushed skin, I step out of my room in a clean T-shirt and shorts.

Jesse's in the kitchen, his hair still damp from our shower, looking vaguely distracted with his phone in one hand and a carrot in the other. When he sees me, he taps a couple times on the screen and drops his phone onto the counter beside him, then returns to preparing dinner.

"I just texted you a thing," he says, sliding the blade of the knife under the chopped vegetables on the cutting board and tipping them into a nearby bowl.

Barefoot, I pad over behind him and slide my arms around his waist. "Yeah?" I murmur into his back. "My phone's in my room. Should I go—"

"Nah, just look at it whenever." He sets the knife down and wipes his hands on a tea towel before turning around to face me.

"Okay." I rise on tiptoe to kiss him. When I pull back, my eyes fall to his neck and a memory swims back to me. "You know that day I cut your hair?"

The corner of his mouth lifts in a lopsided grin as he rubs soft strokes up and down my arms. "Hard to forget."

"Well... I had this thought about biting you right here." I lift up again and kiss the spot in question.

Jesse makes an intrigued sound. "Little vampire fantasy?"

"Mm-hmm." I nip gently at his neck.

"You'd make a cute vampire." He slips his hands over my ass and lifts me up, wrapping my legs around his waist.

I scoff as he carries me into the living room. "If by cute you mean *terrifying!*"

"Sure. Terrifying." He pauses. "Terrifyingly adorable!" He throws me over the back of the couch and onto the cushions, scrambling after me.

I shriek with laughter, kicking my legs. "Take it back, you dick!"

He wrestles his way over me on his knees, snagging my flailing hands and pinning them above my head.

"I'm horrifying! A monster! Pure evil!" I cackle, wiggling to get free. "Admit it!" I jut out my chin in defiance.

"Never," he says, his voice calm enough to get my attention.

I go still, holding his gaze.

His smile slowly fades, and the way he's looking at me has anticipation thrumming through my body.

There's a loud knock on our front door, and we both turn toward the entranceway, then back to each other. My brow knits together.

Who the fuck is that?

A mixture of confusion and concern on Jesse's face replaces the heat from moments before, and he releases my hands, pushing to stand. He straightens his T-shirt and runs a hand through his hair a few times, making an effort to tidy it before heading to the door.

I sit up, tugging my T-shirt down where it's ridden up. I run my fingers through my own damp hair, smoothing it down.

Dread pulls heavy in my stomach when Marcus' voice drifts in from around the corner.

What is he doing here? Why didn't he text?

My head snaps around the room, checking for evidence that could incriminate us, but I see nothing.

Except we both have wet hair.

Shit. Wet hair at the same time isn't a dead giveaway. Or is it? Shit. Shit, shit, shit.

No, it's plausible we took turns in the shower. We would have both wanted to wash off the sunscreen...

Marcus' voice gets louder. He's coming in. Quickly, I force my face to appear casual, despite the way my chest feels like the inside of a pinball machine.

Jesse comes in first, his expression carefully neutral, followed closely by Marcus. Jesse holds up a pair of sunglasses in explanation.

"Hey," I say to my brother.

"Hey," Marcus replies. "Your *roomie* here left his sunglasses with our shit, so I thought I'd swing by and drop 'em off."

"Why didn't you just give them back some other time?" I ask, trying not to sound defensive.

He shrugs. "We were driving right past. Figured I'd pop by."

"Thanks, man." Jesse places the sunglasses on the kitchen counter and clears his throat.

"But, while I'm here," Marcus says, turning to me, "we were gonna head to Seattle tomorrow. Take Jess to visit Claire and do some other stuff. You working? You can tag along, if you want. Figured you might want to hit up that art store you never shut up about."

"Uh, yeah. I have the day off, actually." I rub at my arms and glance Jesse's way, but he's not looking at me. I give Marcus what I hope is a relaxed smile.

"Cool. I'll tell Renee. She's making plans to go to a bunch of places. Shopping probably, if you wanna join."

Shopping in the big city? No, thank you. I'd rather find a weird, potentially haunted art gallery to hide in.

"Will there be an official itinerary?" I ask in a deadpan tone. "Will it be laminated?"

Marcus rolls his eyes and turns to leave.

"Color-coded at least?" I call after him.

"Never mind, you're uninvited!" he calls back, throwing me the finger over his shoulder as he disappears down the hall.

I smirk to myself, knowing he doesn't mean that. I try not to rag on Renee, but we're such different people that sometimes I can't help but point it out.

When the door closes, Jesse runs his hands over his face.

I watch him for a moment. "I think it was fine," I say, trying to reassure him. "Like, I don't think he…"

"Yeah," he says, frowning. He turns toward the sink and flicks on the faucet.

Shit.

I push up from the couch and head to my room—the moment between me and Jesse thoroughly ruined. When I check my phone, the text Jesse mentioned is just a long, cryptic link. I glance up to where he's still standing in the kitchen, and then back down at my phone. I tap on it. The website for the Puget Sound School of Art loads, and my stomach sinks.

24

JESSE

The Seattle trip has already gone sideways and we haven't even left yet. Marcus texted this morning that he and Renee have food poisoning and, when I tell Ada the news, she looks concerned.

"Damn. Hope they're okay," she says, then deflates a bit. "And I was counting on getting to that art supply store too. Shit."

"We can still go. Just you and me. If you don't mind stopping in to see Claire."

She tilts her head. "Yeah, I guess I could drive."

"Actually," I say, showing her the website for the rental place on my phone. "I was kinda thinking about riding into the city." I'd been toying with the idea of renting a motorbike sometime this summer. It's been years since I sold my bike and I miss it; this trip with Marcus falling through is the perfect excuse for a ride.

"Since when do you ride a motorcycle?" She picks up her cereal bowl and leans back against the kitchen counter with amused skepticism.

"I got into dirt biking in Australia. Got my license there and had a bike for a few years."

"Uh, okay," she says, eyeing me. "Putting a pin in that whole" —she pauses and gestures vaguely at my face—"*revelation*... You want me to ride on the back of your motorcycle?"

I laugh. "Yes! What's the big deal?"

"Where would I even get a helmet and gear and stuff?" She finishes the last of her cereal and sets her bowl beside the sink.

"The rental place has all that."

She squints at me, clearly unconvinced. "Don't you need a special class of license or something?"

I wave off her concern. "Got an international one for Thailand. It's valid here." I step toward her and slip my hands over her waist, pulling her close. "Come on. It'll be fun." Dropping my voice low, I add, "I kinda like the idea of you wrapped around me on the bike."

"Mmm," she hums. "Alright. Sold."

"Yeah? You wanna be my backpack?" With a playful growl, I scoop her up into a hug, and she wraps her legs around my waist with a smile. I kiss her and set her down on the kitchen counter. When our lips part, she tucks her hands under the hem of my T-shirt and slides them over my lower back.

"Whatcha thinking about?" I ask, noticing the far-off look on her face.

She snaps back to meet my gaze with a smirk. "Just picturing you on a motorcycle."

"Yeah?" I raise an eyebrow.

She smiles and bites her lip. "I don't hate it."

I run my hands up over her thighs and kiss her again. "Then we should get going. So you can see the real thing. Y'know... for science."

"I love science," she says, tracing her fingers around my waistband.

"So we should... get to the... rental... place." I gesture vaguely over my shoulder, sucking in a breath as her fingers continue their path over my hips and stomach.

"Probably should." She grins back at me, then turns to glance at the clock on the stove. "How much time do we have?"

Following her gaze, I dig my fingers into her thighs and force myself to step back. "Not enough for whatever you're scheming."

"Oh? Well, then, too bad you'll never find out what I was scheming." She hops down off the counter.

I slap her ass as she walks past. "You're gonna be fucking adorable in that helmet."

"I think the word you're looking for is *badass*."

THE RIDE into the city is over too quickly. Oppressive August heat be damned, I can't get enough of Ada pressed against my back. The way her fingers brush small strokes against my stomach while we sail down the highway has my dick half-hard and my chest feeling open in a way I haven't felt in months. It's intimate —both hot and sweet—and I don't want her to stop. And when she hugs me tighter... *Fuck.* The press of her fingers lights me up. I reach down to squeeze her hand, the action saying everything I can barely admit to myself, let alone say out loud.

As the open highway gives way to busier city streets, I pull up at a red light and reach back, tracing slow strokes over Ada's calf. I've been batting around this idea in my head the entire ride, but... *fuck it*; I twist around to face her. Raising my voice so she can hear me through the helmet and the din of traffic around us, I call out, "There's somewhere I want to take you before Claire's."

"Where?" she calls back.

"It's a surprise. You trust me?"

She nods.

I turn back around, smiling to myself as I release the clutch and hit the throttle when the light turns green. After a few blocks, I hang a left and cruise along Rainier Drive, catching our reflection jumping across shop windows out of the corner of my eye. As we round a cluster of office buildings on the outskirts of downtown Seattle, an oasis of green parkland comes into view and I pull off the main road. We follow the winding driveway through the trees and gardens and eventually end up in front of a historic stone building. I park the bike, tugging off my helmet. When I feel Ada climb off behind me, I follow suit, running my free hand through my sweat-damp hair.

"Fuck, it feels good to take that off." Ada balances her helmet on the seat of the bike before dragging her fingers through her own hair. She looks up at the building beside us, then backs up to get a better view, blinking in the dappled sunshine filtering through the trees. "What is this place?"

"The Puget Sound School of Art," I say with a cautious smile, and join her, admiring the English ivy creeping up the face of the stone. This place must be at least a hundred years old. I have to suppress the urge to slip my arm around Ada's waist and press a kiss to her temple, reminding myself we're in public.

She doesn't say anything.

I turn to her. "Thought you might like to come see it in person. You know, check out your options."

She still doesn't speak, keeping her gaze trained on the building. Or maybe through it. She has this glazed look to her—like she's somewhere else right now.

"Ada?" A nervous churning stirs my stomach. "Listen, I know you've been reluctant about college, and I get why."

She finally cuts her eyes to mine. "Do you?"

Her sharp tone puts me on my back foot. "I just wanted you to see there are programs out there that are still viable options. You don't need to write off school entirely. Did you even look at that link I sent you?" I'd thought the hands-on program here would work for her—would work *with* her brain, not against it.

"Why would I?" she asks, frustration simmering in her expression. "I already made up my mind about school, Jess."

"Come on, can you just hear me out on this one?"

She balks, taking a step back. "No!"

"Just no?"

She huffs out a derisive laugh. "Why can't anyone fucking *listen* to me when I say I don't want this? That school isn't my thing? God, you're as bad as my parents with this shit." She walks around me, heading back to the bike.

I spin around, arms out at my sides. "Oh, come on. Don't lump me in with them." The comparison stings a bit, but my disappointment stems more from realizing it's not an unfair one. "And you don't have to do anything you don't wanna do. I just thought—"

"I already tried that art program in London," she says, cutting me off. "You know what that got me? A bunch of tension headaches and an ex-boyfriend."

Shit. I exhale at the reminder.

She meets my gaze. "Can we just go?"

"But I thought... I mean, it's nice here, don't you wanna at least—"

"No. Let's just go see your sister." She shoves her helmet back on her head and clips the chin strap.

I sigh, looking at my feet.

Fuck.

I should never have sent that link—never have brought her here. What I was hoping she'd think of as a sweet gesture has fallen epically flat, coming across as tone-deaf and pushy instead of supportive. She's the opposite of touched—she's pissed. And she has every right to be.

Slowly nodding, all I can trust myself to say is, "Yeah. Okay."

25

JESSE

Claire throws her arms around my shoulders, standing on tiptoe and squeezing me with surprising strength. "Glad you could get away. Mom's doing so much better, huh?"

"Yeah," I say. "A lot better. Still gets tired pretty easily, but she's getting there."

It's been six weeks since Mom got sick. Being able to trust she'll be okay while I'm an hour out of town is... huge.

Claire squeezes a bit harder.

"Oof," I croak out. "You're gonna have to loosen your Hulk grip before I pass out."

She lets go and steps back. "Sorry, Garby."

"Wow. It's been ages since anyone called me Garby," I say with a chuckle, glancing past my sister to where Sam and Hazel sit at the coffee table with paper and colored pencils dumped everywhere. My chest twinges at how much bigger they are. Claire and her husband brought them both out to see me a couple years ago in Australia, but they were too young to remember. Hazel was just a baby.

"Garby?" Ada's amused voice comes from over my shoulder. "There's gotta be a story behind that."

I'm relieved to hear a glimmer of Ada's usual sense of humor returning. The ride over from the art school was... tense.

"Claire, you remember Ada? Uh..." I pause, not sure what to call her. My roommate? Friend? Fuck-buddy? "Marcus' sister?"

"Oh, wow, yes! Hey!" Claire beams, taking Ada in. "Long time no see! And Garby's short for Garbage Mouth."

"Claire—" I start, rubbing my forehead with my fingertips.

This is what we're leading with?

"Garbage Mouth?" Ada repeats, smirking at me. "What, did you swear a lot as a kid, or...?"

Claire slips her arms around my waist again and gazes up at me—somehow still managing to serve big sister vibes even though she's six inches shorter than I am. "When he was a toddler, I found him picking through the trash and putting stuff in his mouth. So, being the creative genius big sister that I was, I started calling him Garbage Mouth, and it just... morphed into *Garby*." She shrugs. "He was always putting the weirdest stuff in his mouth. Mom and Dad had to call poison control twice after he ate snowberries."

"Uh,"—I scoff—"because you *fed me* snowberries, Claire." The attempted murder is canon in our family.

"Accidentally! The *first time*, at least." She throws Ada a guilty glance. "I swear, I didn't *want* him to die, but, you know, little brothers..."

I shake my head. I'm never gonna hear the end of this *Garby* thing.

"Yeah," Ada says. "Younger siblings are the *worst*."

I let out a wry laugh. "Well, Marcus would probably agree with you there."

"Come on in," Claire says, gesturing for us to follow her inside.

As Ada steps past me, I reach out to tug discreetly on the hem of her shirt.

She turns, cautious eyes jumping up to mine.

"I'm sorry," I whisper.

Before she turns away, she holds my gaze for a moment and nods, giving me a small smile. "I know."

And *damn* if that smile doesn't patch up some bruised part of my heart. I let a tiny swell of relief take root in my chest; I know we still need to talk about what happened, but that look tells me we're okay.

I trail Claire and Ada into the living room and tentatively squat down beside Hazel. "Hey," I start, not sure what to say. "Whatcha drawing?"

Hazel peers up at me from under dark brown, frizzy curls. "Dis guy's a monkey. And him's got rainbows." A series of colorful scribbles cover the paper.

"Wow! A rainbow monkey? Sweet." I inspect the paper in front of Sam. "What about you, bud?"

"A dragon," he says quietly.

Claire sweeps over to crouch down beside him, softly rubbing his shoulder. "Sam, do you remember Uncle Jesse?"

Sam gives her a shy shrug.

Claire continues, "We went to visit him in Australia a couple years ago, when you were three. About how old Hazel is now."

"It's okay if you don't remember," I reassure him. "I don't remember anything from when *I* was three."

God, it must be weird for them—to barely know me and yet be told I'm family.

I push down a pang of regret that I haven't had more of a relationship with my sister and her kids. Because of my crappy internet connection in Oz, we haven't even been able to do video chats. Postcards and phone calls only go so far.

My gaze snags on Ada, who's standing near the mantle above

the fireplace, holding a framed photo with an amused look on her face. When she catches me watching her, she turns it toward me; I recognize the shot of me at the seventh grade science fair with Claire posing at my side. She mouths, *"love him."*

I roll my eyes.

"Hey, Sam," I say, keen to shift attention away from the evidence of my awkward years. "My friend Ada over there does lots of drawing. I bet she could draw anything you can think of." I glance her way with a meaningful tilt of my head, silently beckoning her over.

Ada smiles and puts the photo back, then walks over to sit beside Sam.

"Hey, Sam," she says. "My name's Ada."

"Hi."

"So, what are we drawing?" Ada peers at Sam's dragon picture. "Ooh, super cool dragon! Can I draw one too?" When Sam nods, she picks up a red pencil and pulls an unused sheet of paper in front of her.

Hazel scribbles with enthusiasm at my side, and Claire circles around behind me, quietly reminding her to make sure her drawing stays on the paper.

"So, is Sam short for anything?" Ada asks, sketching a rough outline in red. "Samuel? Samson? Sample Sale?" she spitballs, and when he stares at her, she just keeps going. "Sambuca? Samosa?" She drums her fingers on her chin, squinting thoughtfully. "Sammich? I bet it's Sammich."

Sam cracks up. "No! My name's not Sammich!"

"I dunno. You look like a Sammich to me. But maybe I'm just hungry." She smirks and elbows him gently, then leans toward him and stage-whispers, "Don't worry, I won't eat you."

Across the table, Sam's eyes go wide.

Ada makes a *tsk* sound. "Uncle Jesse, though? He's even hungrier than me, dude."

"No!" Sam shouts through his laughter.

"And he eats weird things all the time. Your mom just told me!"

"Hey, that's right, *Garby*," Claire joins in, teasing.

I shake my head.

"Wait a second," Ada says, her tone suddenly serious. "How old are you?"

"Five!"

Ada purses her lips and sucks in a long breath, making a show of cringing. "A five-year-old Sammich? Yikes. Can't eat you. You're probably all moldy." She gives him an over-the-top grimace.

Sam laughs. "I'm not moldy!"

"Jesse, what do you think? Is Sammich here too moldy for us to eat?"

"Definitely," I nod, grinning at her.

"See? You're safe. Uncle Jesse doesn't like moldy Sammiches either."

"I'm not moldy!" Sam squeals with laughter. "And my name's not Sammich!"

She holds up her hands in a defensive pose. "Okay, okay. If you say so."

She's so good at this. Good with kids. Meanwhile, I barely know how to talk to them.

"What color should my dragon's scales be?" Ada asks, eyes glittering. "Should we let Hazel choose?"

Hazel rounds the table and climbs over Ada's lap, picking up a handful of colored pencils and pushing them into her hands. "Dese ones," she says.

"Wow, *all* the colors?"

"Draw him rainbow," Hazel instructs.

"Oh, nice. He's gonna be the most beautiful *and* scariest dragon with all these colors."

Hazel settles in on the slant of Ada's lap and Sam drifts toward her, working on his drawing close by her side.

Claire stands and motions for me to step aside so we can talk. I push off the edge of the table, still smiling at how quickly Ada worked her charm with the kids.

Behind me, I hear Sam ask, "Why do you have blue hair?"

Ada responds simply, "Because I like having blue hair."

In the kitchen, Claire puts on a pot of coffee and pulls down three mugs from the cupboard. While it brews, she gets out some snacks for the kids, and I busy myself by peering at the photo collage on her refrigerator.

"So, just the two of you?" she asks, slicing an apple. "What happened to Marcus?"

I wrinkle my nose. "He and his girlfriend got food poisoning. Ada had some stuff to pick up in the city so she tagged along. It was kind of a last-minute thing."

Claire lifts her chin in a slow nod, something I can't quite decipher flitting across her expression.

"What?"

She gives me a knowing look and turns to pour the coffee. "I didn't say anything."

"Your face did."

She hands me my mug, wisely choosing not to pry. "So, have you talked to Dad?"

The question lands with a thud. Though I cut that asshole out of my life a long time ago, Claire hasn't. She's never understood my hard boundary about him.

"Uh, no," I say. "And I'm not planning to."

"Really? You've come all this way."

"So? Doesn't change what he did to Mom."

"But he's our father," Claire says. "He's family."

"All the more reason he shouldn't have fucked her over in the divorce."

For my sister, family is everything—an unbreakable bond, for better or for worse. But for me? Well, let's just say, whatever mixed feelings I may have about my time in Australia, cutting ties with toxic people has never been something I regretted.

"Okay," she relents. "Sorry I brought it up. I just thought... never mind. Forget I said anything."

"Happily," I say, taking a sip of coffee.

Claire seems to study me for a moment before changing the subject. "So, do you two need a place to crash tonight? Or are you heading back?"

"Nah, we're just here for the day."

"You sure? You could stay here. We've got an air mattress I could set up. Though, fair warning: the kids get up at six and they aren't exactly quiet about it."

"Six, huh?" I chuckle and rub my chin. "Well, wouldn't bother me, but Ada isn't a morning person."

"Yeah. I wish I could say you get used to it, but I'd be lying." She takes a sip of her coffee. "Let that be your reminder to use birth control."

"Claire!"

She laughs. "What? I'm just saying, wear a cond—"

"Mommy!" Sam calls out, running into the kitchen, paper flapping in his little hand like a battle flag.

Claire throws me a wide-eyed glance and puts her coffee on the counter, stooping down to meet him.

"Look at the dragon Ada drew!" He thrusts the drawing in front of Claire's face.

"Okay, lemme see," she says, backing away slightly so she can focus on the picture. She takes the paper in her hands and stands up to her full height. "Whoa," she says in a low voice. "This is..."

"She did it rainbow!"

"I can see that..." Claire turns the paper around to show me.

Ada's artistic skill shouldn't still shock me, but I can't help but gape at the picture. It's fucking *good*. Not only did she draw a dragon better than any I could produce, but it has individual scales, each shaded to appear almost iridescent. How did she do that? And how long did that take her? Ten minutes? It would take me hours, maybe days, to even attempt something half as good as hers.

I turn at Ada's voice and see her piggybacking Hazel into the kitchen.

"Ada, I had no idea you were an artist!" Claire exclaims, holding up the dragon picture before Sam's grabby hands reclaim it.

"Oh, yeah," she breathes with a scrunch of her nose, crouching down to let Hazel off her back. "Alright. Down you go, Hazelnut."

Hazel grabs at Claire's legs. "Mama, I'm hungry."

Claire crouches down and reminds Hazel to use her manners. Once the required *please* and *thank you* have been uttered, Claire guides Hazel to the kitchen table, placing the apples alongside some other snacks for the kids.

Ada puts her hands on her hips, smiling at Claire. "Cute kids."

"Thank you," Claire says distractedly, her gaze fixed on Ada. "Sorry—I'm not over that dragon picture." She gestures over her shoulder toward where Sam ran off with it.

"Oh, uh... I dunno," Ada says, brushing it off. "I was just messing around."

"Uh, no. You've got serious skill," Claire presses.

Ada rakes a hand through her hair and shifts on her feet.

I try to rescue her, painfully aware the subject of Ada's art didn't exactly go well for us earlier. "Claire, maybe she—"

I'm cut off when Sam runs back into the room and heads for the table, sidling up beside the chair Hazel's kneeling on. A squabble about Hazel being in Sam's chair immediately erupts and Claire gets pulled away to intervene, heroically saving the bowl of goldfish crackers before it hits the floor.

My sister returns to join us and takes a sip of her coffee. "What do you do for work, Ada?"

"Bartending," Ada replies, cutting a glance my way.

"She makes a mean Blue Hawaiian," I say, hoping to steer the subject to safer territory. I throw Ada a tentative smile, relieved when her lips twist with a hint of amusement.

Claire turns to me, steering us right back into the rocks. "Jess, did you know she could draw like that?"

"Yeah. I did." I want to say *that's why I keep saying she should apply for art school*, but I figure it's wise to keep my mouth shut.

Ada's smile fades slightly as the unspoken tension thickens once more.

Claire zeroes in on her once again. "So, do you make art to sell, or...?"

Ada stuffs her hands in her pockets. "Uh, yeah. Not too successfully, but yeah."

"Do you have a portfolio or something?"

Oh, God, Claire. Drop it already.

"Sorry," Claire says, glancing between the two of us. "It's just... This might sound random, but have you ever thought about illustration? I work for a children's book publisher. Like, if that's what you can pull off in ten minutes... Wow."

"Thanks," Ada replies, then shrugs. "Uh, maybe? I hadn't really..."

"Like, our art team is always considering new artists. If you want, I can connect you to submit your portfolio." Claire fishes a business card from her purse on the counter. She hands it to Ada. "Gimme a call anytime."

"Okay, thanks." Ada takes the card with a polite smile.

Claire seems to finally pick up on Ada's awkwardness and changes the subject. "Can I get you a coffee?"

HAZEL AND SAM are pressed up to the window over the back of the couch, their little hands leaving smudges on the glass. Waving goodbye, I realize I don't know when I'll see them next. I frown, once again toying with the prospect of being back here for good— and what that would mean for my family. I could be a better brother to Claire, a proper uncle to her kids, and be here for Mom... who's not getting any younger.

And Ada... I clench my jaw. *Shit.* Still not on the table.

We mount the bike and I let out a breath when Ada's arms snake around my waist and she snugs herself against me. I press my gloved hand over hers for a long moment, squeezing once before I start the bike. The short ride to the art supply store with her at my back again makes everything feel easier—and seems to soften whatever tension was pulling tight between us.

A bell jingles above the door as I follow Ada into Different Strokes Art Supplies. I stuff my hands in my pockets and take in my surroundings, feeling a bit out-of-place in the tightly stocked shop. It's one of those places where you have to watch your elbows everywhere you turn to avoid knocking something fragile off a display. Ada makes a beeline for the paints she needs, disappearing down a narrow aisle at the back of the store.

I loiter near the front counter until a heavily pierced employee starts to eye me warily and I go find Ada. She's crouched at the end of an aisle, squinting at the labels on two nearly identical tubes of red paint.

"Shit," she says. "They're out of the color I wanted." She huffs a resigned breath and stands, putting one tube back and tapping the other against her hand as she strolls toward the paintbrushes.

I lean over her shoulder, peering at all the options. "Wow... What's the difference between all these?"

"It's a lot of things. The size, obviously… but also the cut of the bristles, whether they're synthetic or natural hair, how firm they are, what type of paint they work best with…"

I slide a hand over her lower back, pressing an experimental kiss to her temple.

"What are you doing?" she asks softly, withdrawing a bit. "We're in public."

"Okay." I step away, not wanting to push her right now, and try to stuff down the sting of rejection that threatens. "But we're also an hour from home. I don't think we need to be *that* careful."

She doesn't answer, only lifts a brow in thought. Then she pulls down a package of three paintbrushes and opens the plastic flap, skimming her fingertips over the bristles. "Ooooh. Mink hair. These are fucking lush."

I catch sight of the price tag. "Fifty bucks? For *three* paint-brushes?"

She sucks air through her teeth. "Yeah, that's a bit steep. Too bad. They're gorgeous."

I study her in profile as she puts the brushes back, giving them a lingering touch before walking away. I want to pull her into my arms, make things right. I want to kiss her and feel her kiss me back, and I suddenly don't give a shit about being in public.

She strolls down the aisle, poking absently at a few more items, lost in thought.

Checking to make sure she isn't watching me, I pull the package back off the hook and tuck them out of view. Squeezing her arm as I walk past, I tell her I'll meet her outside when she's done.

The employee from earlier doesn't seem impressed by the shady way I keep looking over my shoulder while she rings me through, but she seems to accept that your average shoplifter doesn't drop fifty bucks on paintbrushes and hands me my receipt.

I step out into the sun and tuck the brushes into my back pocket. When I catch myself pacing the sidewalk, anxious about how Ada will receive the gift, I try to settle my nerves and lean up against the brick wall next to the shop.

When she finally emerges, she doesn't see me right away. And in that split second—that small, insignificant moment before she spots me—time seems to slow. Her turquoise hair catches in the golden afternoon sun, glowing almost green around her face, and a slight frown worries her brow as she scans the passing faces on the sidewalk. It's her eyes that get to me. Those eyes that glitter with challenge, that flare in a fight, that soften under my touch... Those eyes that can call me on my bullshit and bring me to my knees in a single glance. Those eyes that see me. *Really* see me.

Those eyes are everything.

And, as she searches for me outside the shop, I realize just how badly I want to be found. How I can't deny it any longer.

I love her.

The corner of my mouth tugs up in a smile as I push off the wall, willing my heart to steady. "Hey."

She turns at the sound of my voice. "There you are."

We fall into step together and head down the block toward the bike. For a minute, maybe two, we walk in silence.

"Listen," I say eventually, glancing at her sidelong. "I know we didn't really get to talk about the whole art school thing before coming here."

"Right," she says, sounding uneasy.

"I'm sorry if it seemed like I was pushing it on you. I didn't mean—I don't mean to act like I know what's best for you. I only wanna encourage you. You've got this talent, and I hope you can find a way to..."

"To what? Make money as an artist?" She frowns, dodging a group of tourists gathered outside a coffee shop.

"No. I mean, maybe? Don't get me wrong, that would be great.

I was gonna say… I hope you can find a way to do something that makes you happy."

"And bartending doesn't make me happy?" She stops as we reach the bike and hugs her arms across her chest.

"Hey, I didn't say that." I dip my chin, getting in her eyeline. "But does it? Be real. Is that what you wanna do?"

She turns away, biting her lip and shaking her head slightly.

"Ada, come on. You can't honestly tell me getting hit on by drunk assholes every night makes you as happy as when you were drawing with Sam and Hazel!"

"Jess, not everyone gets to run around doing whatever makes them happy all the time."

"So you're not even gonna try?"

"I dunno! I'm twenty-five, for fuck's sake! I have time to figure my shit out. I just want everyone to stop *pressuring me* about it!"

"Why are you getting upset? I'm trying to be supportive, here. Look—" I pull out the paintbrushes from my pocket and hold them out for her. "I just wanna show you I'm in your corner."

Her demeanor stutters. She stares at the paintbrushes but doesn't take them. "Why did you do that?"

I drop my outstretched arm in defeat. "Oh my *God*, Ada. Why is it so hard for you to accept that I wanna support you?"

"Because it's like you're telling me what to do! Like I need to do more. *Be* more. Be *better*."

I hold up my hands. "I'm not. I swear. But you're amazing at this. You have a gift. Even Claire noticed how incredible your drawing was. And she could be a foot in the door for an illustrator job. That's legit, paid work!"

"I know that." She frowns at the ground.

"Then why are you resisting this stuff?"

Her expression falls. "Jesus, it's like you're in fucking cahoots with my parents."

"I was trying to do something nice for you."

Something about that makes her snap. "So quit it! Quit doing nice things for me! Stop being so nice!" Her voice is pleading. "Jess... You live in Australia!"

"What's that supposed to mean?"

She doesn't answer, just slings her backpack over both shoulders and picks up her helmet.

"What do you need from me, Ada? What do you want me to say?"

She tenses up in a shrug. "Can't I just... do what I'm doing? And can't we just have fun this summer? Why does it have to be more than that? Bigger than that?"

I step toward her. "*You're* bigger than that. Can't you see?"

We're bigger than that, I almost say.

Ada seems to read my thoughts and gives me a warning look.

"Okay," I say. "If you don't want this, fine. Like I said, you don't have to do anything you don't wanna do. Do I hope you do something with your art? Yes. Not gonna pretend I don't. But I won't pressure you anymore."

She considers me for a long moment. When she speaks, she sounds tired. "Let's just go home."

"Ada..." I say in a low voice. "Come here. Please."

Reluctantly, she lets me pull her into my chest.

"I'm sorry," I whisper, kissing her cheek. I don't give a damn we're out on the street. "I just want you to be happy."

"I know." Ada's brown eyes lift to mine. "Whether you believe me or not, I *am* happy. Right now, anyway."

I let out a breath through my nose. "Ominous."

"Yeah, well," she says, pulling back slightly.

We both know there's an expiration date on... whatever this is. On *us*.

"I'll drop it, okay? The art stuff."

"Really?" She peers up at me.

"Yes, really. I'll chill."

"You'll *chill?*"

"I'll be *super* chill. You won't even recognize me, I'll be chilling so hard."

She smiles. "Thank you."

I don't know how long we stand there, just holding each other, but the fight seems to melt from her as I run my hands over her hair, her shoulders, her back. The thought of leaving her makes my chest ache.

Ada eventually braces both hands on my hips and rises onto her tiptoes to lift her mouth to mine. The kiss is soft and slow, sending a warmth through me that's equal parts incredible and terrifying.

As our lips part, I press my forehead to hers. Neither of us speaks for a long moment.

"Promise me something," I say softly.

"Mmm?"

"Promise me, at the end of the summer, when I go back…" I pause, trying to find the right words. "We'll stay friends."

"Friends who used to fuck?"

"Oh, geez." I lift my head and rub my forehead with the back of my wrist. "Do you have to make everything crass? I mean it, though. Let's not let things get weird. I know it might be a bit weird—possibly shitty… But let's promise not to be shitty to each other, okay?"

She prods me in the chest with a finger. "Jesse Bailey, are you telling me not to break your heart?"

"Is that Ada Russo?" an older woman's voice comes from nearby.

We turn, pulling apart with a speed that only implies guilt.

"Hi," Ada ventures. "Mrs. Nicolosi? What are you doing here?"

"Just getting some shopping done, dear." She lifts the bags in her hands and gives us both a kind smile.

I slip my hands into my pockets, awkwardness quickly giving way to dread that we've run into someone from home.

Shit.

"Jesse, this is Mrs. Nicolosi," Ada explains, her face almost ashen. "She goes to church with my parents."

"Nice to meet you." I force a smile and extend my hand.

She shakes it vigorously, covering it with her other hand as the shopping bags slide over her freckled forearms. She gives me an appraising once-over and turns to Ada. "Nice to see you've found yourself a looker like this one."

I try to suppress the wince but know I must be mirroring Ada's stricken expression.

"Oh, um..." Ada starts, shaking her head, then seems to decide she's not up for picking this particular battle. "Thank you."

Of course this woman would assume we're a couple. We were sure as shit acting like it just now. Hell, I can't deny that line has been blurring for me, too, this last week. Weeks, even. This thing had already left the station well before we gave in to it.

"Anyway," Mrs. Nicolosi says, letting go of my hand. "Don't let me interrupt you two lovebirds!" She turns to pat Ada on the cheek. "Tell your parents I say hello."

"Uh, will do, yeah," Ada says, clearly trying to hide her dread behind a pasted-on smile.

Ada mouths a silent *fuck* as Mrs. Nicolosi heads down the sidewalk.

26

ADA

Running into Mrs. Nicolosi was the wake-up call I desperately needed. Our trip to the city was a flimsy excuse to justify being physical outside the apartment. Huge mistake. Probably one of many in a slippery slope of mistakes I've made since Jesse's been here. I should have ended this a long time ago—or better yet, found a way to stop myself before we started anything.

I tell Jesse I need some space when we get back and, for the first time since we started this, we spend the night in separate beds. It almost breaks me. I have to walk myself back to my own bed on two separate occasions after nearly making it to his door like some pathetic, lovesick puppy.

He'd tried so hard to do something nice for me in Seattle, and I'd panicked and thrown it back in his face. The pressure I'd felt from him was real, but I know my reaction was mostly the frustrations with my parents burbling up to the surface, as always.

By the time I wake up in the morning, he's already gone. A sticky note on the fridge reads *"Off to locate my chill"* with a little arrow in the corner. I peel it off and flip it over.

Text me when you
see this. - J

A warmth spreads over my chest, and I smile to myself. Then, a pang of dread punches me in the gut.

What am I doing?

This man is my brother's best friend. I can't do this. I can't fall for him. Who do I think I'm kidding, here? And, even if Marcus wasn't a factor or we could somehow come clean, the reality is that Jesse lives on the other side of the world's biggest ocean. Best-case scenario, we'd try to keep in touch via email or text. But it wouldn't last. Between the distance and the time difference, it'd be impossible to keep any shred of connection going. And I can't do long distance—can't risk a repeat of what happened with Pascal. The strain from being apart would inevitably push him to find someone else... I feel nauseated just thinking about it.

Fuck. I'm already in too deep.

I find my phone and text him.

ME

Hey, just woke up. Where'd you go?

JESSE

Gym. Then I'm gonna visit mom. Then I dunno. Coffee? Walk? Netflix?? Something chill.

Damnit. Joke bait.

Never one to back down from a punchline, I can't help myself and tap out my reply.

ME

Netflix and chill?

JESSE

That an invitation?

Damn him for being so easy to flirt with.

And yet, I can't deny the way my chest lifts at the thought of getting to be with him again tonight. I miss him.

I already fucking miss him.

ME

Maybe...

JESSE

Well in that case I can't wait to Netflix and chill (the fuck out) at your earliest convenience

(By that I mean fuck your brains out and then be suuuuper chill about it)

Or whatever

(Chill style)

ME

I'm closing tonight... 2am too late for you?

Fuck.

Is the lovesick puppy writing my text messages? Wasn't I supposed to be calling this off?

JESSE

I'm super chill about how late that is for me

Want me to walk you home?

Unable to help myself, I bite the inside of my cheek, already regretting the next words as I'm typing them out. I hit send before I can think better of it.

ME

Yes please. I missed you last night.

JESSE

Missed you too

AT MIDNIGHT, Ros declares herself far too pregnant for late nights and heads home, leaving me to lock up. The bar's closed to the public for a private engagement party tonight, and things have slowed down enough for me to manage on my own—a test run for me taking over as acting bar manager this fall, Ros said. I haven't officially accepted the job, but it seems inevitable I'll step in.

Covertly checking my phone behind the bar, I notice Jesse hasn't texted me since this morning. Shelving my disappointment, I remind myself I'd asked him for space. He's giving me just that. Shouldn't I be happy? Instead, I'm only restless. It doesn't help that time seems to be passing at an intolerable crawl. After serving my next customer, I pick up my phone again.

ME

These customers are boring af

JESSE

Need a distraction?

ME

Depends what you're offering

JESSE

I could tell you about my day

ME

Ok I'll bite.

JESSE

Well it started out so chill, right? The chillest

But then the darnedest thing happened

ME

Yeah?

JESSE

Got to thinking about you...

In the shower

And part of me got way less chill

Heat thrums between my legs at the image of Jesse hard in the shower while thinking about me.

ME

Please tell me you didn't defile the shower at the gym

JESSE

God what kind of animal do you take me for?

I defiled Marcus's shower

ME

Not sure whether to be flattered or horrified

JESSE

Waited until he was out obviously...

(Like a good best friend)

ME

Horny and respectful?

JESSE

Exactly

And no kink shaming please… We all have needs

I bite my lip and smile.

A woman clears her throat and I jerk my head up, dropping my phone on the shelf behind the bar.

"Sorry. What can I get you?"

When I've pulled two pints of beer and taken her payment, I glance around, finding no customers in sight. I reach for my phone again.

ME

Tell me more… about these kinks of yours

Nice, Ada. The one-eighty I've done here—going from wanting to end things this morning to asking him about his kinks mere hours later—is truly impressive.

Where the hell is my willpower?

JESSE

Oh funny you'd ask, because my biggest kink is actually…

…at work right now

ME

I see what you did there

JESSE

I'm a very clever boy

The bad idea is already materializing in my mind.

ME

Clever boys deserve rewards…

What am I doing?

I start looking for a chance to duck away, unable to shake off the simmering thrill. It must be the rosy haze of infatuation fucking with my mind. We've been having too much sex. *Good* sex. *Incredible* sex. The kind of sex that makes you do some soul-searching the next day. Or maybe my brain is melting. That must be it. Jesse is somehow, slowly but surely, lobotomizing me with his cock. There's no other explanation.

I can practically hear my subconscious laughing at me, but I shove it down.

JESSE

What kind of rewards?

The part of me screaming this is exactly what I should *not* be doing has apparently been gagged, bound, and thrown into the fucking river because, when the moment presents itself, I grab my phone and speed walk to the back. My heart pounds as I lock myself into the single-stall staff restroom, but I decide not to overthink it. I set the camera's timer, propping my phone against the sink, and turn to face the wall with my eyes squeezed shut. Lifting my skirt, I hold the pose until the shutter sound clicks, then tug it back down as I spin around to inspect the photo. *Perfect.* After a quick crop-and-enhance treatment, I text it to Jesse.

ME

[image sent]

Consider this my peace offering

When he doesn't respond for a minute, I start to panic. *Shit.* He said he was at Marcus' place. What if he opens it in front of my brother?

What the fuck is wrong with me?

This is reckless.

Walking back to the bar, I remember the last photo I sent Jesse and tap out another text.

ME

> I swear to God if you say "it was cool" about this
> one, I will cut you

Three dots start jumping and I wait, holding my breath.

JESSE

> Jesus I think my heart just stopped

> Might need another shower

I grin, releasing a sigh of relief, kicking myself all the same.
Oh, I'm so fucked.

AT TWO A.M. SHARP, Jesse's eyes lock on mine through Carnival's
glass front door. I'm teetering on the edge of a cliff—heart racing,
muscles tight, and nerves firing in a desperate attempt to avoid
falling. A crooked smile tugs at the corner of his lips, and I know
I'm losing this fight.

Because *Christ on a bike*, Jesse looks fuckable right now, and
the heat simmering in his gaze lays me bare.

*Oh, my God. How am I this starved for him when we've only been
apart for a day?*

His lips are moving, but I can't hear what he's saying through
the glass. Catching myself staring, I snap out of my pornographic
trance and finally unlock the door.

"You okay?" he asks on the back of a confused-sounding
laugh, reaching a subtle hand to squeeze my hip as he moves past
me into the darkened restaurant. Electricity zings through my
core from that one touch, fueling the warmth already there.

I flick the deadbolt again, trying to ignore how good he smells.

"Uh, yeah," I reply, my voice coming out a bit breathless.

"Where's everyone else?" he asks.

"Uh, Theo finished up already, and Ros left me the keys so I could lock up." I don't want to talk about work—not when Jesse has that fucking smile trained on me, the glow of the streetlights illuminating the angle of his jaw. I want to bite it.

"Anyone else in the kitchen?" He scans the place.

My gaze falls to his neck. "No. Just us."

"Well, shit." His eyes trace down my body, leaving heat in their wake.

"Don't get any big ideas," I caution, gesturing to the floor-to-ceiling windows separating us from the street outside.

He steps toward me, his voice low and conspiratorial. "Ada, it's two in the morning. I highly doubt we'd have an audience."

I scoff. "Didn't realize I'd agreed to a performance."

Who am I fucking kidding? He could fuck me up against that window if he wanted to.

"No?" he asks as he steps closer still, one brow raised. "Because that picture you sent me of your perfect ass... was quite the fucking show."

I exhale and cut my eyes away, suddenly self-conscious.

"I haven't been able to stop thinking about you." His voice rumbles deep.

"You really liked that photo, huh?" I tease.

He reaches out to brush the hair back from my forehead. "I did. But even before the photo. It's been killing me to be away from you all day."

Okay, that was unexpectedly sweet.

"Sorry about yesterday," I say.

"It's okay. I know it felt like I was pushing you. I shouldn't have—"

"Yeah but you were trying to do something nice and I bit your head off."

He dips his chin in acknowledgment.

"Thank you, by the way," I add, "for the paintbrushes. They're beautiful. Almost too nice to use."

He stays silent. So silent I'm not sure what to say next.

"What, you're not gonna say *anything*?"

He gives his head a quick shake as if he's snapping out of a dream. "Sorry, I was just thinking about your ass again."

"Hey!" I prod him in the chest.

He laughs, running his hands over my upper arms. "No, seriously. I told you I'd drop it. The art stuff. I meant what I said."

I look down at my feet. Then, both his hands lift my face, angling my head as he dips down. His kiss is soft but charged, his tongue twining in delicious spirals around my own.

I tuck my fingers into the front pockets of his jeans, hungry for his warmth, and an ache throbs between my legs. I shift my hips, already feeling the slip of wetness against my panties.

Oh, fuck.

When I remember where we are, I pull back, breathing hard.

Jesse's blue eyes are almost black in the dark. "Sorry," he says. "You wanted space. I—"

"No, that's not it. It's just..." I whisper. "We can't..." I shift my gaze again to the wall of glass and the deserted street outside, then grab his hand. "Come on."

The darkness swallows us as we weave between the tables, heading for the staircase at the back of the restaurant.

"Where are you taking me?" he asks as I lead him up the stairs. "Shit. It's *you* who's gonna harvest *my* organs, isn't it?"

"Gotta pay the bills," I deadpan.

I push open the door to the private dining room at the top of the stairs—a sort of mezzanine space overlooking the main floor of the restaurant and bar. Skirting the vast table and chairs that take up most of the room, I let go of Jesse's hand and walk to the railing, peering down at the empty expanse below.

"It's so cool up here," I say, almost to myself. I don't have reason to come up here often.

"Don't fucking move." Jesse's voice is rough at my ear as his hands skim up the backs of my thighs. My breath catches when he lifts my miniskirt with a jerk and palms my ass, his fingers kneading into my flesh. "Fuuuuuck." He draws out the word, then nips at the ridge of my ear. "This ass."

My core clenches in tiny, delicious pulses. Reaching behind me, I grasp for his cock through his jeans, but he catches my hands.

"I told you. Don't fucking move." His lips are on my neck as he guides my hands back to the cool metal in front of me. "Keep them on the railing."

My fingers curl around it and I exhale as Jesse drags his palms up both my arms.

"Any security cameras?" he asks, his nose grazing the shell of my ear.

"Not up here." I smile at the low rumble of approval from over my shoulder.

Shoving my skirt higher, he hooks his thumbs into the black lace of my thong and slides it down to the floor. "Fuck, this has to go too," he says, almost to himself, as he rips my skirt down and off.

I step out as he drops to his knees behind me.

"Oh, fuck," he murmurs, his big hands gripping my ass cheeks roughly as he presses kisses to my bare flesh.

I gasp when he surprises me with a quick slap, the sharp sensation fanning out across my skin. He smooths his hand over the stinging flesh and exhales hard.

"So, you like my ass, huh?" I ask with a smirk, pressing back into his touch.

"Mmm," he replies, the sound coming from somewhere deep in his throat. "And I like this too."

I inhale sharply as he trails a finger between my legs—through the slickness gathered at my center—then circles it softly over my clit.

"And I fucking *love* this," he adds as he plunges his finger inside me.

My whole body trembles and I grip tighter on the railing, letting out a soft moan.

He kisses my lower back, right above the cleft of my ass.

"Oh, my God," I breathe, my eyes fluttering closed.

Why the fuck is that so hot?

There's a shuffling behind me as he withdraws his finger, and I squeak out a surprised sound when he grips me by both hips and tugs me back hard. Warm, wet heat envelops my pussy as he licks the full length of me. It's almost too much, and my knees nearly buckle—but he's got me. He holds me up, angling me toward him.

"Holy fuck." I squeeze the railing until I'm sure my knuckles are white—but I'm not looking because my vision won't focus anymore. I can feel only Jesse's tongue flicking into me, his fingers digging into my hips, his soft curses brushing against my flesh.

"Christ, you taste so fucking good." He tears away for long enough to spin around under my legs, sitting on his ass, and then his mouth is on me again. He pulls me to him, and the hard draw on my clit has me crying out.

His eyes blaze as he lowers all the way to the floor, tugging me down with him—but I hold back.

"Sit," he commands from between my legs, squeezing my hips in encouragement. His expression is filled with nothing but hungry, desperate need.

"Jess, I don't wanna hurt you…"

"You won't," he groans. "Just fucking sit, Ada."

"You're gonna dislocate your damn jaw!"

"And it'll be worth it. Now sit on my face." At this, he drives two fingers inside me and curls them, ripping a moan from my throat. "Let me have you. Let me have *all* of you."

He pumps his fingers inside me again—*for emphasis?*—and my back arches on another guttural cry of pleasure.

Unable to deny him, I lower myself and he pulls his fingers out. My thighs start to shake, but I consciously let the tension go, unclasping my hands from the railing and dropping my knees to the floor on either side of his head. I rock and grind my hips, chasing my pleasure with every stroke of his tongue. It's building so fast I think I might be having an out-of-body experience.

The sounds he's making coax me right to the edge—every whimper, every catch of his breath, every groaned swipe of his tongue and nip of his teeth against my aching center... Someone get this man a damn gold medal for using his voice.

God, it's so good. He's *so good.*

"Oh, shit!" My muscles tense, my hands grasping for purchase on his chest, my thighs, his hair, the railing—anywhere. I can't figure out where or how to hold on as I try to ride the wave I can feel coming. So I don't. Instead, I let go. And, when the explosion of pleasure bowls me over, I'm lost in it, crying out, moaning the word *fuck* on repeat, my own voice a deep, foreign rasp. I feel like I might come undone as another wave crests, overwhelming my senses. This time, I think I scream.

When I finally get my bearings, I realize I have Jesse's hair clenched tight in my fist. I release my grip, suddenly self-conscious and worried I've hurt him. I push up and scramble back from him, pressing my fingers to my lips as I sit straddling his lap.

But there's only fire in his expression.

"Shit," I whisper. "Shit, Jess, I'm..." I trail off, breaking eye contact. What do I even say? *Sorry I came so hard I nearly ripped out your hair?*

He sits up and reaches for me. "Ada, look at me."

I reluctantly comply, then tear my gaze away again. I've never lost control this way—never *responded* this way—with anyone.

He dips his head to get in my eyeline. "Hey. *Really* look at me."

When I do, my cheeks are burning.

"Whatever bullshit you're telling yourself right now? Let it go."

I shake my head and swallow.

"Let it *go*," he says again. Those unwavering blue eyes stare into mine. "'Cause that was the hottest fucking thing I've ever seen."

"Oh, God." I drop my head into my hands before peering up at him. "Really?"

"Nearly came in my pants." His earnest smile is everything.

I let out a surprised snort-laugh, the tension evaporating. "Classy."

He pulls me in for a kiss. It's slow, but heat builds between my legs at the slip of his tongue against mine. The tangy taste of my release on his mouth only heightens the promise behind it.

I can't believe how at ease I am with him. How effortlessly he can wash away my insecurities.

"Arms up." Jesse peels off my tank top, then my bra, lifting one breast and drawing my nipple into his mouth.

I push up on my knees, pressing toward him, and he sucks hard, sending an ache straight down the center of me.

Still teasing my nipple with his tongue, he unzips the fly of his jeans, freeing his cock. He strokes it slowly as I pinch and roll my other nipple between my fingers.

"Oh, God," I whisper, drinking in the sight of him touching himself.

He releases me and drags his gaze up my body, reaching up to stroke my cheek. "You're so fucking sexy, Ada."

Leaning into his touch, I press my lips into his palm. When I turn back to him, something about the way he's looking at me darkens. I hold my breath, waiting. I'm not even sure what I'm waiting for—until it happens.

I let out a small cry when he tangles his fingers in my hair, gripping firmly. My eyes lock with his, burning with need and heat and one unspoken word: *Yes.*

I reach for him, desperate to feel his steel heat in my hands, and *oh, fuck,* he's hard. I dive for his mouth, kissing him like it's a fucking crisis and he's the answer to all my problems.

His fingers twine in my hair, tangling and tugging, and I give up control—I want him to show me exactly where he wants me. I can't think anymore—I just *want.* And I want *him.*

I squeeze my fist and drive it up and down over his length. A drop of precum beads at the tip and I moan, massaging it into the head with my thumb. I'm desperate to taste him. I try to move down to do exactly that, but his grip tenses in my hair, holding me in place. "Jesse. Fuck," I whisper.

Not this again. This delicious goddamn torture.

He grins. "Hmm... What is it? You want my cock in your mouth?"

"Uh-huh," I almost whine. Hearing him say it floods me with a rush of need. I try to move down again.

He tugs at my hair, pulling my head back. "Then beg."

Wet heat gathers between my legs. I fucking hate this. And I fucking *love* this. I try to move again, but he holds me steady, his grip unyielding.

"Beg for it."

I think my eyes roll back in my head.

With his free hand, he reaches for mine, bringing it up to his lips. He sucks two of my fingers, then guides my hand between my legs. "And touch that beautiful, soaking wet pussy while you do it." The look on his face is goddamn feral. "Show me how desperate you are for this cock."

"Fuck..." is all I can get out, my fingers swirling over my throbbing clit. "Please," I whisper, trying to keep it together. "Please fuck my mouth."

When he finally guides me downward, the rush of relief is short-lived. He stops me again—just out of reach.

God, it's so close.

"Jesse! Oh, God..." I whimper. "*Please!*"

He draws his thumb over my lips, slipping the pad into my mouth.

I lick it eagerly, dizzy with need.

"Just wanted to hear that one more time," he says, his voice low and rough. "You're so fucking pretty when you beg."

I lift my addled gaze, practically salivating.

When he releases my hair, I dive down and take him deep. His groan of pleasure sends trembling waves of sensation through my core. My lips and tongue slide over his thick length, one fist following along in a slow rhythm while my other hand works my clit. Drawing back, I spit on his cock, pumping and twisting my fist until he's slick with it.

His inhale is sharp. "Oh, Jesus... Ada..."

I take him into my mouth again, speeding up my pace, and his hands are in my hair, guiding me gently.

"You're so good at that," he murmurs. "So fucking good."

I push a finger inside myself as I slowly fill my mouth with him, my moan cutting away to silence when he hits the back of my throat.

His fingers tense in my hair, but I can tell he's holding back, not wanting to push me beyond my limit. His jagged, whimpered sounds tell me he's getting close, and his self-control is crumbling.

"Fuck, Ada." He hums with pleasure, the sound catching as his breath stutters. "Fuck... Stop before I come." His expression is almost agonized. "Get over here." He lifts me up and ravages my mouth with his. With one hand, he quickly coats the head of his dick in my wetness and hisses out a curse as I sink down, all the air leaving my lungs as I take him to the hilt in a single stroke.

I stay there, circling my hips to chase the friction against his skin.

"Yes," he whispers. "God, I love how you feel when you do that."

As I start to rise up and sink down, I bite his lower lip, tugging and licking and sucking however I can, somehow unable to get enough of him.

He grips my hips as he lifts me up and slams me back down over and over again. We move faster, my tits bouncing against his chest, his face buried in my neck. Each plunging impact seems to hit deeper.

When he starts thrusting up to meet me, I know he's going over the edge.

"Fuck!" he cries out, tugging me down hard and wrapping his arms tightly around my back. He holds his breath for a moment as I move my hips in small circles, then he shudders with a long groan as his release spurts long and hot inside me. I tilt my hips, grinding against him to make it last, to take every drop from him.

As he slows, his teeth scrape over my shoulder. Suddenly, he lifts me up, pulling his cock from inside me.

"Ada..." he says only my name, his ragged voice reverent and spent, and flicks his tongue over my nipple. Dragging his fingers between my legs, he gathers the slick of his release as it trickles out, then shoves it back inside. "Mmm... keep that in there."

I hum a soft moan, pressing into his touch.

He feathers smiling lips over my cheek, taking a moment to collect himself. "Well, that wasn't very gentlemanly of me—coming before you could go again."

"It's okay, baby," I reassure him, almost sighing the words. "I already came once."

He goes still, lighting up with amusement, suddenly more alert. "Sorry, did you just call me *baby*?"

I cringe. "It just slipped out. Shut up."

He scoffs. "So, I can't call you *Buttercup*, but you can call me *baby*?"

He's never going to let me forget this.

I groan, arousal and annoyance blending together. Still, I can't help but tilt my hips, moving against his fingers, hungry for the friction he's denying me. "You're the worst."

"The *worst?* A second ago, you were calling me *baby*," he teases. He's fucking *loving* this.

I roll my eyes. "God..."

"Doesn't seem... oh, I dunno..."—he drives two fingers inside me and I gasp—"*fair.*"

"Oh, fuck, Jesse..."

"Make it up to me," he rasps. "Make a fucking mess of my hand when you come again."

It doesn't take much. His strokes start slow and then speed up, my muscles clenching and tight, my fingernails digging into his shoulders. The pleasure quickly builds to a peak, exploding inside of me like it had been caged there, aching to be let loose. My strangled voice rings through the empty restaurant as the waves of my release throb and wash over me in an all-consuming chaos. Jesse slows as my orgasm ebbs, the jump of my muscles grasping at his fingers in soft pulses.

"Attagirl," he says softly, stroking my cheek as I return to Earth, panting and sated.

I give him a drowsy kiss and drop my forehead to rest on his shoulder. That feeling hits me again—the same one from after he read to me on our couch. The one where I feel so safe—so protected—I know I could fall asleep in this man's arms. Not just now, not just tonight, but every day, forever.

Oh, God. I love him.

He rubs soft circles on my back with his free hand.

I'm in love with him.

"God. How long have we been here?" I ask, trying to keep things light. I smile into his T-shirt, inhaling the scent of sex—and of him. "What year is it?"

He twists to kiss my cheek, chuckling. "Come on, let's get cleaned up. I wanna take you home."

Home. He could take me anywhere and it would be home.

27

JESSE

Frank frowns at his watch. "What's the holdup?"

"Oh, you know how Marcus works so hard," Maria chirps, waving a dismissive hand and scooping another helping of lasagna onto my plate before I can protest.

"I'm really good, Maria," I start, trying and failing to stop her before she loads me up with more food than I can eat.

Ada nudges my ankle under the table and shakes her head. Maybe it's better not to refuse food in the Russo household.

"Nonsense! There's so much! Eat!" Maria moves to fill up my wineglass for the second time. "Plus, your mother got good news today, so we have something to celebrate. It's a shame she couldn't join us for dinner."

"Right," I say, halfheartedly. After getting the all-clear to drive and resume light activities, Mom had been so excited she'd decided to celebrate with her best friends; she'd made a dinner reservation before we even left the parking lot at the doctor's office. I try to push down the knowledge that Mom's news means I've been given my own all-clear: to fly back to Australia.

"I know Marcus had some things to wrap up with that

Gilmore account," Frank says, "but it shouldn't have taken *all day.*" He sips his wine.

"I can text him," Ada offers, reaching for her phone. "Or Renee. Was she gonna come?"

"Renee had a client," Maria says. "And don't bother texting. I'm sure he'll be here any minute."

As if on cue, the doorbell rings.

Ada's brow furrows. "Is the door locked or something?"

"Oh," Maria says, like she's suddenly remembered something, "that actually might be Gloria." She pushes up to answer the door.

Ada shoots a curious look at her dad.

"I think she was gonna stop by to pick something up for the bake sale," Frank explains.

"Oh." Ada sounds uneasy and, when I glance her way, she looks it.

"Who's Gloria?" I ask her under my breath.

Ada turns to me and swallows. "Gloria *Nicolosi.*"

It takes me a beat, but I straighten in my chair. *Mrs. Nicolosi.* The one who saw us together last weekend in Seattle.

"Come on in, Gloria!" Maria calls out from down the hall. "It's in the kitchen, through here."

I lower my fork with an uneaten bite of lasagna and wipe my hands slowly on my napkin.

Beside me, Ada prods at her salad, attention fixed on her plate.

"You can say hello to Ada!" Maria calls over her shoulder as they enter the dining room.

"Oh, goodness, I'm interrupting your dinner! Sorry!" Mrs. Nicolosi says. Her gaze then shifts between me and Ada with a flash of recognition. "It's you again!"

"Again?" Frank asks.

"I ran into these two in Seattle last weekend," Mrs. Nicolosi explains. "What, didn't Ada mention it?"

All eyes turn on us.

"I forgot to tell you," Ada says to her mom, her voice flat.

"They make such a lovely couple, don't you think?" Mrs. Nicolosi lifts her chin at us, then does a giddy shrug before turning to Maria for a response.

"Couple?" Maria echoes in confusion, cutting a look across the room to Ada, then me.

"Yes! They were so sweet. So wrapped up in each other like that, you know." The kitchen door swings open and I wince. "Kissing on a busy sidewalk like they were the only two people in the world!"

Marcus drops his car keys on the table. "Oh, hey, Mrs. Nicolosi! I didn't know you were here." He pulls out his chair and sits down. "Sorry I'm so late, Mom." A beat passes. "Who was kissing?" Marcus asks as he takes his seat, then seems to clock the gobsmacked silence in the room. I can almost see the question in his eyes followed by a quick grasp at denial when the answer is clearly written on my face.

Unfortunately, it takes another moment for the other shoe to drop for Mrs. Nicolosi. "Ada and Jesse!"

I wince. *Shit.*

"I was just saying they were..." she trails off, finally picking up on Marcus' reaction.

"*What?*" Marcus sits back in his seat.

"Marcus—" Ada tries.

"Is she serious?" He stares at me, then at Ada. When nobody immediately denies it, he adds, "What the fuck?"

"We didn't wanna make a big deal—" I try.

"Oh, you don't think this is a big deal, Jesse?" He pushes away from the table and stands, his food untouched.

"It's none of your business, Marcus," Ada says. "We're both *adults!*"

"In what universe is it not my business that my sister is

hooking up with my best friend?" He flings an arm my way, barely able to look at me, and runs both hands through his hair.

"Gloria," Maria says softly, putting a hand on her friend's arm, "let me grab you that tray." She guides an apologetic Mrs. Nicolosi into the kitchen.

"How long has this been going on?" Frank asks. Both Ada and I turn at his voice like we'd forgotten he was here.

"Uh, a few weeks, I guess?" Ada replies.

"A few *weeks*?" Marcus asks, incredulous. "You know what? After the day I've had, I can't deal with this shit right now." He turns to leave.

"Marcus, would you fucking relax?" Ada tries again. "We can talk about—"

Maria comes back into the dining room, glancing between the rest of us.

Marcus spins to pick up his car keys from the table, then makes for the front hallway.

"What, you're not even gonna stay to eat?" Maria calls after him.

"Lost my appetite!" he calls back.

I sit there in shock for a moment before I push away from the table to follow him.

He flings open the front door and charges down the porch steps to where his SUV is parked in the driveway.

I jog after him. "Marcus, wait! Can we just talk about it?"

He spins around. "What the fuck were you thinking, Jess?" His eyes dart between mine, as if trying to find the answer in my face. "You know what? Don't answer that. I don't wanna know. *God.* She's my *fucking sister*!"

"Look, I'm sorry."

"Why didn't you tell me?"

I let out a surprised breath. "Are you kidding me?"

"Do I look like I'm fucking joking?" he asks, glaring at me.

"Dude. Ever since we were kids, you've been clear Ada was off-limits."

"What are you talking about? When did I say that?"

"I dunno. Kai made some crack about her once, said something about getting in her pants, and you nearly kicked his ass!"

"Uh, when?" He screws up his face.

"Senior year?"

His jaw drops on a scoff. "And you don't think I've maybe, I dunno, *grown* a bit in the last *decade*? Jesus Christ. We're adults, Jess."

"Okay, fine, but the day I moved in you were all like *she's my sister* and telling me not to get involved, saying it would be messy and shit..."

"And was I wrong?" He throws his hands out at his sides.

"We just... thought it would make things weird. It was"—I catch myself—"it *is* temporary. We didn't think you needed to know."

He paces in front of me.

"I'm sorry. Really." Guilt twists my stomach. This is not how I imagined Marcus finding out.

"What changed, man? You and Ada were friends for years. Why now?"

"I dunno. It just... *changed.*"

He shakes his head with a joyless smile. "I *knew* something was up. I fucking knew. You were all..."—he grimaces—"*weird* around each other. Even before you moved in with her."

"I know. I tried really hard not to... We both did. For a long time."

"Oh, well, in that case, do you want a goddamn prize? Because not fucking my little sister should be the bare minimum of friendship, Jess."

"I know." I look at my feet.

"And yet that didn't seem to matter much to you, did it?"

I lift my gaze. "Dude. No. It wasn't—"

"Don't *dude* me, *bro*." He squints. "You fucked my sister, you kept it a secret from me for weeks, and now I'm the last one to find out? Even fucking *Mrs. Nicolosi* knew before I did. We're supposed to be *best friends*!"

I swallow. "She saw us in Seattle. We didn't mean for it to shake out like this."

"Oh, yeah? And how did you mean for it to *shake out,* Jess? Were you ever gonna tell me?"

I rub my forehead. "I dunno. But we weren't trying to hurt you. It was never supposed to end up like this. Never supposed to be more than just..." I trail off, clenching my jaw. I can't tell him it was supposed to be just sex.

His face falls. "So it's more now? You care about her?"

"I've *always* cared about Ada. You know that."

"You know what I'm asking, Jesse," he says, giving me a warning look.

I press my lips together. I haven't even told Ada how I feel.

He furrows his brow. "You have feelings for her?"

"Yeah," I admit on a harsh breath. "I do... I have feelings for her."

"Fucking hell." He turns away, opening the driver's side door. "Well, sounds like you two need to... I don't even know. I gotta go. I need some time to cool off. Tell Mom and Dad I'll call them later."

"Marcus—"

"Just figure your shit out, man."

28

ADA

When Jesse hadn't come back inside after a couple of minutes, I'd gone after him, stopping short just outside the front door when I caught a glimpse of his back and heard Marcus' angry voice. Knowing I was tucked out of view thanks to the garage, I couldn't help but eavesdrop. I shouldn't have stayed, but when someone asks the man you're in love with if he has feelings for you... well, it's hard to make yourself leave before finding out the answer. My dumb heart was frozen, hoping against all reason he'd say yes.

And then his words nearly took me down.

"I do... I have feelings for her."

That single piece of information simultaneously lobbed me high in the sky and slammed me into the ground. My knees felt like they were made of sand, so I slumped down on the weathered porch, sitting with my back against the wall beside the front door. And there I remain, rooted to the spot—paralyzed by the futility of loving Jesse when I've known I'd lose him from the start.

It doesn't matter how he feels. How *we* feel. There's no future for us.

Marcus' car peels out of the driveway and Jesse turns back toward the house, looking exhausted. When he sees me, he stops in his tracks.

I swallow.

He walks to the bottom of the porch steps, putting his hands in his pockets. "How much did you overhear?"

"Enough," I say, my voice wavering as I force myself to my feet. I glance over my shoulder and descend the steps so my parents won't overhear us. Facing him in the driveway, I'm somehow both desperate to reach for him and determined not to. "Jess, we fucked this up."

Hurt touches his brow. "Yeah."

"It got out of hand. *We* got out of hand. Now we've hurt Marcus... and for what? Some incredible sex?"

He looks stung. "Don't say that shit."

"That's all this was ever supposed to be, Jesse."

"But we both know it's more," he says, shaking his head. "It's been more than that for a while."

I hug my arms tight over my chest. "Yeah, well, letting that happen was a huge mistake."

He clenches his hands. "Do you honestly think we could have resisted this? Avoided each other and still lived together—still seen each other every single day? Still shared everything else?"

"We could have tried!" I exclaim. "We *should* have tried."

"We *did* try!" His shoulders tense in a frustrated-looking shrug.

"Tried harder, then! We should never have let anything happen in the first place."

He huffs a breath through his nose. "Says the girl who insisted it happen in the first place."

I set my jaw. "Hey. Don't put this all on me like I roped you into something you didn't want. I might have taken that first step, but you've been with me the whole way along—enthusiastically, I might add. We *both* did this."

"Yeah." He sighs, regret passing across his face.

Long seconds pass before I speak again. "It stops. Now."

His shoulders drop. "You can't be serious."

"There isn't any future for us beyond this summer, Jess. We knew that from the beginning. You're leaving soon anyway, and—"

"You think we can stop?" he asks, cutting me off. "Flip a switch? Just like that?"

"Jess, we have to," I plead. "It's only gonna hurt more if we keep this going until the bitter end."

"No." He shakes his head as he steps toward me. "Fuck that. What would hurt more is spending my last few days in town living with you and not being able to touch you. Us not spending every second of what little time we have left here together."

"But don't you get it? There's no *together* for us! You're gonna be in fucking Australia! You couldn't get farther away if you tried."

He recoils. "You *told me* to go back."

"I know!"

"What the fuck do you *want*, Ada? You either want me here or you don't. You can't have it both ways."

I don't answer because it doesn't matter. It won't change anything. "I'm not fucking up your friendship with Marcus, Jess, so what's the point in carrying on with this charade?"

"Charade? So this is... what, just an act for you?" His eyes bore into mine, searching for answers. Long moments pass. "What are you saying?"

I look away, trying not to let tears cloud my vision.

"Are you saying you don't have feelings for me?"

I don't trust myself to speak.

"Ada, look at me." He takes a steadying breath. "Do you have feelings for me?"

I know what I have to do. It's gonna hurt and I know it's cruel, but I need to rip off the bandage. I meet his eyes. "No."

The word lands like a physical blow. He stares, lips parted, a slew of emotions taking up brief residence in his quickly changing expression. Shock gives way to a glimpse of raw pain before he quickly bricks it over. "Bullshit."

"W-what?" I sputter, caught off guard.

"That's bullshit." He comes closer. "You've always been a shitty liar, Ada. I might be kinda crap at the whole feelings thing, but that's never been your problem. I can see everything right on your face and I know you feel this too."

"No, I don't." But I can't quite look at him when I say it. It's a low blow.

"Cut the crap, Ada," he grumbles.

I can almost feel the sarcastic cogs humming to life, that well-oiled machine of self-preservation doing what it does best. "Oh, you know best, huh? You're gonna tell me how I feel?"

"About me? Yeah. I have a pretty good fucking idea." The corners of his eyes tense up. "And I'm not gonna let you gaslight me into thinking I imagined all this."

"Gaslighting? Fuck off. You know me so well, huh? Well, then fucking enlighten me, Jess. What do you know about me?" I throw my hands out at my sides.

Jesse steps closer still, his body only inches from mine.

My eyes flare wide as he grips my chin between his thumb and forefinger, lifting my face to his. "Jesse, what the f—"

"I know you have an entire drawer full of tea but you only ever drink coffee. I know your favorite animal is the sea otter because they hold hands and you think that's adorable. I know your greatest fear is earthquakes. I know you got that scar on your right knee sliding into third base when you were fourteen—because I was *at the game.*

"I know you'll fight tooth and nail to protect the people you love because you're a good person. And I know, even though you're a good person, you can still act like a huge pain in the ass."

I cut my gaze away from his.

"No." He tugs my chin back to face him. "Look at me. I know all you wanna do right now is hide behind your snarky bullshit and bury your feelings down deep where they never touch you. I know you think it's easier to blow this up and try to hurt me than to admit what's really going on here."

I open my mouth to speak, but I falter. I don't know what to say.

"I know you," he continues. "You've been trying to downplay how you feel about me for two months. *Two months.* And I know you're scared as hell, and you're trying to put on a brave face."

Fuck. He's not wrong.

"But Ada," he almost whispers, the emotion thick in his voice, "we've known each other way too long for you to hide anything from me. You don't need to pretend. Not with me."

What the fuck am I supposed to do now?

"Jesse..." I step out of his arms, my heart twisting. "I can't. I can't do this anymore."

"Ada, don't..."

I shake my head. "I can't be with you, Jesse."

Silence stretches between us. It's not untrue and it's not surprising. Being together was never in the cards.

But it still hurts to say out loud.

"Look," he finally says, his voice wavering. "If you really wanna end this, I'll respect that and back off, but I won't pretend it's not gonna kill me to do it. So don't insult me by pretending you don't feel anything for me." A muscle in his cheek flickers, the movement caught in the orange glow of the evening light.

The front door pushes open and Dad steps out onto the porch. "Everything okay out here? Where's Marcus?"

Jesse gives me a long, hard look before turning to Dad. "Marcus left. Said he needed to cool off. He'll call you later."

Dad nods.

"And, actually, I was just leaving too."

"We drove here together," I point out softly. "What are you—"

"I'll walk."

"What? Jess, it's like six miles."

"It's fine." He turns again to Dad. "Thanks for having me for dinner, Frank. And for lending me the bed. I'll make sure it gets back to you. Please tell Maria thank you for me. It was great to see you both." He gives Dad a tight smile and turns to go.

We watch him walk to the end of the driveway before Dad's footsteps approach me from behind. "You okay, kid?"

"No, Dad." I wipe my eyes. "None of this is okay."

29

———

JESSE

Taking off: it's what I do best. But I couldn't stay there. Couldn't keep it together another moment with Ada pushing me away. I tell myself I'm giving her what she wants—time and space away from me—and try not to let that thought gouge too deep.

The plan all along was for me to go back. To leave her behind.

She's probably right: this is for the best. But there's a twisting ache in my chest at the thought of sleeping alone tonight—and every night until I leave. And *God damn*, it hurts.

The heat of the day radiates up from the sun-baked sidewalk, and I frown, pulling my T-shirt away from my damp skin. I've been walking maybe twenty minutes and I'm already sweating.

My phone vibrates in my pocket and I pull it out.

UNKNOWN NUMBER

Hey J its Kai. Marcus gave me ur number

ME

Hey

I save him as a contact, not sure why I'm bothering, since I'll be leaving soon. My guilt about being a shitty friend, probably. As I hit *save*, he texts again.

KAI

Ur still in Lennox right

ME

Yeah for another week I think?

KAI

So can u make it 2 the wedding sat

Trying 2 firm up numbers

Kai's wedding. Right.

My first instinct is to bail. Avoid Marcus. Avoid Ada. But I check that impulse, knowing it would be shitty to do that to Kai, who's offered me this olive branch after I basically ghosted him for eight years. No, I can't blow up one more friendship. I'll go to the wedding—try to breathe one last gasp of life into these friendships before I leave. It's the least I can do. Even if Ada will be there.

Besides, what am I gonna do instead? Sit in our apartment and feel like shit?

God, I don't know if I can face going back.

ME

Yeah man I can make it. Thanks again for the invite

KAI

Forgot 2 mention Naomi will b there

Shes friends w/Nadine. That gonna b weird 4 u?

U dont have 2 sit w/her or anything

I stop in my tracks and almost laugh. This fucking town. *Of course* Naomi will be there. *Of course* I'll have to spend the evening dodging both the women who've broken my heart.

ME

Not a problem. I'll put on my big boy pants

Speaking of which...

I need to quit dicking around.

Pulling up the airline's website, I find the flight I've been watching for the past two weeks, waiting for a seat sale. The price has gone down by fifty bucks. As far as airfare goes, it's a drop in the bucket, but I need to shit or get off the pot. I can leave the morning after the wedding on the early flight.

Fuck it. I'll sleep on the damn plane.

I tap through the checkout process, forcing myself not to second-guess. If the wedding ends up being a disaster, at least I won't be sticking around for the fallout.

I pocket my phone and keep walking, climbing a steep hill and pushing through when my leg muscles start to feel it.

I'm really doing it. I'm leaving.

I walk faster, wishing for that familiar burn to consume all my attention—to take my thoughts away from Ada. But I know it won't; no exercise is intense enough to block her out. I push harder, breaking into a run as I crest the hill.

And I don't stop.

Running past parks, businesses, and countless houses, I let the rhythmic drum of my footfalls pound through me, the usual numbing effect giving me no relief. I'm rounding the corner to a long path through a park when my phone rings. I slow to a stop and pull it out, cursing under my breath when I see Marcus' name on the call display.

I brace myself, letting it ring a couple more times before I answer. "Hey," I say, trying not to sound too out of breath—or too devastated.

"Hey," he says back. A beat passes. "You okay? You sound like you're crying or something."

"Or something." I run my free hand over my jaw and push my fist against my solar plexus. Blinking in the glare of the setting sun, I turn to pace along the path.

"Look, Jess—"

"I'm so sorry, Marcus," I blurt out. "I don't know what else to say. I know I don't deserve it, but I hope you can forgive me. She's your sister, and I…" I trail off, not knowing how to make it right. "So, just… whatever happens between you and me, promise me you'll forgive Ada. I'd hate to have fucked things up for your family."

Another beat passes and Marcus' silence makes me anxious, so I continue. "Anyway, I dunno if it's any consolation, but… she called it off. After you left."

"Really?"

I sniff, trying to clear the hot feeling at the back of my throat. "Yeah. Didn't want to drag things out, with me leaving soon."

Marcus makes a small sound of understanding.

"I'm outta here on the twenty-fifth," I add.

"You booked a flight?" Marcus asks.

"Yeah, just now." My stomach clenches as the reality sinks in. I'd been putting off booking that plane ticket, lying to myself that it was about the cost. But it was always Ada.

I'd been holding onto some ridiculous thread of hope that she might feel the way I do—might ask me to stay. *Want* me to stay. She'd wound herself around my fucking heart and I was ready to drop everything to be with her.

But now? She's looked me in the eye and told me point-blank that she doesn't have feelings for me. I don't believe her, but I can't upend my entire life if she won't even be honest with me—or herself.

"So, anyway," I continue, "you won't have to see my face or

think about this shit anymore after next week." This isn't how I wanted to spend my last days in town, with my best friend pissed at me and Ada shutting me out.

"That's assuming I want to see your ugly mug at all," he says.

Ouch.

It's a low blow—and one I totally deserve. I've hurt Marcus. Lied to his face. Fucked his little sister, for God's sake.

Some best friend.

"You have every right to feel that way. I totally understa—"

He cuts me off. "Dude. It was a joke."

I exhale with what should be relief, but all I feel is helpless.

"Jess, I talked with Renee and she helped me... calm down about things."

"Yeah?" I scrub a hand down my cheek.

"Yeah."

There's another long silence and he doesn't elaborate—which is saying something. Marcus is a Russo through and through; he doesn't usually stay tight-lipped. *Oh, God.* I wish he'd just punched me in the face.

"So, are we cool?" I bite my lip as the dead air hangs.

"We will be," he says, sounding resigned. "I'm still not happy about it, but I can get over myself."

"Okay," I say, still uneasy. In reality, nothing about this is okay.

"I mean, if you're leaving next week, I still wanna hang out with you before you go. So let's just try to forget all this."

I wish I could forget—wish I could erase this ache in my chest. "You'll have to make sure to get me drunk at Kai's wedding, 'cause I'm gonna need it. Naomi's apparently gonna be there too."

He makes an *oof* sound. "Well, better to go out with a bang than a whimper."

I laugh and start walking again. "Interesting choice of words."

"Ah, fuck, just... don't bang anyone else."

I smile despite the weight pressing down on my chest. "You got it."

I'M ALREADY FIGHTING with the damn air mattress setup not five minutes in. Two single airbeds—wedged between Mom's TV stand and the coffee table, with a queen-size fitted sheet failing to hold them together—have about as much structural integrity under a man my size as a Riverside Deli sub. My feet hang over the edge by several inches. I thrash and wrestle with the covers, trying to put most of my weight on one side so I don't fall into the *Pit of Despair*. Still, the cavern underneath me gradually widens as the coffee table inches toward the sofa. Defeated, I sit up.

"Maybe you should try the couch?" Mom suggests softly from the doorway, dressed in her pajamas. We both eye the love seat with matching skepticism.

"Sorry. Didn't mean to keep you up." I sigh and gesture in resignation to the pathetic excuse for a bed. Mom had bought the airbeds for Sam and Hazel to use when sleeping over. So, when I called her asking for a place to crash, she was cautiously optimistic we could work something out for a few days. Too optimistic.

Maybe staying here was the wrong move. But I can't face the prospect of dodging Ada for the next week, and I don't have the balls to ask Marcus for another turn on the *trash couch*. I'd gone back to the apartment to pack up my things, but seeing Ada for even that short time was painful. I could tell she'd been crying.

Mom perches tentatively beside me on one of the airbeds. Even in the dark and without her glasses on, she looks so much healthier than when I first arrived. "Hey, kiddo, I know your last few days here aren't exactly working out as planned..."

I grunt a soft sound of agreement, leaning forward to rest my elbows on my knees. "That's putting it lightly."

Mom rubs my back. "But it's been wonderful having you home."

I turn toward her, attempting a smile. "Yeah?"

"You know, I didn't handle things well when your dad and I were going through all that mess with the divorce."

"Ah, you did your best," I say, trying to reassure her. "It was awful. I know."

"It was." She takes a breath, rubbing her hands over her thighs. "But I should have been there for you. Claire, too, but you especially. You were barely out of school. I'm sorry for letting my personal problems take me away from what really matters."

"Mom, you don't need to—"

"No, I do." Her tone is unyielding. "You deserved better. And it's been my biggest regret that we lost touch when you moved away. I missed you."

"I missed you too," I say, sniffing back my emotion.

"You know I'm not the least bit religious," she continues, "but *blessing* is the only word I can think of. This aneurysm—as hard as it's been—has been a blessing, Jesse. And I don't just mean having your help. I mean getting to see you. Spending time with you again." She pulls me over and kisses the side of my head. "The way you raced to my side, like some kind of knight in shining armor!"

I chuckle. "I guess?"

"Only, instead of scoring the beautiful princess, you're stuck with me," she adds, elbowing me.

I blow a breath through my nose and look at the floor.

"I think I got the better end of the deal there."

"You almost died, Mom," I say. "What was I supposed to do? Wait for a seat sale?"

She smiles. "My point is: you've done a lot to help me. You've shown up for me. Over and over again. Thank you."

I nod, thinking for a moment. "I wanna say I'd do it all over again but, please, let's not do *that* all over again, okay?"

She squeezes my hand. "I'll do my best. And you know, I'm gonna return the favor. I'm gonna keep showing up for you. That's what you do when you love someone, isn't it? Even when it's hard. You just keep... showing up."

"Yeah, I guess it is."

We sit together in the dark for a few moments, my gaze falling to some indistinct spot on the carpet.

Mom finally breaks the silence. "So, about that beautiful princess..."

I dip my head on an exhale. "You know, she'd *hate* to know you called her a princess."

"Oh? Well, okay, then. That beautiful... strong, independent, self-made woman." She raises her eyebrows.

"Okay," I say, nodding. "Not bad, not bad."

Mom leans in closer. "Is that the opposite of a princess? I have no idea."

I laugh, but my smile slowly fades as I remember what happened. "Mom, what do I do?"

She thinks for a moment, reaching an arm around me. "You just keep showing up."

"And if she doesn't wanna see me?"

"Give her some time. She needs to *feel her feelings*." At my curious look, she waves her hand and adds, "Claire got me going to this counselor."

"Really?"

She nods. "Seems I suppressed a lot during the divorce. And afterward."

I tilt my head; she's not alone in that. When I speak, my voice is thick with emotion. "I love you, Mom. Thank you."

"Love you too." She pats my cheek, then pushes up to stand. "Now let's fix your bed."

30

ADA

To heartbroken people, weddings are a swirly for the soul: equal parts disgusting, overwhelming, and humiliating and, at some point, you give yourself over to the numb resignation that you're being shoved face-first into your own personal hell.

Living alone in the apartment for the last week has been brutal. There's no one running the coffee maker at six in the morning or smirking at me from the kitchen in a sweaty running shirt—and the hateful silence seems to deliver a fresh sucker-punch to my heart every day. I haven't been able to bring myself to answer Jesse's texts or calls, knowing it would hurt too much. When he told me he'd booked his flight, I'd sobbed for a good forty minutes before pulling myself together enough to re-list my ad for a roommate. After all, my bank account isn't gonna wait around for me to get over him.

The crushing weight drapes over me like a leaden cape and I feel nauseated. Sluggish. Broken. All I want to do is run away from this feeling but, like some kind of emotional *Scream* sequel, the call is very much coming from inside the house.

I just need to survive one more night. One more night and Jesse will be gone.

Only through a combination of spatial jiu-jitsu and pure luck did I manage to avoid sitting next to Jesse at the wedding, using Marcus, Renee, and our old friend Adrian as my human buffers.

"You doing alright, Ada?" Adrian whispers from the chair to my left, his voice filtering through the numb buzzing in my skull. With effort, I translate the inscrutable *womp womp* into English.

"No," is all I say, but the look I give him invites no further questions.

Over Adrian's shoulder, Jesse pinches the bridge of his nose. The few glances I've stolen today—tiny sips of self-inflicted poison—reveal he's not faring much better than I am. His eyes look dull and shadowed. Even four chairs down, he's somehow both too close and too far away from me.

Stop drinking the poison, I remind myself and force my gaze to the happy couple.

Nadine and Kai beam, bathed in the glowing light of the late afternoon sun. A non-denominational officiant gestures in front of them, saying something about love and commitment I can't really hear—or process.

I turn to my right, hoping nature will ground me in the present.

In another headspace, I could acknowledge the beauty here. It's the kind of place that should inspire me to paint: the lush gardens, the quaint Tudor-style bed-and-breakfast, and the incredible view of the river from the open cliffside. Even the name is ethereal: *Starscape Manor.*

Murmurs to my left snag my attention and my stomach drops when I turn to see Jesse leaning close to Marcus, whispering to him and Renee. Roping Adrian in, he gestures for them to shuffle down the row of chairs.

No. Don't. Please fucking don't. Shit.

He sinks down beside me and I angle away, arranging my limbs so we don't accidentally touch. If my leg brushed Jesse's leg right now, I think I might actually ignite—and not in a sexy way. More in the scorched-earth, my-heart-is-a-charred-ball-of-ash kind of way. And nothing ruins a wedding like a guest torching the venue in the middle of the ceremony.

"Hey," he whispers. "Can we talk?"

I glance past him to where Marcus is watching us.

"Please." Jesse's desperation pulls at me.

"There's nothing to say," I whisper.

The woman in front of me glares at us over her shoulder in a silent reminder that we should both shut the fuck up right now.

I cross my arms over my chest and fix my gaze on Nadine and Kai, who are grinning in ways that I'm sure normal humans shouldn't be capable of. It's obnoxious.

"Ada," he whispers again.

Clenching my teeth, I meet his eyes.

"Please," he mouths.

I don't respond and return my attention to Kai and Nadine, who are about to read their vows.

Nadine smiles sweetly and pulls a tiny, folded paper from the cleavage of her dress, eliciting titters from the crowd.

Beside me, Jesse sighs and orients himself forward.

Nadine starts. "Kai, you came into my life when I was least expecting it and turned my whole world upside-down."

I stare down at my lap as she goes on.

"I've never been a big believer in fate, but I can't imagine my life with anyone else—can't imagine loving anyone else the way I love you."

An invisible fist clamps down around my heart.

"You've always supported me in following my dreams, had my back in every fight, made me laugh, and made me feel beautiful. And you've always put up with all my bullshit." Nadine makes a guilty face. "Sorry, Grandma!" she adds as soft laughter floats up all around us.

In the pause, I risk a glance at Jesse, immediately regretting the way his anguished expression gouges deep in my chest. His gaze holds mine for a torturous second before I force my eyes ahead.

"Kai, I promise to love the man you are and the man you'll become. I promise to make you laugh and put up with all *your* bullshit and be your best friend. I love you." Nadine dabs her tears away and folds the paper, tucking it back into her dress with a sweet little laugh.

I feel a light tap on my chest and look down to see a teardrop soaking into the silky red fabric of my dress. I swipe at my cheeks, determined to get through this with my dignity intact.

Good fucking luck.

"Nadine," Kai starts, "I've been an idiot for a long time."

Chuckles rise from the crowd.

"But the smartest thing I ever did was take a chance on you. Loving you has opened me up to what I didn't know was missing from my life."

In my peripheral vision, Jesse lifts a hand to wipe his face.

Kai continues. "No matter how far we travel, no matter what happens, and no matter where life takes us... you'll always be my home. And I promise to be yours. I promise to be everything you are to me for the rest of our lives. I love you with all my heart."

I grip the seat on either side of my thighs and dig my nails in, desperate for any sensation but this.

I barely feel the first tentative brush of Jesse's hand but, when it finally registers, my eyes close, letting loose twin tears that slip down my cheeks and drip off the slope of my jaw. And then I'm scrambling for his fingers, interlacing them with mine and squeezing hard in the privacy between our garden chairs. I hold onto him, the connection of our hands raw and vulnerable. I open my eyes and keep looking forward, but I feel him watching me—sense his pleading gaze.

I send all the words I don't have down my arm and into his fingertips, trying to memorize the way his thumb sweeps softly over the back of my hand.

When the happy couple kiss, applause rises to fill my ears, breaking the spell, and I jerk my hand away from Jesse's. I trust the commotion to drown out the gasping, messy breath that feels like knives against my ribs. When the guests stand to see Nadine and Kai walk arm-in-arm down the aisle, I push past a few vaguely alarmed strangers and head toward the house, intent on finding a bathroom sink to cry over—alone.

I DON'T KNOW how I make it through dinner, but I'm sure dissociation plays an unhealthy role. While drinks are being handed around, a small crew works in the fading light to create a dance floor of sorts, rearranging chairs and erecting lighting stands around the expansive lawn. Twinkling fairy lights have been strung through the trees and overhang the bar, and staked lanterns light the periphery of the garden. The whole place glows.

I snag a champagne flute off a passing tray and immediately slam its contents, then covertly scan the crowd for Jesse—intent on clocking his movements so I can stay the fuck away from him for the rest of the night. When darkness finally cloaks the river over the cliffside, I'm grateful; if I keep to the shadows, I can let myself look as miserable as I feel. I'd underestimated how much it would hurt to be near him again.

"There you are!" Renee chirps, plopping down next to me on a chair, slightly winded from dancing. She gives me a sad smile. "You doin' okay?"

I shrug, worried that speaking will burst the fragile dam holding back my tears.

"Come on," Renee says, squeezing my hand. "Let's take a walk."

We head down a gravel path lined with soft pink strip lighting and descend a small set of stairs to a private garden. Strings of lights drape from posts surrounding an unlit fire pit, the glow illuminating Renee's golden hair as we sit on the cushioned benches.

She crosses her legs and tugs down the short hem of her shimmering blue dress. "You're miserable, aren't you?"

I bark out a wet laugh. "Is it that obvious?"

"I mean... kind of." That sad smile is pointed at me again.

"I keep telling myself I just have to get through tonight." I sniff, holding back the tears threatening to spill out. "But I'm not pulling it off, am I?"

"Hey, y'know, being at something like this is hard right after a breakup."

"But we didn't break up. We weren't even... Fuck. Forget it." I sniff again and shake my head.

"You can talk to me about it, you know."

I give her a blank look.

"I'm not Marcus!" she says with a swat at my knee. "And I don't have to tell him anything you don't want me to."

"Do you really keep things from him?"

"All the time!"

I raise my eyebrows. "Should I be worried?"

"Oh, God, nothing scandalous like that. Unless you count my secret vibrator." She giggles. "A girl's gotta have her secrets."

I can't help but laugh. "You have a secret vibrator?"

"Well, he knows about my main one, of course. We—"

My shoulders tense and I cringe. "You know what? Never mind. I don't wanna know!"

She puts her hands to her face and covers her mouth. "Sorry!"

We both laugh, and I let loose a theatrical shiver as I try to push away any thoughts of my brother having sex.

"Come on. You gonna get this weight off your chest or what?" she presses.

"Okay." I sigh. "It wasn't ever supposed to be more than…"

"Sex?"

I slide my eyes to meet hers. "Yeah."

"And then it ended up more?"

I press my lips together and nod.

Renee scoots closer and rubs circles on my back, her voice soft. "Does he know how you feel?"

"No." I shake my head. "It's better he doesn't."

"How do you figure?" she asks.

"It'll only hurt more. For both of us."

"Honey, it seems like you're hurting plenty right now. And *he* doesn't look so great either." She covers my hand with hers, squeezing softly. "Can you talk to him tonight? Before he leaves?"

"What's the point?" I huff. "He's on a plane in a few hours. It's not gonna change anything."

"The point… is if you keep stuffing down how you feel, it'll eat you alive. Better to say it, don't you think? Even if it hurts like hell. Even if it doesn't change anything."

"I can't," I say, feeling the tears threaten once again. "I can't tell him and then just watch him leave. Watch him choose somewhere else to be."

Pascal fucked someone else. Katie moved out. Hell, even my parents always choose my brother.

No one ever chooses *me*.

Not that Jesse could, really. Not unless he wants to destroy his friendship with Marcus. And I could never live with myself if he gave up his best friend to be with me.

"So you're not even gonna give him the choice?" Renee asks gently.

"There *is* no choice," I reply, looking at the ground. "Besides, getting over someone is hard enough; I don't need to drag false hope into this mess."

"Oh, honey." Renee pulls me into a hug and smooths a hand over my hair. The gesture is almost motherly, and I have to take a deep breath to stop another flood of tears from rolling down my cheeks.

I need to get it together.

Voices from nearby have me pulling away and sniffing. "Thank you."

"You wanna head back?" Renee asks.

"Probably should." I try for a brave smile.

"Come on, let's go find Marcus," Renee says, moving to get up. Then she pauses, studying me more closely. "You sure you're good?"

No.

I nod.

We head up the steps, picking our way across the gravel path. The crowd and music grow larger and louder as we approach and, when we pass a small seating area overlooking the cliffside, anxiety grips my stomach.

"You know what?" I blurt. "You go ahead. I'm gonna hang out here for a few minutes." Staying away from the crowd feels safer right now.

Renee gives me another hug and leaves me to slump down onto one of the wrought-iron bistro chairs. I don't know how long I sit there, staring into the darkness, but my mother's voice eventually cuts through my thoughts.

"Ada! There you are!"

"Mom!" I say, snapping back to the present. "Hey."

"You wouldn't believe it," she says. "I just ran into Roman Esposito."

"Who?" I ask. I've never been able to keep up with Mom's

social life. Between all her church friends—the infamous Mrs. Nicolosi included—and now this Roman guy... she's one of those people who seems to know everybody.

"Mr. Esposito? From church. Don't you remember him?"

"Uh..." I start, searching my memory. "Wait—the bushy eyebrows guy?"

"Ada!" Mom scolds, looking over her shoulder. "Anyway, it doesn't matter. That's not the point. I think you know his grandson, Rolando."

"Oh!" I say. "Yeah. Roly comes to the teen center."

She nods and takes a seat in the chair on the other side of the tiny bistro table, smoothing some invisible wrinkle in her dress.

"He's a good kid," I say, not sure where this is going.

"Well, sounds like he's been struggling in school for a while. But Roman was telling me you've really helped him. With his *dyslexia*." She almost whispers the word.

Whoa. This was not what I was expecting.

I straighten. "Yeah?"

"Yeah. Apparently, this is the first year he's been getting his homework done." Mom throws me a cautious glance. "Roman told me he made some kind of arrangement with his teachers to get the instructions audio recorded."

"Did he really?" I ask. *Smart kid.*

"Listens on his phone or something, I guess." She makes a dismissive gesture. "I don't know how it works. But in any case, Roman kept singing your praises. He thinks it was talking with you about it that made the difference. Helped him take some ownership. Bring up his grades. Made him feel less... alone."

"Seriously? I had no idea." For the first time tonight, my chest feels something other than heavy.

She stares at her hands in her lap. "Ada, I think I owe you an apology. I haven't given you a fair shake, honey. To do your own thing. I guess I've... I've had this picture of what success looks like for you in my head, and I haven't let you do things your way. The way you want to..." She lifts her gaze. "Or the way, I guess, you might *need to*."

My brows draw together. I don't know what to say.

"Your dad and I, we weren't allowed to find our own paths. It was just understood that we'd get a degree and a good job. No discussion. Our parents wouldn't even entertain the *idea* that college wasn't right for us. Not after everything they sacrificed."

"I know." I can only imagine the pressure my mother faced with Nonna and Nonno's expectations looming large.

"But," she continues, "you've always marched to your own drumbeat. I just haven't been ready—haven't been *listening*..." She trails off, visibly struggling to keep her emotions in check. Her brows pinch together. "I'm so sorry. I'll try harder—to respect that you know yourself best. And I'll stop harping on about college. I just want you to be happy. We've been arguing so much lately, and that's my fault."

"Mom..." I inhale an unsteady breath.

"Anyway, what Roman said, it made me realize... You're putting good into the world," Mom says, tears welling in her eyes. She reaches across the small table and squeezes my hand. "That's what counts. If you can pay the bills and you like what you do, I have no right to criticize that. Even if it's not the way I was raised. Or the way *I'd* do things."

A long moment passes before I trust myself to speak. "Thank you."

Mom's voice is tight. "I know I've told you to try harder, but it's me who needs to do that. Dad too. I'll talk to him. But you know that whole thing about old dogs and new tricks... Just be patient with us."

My shoulders sag and I sit back in my chair. This is all I've ever wanted them to do—to try. The relief is immense. I needed to hear this. I *have needed* to hear this for a long time, but especially right now.

How did she know?

"I will, Mom. Thank you. This means a lot."

She smiles softly, scanning my face. "You okay?"

Still no.

I drop my gaze. "Um..."

"I saw you leave after the ceremony." When I don't respond, she continues. "I'm not gonna pry into what's happened between you and Jesse, but I hope you know I'm here for you if you want to tell me."

"Thanks, Mom. I will soon. Just... not yet, okay?"

She nods, the silence hanging for a moment. "Ready to rejoin the mayhem?" she asks, tilting her head at the dance floor.

"Ready as I'll ever be."

We push up to stand, and Mom takes my arm as she walks me back into the glowing crowd of wedding guests. I tell her I need to grab my purse and we part ways. For a second, I watch her weave between a few stragglers on the sidelines until the crowd swallows her up, then turn toward the spot where I left my clutch.

It's then that I spot two figures off to the side of the dance floor, and my lungs seize up. A woman I don't immediately recognize has her hands on Jesse's chest, leaning into him and whispering into his ear.

She turns, and it clicks. *Naomi.*

I stand frozen, blood rushing in my ears, until Jesse's eyes lock with mine.

And then I run.

31

JESSE

"Ada, wait!" I call out, catching only a glimpse of fluttering red before she disappears into the house. Jogging after her, I fight the panicked knot forming in my throat, knowing what she must be thinking. "Ada!"

I race up the porch steps, following her through the front doors and down an empty hallway. I catch her arm as she pushes into some kind of den lined with shelves of books and old movies. We stumble inside and she whirls around to face me, eyes blazing.

"Let go!" She jerks her arm from my grip as the door swings shut behind us. "You asshole. Couldn't wait, could you?"

"It's not like that. Listen—"

"Oh, sure. You seemed pretty fucking cozy with Naomi out there," she spits.

"I know what it looked like, but she was…"

Totally overstepping? Drunk? Both?

I'm grasping for the words to explain. "She was having trouble hearing me over the music."

Oh, God, even I can hear how flimsy that sounds.

Naomi had downed a couple glasses of champagne in my

presence and, from the way she was falling all over me, probably more before that.

"How convenient." Ada glares and moves to push past me, but I block her.

"Stop. Please."

She steps back, the fight in her flaring like she's a cornered animal. "You know what? Fuck you. You could have at least waited until after the wedding before going on the prowl—forcing me to witness that shit."

"*On the prowl?*" I echo. "Who the fuck do you think you're talking to? I'm not *him,* Ada."

She bristles at my reference to her cheating ex. "No? Well, you sure seem to be in a hurry to find the next girl to fuck... and to rub it in my face."

My brows pinch together. She can't mean that. Can't think I care that little for her. That I'd go hit on someone else right away —*Naomi,* of all people—right in front of her. Not after holding onto her shaking hand while she cried during the ceremony.

"What kind of callous asshole do you take me for? There's nothing going on between me and Naomi. There never was, not really."

Ada looks away, shaking her head.

"We were just *talking,*" I try to explain. The reality is, unlike years ago when I would have been thrilled to have Naomi's hands on me, tonight I was repulsed—couldn't wait to get away from her. "She was drunk and being inappropriate. I was telling her just that when you saw us."

"Right." Her sarcasm is palpable. "You know what, though? Who am I to get in your way? Go right ahead. This was just a summer fuck-buddy situation. Not a *real* relationship."

My chest takes the blow, but I force some air back into my lungs. She's only lashing out because she's terrified and triggered.

"Y'know what?" she continues. "I'm not even supposed to

care. This is..."—she gestures between us—"This was never a thing, and now whatever it was is over, anyway, so..."

"Look, I get you're pissed at me, but you're wrong."

"Whatever." She hugs her arms tight over her chest.

"Don't give me that *'whatever'* shit! I don't want to fuck Naomi! Or anyone else, for that matter." I drag my hands through my hair. "God fucking damnit, Ada! You're the only..."

"What? Cat got your tongue?"

"Fucking hell," I groan. "God, why do you always do this? Needle me the moment I so much as *hesitate!*"

She holds my gaze but snaps her mouth shut.

"You want me to talk about how I feel? Then stop fucking jumping down my throat about it." I draw in a steadying breath. My voice is low and firm, but the calm I've managed to muster up is fragile at best. "I don't wanna fuck anyone else. The only one I wanna fuck is *you*. The only one I wanna be with is *you*. The only one who drives me this fucking crazy is *you!*"

"Jesse... stop."

"No." I exhale hard. "This was never just sex. Not for me. I can't leave tomorrow, letting you think you weren't—you *aren't*—more than that to me. If circumstances were different, we could be so much more."

She sets her jaw. "Fuck you for dangling that in front of me."

We both know Marcus isn't going anywhere.

"Okay, I'm sorry," I say. "But it's just the truth. I know I'm gonna spend that entire flight tomorrow feeling like I have a sucking chest wound... But Ada, *fuck*... I can't think about that right now. Not when you're still right here. I've been trying to give you space all week, but I can't do it anymore. This can't be how we spend our last night together."

"Don't do this," she says, her voice thin and distant.

"Do what?"

She comes closer, getting right in my face. "You don't get to lay all these *togethers* and *what ifs* at my feet and then fuck off across the world the next day. What am I supposed to do with that? Huh?"

I wince at her words.

"What's the point, Jesse? Just to make sure it *really fucking hurts* when you go? Rip my heart a new one and leave me bleeding out?"

The pain in her expression cuts into me like a knife. I tug at the choking restriction of my tie, loosening it. "Please, Ada. All I'm asking for is one last night. One more night with you. Please don't push me away."

"Jess." She says my name on a shaking exhale.

"Please." I step into her, pressing my body against hers, and her hands slide up my chest. "Because I can't stop thinking about you. And I can't keep my eyes off you. I've barely slept all week." My voice wavers. I palm her hip, the heat of her skin warming my fingers through the silky fabric of her dress. "I need you."

Fuck, I've missed her.

"You're fucking *leaving.*" She fists my shirt, but the bite in her words is dulled when she doesn't push me away. Try as she might to deny it, the flush of her cheeks tells me she wants this too.

"Not yet. Not tonight." I lean in close, my lips grazing her cheek, and she sucks in air as her back arches. "Tonight, I'm right here." A wave of need swells inside me, my cock already pushing against her stomach. "Tonight, we can be *everything.*"

Her shoulders sag slightly as a crack forms in the wall she's desperately trying to throw between us. I can tell she's doing everything in her power not to feel this.

"God, Ada." I drop to her neck and brush my nose against her thrumming pulse, then slip my hands around to grip her ass, loving the way my fingers sink in. I let out a low groan against her skin, lifting my head and pressing my forehead to hers. "Please. I need you."

This can't be it. This can't be the last time I'll have my hands on her.

I try to push the thought out of my mind, but it's followed by one that makes me feel even more hollow. "If we'd known our last time together was going to be *the* last time..."

She freezes as it hits her, too, her hands still clinging to my shirt like a lifeline. Her fiery eyes drop to my mouth. "Jesse, we shouldn't," she whispers, almost panting.

"I know you've missed me too." I smile softly, tracing her collarbone with a finger. "I see how you react when I get close like this... How your skin flushes and your breathing speeds up."

"That doesn't mean—"

"And I see..." I lower my hand to her thigh and trace my fingers upward, lifting the hem of her short dress, "how desperate you are to pretend it's fine that I haven't been inside you in a week."

She scoffs, but her voice is unsteady. "Cocky prick."

I ignore the barb and lean in close, my lips feathering her cheek. "But it's not fine, is it?"

Ada lets out a jagged breath.

My fingers travel higher, drifting up to trace the edge of her panties. I go slow, giving her time and space to stop me. When she arches into me instead, I quickly slip them behind the lace and grip the fabric, tugging it up tight against her clit.

She gasps, her pupils blown wide, but there's no question, no hesitation in her eyes.

"Because it's not fucking fine with me, either." My lips crash against hers and my tongue sweeps into her mouth with a ferocity even I wasn't expecting.

And she responds. *Oh, God,* she responds. The feeling of her tongue swirling against mine nearly brings me to my knees.

God fucking damnit.

This mouth. I could lose myself in this mouth. The taste of her makes my bones ache.

I tug on her panties again, and she moans, rocking her hips.

She holds onto the back of my neck, tangling her fingers in my hair.

I'm lost in her—unable to pull away. I need to be closer. Need to feel her skin on mine. Need to be inside her.

She tears her lips from mine, pushing against my chest. "Jesse," she whispers, shaking her head. "We shouldn't."

It takes a second for the words to register through the fog of need that's swallowed me up. With effort, I fight against every instinct I have and pull back. "What?"

Her brows draw together; she's clearly fighting her own internal battle. "I want to... *Fuck*, I want to..." Her voice cracks as she says the words. "But, like I told you before, it's only gonna make tomorrow harder."

I groan at the reminder, falling forward again. She presses her face to mine, and we breathe together for a moment.

"Fuck that," I rumble against her cheek. "What would be harder is knowing we wasted our last night together. Wasted our one last chance to have what we both want."

"What I *want*," she says, the edge creeping back into her voice, "doesn't fucking matter. You're *leaving*."

"I know." I start unbuttoning my shirt, something primal inside me taking over. "So make sure I remember. I wanna spend that entire flight still able to feel you." I yank my shirt open, then reach for her hands, lifting them to rest against my heaving chest. My heart races under her palms as I wait. "I want you to mark my fucking skin, Ada."

Her fingers clench—and that's when she snaps.

"Oh God. Fuck it."

With clumsy, desperate grasps, she rips my belt away and frees me from my pants. She lets out a beautiful, soft whimper when she finally fists my cock in one hand, the other sliding up over my bare chest as her mouth crashes into mine.

"*Fuuuuuck*," I grind out. I swear, I've never been this hard before—never been this hungry, this carnal in my need for her. "I need to hear you say it, Ada. That you want this too."

"Yes, okay? Yes." She presses her lips to mine again.

Relief floods me. Wrenching her drenched g-string to one side, I draw a finger through her entrance and my knees bend.

So wet. So ready for me.

"C'mere," I say, my voice almost a growl, and lift her by the thighs so her legs wrap around my waist. "If I don't fuck you right now, I'm gonna lose my damn mind."

"Here? We could get caught," she says, even as she claws at my shoulders, her fingers sinking under the collar of my shirt.

"Don't care." I back her against the nearest wall. Between torturous kisses, I manage to mumble out, "God, baby, I've missed you so much."

Her smirk is so familiar it hurts. "Did you just call me *baby?*"

I match her smile. "It just slipped out. Shut up." Bracing her against the wall, I line myself up with her slick opening, the needy way she rocks her hips nearly obliterating my control. It takes everything I've got to wait. The desperation to push inside her makes me feel like a clumsy virgin about to blow my load. But I need to do this right. Need to know she's sure. "Ada. Eyes on me."

Her heavy-lidded gaze drags up to my face.

"Tell me to fuck you." I'm shaking. "Tell me. Please."

"One last time?" Her arms tighten around the back of my neck and I never want her to let go.

I nod, forcing the words from my chest. "One last time."

"Jesse," she finally says, her voice catching with emotion, "please... fuck me."

I plunge inside, desperate and aching and deep—*so* deep. I cover her cry with my mouth, the kiss claiming and raw, though it only leaves me needing more of her.

"Harder," she says, the word muffled by the crush of my lips. "So I never forget."

Oh, fuck. Don't have to ask me twice.

I oblige, pressing her into the wall as I slam into her. The way she cries out and digs her fingernails into my shoulders pulls a feral smile from me. I stay buried there, grinding against her inner walls like I can leave my mark inside her—someplace hidden that only the two of us know about.

As my hips buck forward again, her glazed eyes wrench up to mine, then loll back in her head as she makes another soft mewling sound.

Slam.

She cries out again.

I run my thumb over her bottom lip, tugging her jaw down. "Let it out. I want every fucking moan, every gasp, every whimper... Never wanna forget how you sound with my cock buried inside you." I thrust in again. "Exactly"—and again—"where it fucking belongs."

Her cries of pleasure are like a drug, and I immediately need more. I want her loud—unrestrained. I pump inside her again and she cries out softly.

"Oh, you can do better than that," I say as I slip my hand to her throat and squeeze gently.

Slam.

She sucks in a breath, her expression flaring with unmistakable need.

God damn. So fucking responsive.

I'm watching her every move, every twist of her features. I shift the angle of our hips and, on the next stroke, a delicious, liquid moan rips from somewhere low in her chest.

"That's my fucking girl," I whisper against the shell of her ear.

Her pussy clenches. She's wound tight already, and I can't wait to see her come undone.

"You're perfect, Ada." I brush my thumb over the knot of her delicate throat and smile, trying to memorize everything about this moment. I plunge in again with a groan, bracing her weight against the wall, and pull down one strap of her dress. Freeing her breast, I cup the soft weight in my palm. "Mmm. So fucking perfect."

She grinds her hips, and I sink into her, rubbing against the tight walls of her pussy. I pinch her nipple, then dip down to take it between my teeth.

"Jesse, fuck!" she cries, her gasps coming faster with every flick of my tongue.

I break away and take her mouth in a burning kiss. With every thrust of my hips, my tongue meets hers, our swollen lips colliding—messy and wild. Urged on by her sweet moans, I grab a fistful of her hair and tug her head to the side, dropping to her neck again to taste her skin.

She slides one hand between us, rubbing quick circles on her clit, and squeezes her legs around my waist. "Don't stop. Please."

Oh, Jesus. Yes.

"Not a fucking chance," I grit out, jerking her up against the wall with each pounding stroke.

Her breathing turns rapid, skittering out unevenly, and her pussy clenches. I know she's close. I love knowing that about her—love *everything* about her. I drink in her taste, the sounds she's making… My own orgasm is gathering with every panting breath, every touch of her tongue, every new angle of her hips. I can't seem to get deep enough. Close enough. I want to lose myself inside her.

I chase the feeling, speeding up as my control starts to crumble.

Ada cries out as her muscles convulse around my cock, her hoarse voice filling the empty space around us when she shatters. Her cunt twitches through wave after wave of pleasure, and she sounds almost tormented.

"I know," I murmur against her cheek, devouring every gasp,

every twist of her features. I try to slow down—just enough that I don't overwhelm her. "It's too much... I know... I know..."

But, oh, *God,* the way her pussy pulses. When the next wave hits, her nails dig so hard into my back that I think she might draw blood. But I couldn't care less—I'd give anything to make this moment last.

"Jesse!" she practically screams.

And that's it for me. If I thought I could slow down, I was wrong. Some untethered part of me takes the wheel, relentlessly pounding inside her, giving her everything I have left. My moans join hers as I go over the edge, thrusting harder and faster than I thought possible.

As we slow and shudder together, I press my sweat-damp forehead against hers. Ada's shaking breaths fan over my face— the only thing I can hear aside from a distant pulse of muffled bass music and laughter. I want to lap up every drop of this moment. Of her. Imprint the taste of her skin in my memory. Because holding her like this is the only thing dulling the cruel knife that twists inside me when I think about leaving in the morning.

I brush my nose against hers and kiss her, soft and slow. As her supple lips melt into mine, I sink against her, knowing there's nowhere else I'd rather be.

I don't even see it coming—see her throw her walls back up.

Until she shoves me in the chest.

32

———

ADA

"**S**top. Stop kissing me, Jesse."

Stricken, he slides out of me and stumbles back.

I almost feel bad for the indignity of it.

Quickly tucking himself back into his pants, he zips his fly. "What the *hell*, Ada?"

"No. No more kissing." I adjust my panties and tug my dress back into place. "No more fucking. And no more sappy feelings talk either." I whirl around and reach for the door. "I can't do this."

Fuck this. He's hours away from going back to Australia. What are we even doing?

"Ada, wait! Just fucking talk to me, please!" He grabs my arm, pulling me back to him. "Why?"

My eyes well with tears I refuse to let fall, and my voice comes out wavering and tight. "Because, Jesse,"—I take a shaking breath—"kissing you makes my heart feel like it's going to bottom out of my fucking ribcage."

"Ada…"

"You got what you wanted, right? One last fuck." I regret the words the moment they leave my mouth.

His expression falls. "That's *not* what I meant and you know it. Don't do this. Please. Don't run off on me."

I shake my head. "I can't stay here."

"You don't think I'm terrified too?" His eyes dart between mine. "That I'm not dreading getting on that plane tomorrow and leaving you behind? Not knowing when I'll even see you again?"

His words squeeze the air from my lungs. Neither of us has said that part out loud—until now. And I hate him for saying it. I hate it for being true.

"Then let's rip off the bandage now." I twist out of his grasp and pull open the door, unable to draw this out any longer. "Don't say goodbye to me. Tomorrow, I mean. I don't wanna see you. I can't. Just... just go."

"Ada, Jesus Christ, don't do this. Ada!"

Jesse's voice fades behind me as I lurch across the hall and into the bathroom, slamming the door behind me and locking it.

He jiggles the knob moments later, then bangs on the door. "Ada! Come on!" His voice is thick and pleading. I can picture the twist of hurt in his expression and squeeze my eyes shut, wishing he'd leave.

I let moments pass and don't answer.

"Fuck!" he grumbles before I hear his retreating footsteps.

Good. This is for the best.

So why do I feel like I'm dying?

The tears finally spill out and I make a quick grab for some tissues. The sticky reminder of what we shared pools between my legs, and I can't get rid of it fast enough—although my heart sinks all the same, knowing I'm wiping away these last traces of Jesse. I clean myself up and wash my hands.

Leaving the solace of the bathroom, I launch down the empty hallway—half expecting to find him there waiting for me—and out into the warm night air. The music and laughter from the dance floor claws at my ears. I blink a few times, then make a beeline for the bar, swiping up my purse from where I'd left it earlier. Fishing out my phone, I call a cab.

"Two shots of gin, please," I manage over the noise. All my senses are on alert for Jesse's inevitable approach, but I refuse to turn around. I told him I didn't want to see him. And I don't. I don't trust myself to look him in the eye without melting into a pathetic puddle at his feet, begging him not to leave like some genuflecting wretch in a Renaissance painting. As I slide a twenty to the wary bartender, I can feel Jesse watching me from wherever he is.

Stop me, I plead with him silently. *Tell me I'm an asshole and stop me from leaving.*

I down both shots, then feel the tap on my shoulder. Bracing myself, I turn to find my brother—smiling, his hair damp with sweat from dancing. I try to hide the way the air is sucked out of my chest—whether from disappointment or relief, I'm not sure, and I'm too tired to figure it out.

Marcus' dopey grin vanishes when he registers my face. "Whoa. You okay?"

I give him the stink eye of a lifetime for even asking, and he takes a step back, like he's worried I'll break a bottle just to cut him with it.

"Okay, clearly not. What the fuck happened to you?"

"*Jesse* fucking happened to me."

"Damn. Do I need to break his knees or what?"

I press my lips together and shake my head.

"Fuck, Ada, this is exactly what I was—"

"Save it, Marcus," I say, cutting him off. "I'm not ready for an '*I told you so.*'"

He studies me for a few beats as I swipe at the fresh wave of tears. "This is serious shit for you, isn't it?"

Immediately enraged, I swat his arm. "Yes! Yes, this is *serious shit*," I mimic him, "you dickbag!"

"Jesus, Ada! Take it easy!"

"He's gonna be on the other side of the world tomorrow, Marcus! So no," I say, squinting with disdain, "I'm not gonna take it fucking easy."

"Okay..." My brother looks like he's trying to figure out how to approach a volatile wild animal.

I push down a sob, clinging in vain to the last shreds of my dignity. I refuse to have a public tantrum at a wedding—kidding myself that I'm not currently mid-tantrum, of course.

"Shit," Marcus whispers, then runs a hand through his hair. "You love him, don't you?"

"Yeah." I suck in another jagged breath as the reality washes over me once more. I might never see Jesse again.

"I didn't realize—" Marcus says, cutting himself off when he follows my gaze over his shoulder to where my cab is pulling into the long, gravel driveway.

I try to steady myself, wiping under my eyes. "Tell Kai and Nadine congrats or whatever," I mutter as I push past him. "I'm going home."

The booze hits my system in the cab, a dull buzzing sensation settling in at the base of my skull. Tears slide over my hot cheeks as I stare out the window into the black nothingness, suddenly and profoundly exhausted.

My driver casts uneasy glances at me through the rearview mirror but doesn't poke the hornet's nest.

Smart man.

I blink away my tears and text Katie.

ME

Gonna need some top tier bestie commiseration tomorrow... The wedding was rough.

In response, I send her a GIF of Artax dying in the Swamp of Sadness from *The Neverending Story* then turn my phone to silent mode and shut off the screen.

When I stumble through the door to my apartment, it hits me all over again. Something about the privacy and silence here is like a kick to my stomach, although you'd think I'd be used to it after a week. But after what happened tonight... It's like the wound has torn right open again.

I knew this would happen.

The sooner he's gone, the better.

I punt my discarded shoes across the kitchen floor.

I barely have enough energy to halfheartedly brush my teeth before I tear off my constricting dress and toss it into the laundry hamper along with my still-wet panties. I don't bother to shower or even take off my makeup, though I know I should do both. Instead, I yank on a tank top and pajama shorts and fall into bed. Curling into the fetal position, I pull the covers over my head.

Through the haze of gin and tears, Jesse's words thunder back: "*Tonight, we can be* everything."

I can almost feel it again—his voice rumbling against my cheek. I jerk my head to the side, rolling over like I can get away from the memory—like it isn't trapped inside my heart, indelibly inked into my very being.

And he'd made me give in—pressured me into being with him one last time. Coerced me into sex.

Bullshit! my conscience screams, the lie so glaring that I can't even buy my own crap. All he'd done was speak the plain truth— that he can read me like a fucking book. That he knows how I feel. That I've fallen hard. That I want him. That I love him.

I love him.

I love him and I shoved him away—*literally*—and told him to go. *God*, I don't want him to go.

The weight on my chest threatens to shatter my ribs into little spears of bone that pierce my heart, one by one. I try to inhale, but the air is hot and jittery, my lungs fighting both for and against the oxygen. I pull the blanket away from my mouth and try to draw a deeper breath, but the room feels suffocating. My pulse hammers and nausea swirls in my gut; I'm frantic. Shivering. This is what I imagine freezing to death must feel like, except I'm somehow too hot. I'm so tired, and yet so painfully, acutely awake.

I must lie there in a devastated trance for some time because, eventually, I let myself close my eyes.

I should apologize.

The thought dances lightly—too lightly—through my mind.

I should talk to him before he leaves. Tell him I love his stupid face.

But my limbs feel leaden and my phone's on silent somewhere in the carnage of my discarded belongings. The idea of swimming my way back to the land of the living escapes my clumsy mental clutches.

I already miss him.

I imagine his arm around my waist—the warm, familiar weight of it—before the hazy molasses I'm drowning in finally delivers the knockout punch and I drift to sleep.

33

JESSE

It's my last night here and everything's fucked. I'd known it was gonna hurt. *Of course* it was gonna hurt. But, like all pain, you can't really grasp it—can't feel it—until it's happening and you realize how wildly unprepared you were.

The cab pulls up to our apartment—no, Ada's apartment now —and I exhale, unclipping my seat belt and pushing out into the darkness. The door feels like it weighs hundreds of pounds. When I straighten, Marcus has climbed out on the other side of the car. He leans in the open window, talking quietly to Renee, who's still in the back seat.

"See you at home, okay?" is all I catch.

When I'd tried to give him Ada's key, he'd refused to take it, saying I had to give it back to her myself. I'd had no fight left in me to argue.

The cab pulls away and he walks toward me, slinging an arm over my shoulder and pulling me toward the backyard. "Come on."

I don't even question him staying behind; I've been a wreck since Ada locked herself in that bathroom and I haven't exactly been able to hide it. Numb and exhausted, I shuffle along beside him. I have to head to the airport in a few hours and I'm a heartbroken, useless shell of a person.

Fuck. Why did I think going to this wedding the night before my flight was a good idea?

My chest tightens at the memory of Ada shoving me away and telling me not to say goodbye.

Marcus pulls out what he affectionately refers to as the *tetanus chairs* and gestures for me to sit across from him.

I slump down with enough force that something in the chair pops, but I'm too tired to care whether it'll give out. If it collapses, it'll be the least painful thing to happen to me in the last few hours. I lean forward and rest my head in my hands, letting out a muffled groan.

A few beats pass before Marcus speaks. "So, is this for real, or what?"

I lift my head just enough to meet his eyes in the darkness. "What?"

"You and Ada. Is it the real deal?"

There's a twisting sensation behind my sternum. Long seconds tick past as I look at my best friend with a swirling mixture of pain and regret. He'd warned me from the jump that this was a bad idea. I slowly nod.

"You love her?"

I drop my head back into my hands and drag them over my face. "Yesh," I groan against my palms, then suck in a quick breath and sit back in the chair, trying to wake myself up. "I do. I love her." Saying it out loud almost hurts. "And I didn't even have the balls to tell her."

He inhales slowly and nods, peering around the yard, then slouches back in his seat. "So, on a scale from one to *bag of trash,* how bad are you feeling right now?"

I exhale. "Well, it feels like there's a small car sitting on my chest, knowing I have to leave in...”—I check my phone, then pinch the bridge of my nose—“fuck... just under three-and-a-half hours.”.

“Shit, man.”

“And she doesn’t even wanna see me again before I—” I cut myself off, the knot in my throat making it difficult to speak. I run a hand over my jaw. “I fucked this all up.”

“Maybe. But Ada talks a big game. You know that as much as I do.”

“What do you mean?” I ask.

“You know how she is. All bluster and shit. All *Sturm und Drang*.”

I give him a skeptical look. “You didn’t hear what she said.”

“Fair. But I saw her before she left the wedding. And? I know my sister.” He tilts his head at our front door. “I guarantee you, she’s in there right now bawling into her pillow over you—” He cuts himself off with a derisive head shake. “Oh, *God* this is so weird, trying to hook you up with *Ada*... For fuck’s sake. How is this my life?” He slumps down onto his elbows and rubs his temples.

I can’t help but smile in my confusion. “Hook me up with Ada? I thought you didn’t want us getting involved.”

He tilts his head in acknowledgment. “I just thought it could get fucked up in a hurry. Didn’t want either of you getting hurt— and didn’t wanna get stuck in the middle of your drama.”

“Right. Like *this,* you mean?” Regret stabs at me again, though I know full well we couldn’t have avoided this.

“Yep.” He raises an eyebrow but doesn’t push the point. “But dude. I shouldn’t have even... I mean, you’re both adults. It’s really none of my business.” He points at me. “Don’t get me wrong, it’s fuckin’ *weird*. And I don’t have to like it... but I can deal.”

The iron anchor dragging my heart into the dirt threatens to lift.

Is he serious right now?

I straighten in my seat and swallow. "Really? You mean that?"

"Yeah. The part I was pissed about was you didn't tell me. I'm your *best friend*. And, like, I know she's my sister, and I get telling me would be fucking awkward…"

"I know," I say. "But it was shitty of us to keep you in the dark. I really am sorry."

"Hey, man, people fuck up, though. I get it. No one knows how to handle these things. You two wouldn't be the first or last people to make questionable choices when"—he shudders—"*sex* is involved."

I stare at the ground, begging the hamster wheel in my exhausted brain to pick up the pace.

If Marcus can deal…

"And I didn't realize," he continues, "like, if this is serious"—he taps a finger on the armrest of the chair—"if this is some heart-stopping, can't-live-without-you shit? If she's gonna have to run slow-mo through the airport to stop you from leaving? Nobody likes to drive to the airport. Save her the trip."

"The *fuck* do you mean?" I ask, lifting my gaze to his. It's too late and I'm too foggy for this.

"Fuck you. It's after two in the morning and I'm still drunk." He sighs. "What I mean is this obviously isn't just… *gross*, nope, not even gonna say it." He shifts in his seat and tries again. "I mean, it's clearly not just some stupid fling."

"No, but that doesn't change the fact that I'm flying back."

He rolls his eyes. "Cancel your flight, dipshit!"

The weight on my chest lifts just enough to let a swirling fizz of hope creep in. That, or I'm about to throw up.

"And my job?" The question is almost rhetorical; I've tossed around the idea of quitting more times than I can count. But I don't dare let myself read into this. Into what I think he's saying.

He shrugs. "Quit! Did you know there are other jobs? Even *here*, if you'll believe it." He's smirking now.

Prick.

"Marcus..." The hope starts to swell, expanding and spilling into all the cracks and tears wrought when Ada shut me out.

This... I wasn't expecting this.

"I mean, fuck, they could probably ship you whatever shit you left behind, right? Plus, I assume your mom and Claire would be happy if you stuck around."

I cover my mouth with both hands and stare into the middle distance, reeling. This changes everything. Well, *almost* everything.

"Don't get me wrong," Marcus continues, "it's gonna be weird as fuck knowing you're with my sister. I don't want any details, okay? And I reserve the right to crack jokes about all of this. Forever."

I narrow my eyes, still not letting myself believe it. He's talking like Ada and I are together, when what we are is a mess. "What are you saying?"

"Oh, my God, Jess. You're thicker than usual when you're in love," he deadpans, reaching over to deliver a rough swat to my knee.

"Fuck off," I say, too tired to flinch. "I need to hear you say it, okay?"

"Look. If you make Ada happy, and she makes you happy, you should goddamn be happy *together,* alright? I'm saying you have my fucking blessing, dumbass."

I hold my breath. If he's really giving us the green light... I glance at our front door.

I need to tell her. Need her to know this could work...

"I'm saying"—Marcus says again, this time putting on his best impression of *The Godfather*, his voice strained—"welcome to the family."

All the air leaves my lungs in a surprised laugh, a flood of relief and anxiety hitting me all at once. I should be jumping for joy, but I can't forget the twist of pain on Ada's face when she shoved me away at the wedding. I swallow past the knot in my throat.

"Now, the fuck are you doing still talking to me? You gonna cancel your flight, or what?" Marcus stands and pats my shoulder, then turns to leave.

Stunned, I watch him plod back toward the gate. He pulls out his phone, probably to call another cab.

"Hey, Marcus?" I call out quietly, not wanting to wake Mr. Wozniak.

He turns. "Yeah?"

"Thank you. You have no idea what this—" I cut myself off and press my lips together, not trusting my voice to stay steady.

He bobs his head thoughtfully, then walks back to me. Clapping a hand on my shoulder, he stoops down to look me in the eye. "Hurt her and you're a dead man, Bailey."

I only nod, breathing out a strained chuckle.

Fair.

I silently resolve to do my damnedest never to find out how Marcus would choose to murder me. Though, truth be told, I don't know how to fix this—fix the hurt I've already caused. But I'm damn sure gonna try.

He turns to leave again.

"And hey," I say again and he turns to me once more, walking backward. "Nice vocab, my guy." At his confused face, I add, "*Sturm und Drang*? You been readin'? Like... something other than the smut you claimed was Renee's?"

He shakes his head, although he can't fight the smile. "Fuck off."

"And your Brando needs some work," I add.

He points a finger at me. "Thin ice, Jess... thin fuckin' ice."

34

ADA

The mirror above my dresser reveals an unrecognizable, raccoon-like creature. As I shift on my bare feet, a beam of morning light zaps straight into my retinas and I wince. I move out of the direct sunlight and lean forward to frown at my reflection. My black eye makeup is smeared and I've got hair sticking out in all directions. Like I'm moving in slow motion, I pull a loose bobby pin from where it dangles in front of my nose and toss it on the dresser. I drag my wild hair back into a messy ponytail and try to swallow past the raw lump in my throat. My lungs ache.

He's gone.

Shoving one arm through the sleeve of Jesse's hoodie, which he forgot to grab before he left, I gather the fabric against my face. I breathe in deep, like I can store him inside my chest cavity. I hate myself for doing it, but I don't have the willpower yet to make better decisions.

Determined to at least pee before I start crying again, I pull open my bedroom door and yank the hoodie over my other arm. As I plod to the bathroom, I rub the heels of my hands into my

eyes. My makeup's already a fucking mess, so I might as well lean
into it.

I slump down on the toilet, making a clumsy grab for the
mouthwash. It's only when I go to spit and wash my hands that I
catch sight of the sticky note on the mirror.

Turn over.

I look over my shoulder in confusion, suddenly not sure I'm
alone.

What the hell?

I shake it off; his flight left hours ago. He never gave me back his
key, so he must have come by to drop it off. Knowing he was here—
even briefly—while I slept threatens to wrench my heart from my
chest. I almost don't reach for the note, but I'm too desperate for
any scrap left of Jesse. I peel it off the mirror and flip it over.

Follow the clues, Buttercup.
#1: Where you kicked
my ass at Mario Kart.

Brow pinched in confusion, I drift out the door, peering into
the living room with my heart in my throat. When I spot another
note stuck to the TV, I hurry to snatch it up.

You were such a shit.
And I wanted to let you win every
race just to see you light up again.

I cover my mouth with one hand and stare at Jesse's words,
trembling. The little arrow in the bottom right corner prompts me
to flip it over.

#2: Where you cut my hair.

I spin around to scan the kitchen, remembering how Jesse sat patiently on the chair in the middle of the floor. My gaze falls and I round the couch, laser-focused on the note where that chair had been. I crouch down to pick it up, already drinking in his words as I slowly stand.

You were bossy as fuck.
And I was so desperate for you to
touch me, I couldn't think straight.

Memories of that haircut rush back to me—the way Jesse's body had felt like a siren song pulling me into the rocks. The way his strong hands had gripped my hips and yanked me down into his lap. The way his lips had brushed against mine as he breathed my name...

Snapping out of my trance, I flip the note to read what's on the back.

#3: Where you made
too many margaritas.

Like a shot, I'm at the kitchen counter, peeling off the next note.

You tried to seduce me that night.
And it fucking worked. I was ready
to take anything you'd give me.

The air falls from my lungs. I feel like I'm moving too quickly between these precious remnants of Jesse, yet time simultaneously feels like it's slowed to a crawl. I can't gulp his words down fast enough. I turn the note over.

#4: Where you forced me
to confess everything.

My mind reels. *Everything?* He can't mean last night at the wedding. I scan the apartment until my eyes snag on the wall across from the bathroom door, the little yellow note catching my attention immediately. The night we fought and he told me he wanted me. When he caged me up against that wall. I rush over.

You pushed me until I snapped.
I felt like my heart was
gonna hulk out of my chest.

I smile despite the tight knot in my throat. If he only knew what it had felt like for me that night. I brush my fingers across his scrawled words before I flip the note over.

#5: Where I kissed you the
first time. (Fucking finally!)

I whip my head to Jesse's bedroom door and run. When I push inside, it's empty, save the bed my parents loaned him. As I scan for a little yellow note, I remember how he'd finally kissed me when I'd been standing just inside his... I nearly rip the door off its hinges in my desperation to find the note. And then I see it.

You told me to fuck you.
And I felt like my dick was
gonna hulk out of my pants.

I laugh, the sound messy and wet as the tears roll freely down my cheeks. I turn the note over in my hands, blinking hard so I can focus.

#6: Where my book took
an unexpected turn.

I fly out from Jesse's room and back to the living room.
How did I not find another note here before?
Heady confusion rushes through me as I circle the coffee table and inspect the floor. The notes I've collected so far are crushed in my grasp, damp with sweat and tears. *What is all this? What does it mean?*

It's harder to spot, but I finally find the note tucked between two sofa cushions. I tug it free and wipe my tears away so I can read it.

You were so fucking greedy.
And I loved when you crawled
into my lap afterward.

My heart seizes up at the memory: nuzzling into his neck, wanting to stay there forever. Following the little arrow once more, I turn the note over.

#7: Where you told me you
weren't wearing any panties.
(Scandalous!)

I smile again, the memory of Jesse bending me over the table after we got home from the river still as vivid in my mind as the day it had happened. I remember his urgency to get in the apartment and the way I'd teased him with my little secret outside our front door.

Nearly crashing into the coffee table, I launch into the hallway. I don't bother stopping to put shoes on—I just pull open the front door and stumble outside.

And then I can't breathe.

Jesse's asleep on the stairs, sitting up with his head propped against the railing on a folded-up sweatshirt. And, stuck to his chest, right above his crossed arms, is a yellow sticky note.

Still not Katie.

I'm spinning out, a million questions flooding my mind.

He's still here? How long has he been waiting outside?

I take a step toward him and then freeze when I remember how I look. I squint at my reflection in the nearby window, taking hasty swipes at the remnants of my smudged makeup until it's giving a bit less melted goth and a bit more smoky-eyed emo.

When I turn back to Jesse, I'm suddenly at a loss for what to do. With one foot, I nudge the toe of his shoe.

He stirs, a sleepy grimace playing on his features.

I smile and tap his foot again, harder this time, and he cracks open an eye. The moment he registers me standing in front of him, both eyes fly wide and he sucks in a gulp of air, his arms uncrossing as the sweatshirt pillow falls to the ground.

Before he can speak, I climb right into his lap, burying my face in his neck.

He pulls me in tight—cupping the back of my head with one hand and rubbing soft strokes up and down my back with the other. We speak strained words of relief and apology into each other's skin, and he whispers my name like a prayer between uneven breaths. I nuzzle into his neck, my hot tears soaking the collar of his T-shirt.

I finally pull back, searching his tired face, and wipe at the wetness on his cheeks. "You missed your flight," I whisper.

"Not missed." His voice is rough as he wipes my own tears away. "*Canceled.*"

"Canceled? What about your job?"

"I quit."

The twisted knot in my stomach dares to uncoil half a turn. "You what?"

"I quit," he says again. "Emailed my resignation at three in the morning like some drunk teenager." He's smiling. The fucker is *smiling* at me. I don't trust it.

"And Marcus?"

He shakes his head. "Talked some sense into me."

"What?"

"Your brother, by the way, does a terrible Marlon Brando impression."

I frown in confusion. "Wait, what? What the fuck are you—"

"He gave us his blessing, Ada." He brushes his thumb over my cheek.

"What?" I laugh-sob the word out, searching his eyes for confirmation that this is real.

"Helped me see what was right in front of me this whole time." Jesse's lips meet mine, soft and tentative at first, then deeper. The kiss is exploring, apologetic, drugging.

I feel torn in half and sewn back together all at once. Raw.

He breaks the kiss and smooths the hair back from my forehead, then brushes his nose against mine.

"I love you," I whisper.

He exhales hard.

"I love you," I say again, pressing kisses to his cheeks, his forehead, his nose. "I love you."

I repeat it again and again, breathing my love for him against his lips. I feel like I'm dying—like the words are the only thing keeping me alive.

"I love you, Jesse. I'm so sorry. I should've told you before, and I—"

"I love you too." His voice wavers. "Ada, I'm so fucking in love with you that I don't know what to do with myself." He clenches his jaw and shakes his head. "I couldn't go. The thought physically hurt."

"Are you sure, though? You're giving up so much. I can't ask you to do that. I wouldn't—"

He cups my cheek. "Nothing in Australia is important to me. Not like this. Not like you and me."

"But you *love* your job."

"I don't," he says. "I might have made it sound a bit better than it is." Guilt furrows his brow. "The reality is, it's long hours and really fucking hard work. And... Ada, I thought I'd built a life there, but I wasn't living. I was just *existing*. But now?" He presses his lips together.

I exhale and a tear slips down my cheek.

"My heart didn't break when I thought about leaving my job. But it almost broke thinking about leaving you." Emotion clouds his eyes and he pauses to collect himself. "I'd been thinking about staying, but then you told me to go, and... I guess it wasn't until Marcus gave us his blessing that I realized... I *could* have a life here again. With you." He kisses me softly. "So I'm not going anywhere. I'm yours, if you'll have me. If you want me to stay."

Another tear spills over my cheek and I smile. "Yes. Stay. God, please stay."

His relief is potent. He wipes the tear away with his thumb and kisses me again.

"I've never seen you cry before," I say.

"I've never been this scared before." He exhales hard through a smile, and cradles my face in both hands. "Or this relieved."

Tell me about it.

I touch his cheek. "I can't believe you passed out on the stairs."

He rolls his shoulders and winces. "My back can sure fucking believe it."

"Shit, sorry," I say on a laugh. I move to climb off his lap, but he tightens his grip on me, shaking his head.

"Don't you fucking move. I'm not letting you go yet."

I give him a soft smile and kiss him again.

I never want to stop kissing him.

"Why didn't you wake me up?"

"I wasn't going to just skulk into your bedroom like a *weird lurker*." He smirks.

"I actually thought you might be hiding somewhere inside... like you were gonna leap out of a closet and scare the shit out of me."

He laughs. "Well, nothing says *I love you* like a jump scare."

I smile just hearing him say it again, and my gaze falls to his chest.

"But why all this?" I ask, touching the half-crumpled note still stuck to his shirt. "Still not Katie?"

"Turn it over." His teeth skim over his bottom lip.

I peel it off his chest.

On the back are two stick-figure people with a big heart between them and the word *now* underlined three times inside it. There's an arrow pointing at the one with longer hair with the word *you* in capital letters.

I can't tell whether I'm laughing or crying. "Jesse, this is..." I start. The words are barely a whisper. Then I do start to laugh— and turn the drawing around to face him. "I mean, what the hell is this?"

He squeezes my hip, laughing with me. "Hey, I'm not the artist, here."

"Seriously. All the notes... This. Why?"

His smile is soft. "Last night, everything was so rushed. And *harsh*. You deserve so much more than that. That's not how I wanted to tell you how I felt—how I *feel*: just shouting at you like an asshole. I wanted to show you."

I gaze down at the stick figure drawing still clutched in my hand. "This is really the most..." I pause, touching my fingertips to the crumpled note before meeting his eyes, "... pitiful little drawing I've ever seen."

He pulls back and glances at his wrist like he's checking the time. "You know, I think I can still make that flight," he deadpans.

I swat his arm. "Shut up. I love it."

With a smile, he circles his arms loosely around me, tucking them under the hem of my hoodie to rub my back. "Every note... each one is a moment when I fell more in love with you." The emotion is thick in his voice. "Ada, I haven't felt like I was *home* in eight years. My family fell the fuck apart, the house I grew up in got sold off, and this town felt like it was pushing me away every chance it got. And in Oz... I was always "the American". Always foreign. People would comment on my accent and shit. It was never the same. It was never *home*." He stops to brush a stray hair out of my face. "And then... *you*."

"Me?"

He smiles and shifts his gaze away, almost embarrassed. "This is gonna sound so fucking cheesy—you're never gonna let me hear the end of it." But the look on my face must be enough to coax him to continue. "It's like I could finally see clearly again, after years of everything being blurry. I could see what home looked like. And all I could see was you, Ada. It's you."

35

JESSE

Ada has a thousand questions. We stand under the shower spray as I explain everything, exhaustion soaking deep into my bones. I lose track of how many times she asks if I'm sure. The truth is: I've never been more sure of anything in my life.

"Time to grow up, you know?" I explain. "I gotta deal with what I've been avoiding all these years. And I know I haven't really... done this relationship thing before. I have crap to work on. But I promise to do the work. I'll go to therapy. Sort my head out."

I should probably talk to someone about what went down with my dad, for starters.

I step in close, taking her face in my hands and pressing a kiss to her forehead. "I'd do anything for you."

She pulls back, fixing me with a serious look. "Hey. If you go to therapy and work on your shit... do it for *you*, okay? Not me."

I nod, rubbing my thumb over the furrow of worry creasing her forehead. Her brow smooths out under my touch. She's right. If I want to keep showing up for her, I need to start showing up for myself.

"I should go too," she says, her voice quiet. "To therapy. I mean, clearly, what happened with Pascal fucked me up a bit." She looks down at her hands on my chest. "And all the shit with my parents."

"Yeah?"

"Yeah. Although, maybe we've turned a corner. Remind me to tell you later about what my mom said at the wedding."

"Okay..." I'm not sure what she means just yet, but something like hope touches her features when she mentions her mom. That's new.

"Anyway, what I'm trying to say is: I'm sorry for blaming you when it was my own bullshit. I don't want that to get in the way of this. Us." She lifts her gaze to meet mine, her lips curling in a wry smile. "You sure you're not regretting sticking around for this *huge pain in the ass*?"

I chuckle, tugging her in close. "Hey, I knew what I was signing up for."

Her amusement falters as she searches my face. "What's wrong?"

Now *I* must be the one frowning.

"Nothing. Fuck, Ada. Everything's right for once." I don't know what to do with this feeling, this fullness in my chest.

Wet lashes blink up at me as the shower spray speckles her cheeks, and she lifts on tiptoe. When we kiss, it feels like a promise—to give this everything we've got.

"Hey," she says when our lips part, "I dunno if it was adrenaline or that I was so caught up in everything or what, but your notes were, like, kinda easier to read for me..." She trails off like she isn't sure what to make of it.

I let out a relieved breath, running my hands over her back. "Good. I was hoping it would work."

She looks both surprised and confused. "What do you mean *it*?"

"Uh, well," I say, rotating us in the shower so she doesn't get cold. "I was reading about this font that's supposed to be easier for dyslexic people to read, so I sort of… tried to make my writing more like that. Wasn't sure it'd work, but…"

"You changed your handwriting so I could read it?"

"Yeah," I say with a shrug. "I meant what I said. I'd do anything for you."

"Jesse…" She sinks into my chest and grazes her nose against my neck, wrapping her arms tight around my ribcage. Her voice is quiet but, despite the hiss of the water, I can hear it's heavy with emotion. "Thank you. No one's ever done anything like that for me. No one's ever tried to help me—to meet me where I'm at. Like it's just *what you do*. No big deal. No judgment." She moves back just enough to meet my eyes. "The onus has always been on *me* to cope. Or to try harder… struggle through."

"Well, we're a team now, okay? I'll always help you if I can. Whether that's finding reading hacks or having your back when your parents give you shit… or screaming into the void with you, if that's what you need." I lean down, brushing my nose against hers. "I love you, Ada."

"I love you, too…" She flashes me that beautiful grin, and adds, "*Garby*."

I groan. "Can't wait to make Claire pay for that."

"For the record," she says, pulling me close, "I think you make *excellent* choices about what you put in your mouth."

I bark a laugh, then hum my agreement against her smiling lips. "So, can I move into your bedroom now, or what? Hear me out: I was thinking you could use my room as a studio and—"

My voice is squeezed tight when she crushes me in a hug, and I kiss her wet hair. "So, uh, I take it you like that idea?"

"I love it," she murmurs. "I fucking love it. Yes. Thank you, thank you, thank you."

I hold her close, only letting go when I'm reminded we can't stay in the shower all day. "Here, let's get cleaned up." Guiding her under the stream of water, I lift her face, angling the shower head to wet her hair. I comb my fingers through the tangled turquoise ribbons, massaging gently.

"What are you doing?"

"What do you think? Washing your hair."

"You don't have to do that," she says, brushing her fingers up and down my spine. "But also please never stop," she adds, laughing. "It feels so fucking good."

"Good," I rumble in her ear. My hands go still when I find a bobby pin and pull it out. With a smirk, I toss it over the top of the shower door and reach for her shampoo. I shift my hips to adjust my erection and press it against her stomach, leaning in close. "Because I think making you feel *so fucking good* is my kink, Buttercup."

"Mmm," she hums with a soft smile, slipping her hands over my hips. "I still *really* hate that nickname."

"Liar," I tease. I work the shampoo through her hair and press light kisses to her cheeks, her nose, and her jaw, then tilt her head to rinse out the lather.

Her hands skate low over my stomach. I try to keep it together when she runs a thumb down the side of my cock, though I can't help the way my hips kick forward.

"What's your—" I start, then clear my throat. "What's your um... hair regime, here? Condi... conditioner?"

"Something distracting you?" she asks, feathering her fingers over my balls and back up my shaft. She bites her lip. "And yeah, conditioner, please."

I shake my head, then when she takes me fully into her fist, I shudder, nearly fumbling the bottle.

A grin lights up her features at my reaction.

I furrow my brow in concentration as I squirt conditioner into my hand, then pause, suddenly unsure how to proceed. My hair used to be long, but I'd never bothered with conditioning it. "How do you..."

She rolls her eyes and scoops up the dollop from my palm and rubs it over both hands, then slides the slippery cream over my cock. "Like this."

I groan.

Jesus fuck.

Taking her face in both hands, I kiss her deep and long. When I tear my mouth away, I'm practically panting. "Are you fucking kidding me?"

She chuckles softly, still working me between her slick hands. "Your dick's gonna smell like coconut."

I laugh. "Well, that's probably the weirdest thing anyone's ever said to me." I hiss as she pumps me harder. "Ada. Shit. I'm gonna blow my load if you keep that up."

"I dunno," she says. "Could be a good way for me to thank you."

"For what?"

"Fuck you *for what*," she says through a guffaw, her hands slowing to soft strokes. "For staying."

"Wow, from *thank you* to *fuck you* in two seconds flat. That's impressive, even for you."

"Well, I'm extremely talented at being—what was your term —a *snarky little bitch?*"

I smile, then meet her gaze as my expression turns more serious. I run a hand over my dripping face. "Ada, you don't need to thank me like I'm doing you some favor, here. There was *no way* I was getting on that flight. Even seeing my packed suitcase was nearly giving me a panic attack. Leaving you would have been leaving a piece of myself behind. You've got my heart in your hands."

Amusement dances over her features. Then, as if on cue, our eyes fall to what Ada's *actually* holding in her hands.

"Your *heart* doesn't look right," she says, barely controlling her laughter. She presses her lips into my shoulder, biting at my collarbone in what appears to be an effort to avoid completely ruining the moment. The struggle has her shoulders shaking.

I search the ceiling for patience.

Then she snorts. *She snorts!* "You should really get that checked out!"

With a warning grumble, I pull her face to mine and shove the bar of soap into her hands. "Alright, laugh it up, *Buttercup*. You've got two minutes to get clean before I make you pay for that."

36

ADA

Fleetwood Mac's *Dreams* plays from the small speaker beside me, drowning out the soft scratch of my pencil against the paper. My knees are pulled up, my heels perched on the edge of the kitchen chair and my sketchbook on the slant of my lap.

Jesse emerges from our bedroom and walks up behind me.

"Hey," I say absently, totally engrossed in my drawing.

The sketch, currently only a rough outline, is of a woman's figure suspended in midair, her back in a deep, almost gymnastic bend. Her stomach is drawn up toward the sky and her arms hang down below her. One knee is raised at a graceful angle, the other leg outstretched, and rippled lines explode outward from her chest and abdomen.

"What are you drawing?" Jesse's voice rumbles close.

Resisting the urge to snap my sketchbook shut, I run a hand through my hair and remind myself he's had nothing but praise for my art. Still, showing Jesse the beginnings of this piece puts a distinct twinge of self-consciousness in my chest.

"I'm not sure yet," I hedge, glancing over my left shoulder and absently reaching my hand up to him. It's half-true.

Stevie Nicks' quivering voice sings about keeping her visions to herself, and I smile softly at the appropriateness of the lyrics.

He twines his fingers between mine, then lets go to lean down for a closer look.

"It's just an idea I had," I explain, filling the silence brought by his scrutiny. Skimming over the page, I try to imagine what he might be seeing—or thinking. "I'm not sure if it's gonna work yet." I bite the inside of my cheek, not ready to tell him what it represents—the shift inside me lately.

"I like it." He pauses. "What's holding her up?" His warm hands slide over my bare shoulders, a fingertip lifting the strap of my tank top and tracing my collarbone. "Is she floating, or—"

I lower my feet to the floor and put the sketchbook on the table, scoffing softly. "Something like that," I say, leaning forward to continue drawing.

Jesse's hands move forward with me. "Are you always this mysterious?" he murmurs, bending low to press his lips to the side of my head. The coarse brush of his beard pulls a few strands loose from my half ponytail, and the warmth of the contact rapidly renders me boneless in the chair.

"Yup. Always," I say, my voice breathier than I want it to be. I manage to force my focus back to the drawing and put pencil to paper once more, sketching the curve of the woman's calf. "You'll have to hire a PI or something to figure me out." I smile at the soft chuckle from behind me, then gasp when he grips my ponytail in his fist and tugs my head back—gentle, but firm.

"Oh? I dunno," he teases, his voice low. "I think I have a pretty good idea about what makes you tick."

"Fuck you," I whisper without a hint of menace, my eyes closing as his lips feather over the slope of my neck.

"Soon," he rasps, kissing his way from my neck to my shoulder and biting gently. Still gripping my ponytail, he angles my head to bare my neck and licks his way back up, his free hand gently gripping my throat.

Oh, yes, please.

Waves of heat travel through my body, and sizzling pulses of sensation radiate down my arm and into my fingertips. I feel the warm wetness already pooling between my legs and squirm in my seat.

With teasing flicks of his tongue, he moves up the side of my neck to my earlobe, then draws the soft flesh into his mouth, tugging gently.

The pencil drops from between my fingers and slowly rolls away, falling to the floor with a clatter, and I press my forearms into the table's edge.

I'm putty. I'm goo. I'm a liquid, former human.

Releasing my earlobe, Jesse kisses along my jawline and over my already-flushed cheeks. He sweeps his fingers along the front of my neck, over my collarbone, and across my chest, keeping them just above the fabric of my tank top.

He lets go of my ponytail and pushes his fingers firmly into the hair at the nape of my neck. My head drops forward as the air leaves my lungs in a rush. I'm completely at his mercy as he moves me where he wants me, nipping and licking my shoulder, my ear, my neck...

Can you die from being turned on? Because I'm definitely dying. And what a fucking way to go.

His free hand sweeps up to cradle my face as he scrapes his teeth over the back of my neck, kissing his way up and forward until he reaches my cheek.

I turn toward him, desperate to taste him, and he hovers his mouth over mine for a few aching, endless moments before he angles my head away and dips down to my neck again—denying me the kiss.

"Oh, God," I almost whimper, making a mental note to murder him later, sexually, for that cruel move. But his warm tongue on my skin distracts me from forming coherent sex-murder plans.

Damn him.

Sweeping soft kisses back toward my shoulder, he pulls down the straps of my tank top and bra. He's licking and biting and... *oh, God, it's only my shoulder; what is happening?*

I drop my head into the gentle cradle of his hand, each touch of his lips and tongue teasing every nerve ending under my skin.

He reaches his free hand to my chin and, gripping it firmly, turns me toward him.

For a moment, the only sound is my shallow breathing, and I realize how quiet he's been. He's normally so vocal, but this... this has been all about me. All *for* me.

So, when his lips crash into mine, I moan and don't hold back, giving myself over to this moment—to the way his tongue plunges into my mouth in a claiming kiss that has my core muscles twitching and pulsing.

Oh, sweet baby Jesus.

He breaks the kiss and meets my heavy-lidded gaze with a crooked smile.

I want to devour him whole.

"Well," he says suddenly, standing up, leaving an aching vacuum between us that I almost fall into.

I catch myself by grabbing the table, my eyes widening.

"I was gonna... head to the grocery store." He slowly slides the straps of my bra and tank top back into place and winks at me, his expression playful like he didn't just melt my panties with his tongue—without coming anywhere near them.

"What?" I exhale hard when he turns to go. Baffled, I raise my hand slowly to my lips, then my cheek. It's burning.

Yep. I'm dying. I have sex fever.

"See ya in about an hour!" Jesse cheerfully declares as he walks backward toward the door with a smug grin on his face—clearly eating up the gobsmacked look on mine. He turns and, without a second glance, leaves the apartment. I think I hear him *whistle* as he closes the front door.

When it clicks shut, I gape at the floor, letting out a scoff.

The fucking nerve of this man.

It takes me a few minutes to get my bearings enough to trust my knees won't give out when I stand. When I do, I drift in a trance to the bathroom and stare myself down in the mirror. My cheeks are pinched-pink like I'm drunk. I *feel* drunk. I splash cold water on my face and grab the closest towel to pat it dry. When I realize it's Jesse's towel and it smells like his soap and his clean, gorgeous body, I think I might actually pass away right here in this bathroom. I inhale deeply, ensuring the torture is complete, then hang the towel on the hook behind the door.

No way is he going to get away with that.

No way.

I head back to the kitchen table, stooping to retrieve my fallen pencil with a smirk, and pick up my phone. I shut off the music and settle back into my seat to compose the message.

ME

Dirty move, Bailey.

JESSE

What are you talking about?

ME

Fuck off.

JESSE

Oh god, don't tell me YOU wanted to do the grocery shopping

(How embarrassing for me)

ME

Ya know what? I'm just gonna wait for you in bed until you get back. Plot my revenge.

JESSE

Ok perfect, then I can apologize in person

(For the grocery oversight of course)

ME

You better be ready to beg on your knees for forgiveness.

JESSE

I can think of something far more fun I can do for you on my knees

Biting my lip, I get up and pad to our room, throwing my phone on the nightstand and pulling out my vibrator from a small drawer below. I strip off my clothes and climb under the covers, nearly melting all over again at the scent of him on the sheets, then reach for my phone.

ME

I'm naked in bed. It's a shame you left. I'll have to get started without you.

You fuck around, you find out.

Satisfied and, with nothing else to do but kill time, I put on a sexy playlist and ponder how long I'm willing to give him before I take care of things myself. I pinch my nipples, stoking the heat between my legs. I've barely gotten started when the front door slams and footsteps jog toward me. A smile tugs at the corner of my mouth as I slowly sit up. When the bedroom door flies open, it reveals Jesse, bent at the waist and out of breath.

"Where are the groceries?" I ask, feigning innocence.

"Fuck the groceries," he puffs out as he kicks off his shoes. His gaze is locked on my tits as he peels off his T-shirt.

I drink in the quick rise and fall of his chest, the muscles rippling beneath his skin. My lips part with hunger. "Okay, but fuck *me* first."

He blows out a laugh. "You win this round," he concedes, raising his brows and pointing at me. "But you play dirty too."

"Hmm." I tap a finger against my chin. My eyes travel south as he slides his shorts down, and I lift the vibrator out from under the blanket. Switching it on, I catch the fire that flares in his expression when it starts to hum. "I regret nothing."

I squeal when he dives for the bed, greedily pulling the heat and weight of him down on top of me.

He crushes his lips against mine, his tongue sweeping into my mouth with eager strokes. Breaking the kiss, he looks down at me and brushes the hair back from my forehead.

"Don't you ever threaten to start without me again," he says, still panting slightly from the run. "I almost walked into a fucking lamppost."

37

JESSE

The street market is buzzing. Easily half of Lennox Valley has turned up to check out the food trucks and sidewalk sales. Riverside Avenue is closed to traffic and every shop on the street has some kind of offering out front.

As we wind through the humming crowd, I grip Ada's hand, lifting our arms to let a little girl run between us. Her screeching is more or less incoherent, but I catch something about mini doughnuts. Ada smiles over her shoulder at the kid. Following her gaze, I watch as the girl, who must be about Hazel's age, slams into the thighs of a barrel-chested man holding a toddler. He stoops to hear her request with the tired patience only a father could possess.

I interlace my fingers with Ada's and pull her along to the next set of stalls. Her hand is warm and her thumb brushes over mine. I love that we can be like this. Together. In public.

No more hiding. No more rules about not touching. Because I fucking love touching her and, now that I'm allowed to do it openly, I want to do it all the time. I'd stop in my tracks in the middle of this crowd to make out with her if... *wait, why am I not doing that right now?*

I stop and pull her into me, smiling at the wide-eyed confusion that blooms in her features. "Jess," she breathes. "What the f—"

"Ugh, you two are *barf-level adorable*," a familiar voice calls out. I spin around to find Katie and Dimitri approaching us from the doorway of the Gareth Mason Art Gallery.

"Hey!" Ada says, slipping out of my arms to give Katie a hug. "You're not asleep! Or at work! Who *are you?*"

Katie laughs. "I know, right?"

"Hey," Dimitri says, lifting his chin at me with a genuine smile. "Good to see you again, man."

"Likewise," I say, shaking his hand.

"Oh, hey, Jesse... I should introduce you to Jude—my boss. Pretty sure he's still around here somewhere," he says, taking in the crowd over his shoulder. "I'll see if I can flag him down. I know he wanted to ask you more about that grazing rotation thing you told me about."

"Sure, that'd be great," I say. Since deciding to stay in Lennox, I've been texting with Dimitri quite a bit about the homesteading project.

"What's going on in there?" Ada asks Katie, gesturing to the open door of the gallery, which hums with soft chatter.

"Silent auction," she replies. "It's a fundraiser for the hospital, so I thought I'd check it out. Pretty swish shit up for grabs. I put a bid on a night at this bed-and-breakfast... Starscape Manor, I think it's called? Looks gorgeous."

"Oh, that's where Kai had his wedding," Ada says, glancing at me.

"Shut up!" Katie exclaims. "Is it amazing there? Did you get to go inside?"

"Uh, yeah," she replies, a hint of color rising in her cheeks. "We went inside."

Fuck, we sure did.

Her eyes snag on mine again, and we share a private smile.

"Speaking of going inside," I say, rescuing her before Katie notices anything, "did you wanna?" I tilt my head at the gallery.

"Nah, it's all good," Ada says quickly, but her gaze lingers on the scene through the window.

"You should check it out, Ada. There's good stuff in there!" Katie assures us.

I slip my hand into Ada's again. "Yeah, c'mon. You said you loved art galleries."

"Catch you later?" Dimitri asks, and we agree to find each other again when we're done at the auction.

As I tug on her hand, Ada casts another lingering glance at the crowd inside the gallery, then pins me with a curious look. "When did I tell you that?"

"Tell me what?"

"About loving art galleries."

"Uh, at the deli. You told me you went to every one you could find in Europe."

"After we went shopping?" Her brows draw together. "You remembered that? That was like two months ago!"

"Of course I remembered that."

"Aww," she teases.

"I was hanging on your every word. Couldn't stop staring at your mouth." At her confused expression, I add, "There was mayo, like, *everywhere.*"

She swats at me. "Fuck off."

I grin and wink.

"Did you just wink at me?" She rolls her eyes. "You're such a tool."

"*Come on,*" I say, dragging her through the open door. "Let's go pretend to be fancy people."

We stop inside the doorway, taking in the gallery.

A stylish woman with blonde, curly hair piled into a knot on top of her head winds between people, answering questions and rearranging the displayed items. When she spots us hovering in the doorway, she strolls over, beaming at us with an infectious smile. "Hey! Welcome!"

"Hey," I say. "So, how does this all work?"

"Right." She claps her hands softly together. "Okay, so tickets are fifteen dollars. After you pay, I assign you a bidding number, which is what you write on the sheet next to your bid. Bidding's open until seven, so there's still a bit of time to have a good look around."

"Okay, cool." I nudge Ada. "You up for it?"

"Sure," she says, her attention trained on the paintings lining the walls beyond the auction items.

I dig out my wallet and hand the woman fifty bucks.

"Oh, great! I'll just grab you some change."

"Don't worry about it," I say. "It's for a good cause."

"Well, that's very generous, thank you! My name's Caroline, by the way. I'm the Event Coordinator here."

Caroline leads us to a table with a sign-up sheet, and we quickly scribble down our information. When she takes the clipboard from Ada, her eyes snap up.

"Ada Russo?"

"Yeah?" Ada sounds uneasy.

"Oh my God! You paint all those dark surrealist pieces, right? Lots of red and black? I follow you online!"

"What? Seriously?" Ada scrunches her nose.

"I had no idea you lived in Lennox! I *love* your work! I've been trying to find some young artists to pitch to the curator here, and you're actually on my list."

I nudge Ada's arm, raising my eyebrows.

Fuck yeah.

She glances at me before turning back to Caroline with an uncertain smile. "Wow, um... thank you."

When Caroline sets us loose on the auction and drifts away to check on the rest of the patrons, I dip my head down to Ada's ear. "Hey, check you out. All *on someone's list* and shit."

"Shut up," she says, tucking her hair behind her ear before she lifts her chin to kiss me.

We wander around the tables, perusing the items up for grabs. There are gift baskets, a catering package from Riverside Deli, gift certificates for anything from spa treatments to pest control, hand-carved wooden figurines, yoga classes... Katie was right; there's some nice stuff here. I lean down to bid on the night at Starscape Manor.

"If Katie finds out you outbid her, she's gonna shit," Ada says under her breath. Then she sees the bid. "Wow, you're really throwing the dollars around for someone who hasn't got a job here yet."

"I'll be alright for a bit," I say as I step over to check out the next item on the table, squeezing her hand. "Don't worry. Plus, the nurses were amazing when my mom was sick, so it's worth it. It's important."

"Hey, Jesse?" Dimitri's voice comes from behind me.

I turn. "Oh, hey, man. What's up?"

"You got a sec?" He motions over his shoulder for me to step outside.

"Uh, sure?" I tell Ada I'll be right back and follow Dimitri out into the street.

Katie's holding half a mini-doughnut in one hand and a paper bag in the other, laughing with a couple I don't recognize.

"Jesse, this is my boss, Jude," Dimitri says.

"Quit it with the *boss* stuff, man," Jude says, giving him a good-natured nudge. "You're not on the clock." Then he turns to me, lifting his chin. "Good to meet you. Jesse, right?"

"Yeah, hey. You too." I shake his hand.

He's a good-looking guy—tall, broad. A sleepy Golden Retriever is slumped at his feet, the slack leash in Jude's hand not seeming terribly necessary.

"And this is Olena," Dimitri adds, then tilts his head in her direction. "Badass landscape designer."

"Nice to meet you," I say, shaking her hand.

"You too." She smiles, then drags a few strands of long brown hair away from her face.

"So," Jude starts, "Dimitri tells me he was talking your ear off about urban farming a while back."

"Yeah. Back in July, I think?"

Olena reaches to take the leash from Jude. "I'm gonna take Murphy to visit Wyatt at the deli tent... let you guys chat."

"We'll come with you," Katie says, motioning for Dimitri to follow.

"Okay," says Jude, "but no sneaking him scraps of cheese and salami this time. He's too old to eat random shit."

"Hey, some of us *survive* on random shit," Olena teases back, then kisses Jude on the cheek. "Plus, he deserves it. He's a very good boy. Come on, Murph."

Murphy pushes up slowly.

Jude blows out a breath and shakes his head as he watches them walk away, then turns to me. "Anyway, I hear I should pick your brain about homesteading."

"Uh, well, I don't pretend to be an expert, but I've got farm experience—in Australia, though. Not here. What are you planning on doing?"

He tells me about his idea: offering new landscaping services geared toward folks who want to grow their own food, from simple veggie gardens and backyard chickens to—

someday—full-scale off-the-grid setups. Apparently, he's been trying to find someone to consult with and hasn't found anyone local.

"Realistically, we'd probably start installations early next year —we're gonna be slammed doing deadfall cleanup for the next few months, and then it'll be winter."

"Makes sense," I say, nodding.

"You looking for work?" Jude asks, putting his hands in his pockets. "Dimitri said you just moved back."

"Uh, yeah, actually."

"We could use an extra body starting in a couple weeks. If you don't mind a few months of grunt work, we could talk about the homesteading thing closer to the new year..."

"Uh, yeah, that sounds right up my alley."

Ada appears at my side. "What's up your alley?"

I quickly introduce Ada to Jude, then glance between them when it becomes obvious they recognize each other.

It seems to click for Jude and he snaps his fingers. "The bartender from the engagement party a couple weeks ago! With the roommate drama, right?"

"Oh, yeah!" Ada says. "Good memory!"

"You never did tell me that story."

"Well, he's standing right here." She turns to me, slipping her arms around my waist.

I plant a confused kiss on her hair and tug her into me. "Hang on. *I'm* your roommate drama?"

She arches a brow.

I chuckle softly. "Yeah, okay, that tracks."

"Hey, Jesse," Jude says, digging something out of his wallet. "We don't need to get into details right now, but gimme a call if you're interested in the job." He hands me his business card.

"Thanks, man," I say, reading the card. *Sharpe Blades Land-scaping.* "Will do."

Olena reappears, apparently having left the dog with Dimitri and Katie, and I introduce her to Ada.

"I *love* your hair color," Olena says, beaming. "And your tattoo!"

"Thanks!" Ada replies, then casts a long look at the nearby marquee tent for Rare Bird Tattoos, where customers are draped over chairs, getting inked out in the fresh air. "I keep thinking about getting more."

"Then let's go check it out!" Olena and Ada drift to the table in front of the tent, and Jude and I follow not far behind. They flip through a binder full of tattoo designs, chatting brightly about which ones they like.

I come closer, peering over Ada's shoulder. "You really thinking about another one?"

"Always," she replies, glancing at me before returning her attention to the binder. "They're addictive. But actually..."

I raise a brow.

She turns, sliding her hands over my hips. "I was thinking about how *you* should get a tattoo."

"Oh, yeah? Like what?"

"Probably, like, a *huge* tramp stamp," she deadpans.

I blow out a laugh. "Obviously."

"Right here," she whispers, tracing her fingers over my lower back as she bites her lip, failing to fight off a smile.

"Can you even say that anymore?" I ask, frowning. "*Tramp stamp?*"

Ada thinks for a moment. "Yeah, I guess it sounds kinda slut-shame-y? Fine, then. *Sexually empowered woman stamp.*"

"Well, I *am* a sexually empowered woman." I lean down to give her a quick kiss. "But I'm not getting some random tattoo on a whim."

"You'd look hot with tattoos, though." Ada pulls out of my arms, backing up a step to inspect me.

"Tattoos? Plural? Get outta here."

"It's true, though," Olena chimes in. "Tattoos are hot."

I cast a glance at Jude, who crosses his tattooed arms over his chest with amused patience, then turn back to Ada and Olena, who are both eyeing me up and, apparently, conspiring to get me inked right here and now.

"I dunno," I hedge, frowning at their scrutiny. "I've thought about it. But I don't even know where I'd wanna get one, I mean—"

"*Forearms,*" they blurt in unison, cutting me off with what I can only describe as a *concerning* level of intensity.

Jude laughs behind me.

"Uh..." I clear my throat, motioning to Ada. "We should get going before I let you talk me into something." Then I remember we're waiting on the auction to wrap up. I check the time on my phone. "When did they say they were closing bids? Seven?"

"Yeah," she says.

Olena asks, "Bids? For what?"

"There's this silent auction. In the art gallery." Ada gestures to the doorway nearby. "There's still a few minutes left to check it out if you—"

Olena laughs awkwardly. "Oh, no, that's okay. Art galleries aren't my thing."

"Why not?" asks Ada.

"Oh, I uh..." Olena hedges, like she's not sure how to answer. "I don't really *get* modern art."

"Y'know," I say, "Ada's an artist... She draws and paints."

Ada's eyes widen and she shakes her head at me as if pleading for me to shut up.

"You do?" Olena asks her, appearing genuinely surprised. "But you're so... relatable. Normal. Not a stuffy snob, I mean."

"Aww," I tease Ada. "Did you hear that? Someone thinks you're normal."

"I CAN'T BELIEVE you outbid me," Katie grouses, handing me back the gift certificate package for the night at Starscape Manor. She turns to Dimitri. "We'll have to figure out some other place for our wedding night, I guess."

"I'm not too worried about it," he replies, then kisses her. "We've still got lots of time."

Ada finally emerges from the gallery, looking pleased with herself as she joins us on the street outside. She's holding an envelope in her hand.

"Alright, big spender," I say, lifting my chin at her. "Whaddya got there?"

She opens her mouth to speak when she spots Murphy behind me. "Oh, hey, buddy!" she croons, tucking the envelope under her arm and crouching down to say hello.

He pushes his nose into her, licking one of her hands as she ruffles the fur around his collar with the other.

"He likes you," Olena says. Then, when Murphy pushes into Ada with renewed enthusiasm, tail whipping back and forth, she laughs. "Uh, *really* likes you."

I know the feeling, pal.

"Murphy's a good judge of character," Jude offers, putting his arm around Olena.

I smile down at Ada.

She peers up at me, laughing in surprise when Murphy licks her cheek. She's beautiful.

"So what did you win, anyway?" I ask, eyeing the envelope she has tucked away. "I didn't even see you bid on anything."

She stops petting the dog long enough to hand it to me.

I turn it over in my hand. The logo for Rare Bird Tattoos is stamped on the front. I give her a look.

"I'll design you one," she promises. "If you want, I mean. And if you don't want to use it, I can—"

"Nah," I say, tapping the edge of the envelope against my open palm. "I'll use it. And actually... I've already got an idea of what I might want."

EPILOGUE
ADA

Six months later

I start the car to get the heat blasting as Jesse climbs in, then tug my scarf up around my chin; it's fucking cold, even for early March.

"Okay... well?" I tuck my hands under my thighs for warmth.

"Well what?"

Is he fucking kidding me?

"Seriously, Jess, the secrecy is going to destroy me. Can you just show me already?"

"So impatient. You don't wanna drive home first?"

"I've been plenty patient!" I twist in the driver's seat to face him. "You've been putting this off for *months* and wouldn't even let me know what the design was. Or watch you get the damn thing done."

"I told you..." He reaches over and cups my jaw, pulling me in for a kiss. "I didn't want you to try to talk me out of it."

I drop my shoulders. "That only makes me assume the worst."

He smirks, sitting back in his seat. "I promise it's not something ridiculous."

"Do I have to rip your clothes off myself, or what? Come on." I gesture at his body, scanning him like I might spontaneously develop X-ray vision to see under his clothes and find this fucking tattoo.

"Okay, okay," he says, unzipping his thick hoodie and shrugging his left arm out from his sleeve. "Here."

He rests his arm on the center console of my car, his palm facing up. Tracing a path up the inside of his forearm, covered by the clear dermal wrap, is a simple black line that branches off four times into different leaves and flowers.

I flick my eyes up to his. "This was your big secret? *Plants?*"

He feigns hurt. "Hey, judgy pants, will you look a little closer?"

I drop my gaze to his arm.

"This is my... wait..." I trail off, momentarily speechless, and swallow. "You got my art tattooed on you?"

"Well, two of them are yours. The others I had the tattoo artist design, matching your style." At my confused expression, he continues. "You posted your flower sketches online, remember?"

"Wait, what?" I breathe. "*You're* the friend Olena texted me about? Who wanted to get my permission to use them?" I'd been so flattered; it had never occurred to me she'd been scheming with Jesse.

He gives me a guilty smile.

Sneaky bastard.

"Okay, lemme explain." He shifts in his seat to face me better. "So, these are pink carnations—my mom's favorite, as you know. Then these"—he points to the next branch up his arm—"are snowberries, for how Claire tried to kill me that one time." He smirks. "And these are apples and a rice plant, for my time in Australia." He points to the next design. "And the last one..."

I look up. "Buttercups."

He nods, blue eyes sparkling above a half smile.

"Jesse," I whisper, barely getting his name out past the knot in my throat.

"*Ada.*" He's trying to fight off a grin.

I swallow again. "You did *not* just mark yourself permanently with something that represents *me.*"

"I think you'll find I did."

I exhale and sit back in my seat, turning toward the window.

"Hey, if you hate it... or if you're mad or something... I mean, no one other than you and me would know what it meant anyway, and—"

I turn back to face him, my throat burning.

"Oh, baby, c'mere," he says, reaching for the back of my neck and pulling me in. He rests his forehead against mine, and my tears squeeze free, slipping down my cheeks. After a few moments, he reaches past me. There's a jangle of keys, then the engine cuts to silence.

"No one's ever..." I whisper in the quiet, then pull in a shaking breath. "You're really not leaving, are you?"

He pulls back, his expression patient as his thumb grazes over the line of my jaw. "I don't think you've been paying attention."

My brow quirks in confusion.

"How else do I need to say it? You think *this*"—he gestures to his new tattoo—"is a big commitment? This is nothing. Shit, I'd get every inch of my skin inked with your *name* if it didn't make people think I'd lost my fucking mind."

A watery laugh bursts from my lips, and I wipe the tears from my cheeks. "Please don't. I'd hate to have to send you to live in the woods."

"The woods?" Now he's the one who looks confused.

"You know, to avoid scaring the townsfolk." Then I grab his

shoulder with a gasp. "But maybe that's your Sasquatch destiny! You could grow your hair out again, and—"

He rolls his eyes.

"Aw, c'mon!" I continue, playfully prodding him in the chest. "The kids I work with still call you *Man Bun*, you know."

"Ada. Focus."

"Sorry. Sorry." I press my lips together.

Fuck, I love him.

"I'm serious, okay?" He leans in to kiss me, the brush of his lips a silent promise. "I love you. And not like how people throw that word around, talking about how they love tacos and shit. *I love you.*"

"You love me more than tacos?"

Now he laughs. "Your ability to talk a bunch of bullshit in an otherwise tender moment is truly impressive."

"I love you, too, Jesse," I say. "More than a thousand tacos." I grab his face and lean in to kiss him again.

"Listen," he continues when our lips part. "I just know... This is it. You're it for me. And... ah, fuck." He sniffs and blinks back his own tears. "I wanna spend the rest of my life with you, Ada."

"Are you...?" Another tear slips down my cheek, and I swipe at it with my jacket sleeve.

He shakes his head with a laugh. "I'm not. C'mon, give me some credit. I wouldn't propose to you in a freezing fucking car outside a strip mall."

I smile.

He looks pensive. "But I will. Someday. I want this... this stupid shit we do? I want the forever package. I wanna travel with you, and marry you, and have babies with you, and then show them how to destroy Uncle Marcus on Rainbow Road."

I laugh. "Really?"

"Hell yes!" He takes both my hands in his, rubbing my freezing fingers. "We'll teach them all our stupid shit. I wanna do all that stuff. As long as it's with you."

I take a breath and let it out, nodding. "Stupid shit forever?"

His smile is everything. "Stupid shit forever."

BONUS EPILOGUE

Want more Jesse and Ada?

Subscribe to my newsletter to get a FREE bonus epilogue featuring Jesse and Ada getting... messy!

Get your FREE bonus epilogue:

https://BookHip.com/ZFVVXSV

Enjoy that sarcastic banter you know and love, Jesse leaning into his possessive side, and some seriously spicy use of art supplies, all from Jesse's point of view!

ALSO BY HANNAH BRIXTON

Loved *Jesse's Girl?*

More from the *Lennox Valley Chronicles* series:

Book one:

Hey Jude

https://mybook.to/heyjude

Book three:

Sweet Caroline

https://mybook.to/sweet_caroline

ACKNOWLEDGMENTS

I have so many people to thank for their help with making this story a reality.

Genesis Bird, Laura-Elise Bishop, and Cherry Keeley: thank you for being my OG writer pals and for lending your eyes and brains to early drafts of Jesse's Girl. Not only has your incredible feedback helped shape this story into what it is, but your friendship and empathy has been such a gift. I feel so lucky that we found each other!

My other fabulous author pals (especially Miley Howard, Katie Van Brunt, Valentina Burns, Albany Archer, Kate Cole, and Bailey Hannah): gold stars and shirtless dudes for you all! Thank you for keeping me sane and cackling every day of this weird and wonderful spicy romance journey—and for all your help, your kindness, your humor, and for indulging in my nonsense.

To my wonderful beta readers: Sara, Danie, Caitlin, Alexsis, Alyssa, Kelly, Prerna, Nikki, Jess, Heidi, Allie, and Jenna: thank you from the bottom of my heart for your time, energy, and hugely helpful feedback! You all were amazing and I couldn't have done this without you.

To my editor, Myranda Bolstad, who both beta read *and* edited this book (which involved reading it *three times*): you've been an incredible support and resource to me and I am hugely grateful for your time and energy in diving into the nitty-gritty details of this story! You really went above and beyond with this book and I am forever grateful! Thank you for everything—ridiculous memes included!

To Andrea Bugslag: thank you for being my long-suffering sounding board and always reassuring me that no actual suffering is being endured as you listen to my story babbling! I love and appreciate you more than I can express!

To my husband: Thank you for making sure I ate dinner every day, for schooling me on Mario Kart trash talk, and for giving me the line "loser wears the popcorn." I can't think of a better partner to do stupid shit forever with. (Oh, and I think you left your car parked down at the Y.) Love you!

To my kids: Thank you for being pumped about my writing and giving me the time, space, and grace to do it. You're three damn cool human beings and I'm so excited to watch as you find your own paths. Please don't read this book ~~until you're eighteen~~ ever. I love you so much!

To my mom: This book has far more f-words than the last one, so you probably shouldn't read it. Thank you for loving me even though what I write is very sweary. I love you!

ABOUT THE BOOK

Jesse and Ada's story was a slow burn for me—one that I had to wrestle with a bit before I could tame it. Call it second novel syndrome if you will, but it was a much messier process than writing my first book. Ada and Jesse were tricky characters to get just right, and there were many bumps along the way in getting to know them and showing them the journey and happy ending they both deserved. But it was so worth it.

In this book, I wanted to continue on with the theme of neuro-divergent representation that started with book one in the *Lennox Valley Chronicles* series, *Hey Jude*. In *Jesse's Girl*, Ada's dyslexia impacts her in small and big ways throughout the story and is an integral part of her experience throughout her life. It also has secondary impacts on her relationships that I felt were important to highlight as a (differently) neurodivergent person myself, espe-cially around the theme of being misunderstood. I hope readers feel that I handled this topic with the care and respect it deserves.

Sidenote: At time of writing, there does not seem to be strong scientific evidence for the use of certain specialized fonts (e.g., OpenDyslexic, Dyslexie, etc.) as a way to improve reading rate and accuracy for dyslexic readers. Despite this, I chose to include this element in the story (where Jesse mimics the look of one such typeface in his handwritten notes to Ada) as there seems to be substantial anecdotal evidence that certain readers with dyslexia find these fonts easier to read. The inclusion of this information in the story does not constitute an endorsement of any particular font or approach to managing dyslexia; it is simply a fictional romantic gesture—based on a real-life experience shared with me by one of my beta/sensitivity readers; thank you, Alexsis! (shared with permission)

I deeply loved writing this story, and I hope these two messy, snarky characters come across as the broken-yet-lovable goons that exist in my heart. There are pieces of me in both of them, from Ada's sarcastic quips to Jesse's almost naïve faith that doing the right thing will make everything okay... They're flawed works in progress—as are we all.

I hope every snarky little bitch who reads this book feels seen, feels loved, and finds someone who'll both brush the hair back from their forehead and rail them into next week. Oh, and sorry-not-sorry for using the phrase *throbbing manhood*. I hope it made you laugh.

♡ Hannah Brixton

ABOUT THE AUTHOR

Hannah Brixton lives with her husband, three children, and two cats on beautiful Vancouver Island in British Columbia, Canada. In her spare time, she loves to read, listen to podcasts, and sing along loudly to music that embarrasses her children.

Hannah Brixton's books are available on Amazon

Contact Hannah:
Email: hannah@hannahbrixton.com
Website: www.hannahbrixton.com

Subscribe to Hannah's Newsletter:
https://hannah-brixton-author.kit.com/f8158e2beb

Follow Hannah:
@hannah.brixton on **Instagram**
@hannah.brixton.author on **Tiktok**
@hannah.brixton.author on **Facebook**
@Hannah Brixton on **Goodreads**
@hannahbrixtonauthor on **Pinterest**